Florence Warden

A Woman's Face

A Romance

Florence Warden

A Woman's Face
A Romance

ISBN/EAN: 9783337348878

Printed in Europe, USA, Canada, Australia, Japan

Cover: Foto ©Andreas Hilbeck / pixelio.de

More available books at **www.hansebooks.com**

A WOMAN'S FACE.

A Romance.

BY

FLORENCE WARDEN,

AUTHOR OF

"THE HOUSE ON THE MARSH," "SCHEHERAZADE,"
"A PRINCE OF DARKNESS," ETC.

IN ONE VOLUME.

London:

F. V WHITE & CO.,

31, SOUTHAMPTON STREET, STRAND, W.C.

1890.

POPULAR NEW NOVELS.

Now Ready, in One Vol., the Seventh Edition of

ARMY SOCIETY; or, Life in a Garrison Town. By JOHN STRANGE WINTER, Author of "Bootles' Baby." Cloth gilt, 6s.; also picture boards, 2s.

Also now ready, in cloth gilt, 2s. 6d. each.

GARRISON GOSSIP, Gathered in Blankhampton. By JOHN STRANGE WINTER. Also picture boards, 2s.

A SIEGE BABY. By the same AUTHOR. Also picture boards, 2s.

BEAUTIFUL JIM. By the same AUTHOR. Also picture boards, 2s.

MRS. BOB. By the same AUTHOR.

BY WOMAN'S WIT. By Mrs. ALEXANDER, Author of "The Wooing O't." Also picture boards, 2s.

MONA'S CHOICE. By the same AUTHOR. Also picture boards, 2s.

A LIFE INTEREST. By the same AUTHOR.

KILLED IN THE OPEN. By Mrs. EDWARD KENNARD. Also picture boards, 2s.

THE GIRL IN THE BROWN HABIT. A Sporting Novel. By the same AUTHOR. Also picture boards, 2s.

A REAL GOOD THING. By the same AUTHOR. Also picture boards, 2s.

A CRACK COUNTY. By the same AUTHOR. Also picture boards, 2s.

STRAIGHT AS A DIE. By the same AUTHOR. Also picture boards, 2s.

OUR FRIENDS IN THE HUNTING FIELD. By the same AUTHOR.

LANDING A PRIZE. By the same AUTHOR.

TWILIGHT TALES. By the same AUTHOR. *Illustrated.*

IN A GRASS COUNTRY. By Mrs. H. LOVETT-CAMERON. Also picture boards, 2s.

A DEVOUT LOVER. By the same AUTHOR. Also picture boards, 2s.

THE COST OF A LIE. By the same AUTHOR. Also picture boards, 2s.

THIS WICKED WORLD. By the same AUTHOR.

A LOST WIFE. By the same AUTHOR.

THE OUTSIDER. By HAWLEY SMART. Also picture boards, 2s.

THE MASTER OF RATHKELLY. By the same AUTHOR.

LONG ODDS. By the same AUTHOR.

SHE CAME BETWEEN. By Mrs. ALEXANDER FRASER.

DAUGHTERS OF BELGRAVIA. By the same AUTHOR.

THE CRUSADE OF THE "EXCELSIOR." By BRET HARTE. Also picture boards, 2s.

DREAM FACES. By THE HON. MRS. FETHERSTONHAUGH.

THE HONBLE. MRS. VEREKER. By the Author of "Molly Bawn," &c.

THE DUCHESS OF ROSEMARY LANE. By B. L. FARJEON.

TOILERS OF BABYLON. By the same AUTHOR.

A YOUNG GIRL'S LIFE. By the same AUTHOR.

VIOLET VYVIAN, M. F. H. By MAY CROMMELIN and J. MORAY BROWN.

THE RIVAL PRINCESS. By JUSTIN MCCARTHY, M.P., and Mrs. CAMPBELL PRAED.

F. V. WHITE & CO.,
31, Southampton Street, Strand, London, W.C.

A WOMAN'S FACE.

CHAPTER I.

I⊤ was half-past six o'clock on a bleak evening in January.
A black starless sky above, frost-bound snow-covered
earth underneath, and a film of sleet falling made the
hills and valleys of beautiful Westmoreland dreary and
desolate as the shadowy limboes of the Inferno, where
Dante describes unbaptized and heathen souls as wandering for ever in still and joyless gloom. Between two
ridges of bare and rocky hill a market-cart was jogging
slowly along the whitening road, and the thud of the old
horse's hoofs and the rattle of the wheels were the only
sounds that broke a stillness which was vault-like in the
narrow valley.

From under the rough canvas hood of the little cart
peered out two men's faces, not clearly visible even to
each other; as the cart entered the valley its occupants
had dropped into silence, which was not broken until a
light began to twinkle in the dimness on the road ahead
of them. At sight of the little thread of brightness
across the path one of the men started and the other
laughed good-humouredly.

"Eh, but there's no need to be feared, sir; there's no
moonlighters hereabouts," said he cheerfully, as he encouraged the old horse to mend his pace by a gentle
shake of the reins. "I've lived at Mereside sixty-five
year, and I've been to Conismere and back every Thurs-
day nigh on fifty year, barrin' when the snow had drifted
too deep, and I've never come to no harm on this road,
lonesome as it be. But I can understand how a gentleman like yourself, from Lon'on mebbe, should find it a
bit solitary-like."

"Solitary! Well, yes, it is solitary, there's no denying that," answered his companion in a deep, mellow voice that conveyed a volume of information, true or false, concerning the owner's pedigree, disposition, and education; and all in his favour. "But I mustn't let London suffer for my nervousness. I'm as nervous as a cat to-night, I confess, and for my life I couldn't tell why! I'm a Yorkshireman."

"Eh, not from Lon'on!" exclaimed the old villager, glancing back involuntarily towards the place where the stranger's Gladstone bag lay in the bottom of the cart.

The young Yorkshireman smiled.

"I come from London just now, certainly, as my luggage-labels attest," he said. "But that doesn't make me a Londoner any more than the fact of my being on my way to Scotland makes me a Scotchman."

"Scotchman! Eh, no, you don't need to be that," struck in the old man with decision. "I've no greet love for Scotchmen myself, though we've got one of them for landlord now, and he's not a bad sort isn't Lord Kildonan. But surely, sir, if you're journeying to Scotland, it's a good bit out of your way to go to Branksome. It's getting southwards again like."

The gentleman did not answer, and the villager, after a short pause, went on in reluctant apology:

"Of course it's no business of mine, sir, and I ask your pardon if I've been too free like, but—— "

The stranger cut him short, speaking slowly and with a sort of drowsiness in his manner.

"It is an accident altogether, this going to Branksome. I made a stupid mistake at Haverholme Junction, where I got out of the train, taking my bag with me by an unaccountable bit of luck. I walked up and down the platform a few times to warm my feet, and by a feat of stupidity which I cannot in the least explain, got into the wrong train, and found myself presently at Conismere, where, as you know, the branch line ends; so, as there was no train back to Haverholme before to-morrow morning, I made up my mind to inflict myself for the night upon an old acquaintance of mine, Dr. Peele, of Branksome."

"Dr. Peele!   Oh, ay, I know 'un."

"And you were kind enough to offer me a lift as far as Mereside.   Branksome is about four miles further on, they say."

"Ay, a matter of four mile or so, and a straight road eno'—t' coach road.   But if you don't know these parts, I should advise you to bide at Mereside till morning, for t' wind will make drifts by-and-by on t' roads by t' lake. There is a hotel and two good inns at Mereside where t' coach starts from, and t' owd doctor's ill, so there won't be much of a welcome for ye at Branksome Lodge."

"The doctor's ill, is he?"

"Ay, and t' missis won't be in t' best o' tempers. She's not one o' t' meek 'uns, isn't Mrs. Peele, though she's a good lady, and it's my belief she's saved many a one of her husband's patients by chuckin' his pills and his draughts into t' fire, and sending t' boy off wi' a pie and a bottle of port wine in place of 'em."

The Yorkshireman laughed.   "I don't say there may not be occasions where a little more food and a little less physic is not a bad prescription; but you mustn't disparage medical science to me, for I'm a doctor my-self."

"Lord, and are ye now?   Well, I thowt I was travellin' in better company.   No offence, sir, but it's a sore point with us hereabouts just now, is that of doctors.   There's been a bit of a bother about a young partner Dr. Peele took, who got into little difficulties with some o' t' doctor's patients, and had to go away a bit sudden-like in consequence."

"Difficulties!   What sort of difficulties?"

"Well, two of t' patients under his care—poor men both, a labourer one was, and t'other a man as kept a small stationer's shop, were took ill wi' t' same sort of symptoms; and one died."

"Well?"

"At t' beginnin' one had rheumatic fever and t'other a broken rib.   They ain't t' same thing, sir, are they?"

"No; very different indeed."

"Well, it seemed odd, so folks thowt, when by-and-by they was both took same way. It was so odd that it got about, and people talked."

" And what did they say ? "

" Why, that t' young fellow 'd got a bit careless-like, and was a little too fond of the same drug in his prescriptions."

" And what drug was that ? "

" Laudanum, I think 'twas."

" People said something more than that, I suppose ? "

" A deuced sight more. They said——But here I be a-tittle-tattling like ne'er an old woman——"

" Well, well, it's talk for a winter's night, nothing more. For I know no one in this part of the world but Dr. Peele, I've never been here before, and I'm not likely to come here again : so the gossip can't do any harm, especially as I don't even know the names of the people you speak of."

" Ay, that's true, and so I won't tell 'ee their names. The gossips say this young spark had had 's head turned by a leddy, and a fine leddy too, but who had a husband a'ready, and that his head was runnin' on something that 'ud do away with himself. I don't suppose there was much truth in it, but it's always fine soil for a story where a handsome woman's planted, as I dare say you know, sir."

" What, is this handsome woman a local beauty, then?"

" She lives hereabouts, sir, if that's what you mean. But she's a Lon'on beauty too, so I'm told ; and well she mebbe, for there isn't an eye, young or old, gentle-folk or village-folk, that can look at her bonny face once and not care to look twice. She's worth walking a good mile to see, is Lady Kildonan."

" Lady Kildonan ; oh, she is the wife of the principal landowner about here, then ? "

The old man evidently regretted that he had let slip the name of the subject of his talk. He answered rather reluctantly, and in a more cautious manner :

" Ay."

" They are popular in the district then, Lord and Lady Kildonan ? "

"She makes him popular, bless her. He's always porin' over 's books, is his lordship, but she's all over t' place like a sunbeam, on her horse, or in her carriage, or her little sleigh, leavin' a pound o' tea here, a can o' jelly there, with a word for every woman, and a smile for every man, and a kiss for t' children. She's a sight for sore een, she is."

"Is she young ? "

"Let me see ; she was born t' year my girl Janet was married, that's twenty-four year ago."

"And Lord Kildonan, what sort of an age is he ? "

"Well, there's a matter of thirty years or more between him and 's wife."

"And his heart is bound up in his library?"

"So they say. Indeed, I think he'll turn into a book himself some day, for he's as dry as parchment, and has ne'er a word to give of his own accord, though they do say he's chock full o' learning. But he's a kind gentleman, and the poor have no more to greet about now than they had in the time of her ladyship's father, Mr. Dighton."

"Oh, then the property came through her ? "

"Ay. His lordship hadn't much but his title and his books, they say."

"Surely she might have found a better mate than an old Scotch bookworm ? "

"Well, she was a bit of a madcap, as a lass, and they say old Mr. Dighton was glad to get her off his hands, and married to a honest man. And she don't fret for him and his books : she has too much life in her for that," the old man added with evident admiration.

The young doctor was rather surprised at the wide latitude which this old peasant, who by all precedent should have been a rigid censor of the manners and morals of his juniors and superiors, allowed to a lady whose conduct seemed, by his own showing, to be open to severe criticism. He was about to put a question to the old man with the view of getting an explanation of this singular indulgence, when certain faint sounds, which seemed to come from some distance behind them, broke upon his ears and caused him to again start as he had done at sight of the light on the road in front of them.

"You've no such strong nerves for a doctor, sir," said his companion jocularly. "You started at sight o' t' light in John Barlow's cottage yonder, and now at t' sound o'—why of her ladyship's sleigh-bells," he ended, after listening a moment to the rapidly approaching sounds.

"I dare say you don't believe me, but I don't remember such a thing ever to have happened to me before ; and I can swear I never before made such a fool of myself as I have done to-night in getting out of the right train to get into the wrong one, and then coming through the snow on a wild-goose chase to see a person who is not even a very old friend of mine, instead of putting up at Conismere for the night, so that I might get into the right track again the first thing to-morrow morning."

He spoke with considerable irritation and self-scorn, and his companion was emboldened by his tone to be franker in comment than ever.

"Eh, but I was thinkin' it was a queer thing to do, if you were at all hurried-like on your journey."

"Yes, it's more than queer, it's mad, and I shall do the best I can to bring myself back to saner thoughts and saner conduct by staying at Mereside to-night and returning the first thing in the morning to Conismere to continue my journey."

He was speaking with impatience which seemed unnatural to him, and his companion observed that his feet tapped the floor of the cart in a restless and excited manner. The noise of the sleigh-bells grew louder and louder behind them, and the dull sound of horses' quick steps upon the snow; while the bright notes of a woman's laughter rang out clearly, and filled the young Yorkshireman with a strong curiosity to see this lake-side siren, the very sound of whose voice bore exhilaration to its hearers. In a moment more the sleigh had dashed by, with its twinkling lights, its jingling bells; and all that the doctor could see through the darkness was, that it contained two people, sitting side by side. But as it passed with a whir-r-r and a rush of cold air, something, light and soft and scented, fluttered up like a curled white leaf, and fell on the young man's knees like an unconscious challenge of fascinating, warm-blooded coquetry: a lady's handkerchief, filmy and lace-edged, sweet with a perfume that whispered through the senses to the imagination, and brought up fancies of delicate white fingers that had held the dainty toy. The old villager, however, was not troubled by superfluous poetry; on catching sight of the handkerchief, he began to call out lustily:

"Hey! Woa! Stop! You've dropped summet. Your ladyship, hey!"

The sleigh was rapidly approaching a dip in the road where a group of rough stone cottages, one of which was an inn of the humblest kind, broke the straight line of the roadside, and threw little streams of light across the snow through their latticed windows. At the sound of the old man's cries both occupants of the sleigh turned their heads, and at last, as he still shouted, the jingling of the bells subsided to a faint tinkle, the sleigh drew up just out of the gleams of light from the cottage windows, and a man's voice called out impatiently:

"What is it?"

The young doctor, holding the handkerchief, had already leapt down from the cart, and was running over the snow as fast as limbs stiffened by cold and a cramped position could carry him. Even as he ran and the rapid movement dispersed the fanciful reveries which novel circumstances and his new and strange perversity had induced, a superstitious and dreamy idea took possession of him that this trifling accident had some meaning for him, some bearing upon his future life; and at the same time an entirely mundane and explicable curiosity arose in his mind concerning the companion of the lady. His voice was young, therefore he was not her husband; it was that of a gentleman, therefore he could not be the coachman. The Yorkshireman was filled with interest by the time he reached the sleigh, which was drawn up on the left-hand side of the road. It was the lady who held the reins, sitting high on cushions at the right.

But if, on the strength of the old villager's tattling
stories, the doctor had scented a scandal, he was disappointed; for the man beside her, sitting respectfully
upright with folded arms, was in livery, and could be no
other than the groom.

"Well, what do you want?" asked the lady im-
periously, before the stranger had appeared beside her.
" Hard times, I suppose, and you've been out of work
for weeks, and have a hungry family, and want a night's
lodging. Well, here you are, but you ought not to stop
people on the public road, you know; it looks like an
attempt at highway robbery without the romance of it."

She ended with a ripple of most pleasant, low-voiced
laughter, as if it was quite impossible for her happy
nature to keep up even the faint semblance of annoyance with which her words had begun. She was feeling
in her purse, with her head bent over it, by the time the
young Yorkshireman had reached her side and had recovered breath enough to speak. Just as he was raising
his hat, and holding out the handkerchief, the ponies
started off; and the few paces it travelled before being
pulled up by a quick hand on the reins, brought the sleigh
within the light from the cottage windows, which flashed
upon the faces both of the lady and of the stranger who
stood beside her.

The Yorkshireman held his breath. By some odd
result of this sudden revelation of her beauty to his
dazed and dreamy mood, it seemed to him that not
a flesh-and-blood handsome woman of the nineteenth
century, but the incarnate ideal of the Italian painters
of the Renaissance, looked straight into his eyes with the
frank and fearless gaze of a pictured goddess, and flashed
upon his dazzled sight the rose and ivory tints of her
skin, the gleam of her blue eyes and of her pearl teeth,
the shining coils of her pale golden hair. Lady Kildonan's beauty was that of incontestable, triumphant,
sensuous sort which attacks and subdues at first sight,
needing no wiles of subtle allurement, no attractions of
intelligence or amiability, to establish its claim to allegiance. What sort of mind dwelt in that beautiful body
might become, when longer acquaintance had dulled the

first impression produced by her face, a question of interest; but in a creature of so much loveliness it was of necessity a secondary matter, and although every woman of her acquaintance bewailed what one called a lack, and another a sameness, of expression, and united in regretting that this variously described defect "quite spoiled a face that would otherwise have been good-looking," the less discerning sex overlooked this blemish with generous unanimity, and yielded her that un-questioning homage which has been man's tribute to royal beauty, and the thorn in good plain women's sides since the world began. The young stranger was con-quered at once, and the words he had had ready failed him. On her side, however, the lady seemed to be as much struck with the appearance of the supposed tramp as he was with hers ; the pink colour in her cheeks grew a little deeper, and she held out her hand for the handker-chief with head bent as if in humble apology, while her full blue eyes looked up in his face with a deprecatory expression which would have washed away the memory of a hundred insults.

"I beg your pardon. I'm so awfwlly sorry. I made a dreadful mistake," she said, in a low winning voice that had a strangely moving quality.

"Not at all, madam," answered the stranger, recover-ing his voice, but not all his self-control. "You were quite right. The times are very hard, and I am in search of a night's lodging, though it is true I had no intention of waylaying you for the means to pay for it. You dropped your handkerchief, and I picked it up ; that is all."

"Oh, but it's not all. I'm so much ashamed of myself," broke out the lady, who seemed to enjoy the adventure with all the zest of a young girl. "You are a stranger here, I see—for I know every face in the neighbourhood. Let me offer you the hospitality of my home—The Crags—for the night. My husband, Lord Kildonan, will be delighted to welcome you. Poor man, he's used to making the *amende honorable* for his wife's escapades !" she ended with another peal of the bell-toned laughter which seemed to be a more natural expression of her happy, sanguine temperament than the colder medium of words.

The doctor noticed, even as he excused himself from accepting this headstrong offer of hospitality, that the groom appeared strangely sensible of the want of dignity betrayed by his mistress's rash invitation to a stranger, for the man gathered up the reins which the lady had let fall, as if respectfully to remind her that the time was slipping by.

"You must at least call upon us to-morrow—ah, but I insist upon that," she said, after hearing his answer. "I can't insult people and forget all about it in a moment like that. I must be allowed to make amends in my own way. If you are a visitor to Conismere you have no idea how much an old resident can help you to make the very most of your stay."

The groom gave an admonitory pull to the reins, but Lady Kildonan laid an imperious hand upon them while she listened to the stranger's answer.

"You are very kind indeed, and you have nothing in the world to apologize for, madam. I am a visitor, but a visitor who has to count even the minutes of his stay. I have a business appointment of the highest importance to me to keep in Glasgow to-morrow, upon which my hopes of getting a practice rest."

"A practice! Are you a lawyer, or a doctor then?" the beauty asked with ingenuous interest.

"I'm a doctor, or at least I shall be when I get any patients."

"Well, I hope——"

But before she could get any further with her speech the ponies, whether of their own accord or not it was impossible to say, had started off at a smart pace, and the young Yorkshireman was left standing in the middle of the road, feeling like the hero of a fairy tale when the spell has broken and the enchanted palace melted away. The cart in which the old villager had brought him thus far on his journey now jogged up and stopped for him to mount into it again.

"Well, what dost think o' t' leddy?" asked the old man with interest.

"Why, she—she is very handsome," the doctor answered stupidly ; and he turned to get up into the cart again.

As he did so he caught sight of something on the snow-covered ground at a little distance from his feet. With a quickened pulse, and yet with a conscience-prick, he made two steps forward, and discovered that it was indeed, as a sense even keener than his bodily vision had told him, the same little handkerchief that he had restored to its owner a few moments before. An odd coincidence surely, that she had dropped it again so soon ! Or was it a little wile to secure that call at The Crags on which her fancy seemed so obstinately bent? Whichever it might be, it was not in flesh and blood of seven and twenty to resist any longer the chance of another glimpse of this lake-side goddess. He got into the cart silently, wondering more than ever at the strange influence which seemed to have been at work upon him that day, and so effectually to have made havoc with his usually sober and practical nature, that he thought less of the appointment at Glasgow, with the practice for which he was sighing, than of the scrap of lace and cambric he had hastily hidden in one of his coat pockets from the curious eyes of his peasant companion.

CHAPTER II.

THE cart, with its oddly-assorted occupants, jogged on without further incident until, emerging from the monotonous road, with its enclosing walls of bare and steep hills, the old man announced that they were now "nigh t' village." There had been little conversation between them since the adventure with the sleigh, the villager having been satisfied with the stranger's full acquiescence in the local admiration of Lady Kildonan's beauty. A trifling incident, however, again brought forward the topic.

They had come to a point where a steep and narrow lane joined the main road. Just within the lane stood a tumbledown stone cottage, from the door of which, at the moment the cart jogged by, a man was issuing. The occupants of the cart saw his figure against the faint light of the interior of the cottage, and the old man said :

"Eh, but there's my lady's groom a leavin' something good for poor old mad Peg, I'll warrant ! There's an owd Irishwoman lives in that cottage, sir, as won't let t' parson come nigh her, bein' one o' them as worships t' saints, as they call 'em. And she ain't far wrong, for she's found as good as a saint to look after her. There's hardly a winter's day goes by but what my lady brings a pretty substantial blessing of half a pound o' tea or what-not to t' owd woman. Good evenin' to you, Mr. Martin."

The man, thus addressed, answered very shortly "Good evening," and hurried on towards the spot a few yards further on, where his mistress was waiting in the sleigh. The young doctor peered out at him in the darkness curiously, possessed with the odd idea that the man was disguising his voice. As they passed the sleigh the doctor heard the groom say something about Peggy's humble duty, and she had been laid up since yesterday with the rheumatiz' ; and then a new idea concerning the man's voice occurred to him. A moment later the sleigh scudded rapidly by and its lanterns were lost to sight by a turn in the road, though the jingling of its bells was heard in fact for some minutes, and in the doctor's fancy for some hours longer.

"I should think this admiration of yours, this Lady Kildonan, must find it rather dull in winter time to be shut up in a country house with a book-worm for a husband."

"Dull !" echoed the old man, and he stopped to give an admiring laugh. "Dull ! You don't know Lady Kildonan. Did ye not see her face ? She'd enjoy herself in the county gaol would her ladyship, bless her !"

"I suppose they keep the house full of visitors ?"

"No, not so much that ; his lordship's too quiet-like a man for that. But she goes ridin' an' drivin' about as you've seen her, and she's sunshine in herself, she is.

She's settled down a bit since her marriage, as a lady should, but Lord, the pranks she and young Master Ned, the dentist's son, used to play. They kept the country-side alive, did those two. They say he went nigh distracted when her father married her to Lord Kildonan."

"Was she married against her will, then?"

"Well, some said one thing, some another. But I don't think myself she was t' sort o' lass to be drove to marriage more'n t' aught else she'd no mind to. An' she was proud, and 'ud never have married t' son of a dentist, though young Master Ned, as we called him then, had a college schooling like t' best of 'em."

"And what became of him?"

"Oh, he went to Lon'on, and when he came back he brought a wife wi' him. And her ladyship didn't forget her old playmate, for she got him t' post of agent to his lordship."

"Oh!" said the doctor quite simply.

The gossiping old villager had spoken in perfect good faith, and his listener felt rather ashamed of the less ingenuous interpretation which his own impressions of the lake-side beauty had suggested to his mind. Therefore he discreetly allowed the subject to drop, and a few minutes later, having by this time reached the outskirts of the village, the horse stopped of his own accord before the third of a row of fair-sized cottages, with gardens in front of them.

"T' owd horse knows his home," said the old man as he got down from the cart and gave the animal a rough caress down the nose. "He won't go no further to-night, won't Smiler, but you're only a few steps from t' hotel now, sir, where t' coaches start for Branksome and Conismere, and if you'll take t' advice of a man as knows t' country hereabouts, you'll stay there and not be goin' on to Branksome till t' day breaks. T' wind's gettin' up, and t' snow'll be driftin', and on a night as black as this you might hap to miss t' road, and a turn to t' right in t' darkness might take you bang in t' lake."

"Thank you heartily. I shall certainly take your advice, and when the night's rest has cleared my brains a bit, I shall get back to Conismere, and on with my journey as fast as I can. But by the bye, I should like to renew our acquaintance if I ever chance to come this way again. My name is Armathwaite, Frank Armathwaite——"

"And mine's Haynes, Luke Haynes. As for renewing of acquaintance, doctor, if it's as man and man, and not as doctor and patient, I wish we may. And good luck to you on your journey."

With a hearty hand-shake of warm mutual approval, the gentleman and peasant parted, the latter leading his horse to the stable on the opposite side of the road, while the former made his way to the hotel indicated by the old man. This was a large, solid-looking corner-building, in the centre of the village, erected at an angle formed by the meeting of two roads. The snow was falling so thickly by the time Frank Armathwaite reached this place of refuge that he made up his mind that nothing should induce him to leave its sheltering walls that night, if the interior should come near to fulfilling the promise of comfort held out by the exterior. On entering the low, wide hall, the traveller found that this promise was more than fulfilled; it was exceeded. He was received by the host, a man of about thirty-five, quiet, courteous, intelligent, resourceful; shown to a room where a mahogany four-post bedstead, high old-fashioned chimney-piece, and candles in tall metal candlesticks, gave further promise of the solid, stately comfort which had refreshed at least a couple of generations of travellers; and lastly led by a stream of light and a welcome fragrance of dinner to the coffee-room, where a grave elderly man, who was head waiter in the season and sole waiter out of it, inducted him with honour to a seat at a table near the fire, where the cheerful sight of the flames leaping amidst a pile of coals crowned by a glowing log, chased away the last lingering vestige of the gloomy and fanciful melancholy which had fastened upon him since the morning.

The dinner was well cooked and good; the ale, which he frugally ordered after a glance at the wine-list, excellent. When, his hunger satisfied, Frank Armathwaite drew an arm-chair up to the fire, and running his eyes carelessly over the *Mereside Herald* and the *Mereside Gazette* of the preceding Friday, found nothing new enough or untrue enough to arrest his attention, his thoughts travelled back naturally to the incidents of his broken journey; to the dozing state into which he had fallen just before reaching Haverholme Junction; his unaccountable escapade in getting out of the Scotch express and into a train bound for Conismere; his foolish freak of deciding to go out of his way to call on old Dr. Peele; and finally to the cold drive in the darkness and the falling snow, and his weird introduction, by a chance light from a cottage-window, to the dazzling beauty of Lady Kildonan. At this point of his reverie he heard the well-secured shutters of the two windows rattle loudly, as with a whistle and a shriek a gust of wind caught the side of the old house, and died away into a moan that made him draw his chair closer to the fire, with a shiver and a muttered exclamation of surprise at his own folly in having ventured out at all on such a night. At every fresh gust there was a hissing noise against the window-panes, as the falling snow was whirled in a thick mass of large flakes against the glass.

"A bad night, sir," said the waiter respectfully, as he made up the fire.

"Bad indeed, but it gives a wonderful charm to a blaze like this," said Armathwaite lazily from out of the cozy depths of his chair.

And he sat gazing into the mass of dark rocks and glowing caverns, watching the spiral flames as they shot up amidst clouds of black smoke, until he fell into that pleasant dreamy state induced by warmth and light after cold and darkness, and began to fancy that he felt again the rough jolting of the market cart, that he heard the jingling of the sleigh-bells, the sharp trot of the horse on the frozen snow, and the lady's bright laughter; that he saw again the beautiful sparkling face peering out from its nest of rich furs. But then, even as his open eyes seemed to gaze upon the tints of rose and cream and the red, moist lips, the face appeared suddenly to change, the vivid colouring to fade and grow duller, the bright blue of the eyes to melt into a soft brown, the classical, sensuous mouth to alter in outline, and the whole countenance, while it seemed to recede before his fixed and eager gaze, so that its very features were dim and hardly to be discerned, assumed an expression of mournful, desperate longing that sent a throb of impulsive compassion through the young man's heart. He tried to move, uneasily conscious that this most strange and touching experience was only the result of a rather disorganized imagination ; but he seemed to feel that he was powerless, while at the very same moment the face changed once more, and became near and clear to him : he was gazing again at the handsome, happy face of Lady Kildonan. And an impulse of another sort, of strong, hearty, involuntary admiration, moved the young man as the face re-appeared in his fancy, only to change again in a moment to the shadowy unknown countenance that seemed, this second time, to be further off and dimmer in outline than ever, while the sense of sadness with which the vision filled him was stronger than before.

Another and wilder gust of wind shrieked round the house, and shook the window-sashes in their frames. Frank Armathwaite started to his feet and stared about him like a man who is wakened from a heavy sleep by a violent shock. He listened to the dying wail of the blast which had roused him, and glanced at the fire, the flames of which were now rising more steadily from the glowing mass of co l. He was alone in the room. The loud tick of the clock on the high mantlepiece above his head caused him a strange irritation, while the remoter sounds of the voice of the landlord in the hall, the laughter which came faintly from the bar, or the step of a maid upon the stairs, seemed to fall upon his ears like noises heard in a dream. Hardly knowing what he did. and conscious only of an odd murmur in his head, which seemed to direct his movements in spite of himself, he walked towards the nearest window, unfastened the shutters, and was on the point of throwing up the sash, when the grave waiter, having heard the clatter of the falling bar, entered the room and came up to him.

" You had better not open the window, sir," suggested

the man, respectfully. "The wind blows on this side of the house, and the room would be half full of snow in a minute."

The traveller desisted from his attempt at the first word, but he stood with his face close to the glass, peering steadily out into the blackness of the night, from which the large white snowflakes seemed to detach themselves as they whirled against the window, and falling, swelled the high drift upon the ledge.

"You are right," he said, after a pause. Then he added, in a brisker tone, "You know Dr. Peele, of Branksome?"

"Oh, yes, sir; everybody in these parts knows Dr. Peele."

"How far is it to his house from here?"

"Four miles, sir, I should say. It's just through Branksome, and up to the left a little way."

"Have you a saddle horse you could let me have? I—I have decided that I had better not wait till the morning; I must get to Branksome to-night."

There was some anxiety in his manner, which the grave waiter interpreted according to his knowledge.

"I hope, sir," he began with some concern, "that you haven't been sent for to the poor old doctor! We heard it was nothing more than a bad cold. There isn't a man in the district but would be sorry to hear that anything had happened to Dr. Peele."

"No, no, I haven't been sent for; that's all right," answered Armathwaite quickly. "But I knew him years ago and——Just see about the horse as fast as you can, will you?"

The waiter withdrew, and Armathwaite, again possessed by the overpowering restlessness which had driven him like an evil spirit throughout the day, prepared for his cold ride with an irritable consciousness that he was making a fool of himself. He had ordered the horse on the spur of an impulse he could not define, but which he had in vain attempted to resist. Left to himself, he at first thought he would countermand the order, as common sense loudly suggested. This Dr. Peele, so far from being a very dear old friend of his, was a man he had only met a few times, and whom he scarcely remembered; he was not seriously ill, that he should need a brother-doctor's services, but he was just ill enough, according to report, to make a visitor unwelcome. But, although by no means inordinately superstitious, Armathwaite began to feel acute curiosity concerning the series of unaccountable and apparently crazy impulses by which he had that day been led out of his course, and, in spite of himself, he was inclined to impute to them some significance. Besides this he had to recognize that the cosy evening by the fireside which he had promised himself had now become an impossibility. He could not sit still; his very limbs seemed no longer to be controlled by his own will, but to be under the command of some unknown agency which decreed that they should not rest. When he placed himself, ready dressed for his ride, again for a moment in the chair he had occupied before the fire, he was seized with a dread of a repetition of the vision he had seen ten minutes before; and jumping up hastily, he went out into the hall, where the landlord, with a lantern in his hand, met him, and accosted him dubiously.

"It's a pity you have to go on to-night, sir. What with the wind and the snow it will be a nasty ride. I suppose you know the road pretty well, sir?"

"Not very well, but it's fairly straight, as far as I remember," answered Armathwaite. He had never in his life before been in this part of the world, but he would not confess to this, being afraid lest some obstacle should be put in the way of his purpose.

"Ye-es, it is straight enough, but there are one or two places where you'll have to be careful on a night like this."

The front door had in the meantime been opened by the waiter, and the horse, a powerfully-built dapple-grey, who looked as if he had been used in the season for coach work, was standing close to the step, with the ostler at his head. The front of the house escaped the full fury of the wind, but even here the snow was drifting into heaps and ridges in the road. The landlord himself fastened the lantern to the saddle before the traveller mounted.

" You'll put up at Branksome for the night, I suppose, sir ? " he said, as he stepped back upon the doorstep.

" I suppose I shall have to. Plenty of places there where I can get a bed and put up the horse, I suppose ?"

" Yes. ' The George ' is the best, I think."

" All right. Thank you. I shall be back in time for the coach to Conismere to-morrow morning. Good-night."

Before Armathwaite could start, however, the ostler, a wrinkled, white-haired man, saluted him, sidling up rather mysteriously on the near side.

" Beg pardon, sir," he said in a strong North-country dialect, rendered still more unintelligible by the loss of his teeth, "but ee'd best go by t' low road, and not oop past t' loontic 'sylum."

The landlord, who had been on the alert, overheard these words, and broke in with some asperity of tone :

" John, what's that stuff you're talking. There hasn't been any asylum about here since you were a boy."

John, however, unabashed by the snub, only gave a chuckle of superior knowledge, and muttering his belief that if the gentleman went by the high road he would "see summet," he shambled off to the stables. The landlord, shivering in the cold, glanced after him angrily, but felt that some word of explanation was due to his guest.

" The fellow's got a tile loose, sir, I believe. But he's been ostler here for years before I was born, and you don't like to turn off an old hand like that. He wouldn't live three months away from his horses."

" And he has delusions, you think ? "

" Full of them, sir."

" And what's this about an asylum ? "

" I don't know, I'm sure. I've lived here eleven years, and I've never heard anything about any asylum within five miles of the place."

" Ah, well, we've most of us got a bee in the bonnet a good many years before we reach his age. And I've had something to do with lunatics, so there's nothing less likely to frighten me. I won't keep you talking in the cold any longer."

The landlord, however, as he was stepping inside the door, changed his mind, and ran out a few steps in the snow, calling to his guest as the latter rode away. Armathwaite checked his horse, and turned round in the saddle.

"I wanted to tell you, sir, that you had better follow the old man's advice, and keep to the lower road—the one to the right at the fork at the bottom of the hill. Not that there's any fear of 'seeing summet,' as he puts it, but because the higher road rejoins the lower with rather a sudden dip, and on a dark night like this you might make straight through the trees for the lake, and be into it before you knew you were off the road."

"Thanks. I'll certainly follow your advice. Good night."

"Good night, sir."

A few seconds later Armathwaite heard the hotel door close as he rode slowly down the hill, watching the lights in the shops and houses, and the dancing reflection on the snow of the lantern he carried at his saddle-bow. The cold was intense; the wind, which blew straight towards him, dashed the snow-flakes into his face and made them whirl before his dazzled eyes until, benumbed by the frost and excited by the storm, he lost control of his thoughts, and rode on oppressed by a nightmare of vain imaginings, in which the new faces he had seen that day seemed to fight for mastery with those of his old acquaintances, until they all melted into one blurred mass, out of which loomed mistily the vaguely discerned features of the unknown face he had seen in his vision by the fire. He had reached the bottom of the hill; the irregular street of shops and houses now dwindled into a broken line of occasional villas and cottages, the twinkling lights in the windows of which still proved a sufficient guide. The horse seemed to know the road, and kept up a good pace over the level ground; so that Armathwaite, keeping what look-out he could in the blinding snowfall and the driving wind, began to think that both hotel-keeper and ostler had exaggerated the difficulties of his short journey as much as he himself had over-estimated its inconveniences. For the fight

with the storm had raised his spirits just as listening to
its fury from within snug walls had depressed them : he
was a healthy, warm-blooded young fellow, in a chronic
state of need of a little gentle spur from without to show
him at his best, but able to give a good account of
himself when the occasion came.

He rode on in a pleasant sense of mingled excitement
and security until, by the slackening of the horse's pace,
he suddenly became aware that the ground was rising.
A few paces further the ascent became quite steep, and
he could no longer doubt that, in spite of the look-out he
was keeping, he had done what he had been warned not
to do, and taken the higher road. There was nothing
for it but to go forward very carefully, and to be specially
cautious when the road began to dip again. While still
on the ascent he passed various dwellings which, though
he could see nothing of the buildings themselves but an
occasional light in the windows, he judged, from the
gates and the tall, snow-laden evergreens which formed a
screen parallel with the road, to be villas and ornamental
cottages. These were chiefly on the right-hand side, and
they were further apart as the ground still rose ; he then
noticed that the road by which he was travelling skirted
a hill, which rose up steep and black on the left. He was
keeping, through an instinct of natural curiosity, a sharp
watch for the building which the ostler had spoken of as
a lunatic asylum.

Just as, after a few yards of particularly steep ascent,
the road took a pretty sharp turn to the left, a long, low-
built house, standing back only a few feet from the road,
but on ground so much higher as to give it an imposing
appearance of dignity, sprang quite suddenly into view,
and caused Armathwaite to give an instinctive nod
towards it, as he said to himself, " That's the place ! "
The house was built just where the road, having reached
its highest point, began to descend again. A solid stone
wall, about four feet in height at its commencement and
at least twice as high at the end where the ground sank,
rose up straight from the road and terminated in a large
and heavy iron gate, which led into a small square of
steep and rocky garden. The front door, approached by

a flight of steps and adorned with a very deep portico, was at this end of the house; so that the side of the building which faced the road, with its long row of smallish upper windows and the bars in front of most of the lower ones, was decidedly that of the workhouse or asylum order of architecture. Two things only broke up the monotony of its aspect without increasing its cheerfulness; the one was a rather unkempt looking mantle of ivy which, rising from a thick stem between two of the lower windows, spread itself over a great portion of the upper part; the other was a very narrow conservatory, built barnacle-wise in front of a large window near the garden end of the house. Armathwaite unfastened his lantern from the saddle, and checked the horse to make a swift examination of this desolate-looking residence. Except at the upper, or servants' end, where the rays of a huge fire streamed brightly through the barred windows, there was only one light to be seen in the house; this came weakly and dimly through the blurred glass of the conservatory. The result of Armathwaite's inspection was the conviction that if a person not a lunatic were to live there a month in the winter time he would stand a good chance of being a lunatic by the end of it.

He rode past, holding the lantern still in his hand, giving a last backward glance at the dreary house, which interested him and filled him with curiosity to know what people, mad or sane, lived there. The descent now became very steep, and mindful of the hotel-keeper's warning, Armathwaite proceeded with the greatest caution, peering forward into the darkness, his lantern held now high, now low, watching eagerly for the junction with the coach-road. The snow was now falling in larger flakes than ever, and just as man and horse got on to more level ground, the animal slipped and fell with his rider into a deep drift by the side of the road. Armathwaite soon extricated both himself and the horse, but in the tumble the lantern had fallen from his hand. He recovered it after much groping, the wind being too high for the matches, which he struck rapidly one after the other, to aid him in his search. The glass proved to be broken and the wick damp, so that after a few vain attempts to re-light it and a little muttered strong language, he used his last match in trying to light his pipe, and failing in that also as a gust of wind came swooping down upon him and put out the weak little flame, he laughed aloud to assure the wind amiably that he was not conquered after all, and taking the horse by the bridle with a few encouraging words, proceeded to lead him, as the safest means of progression until the road should be safely reached.

How to know when it was reached—that was the question. Armathwaite felt that the tumble had made him lose his bearings, and it was only by the direction of the wind that he was able to fix with any certainty the course he was keeping. It seemed to be growing darker, too, while the snow began to fall less thickly and the wind to blow with less violence. Then a hissing and crackling on each side of him roused his attention to the fact that he was among sparsely-scattered trees, and at the same time the unevenness of the ground told him that he was off the road. He stopped a moment, and, tying his horse to a tree, proceeded a little way ahead to reconnoitre. The ground was growing more broken and more steep, but he now perceived in front of him a clump of snow-covered bushes, and behind that something which he took for a high black wall; he made straight for this wall with rapid steps, and had reached the bushes, when a figure moved quickly out from behind them, raised a lantern high in the air, and cried : " Stop ! "

Armathwaite, with a sharply-drawn breath, reeled backwards, horror-struck and bewildered. For, by the light of the lantern he saw that what he had taken for a wall was the dark water of the lake, into which a moment later he would have stumbled ; while in the countenance of the woman who had preserved him his excited fancy made him see the dreamy eyes and sad expression of the unknown face which had appeared to him in his vision by the fire.

———

CHAPTER III.

IT was some moments before Frank Armathwaite recovered enough self-possession to try to thank the unknown lady whose well-timed appearance had saved him from drowning in the lake. The young Yorkshireman was generally considered well endowed enough with the splendid British virtue of stolidity. But the unusual experiences of the past day had somewhat shattered his normal placid self-confidence, and he stared at his preserver in a dazed manner, as if half-prepared to accept the intervention as miraculous. She, on her side, still said nothing, but remained stationary, holding the lantern above her head and looking at him fixedly through the veil of falling snow, apparently without either surprise or curiosity.

"You are on foot?" she said at last, as, lowering her eyes, she noticed the riding-whip in his hand. Her voice was pleasant enough, but entirely human and colloquial, the voice of a young, well-bred woman.

"I have ridden from Mereside, madam, but a minute ago I lost my way and tied my horse to a tree to reconnoitre. I can't thank you enough for——"

She interrupted him, lowering the lantern she held, and with a glance directing him to turn back and walk with her.

"Yes, it was fortunate for you I was there, certainly."

She said this in a low voice as if talking to herself, and Frank noticed that she smiled at some thought which passed through her own mind. With a few paces they had reached the spot where the horse was tied up. The animal pawed the ground impatiently as they approached, and straining at his bridle, put his nose into the lady's outstretched hand.

"Gray Friar! My old Gray Friar!" cried she in such a plaintive heart-voice that Armathwaite, whose armour under the influence of the exciting situation was not as strong as usual, felt touched to the quick by it.

She drew one arm out of the voluminous, hooded cloak which shrouded her from head to foot, and flinging it impulsively round the horse's neck, pressed her cheek lovingly against his shaggy mane, to which the snow-flakes clung in a cold, damp mass.

"He was my horse, my own horse, and I had to sell him," she said very quietly as she recovered herself, and, unfastening the horse's bridle, proceeded to lead him back to the road. "Mr. Greenfell, at the hotel, is very kind to him, I know; but he will never be so happy again as he was with me. No, let me lead him, please; I like it."

Armathwaite could only walk by her side in silence. He scarcely dared to put questions to this strange woman with weird sad eyes, who, after saving his life, seemed to have taken possession of him body and soul, and to deem it unnecessary to enlighten him as to the disposal she meant to make of either. They left the trees and the uneven ground behind them—and, the wind being now at their backs and the snow therefore less blinding, Armathwaite could distinguish without much difficulty the point at which they reached the level road.

"This," said the lady, indicating the way from left to right, "is the high road from Mereside to Branksome."

She crossed it without further comment than her companion's polite if rather futile "Oh, indeed," and they began to re-ascend the steep road on which he had come to grief. One thing the young man knew without asking: this mysterious lady who had apparently been on the look-out for human flotsam and jetsam on this boisterous night, came from the gloomy house which had aroused his attention half an hour before. Dwelling and occupant fitted each other like the nautilus and its shell. The soft brown eyes of the woman—they were brown, he could swear, though he had had no chance of optically assuring himself of the fact—had just the same saddened, desolate attraction as the large window through which he had seen a dim light filtering weakly between the dark leaves of the plants in the little conservatory.

As he had expected, the lady who seemed to think further conversation superfluous, stopped before the heavy iron gates and pulled the handle of a long rusty chain which hung beside them. This immediately set

jangling a bell, the funereal tones of which struck as
great a chill into Armathwaite as if it had been the passing bell for his own soul. She then pushed open one
side of the gate, led the horse in, and invited the apparently less important human creature to enter also.
Armathwaite thought, as he watched her playing affectionately with the bridle of her old favourite, that she
had forgotten the rider in the interest of this meeting
with the horse, and had led him home as an accidental
adjunct of the animal, to be considered at her leisure.
But the appearance at the door of a young maid-servant
who seemed struck with amazement at the spectacle
before her, roused the lady from her abstraction, while
an old mastiff ran down the steps and licked her hand.
She turned to the stranger and said very graciously :

"Are you anxious to get to Branksome to-night ? You
would hardly be able to see Dr. Peele before morning,
and we should be very happy to give his friend shelter
for the night."

Armathwaite felt so certain that he had not mentioned
Dr. Peele's name, and therefore so utterly amazed at the
lady's knowing his destination, that he stammered and
answered in a low, shy tone with great confusion. She
entered the house with a grave gesture of invitation to
him to follow, and told the servant to take the horse to
the stables. Just as the girl was about to obey her
order, she turned quickly and asked in a harder voice,
"Is your master in ? "

"Not yet, ma'am," answered she, and she went out,
closing the door behind her, to the grey horse, which
stood patiently and placidly waiting at the foot of the
steps from which his old mistress had so often mounted
him. Armathwaite was too much absorbed by his
interest in the lady herself to examine very minutely the
hall in which he was standing. He perceived that it
was long, wide and lofty, that one wall was well-lined
with whips and guns and fishing-tackle, and that there
was a hat-and-coat stand covered with masculine garments. This was interesting, inasmuch as all these
things must belong to the lady's relations, concerning
whom Armathwaite longed to know more. He hoped,

as a young man instinctively hopes on making acquaintance in a romantic manner with an attractive woman,
that she was not married, and in spite of a certain dis-
couraging dignity in bearing and repose in her manner,
he had an undefinable conviction that she was free. He
offered to help her as she disencumbered herself of her
outer garment, which proved unmistakably to be a
French cavalry cloak. She thanked him, but shook her
head and begged him to take off his own overcoat, which
was covered with snow. When he had obeyed, she stood
before him transformed. Rather above the middle
height, but looking taller, Armathwaite saw a lady of
about twenty-two years of age, dressed in a sapphire-blue
velvet gown as plain as a habit, with a square-cut bodice.
From her neck to her feet hung a long gauzy dark-blue
drapery like a night-cloud, which glistened with bright
drops, the colours of which changed as she moved. The
skin of her face and neck was fair, with a warm, pinkish
healthy fairness ; her eyebrows and eyes were dark ; and
her hair, which seemed to be abundant to the verge of
unmanageableness, was a goldy-brown where it fell over
the forehead, and a brownish-gold where it lay in coils on
the top of her head. Her features were regular, but not
strikingly handsome ; and Armathwaite's first impulse, in
spite of the admiration inspired by the distinction of her
appearance and a certain attribute which old-fashioned
people call elegance, was one of distinct disappointment.
The poetry was gone from her. In this handsome
dinner-dress she might be the central figure of a novel ;
in the hooded cloak, with the snowflakes in her hair, she
might have been the heroine of an epic. At least so
Armathwaite thought as he looked from the crown of
bright hair on her head to the train of glossy velvet
which, seeming to have sprung into existence suddenly,
now lay curled round her feet. The transformation
mitigated the faint disappointment he felt when, glancing
at her hands, he saw that she wore a wedding-ring.
Her manner too seemed to have changed with her
dress; instead of the grave, abstracted silence which
had awed and charmed him, she now seemed to fall
naturally and easily into a pretty, but more conven-

tional, mood of graceful apology for her unconventional conduct.

"I am afraid you must think me a lunatic for carrying you off in this unceremonious way," she said kindly, but with a great deal of dignity. "I believe some of the villagers declare that this house was once a lunatic asylum, and I am sure, after the way in which you have been treated, you will not fail to agree with them. Did you not take me for a mad-woman?" she asked in a suddenly serious tone, looking steadily, almost anxiously, up for his answer.

"No, madam, certainly I did not," said Armathwaite heartily.

The lady seemed relieved, and a touch of her old earnest and pensive manner came back upon her as, instead of immediately speaking again, she fixed ingenuously searching eyes upon the stranger's face, and after gazing at him intently for some moments, withdrew them, leaving Armathwaite, much to his own surprise, in the peaceful conviction that she was deeply interested in and satisfied with her own impressions.

For the lady saw a broad-shouldered, deep-chested man, about seven-and-twenty years of age, just over six feet in height, erect and muscular, of the handsomest type of North-country Englishmen, fair-skinned, blue-eyed, with clear-cut aquiline features, a moustache of the colour which in women's hair is called golden, and hair a shade darker, already worn a little thin on the temples. He had the open, honest expression which belongs to this physical type irrespectively of character, and a certain grave kindliness of glance not so common or so apt to be misleading. Frank Armathwaite was altogether a person on whom both men and women instinctively looked with favour, but it had never before happened to him to read that favour expressed so frankly and so seriously in the eyes of any human being as in those of this mysterious unknown lady.

"Come into the drawing-room," she said, when her inspection was over. "I will introduce you to Mr. Crosmont. My name is Alma Crosmont. Yours is Dr.——"

She paused and looked down, knitting her brows as if she had forgotten. More astonished than ever, the young Yorkshireman supplied the information in a low voice.

"Armathwaite—Frank Armathwaite."

She repeated it after him slowly, however, as if the name was new to her. For the first time the very natural suggestion flashed across his half-benumbed mind that a physician had been sent for to see Dr. Peele, and that Mrs. Crosmont had mistaken this chance traveller for the expected visitor.

"I am afraid, madam," he said, standing still as she invited him to follow her to the narrower part of the long hall, on to which a row of doors opened on the left-hand side, "that I have had the good fortune to receive a welcome not intended for me. My visit to Branksome—if indeed I shall ever get there—is quite a chance one."

But the lady, standing also quite still, and watching his face as he spoke, gave a curious smile.

"Chance!" she repeated softly; and then after a short pause she added gravely and courteously, "Well, call it chance if you like, you are welcome all the same."

It was such a pretty speech, so graciously said, and the lady seemed so perfectly mistress of the situation, that Armathwaite could only bow his thanks and follow her as she turned and moved slowly on, and await his introduction to Mr. Crosmont with curiosity and interest only exceeded by that which he felt concerning the lady herself. He had read—or, excited by the romantic circumstances of his meeting with her, he had fancied he read in her soft eyes a helpless, hopeless unrest which belied the idea that she could be a happy woman; and given the case of a young woman, married, attractive and unhappy, where can the fault be in the eyes of a man seven-and-twenty, but in the brutal or unsympathetic husband? Frank Armathwaite felt with perfect loyalty that he already hated Mr. Crosmont, that he did not want to see Mr. Crosmont except to satisfy himself in what fleshly guise that soulless creature walked the earth. Just where the hall narrowed suddenly to half its first width there was a door on the left which the lady opened, and Armathwaite followed her into one of those rooms which, having acquired, partly through harbouring generations of gentle owners, and partly by the mellowing lapse of years, a physiognomy distinct and eloquent as a noble human face, once seen are never forgotten.

It was an oblong, rectangular apartment, of fair size and lofty, with two large windows, one at the end of the room overlooking the garden, with a wide, cushioned window-seat; the other at the side facing the road. Before this latter window, which reached to the floor, was built the little conservatory, which afforded a narrow and draughty but at any rate covered walk, with a glimpse of the lake and a view of the hills on the other side. There was no prevailing colour in the room; time and wear and the sun had mellowed every tint to a harmonious and restful shabbiness, working their gentle will on loud-toned, large-patterned cretonne, decided wall-paper and striking carpet, until the taste of past generations was vindicated, and blue roses and orange dahlias as large as saucers blended into that harmony which more modern upholstery vainly seeks in brownish yellows and bilious greens. The mantelpiece, of red marble with lighter veins, was low and broad; it was hung with a valance of faded needlework, and upon it stood no clock, but a Dresden group of shepherds and shepherdesses under trees, mounted on a red velvet stand and enclosed reverently under a glass shade. On each side of this treasure stood a tall silver branched candlestick, and about the feet of these principal objects was a cluster of fortuitous atoms : a tiny bronze statuette of a Roman warrior, with a wonderful amount of fierceness for his size; a Venetian gondola, which had evidently suffered at the hands of admiring children ; a Swiss cottage, two small, empty flower-vases, a handsome chased gold snuff-box, and a quantity of bits of quartz and spar. To each corner was fastened a movable banner-screen in worn tapestry needlework. To a Londoner the absence of a clock gave a pleasant, soothing sense of time being no object with the occupants of this quiet room. And the small sheet of looking-glass, in an old-fashioned gilt frame, which stood at the back of the mantelpiece, was only just high enough to reflect the light of the candles and to show the back view of the trees and the shepherds and shepherdesses, and not imposing enough to suggest the pomps and vanities of the far-off world. In the corner opposite to the door, and close to the conservatory window, stood, well away from the wall, an ancient semi-grand piano, of only six octaves' compass. No other object in the room was striking enough to arrest the attention except a pretty little modern work-table, evidently a recent present, which stood by the sofa near the fire-place, and bore a dainty freight of bright-coloured silks, a volume of Shelley bound in Russia leather, a tiny old-fashioned timepiece in the shape of a brass figure of Atlas bending beneath the weight of the globe, and a Venetian glass vase containing a single rose.

In an arm-chair by the fire, with his back to the door, sat a middle-aged man, the top of whose head was completely bald ; he was reading by the light of a candle fixed to his chair. As the door opened, he said in a kind voice, " Well, little one, and what have you been up to now ? " and held out his hand without turning round or putting down his book. Armathwaite was much struck by this circumstance. There was a warm, loving sympathy in voice, action, and manner, which charged the whole atmosphere of the old room with the fragrance of home. His first impression that this must be the lady's father was strengthened by her response to his greeting. She took his outstretched hand in one of hers, and kissed his forehead as she said :

" I've brought a gentleman to see you, daddy."

The book was put down at once, with a start of surprise. The new-comer came forward, and the lady said simply :

" Dr. Armathwaite—Mr. Crosmont."

" Not her husband, surely," thought Frank.

Mr. Crosmont rose, taking off his reading-spectacles hastily, and held out his hand. He was a man of middle height, with a beard and a fringe of reddish hair turning rapidly grey, undistinguished features, and mild, dreamy blue eyes.

"I daresay you know, Dr. Armathwaite, that a stranger in this part of the world, at this time of the year, is worth a king's ransom," said he, with evident pleasure at the meeting, which was, it was also easy to see, quite unexpected on his side.

"But if you once let the world know how they may expect to be treated here, you will be overrun with them," said Armathwaite gratefully.

Mr. Crosmont glanced inquiringly at the lady, who seemed for the moment rather disconcerted; at least, she answered with her eyes cast down.

"I was at the corner of the road by the lake, when I saw someone making straight for the water; in another moment he would have been in, would you not?" she ended, turning appealingly to the young doctor.

"Indeed I should," said Armathwaite earnestly. "I had lost my way altogether. You saved my life."

"But what were you doing out there by the lake on a night like this?" asked Mr. Crosmont, not at all satisfied.

"Oh, never mind, daddy, it was only one of my pranks; these high winds always get into my head, you know, and blow all the brains away."

"Were you waiting for Edwin?" he then asked, in a very gentle and sympathetic tone.

She hesitated like a school-girl, then raised her head with what seemed to be an impulse of straightforward, almost defiant honesty.

"No."

"H'm, I thought not," muttered Mr. Crosmont, and then he turned again to the visitor. "Do you know the lake country well?" he asked. "It is rather a risky thing to travel about here at night if you do not."

"It is my first visit; and I can't hope to see much of it, for to-morrow afternoon I must be in Glasgow."

As he said this, some impulse he did not recognise made him turn to look at Mrs. Crosmont. She was sitting on a sofa, and was unrolling one corner of a large piece of some bright-coloured needlework. The moment his glance fell upon her she slowly raised her eyes until they met his, and at the same time he felt a conviction break in suddenly upon his mind that the next evening would find him still in the lake country. And then again came upon him the same unaccountable impulse that had before moved him, his present surroundings dimly fading till he saw again before him the flashing eyes and superb beauty of Lady Kildonan. This intuition was instantly followed by a fierce impulse of rebellion against the will that dared to assert a power to overcome his own. He looked a second time at the lady, this time with a strongly antagonistic feeling; again he met her eyes, but his irritation melted instantly, for he saw only a very sweet woman's face wearing a plaintive and, as it seemed to him, beseeching expression. Armathwaite, who was sitting in front of the fire between his host and hostess, felt that, in spite of all the excitement of his journey and of his introduction to this kindly household, he was going off again into a strange and feverish reverie like that which had possessed him at the Mereside hotel earlier in the evening. He made an attempt to rise, but so clumsily that it attracted the attention of his companions, and at a sign from the lady, Mr. Crosmont put his arm within that of the young man, and suggesting that the room was too warm after the keen night air, led him off to have a glass of wine. Armathwaite felt grateful for this kindness, and indignant with himself for needing it. A proverb among his acquaintances for power alike of mind and of muscle, how on earth came he to double up morally and physically under the puny influences of a warm room and a woman's not particularly handsome eyes?

He felt better as soon as he got into the cooler air of the hall, or out of the radius of the eyes; he was not sure which was the restorative. At any rate, by the time they had reached the dining-room, and Mr. Crosmont had poured him out a glass of sherry, he was himself again, was secretly scoffing at his feverish and ridiculous fancy concerning a kind-hearted lady who had saved his life and treated him with unexampled hospitality, and was wondering hard what it was that, in spite of the mutual affection of its master and mistress, the charm of the old rooms, and the warm kindliness of the welcome he had received, made a false note in the harmony, and impressed him, stranger that he was, with the belief that in this peaceful-seeming household there was something wrong. In the dining-room he noted a circumstance, however, which might possibly afford a clue to the mystery.

The end of the long, wide dining-table nearest to the fire was laid for dinner for one person. Was there some third member of the household whose presence was a discord? Who was " Edwin," of whom mention had been made? Two dogs lay stretched on the rug by the fire, a Newfoundland and a retriever; they raised their heads as the gentlemen entered, gave a languid wag of the tail in greeting to the one they knew, and relapsed into a comfortable doze.

" Are you fond of animals ? " asked Mr. Crosmont, as he walked to the hearth-rug where the dogs were lying.

" Well, I think I like any dog better than most human beings, and a good horse better than my best friend."

" Well said, though you don't mean it. At any rate, you believe in their intelligence. These brutes are half human. Look here." He looked at the two extended, sleepy heads, and said in the same tone : " I wonder where the little one is."

Instantly both heads were raised with ears pricked on the alert.

" They know who I mean, you see. Up here in the wilds one must make friends with the beasts, or be solitary. It's a dull life, I can tell you."

" I hardly think I should find it so under the same circumstances. For a bachelor living by himself it would be dreary enough. But with a charming wife and——"

" Did you think the little one was my wife ? " asked Mr. Crosmont, with evident pleasure. " I wish she were ; though Autumn and Spring don't go well together. I am Uncle Hugh. She is my niece, my niece by marriage, and my child by affection. I would walk into the lake for her any day. Some day I shall walk her husband into the lake, if he doesn't look out," he added in a gruff comment to himself, which was a little embarrassing to his hearer. There was a pause of a few seconds, during which Mr. Crosmont remembered that he was speaking in parables, and explained briefly, in his usual abrupt manner : " My nephew is Lord Kildonan's agent ; he's a good boy enough, but he gets his head a little turned, up at The Crags, between my lord's confidences on the one hand, and my lady's on the other. In fact, the big house takes the colour out of the little one, you see. I suppose it's natural enough, but it's a pity ; and one can't say a word to him, because of course if one does it is all zeal for his employer's interests ; and they really have been very kind to him. Still, it's a pity."

Armathwaite thought so too, and felt filled with compassion for the soft-eyed wife, obliged, in the zenith of her beauty and charm, to fall back upon the companionship of a middle-aged relation of her husband when she should have been enjoying the devotion of the husband himself. He was trying to evolve a remark which should show enough, but not too much of the sympathy he felt, when·sounds of a man's angry voice and a man's heavy tread were heard in the hall, and at the same moment the curious phenomenon was witnessed of the two dogs rising slowly from the hearthrug and concealing themselves under the table at the end furthest from where the dinner was laid. Armathwaite was listening with great interest to the tones of the unseen man's voice, as he gave an order to one of the servants with his hand upon the outer handle of the dining-room door.

"That is my nephew," said Mr. Crosmont, shortly.

Armathwaite rose to his feet, feeling very uncomfortable. For he recognised the voice as that of the man who had been driving Lady Kildonan's sleigh when she dropped her handkerchief, and whom, from the livery he wore, he had taken for the groom. Little as he knew of the duties of an agent to a country gentleman, Armathwaite felt certain that the wearing of the latter's livery must be less than optional, and he had an awkard conviction that he had been an undesired witness of the fact that the pranks of Miss Dighton and Master Ned had not ceased when the former became Lady Kildonan and the latter "agent to my lord."

CHAPTER IV.

THE door was thrown open roughly, and Mr. Edwin Crosmont, stalking in with the amiable expression of an enraged bulldog, stopped short on finding himself in the presence of a stranger, and gave Armathwaite an opportunity of noting well every detail of his personal appearance. He was a man of about five feet nine inches in height, so well-built and erect that he would have passed as handsome, in spite of an ill-featured face, to which prominent grey eyes, a short nose, and protruding lips gave a canine cast, which was rendered more unprepossessing by an expression which, on this particular occasion, was alternately morose and savage.

He had black hair, a small dark moustache, and a rather sallow skin ; he was dressed in a Norfolk suit, and riding boots, a costume which showed off the proportions of his figure to great advantage ; while his hands, one of which still held his gloves and riding-whip, were white and well shaped.

"Who's this ?" he asked shortly, and in the dogged voice of a person who had been prepared for an unwelcome encounter and meant to make himself as disagreeable as he could over it. "And where's Alma ? And what's this I hear about her going out by herself at this time of night ? It's not proper ; it's most improper, and I won't have it, and so she must understand. Where is she ? "

Armathwaite, who was watching him steadily, making up his mind that this was quite the most offensive brute he had ever seen, saw, from a look which passed suddenly over young Mr. Crosmont's face, that the latter had recognised him, and that the recognition had the effect of frightening him and calming him down. Before the irate gentleman had had time to do more

than make a half-turn towards the door, Armathwaite
had reached it in two long strides, and looking down
with the expression of superb contempt which his
superior inches enabled him to assume with particular
effect, he said coldly :

"You have forgotten to hear my name : it is Francis
Armathwaite. I am sorry you should think my presence
an intrusion. Mr. Crosmont and Mrs. Crosmont were
kind enough to take pity upon a traveller and a stranger.
I deeply regret that their generous hospitality should
seem to you ill-timed, as it was certainly undeserved. I
will not obtrude myself upon you any longer, but I beg
you to receive my thanks for the kindness shown to me
by your wife and by this gentleman."

He bowed and opened the door quickly, but started
on seeing Mrs. Crosmont, who entered very quietly,
glancing from him to her husband as if she apprehended
the situation. Armathwaite, eagerly on the alert to
notice the demeanour towards each other of this
apparently ill-mated pair, saw that the lady fixed upon
her husband a look so eloquent with dignity, pleading,
and wifely submission, that it seemed a revelation of
noble depths in the woman's character, and filled him,
the onlooker, with admiration and reverence. The
husband, however, would not even meet her eyes,
although he hastened to apologize to the stranger with a
manner which, although still somewhat sullen and not
particularly well-bred, showed rather more grace and
sense of propriety than his previous demeanour had
promised.

"Yes, yes ; I beg your pardon. You must excuse
my hastiness. I am very glad if they have been of any
service to you. People who come here have to take the
rough—that's me, with the smooth—that's my wife and
uncle. Pray stay and dine with me ; I shall be heartily
glad of your company."

"Thank you very much," said Armathwaite, speaking
still rather stiffly. "I dined at Mereside some time ago,
and I must get to Branksome to-night. If Mrs. Crosmont
will allow me——"

He turned to the lady, and stopped short. Her eyes,

which began to fascinate him by an eloquence which seemed to him preternatural, looked straight into his and commanded him to stay. There was a rather awkward pause, which was broken by Uncle Hugh, whose abrupt but genial voice struck upon the ear with a certain soothing persuasiveness, which suggested that he was in the habit of remaining on the alert to resolve family discords as he saw the opportunity.

"Come, Dr. Armathwaite, you won't want us all to go down on our knees to induce you to stay, I'm sure. We have a reputation for hospitality to keep up, and we should have each to do private penance if we let you go before morning. Come now, say you're persuaded."

He passed his arm through that of the young man, and as his nephew had now recovered from his ill-temper enough to echo the hospitable words with a moderately good grace, Armathwaite allowed himself to yield without much difficulty, and without betraying his secret eagerness for a better acquaintance with the interesting household. In a very few minutes it became clear to the visitor that his presence was a welcome relief, even to the surly host himself, who explained that he had been hard at work all day riding about the estate on his various duties, and that this life, involving as it did long waiting for his dinner—which he owned he considered the greatest of the ills which flesh is heir to—was very trying even to the best of tempers. So dinner was brought in for him, and Armathwaite sat by and talked to him, while the other two placed themselves by the fire behind the master of the house, with each a dog for company.

Every moment that he sat conversing with this man, who seemed at this stage of the acquaintance to be a person of strong passions, narrow mind, and conventional ideas, Armathwaite became more interested in the singular union of two human beings whose natures seemed on the surface so utterly antagonistic as those of the husband and wife. He glanced furtively from time to time at the lady, as he could do without fear of detection, for Mr. Crosmont's interest in the viands before him was absorbing and sustained; she made an entrancing picture as she sat with almost statuesque tranquillity by the fire, her white hand resting on the head of the retriever, her eyes cast down as if in deep thought, while the flames threw a softening glow on her somewhat set features, and made the bead-drops on her dress glisten like fire-flies. It seemed to the young Yorkshireman, who was chivalrously ready to believe her a gentle and faultless martyr to the indifference of a soulless boor, that the very curve of her fingers round the dog's shaggy ears revealed a capacity for tenderness unexercised, unsought : the shape of her heavy, drooping eyelids, of her red-lipped and not very small mouth, seemed to him to denote depths of feeling, of sentiment, of passion which to the eyes of her negligent lord and master were as invisible as a jewel in a room without light. These musings filled his mind even while his lips were busy assenting to such broad principles as that " You can't expect a man whose days are occupied with numerous and harrassing details of management to be able to interest himself in dry and abstruse subjects in the evenings." Armathwaite wondered whether these and kindred remarks were directed at Mrs. Crosmont, the intellectual cast of whose face suggested that the "numerous and harassing details " of domestic management would still leave her mind room for more elevated subjects.

"Still, the world would be a dull place if we could not sometimes forget our own immediate surroundings and the wearisome routine of perhaps distasteful duties by the help of art and books, wouldn't it ? " ventured Armathwaite, addressing the husband, but aware that he was appealing to the wife.

Even as Mr. Crosmont, who had now risen from the table and was stretching himself, returned a characteristic answer to the effect that "By Jove ! books only made life duller, and he didn't think the world would be a penny the worse if all the writers and artists in it were drowned in Conismere to-morrow." Mrs. Crosmont raised her eyes and conveyed, with one straight look, her entire, her passionate concurrence in the stranger's views.

" My wife reads a great deal, but it certainly doesn't

make her any livelier," continued Mr. Crosmont, who had not seen his wife's look for the reason that, as Armathwaite particularly noticed, he systematically avoided meeting her eyes. " I consider that it's a very poor head that can't get ideas of its own, without going to books for somebody else's. If you read a book of travels, which is supposed to tell you facts, why how can you answer for it that they are facts ? And as for novels and poetry, it is my firm belief, which nothing can alter, that it's to their pernicious influence we owe the deterioration in our daughters and wives."

As Mr. Crosmont was evidently still a year or two short of thirty, it was plain that his firm belief could not be founded on a lengthened experience of the decadence of womankind.

"What is the use of spending money and patience teaching a girl to paint a picture that nobody'd have on their walls while there are chromos to be bought, when in half the time she might learn how to make a very good pudding ? " he continued, with the solemn arrogance which creeps over even a young man at the conclusion of a very heavy dinner.

" But then the chances are that the girl who couldn't learn to paint a picture of more value than a chromo, would never get beyond a bad pudding," remarked Armathwaite.

" And, Ned, I helped to make the fritters you have just eaten. Do you think they would have been lighter if I had not learned to paint ? "

For the first time a spark of genuine good humour came into Mr. Crosmont's prominent eyes.

" Well, no," he admitted ; and then added with his first touch of pleasantry, "but there might have been more of them ! "

There was a little laugh at this, and Mr. Crosmont, humming an air as he crossed the room to his cigar-cabinet, asked his visitor in a genial voice if he would smoke. Armathwaite excused himself, feeling that to puff tobacco smoke into the air which surrounded that dainty lady would be like profaning the temple of a goddess. She seemed to guess the reason of his refusal, and look-

ing at him with a gracious smile, said she did not mind
smoke in the least.   Drawing a chair to the fire between
his uncle and Armathwaite, Mr. Crosmont observed that
they would not go into the drawing-room ; it was such a
mouldy old place.   If he were superstitious, he should
think it was haunted.

"They do say in the village that this house is
haunted," observed his uncle.   "The servants have
heard the story too ! their rooms are just over my head,
you know.   And I hear them scurry upstairs at night in
a body, like mice in the wainscot, with a little chorus of
shrieks if one of them calls out 'Boh!'   Not one of
those silly girls would come down-stairs between the
hours of ten at night and six in the morning, if you were
to offer her a new bonnet with the longest feather that
has ever been worn in Mereside."

Apparently this fact was already known to young Mr.
Crosmont, for he betrayed no surprise.

"Have you ever questioned them on the subject,
then ? " asked he quietly.

"Yes.   Agnes is the most communicative on that, as
on any other subject, and she assured me that the corridor—it's always the corridor, you know "—Armathwaite
noticed that at this point young Mr. Crosmont's hand
became suddenly rigid as he was in the act of conveying
his cigar to his lips—"was haunted by a lady who of
course was dressed in white, and who equally of course
had the correct blue marks of strangulation on her throat.'

His nephew laughed.   "They have seen the lady, I
suppose ? "

"There seems to be a doubt upon that point.   But
Nanny is ready to swear by her coral necklace and everything else in the world she holds sacred, that she has
heard unearthly moans and groans in the Dolly Varden
room."

"Don't, uncle ; you will make me so nervous that I
shan't be able to sleep," protested Mrs. Crosmont, in
earnest entreaty.

"Stuff and nonsense ! " said her husband roughly.
" What is the use of the education you think so much of
if you can be frightened by the silly fancies of a lot of

foolish, chattering maids ! I never yet heard of a sensible woman believing in ghosts."

"I don't believe in ghosts, Edwin," she said very humbly. "But you know that when I get very much excited—and it is so easy to excite me—I fancy I see all sorts of things ; and though I know very well all the time it is only fancy, and that they are not really there, yet if the fancy is very strong, it is quite as dreadful as reality."

She spoke dreamily and absently, in a low, awe-struck voice, with her eyes fixed before her, as if the remembrance of some of her fancies of the night were filling her with vivid horror.

"Of course, if you will read trashy novels and fill your head with imaginary crimes and mysteries just before you go to bed it's no wonder you can't sleep ; I couldn't myself under the same circumstances. As for the Dolly Varden room, the draught comes in at the window, and that's the worst you can say for it."

"Yet you chose it for your own room, and gave it up after sleeping in it only one night ! "

"That was because of the draught, I tell you. The least superstitious person in the world doesn't care to sleep in a gale of wind."

The lady raised her eyebrows very slightly, and looked more than slightly incredulous.

"Colonel Lawes slept there last summer, when it was so hot we all had to keep our windows open ; but we had to change his room the next night. I forget what pretext he gave, but he wouldn't sleep there again," she said.

"Whatever pretext he gave it wasn't ghosts," said her husband shortly.

"Since you have done me the kindness to offer me a shelter for the night, may I ask as a favour if I may sleep in that room ? " asked Armathwaite. "I have no superstitions on the subject of supernatural appearances. I am a light sleeper and have extraordinarily quick ears ; so that if anybody can find out the cause of the prejudice against the room and set Mrs. Crosmont's fears at rest, I ought to be that person."

"Done ! " cried Mr. Crosmont, rising to ring the bell.

" And we'll compare notes at breakfast-time as to our ex
periences in the room."

Everybody looked at him with awakened interest ; it
was plain from the eagerness with which he welcomed his
visitor's proposal that he awaited the result with some
curiosity ; and when a neat and pretty maid-servant, who
answered the summons of the bell, showed manifest consternation at the order to prepare the Dolly Varden
room, Armathwaite felt a little pleasurable excitement at
the adventure. If it were only a rat behind the wainscot-
ing that he was going to discover after this exciting pre-
lude of masculine curiosity and feminine terrors, it would
be at least a satisfaction to set at rest the mind of his
beautiful and interesting hostess.   While Mr. Crosmont
walked away from the fireplace to chaff the maid on her
evident reluctance to fulfil his order, his wife turned to
Armathwaite with a serious face.

"You are very strong-minded," she said. "All doctors
are, I suppose.   Do you know, I think if I were forced
to sleep alone in that room with the door locked on the
outside, I should be found in the morning a raving
lunatic ! Even the sound of a coal dropping out of
the fire in the drawing-room, underneath my room,
makes me start up and tremble, although I know perfectly well what it is. You think this nonsense, of course ;
although, equally of course, you are too courteous to tell
me so."

"No doctor would presume to call it nonsense. If it
were nonsense, so would every symptom of every disorder be."

" Disorder ! "

"Certainly. It proves an entirely unhealthy state of
the nervous system, the result probably of some shock
or over-strain.   Tell me, does your own doctor think you
are in robust health ? "

"No-o, I don't think he does. But I don't know."
Her tone changed, and she spoke with some sadness.
" I never see Dr. Peele now."

" But you are wrong. Don't you feel yourself that you
are wrong ? You have not always trembled at the sound
of a coal falling out of the fire ? "

"No-o."

" You probably know yourself how long it is since you began to suffer like this—for it is suffering."

"No, that is just what I don't know, what I cannot understand. It has come upon me so gradually that I can't remember a beginning to it, but it is since the winter came on that I have become conscious of what seems like a weakening of the powers of my mind. I do things without wishing to do them, without even knowing why: I seem to be losing touch of the things which exist around me, and to start back into actual life with a painful shock at any call for an effort of my own will. Perhaps you understand now my strange conduct towards you, and the babbling loquacity with which I am telling all this to a stranger."

She seemed at that moment to call herself abruptly back into reality, and cast at him, blushing, a quick, shy glance, to see whether he had received her confessions with any astonishment. But the grave, open and kindly gaze of his eyes reassured her.

"Does your husband know ? " he asked.

" Yes, he has been very kind and anxious about me. You haven't seen him at his best," she continued hurriedly, as at that moment the sound of his voice in the hall, scolding the servants, broke upon their ears. " He is a hasty-tempered man, but he has many good qualities. You must not judge a man when you see him harassed with his work, as I'm sure he is at present, though he never complains."

Armathwaite murmured in suitable terms his admiration for his host's exquisite qualities, and the lady spoke again.

"Tell me," she said. "You have seen other people in the nervous state in which I now am ? "

Armathwaite considered.

" I can only remember one," he said, " whose symptoms were exactly the same as you describe yours to be. It was a very singular case, but the cause had nothing in common with yours."

" What was the cause ? "

" A professor, as he called himself, of spiritualism, or

spiritism, an impudent charlatan enough, but with some undoubted powers which I consider purely physical, had employed as what they call a medium, a young girl of extremely sensitive and nervous temperament, who, after having assisted him at these *séances* for some months, became so utterly unhinged in mind and body that she was obliged to put herself under medical advice. Her symptoms were very much like yours. But it certainly cannot be mesmerism which——"

She interrupted him with a quick movement of her head as her husband was heard approaching the room again. "Not a word of mesmerism before him——" she began.

But it was too late. Mr. Crosmont entered, with a frown on his face, and marching up to the hearth-rug, looked from his wife to his guest and back again with evident displeasure. With the same strange and attractive mixture of dignity and submission which Armathwaite had noticed in her before, she rose and held out her hand to him, bade him good night, kissed her uncle, and taking the candle her husband gave her, glided out of the room, looking to Armathwaite's eyes, which were a little dazzled by her strange beauty and her unexpected confidences, like a golden-crowned queen of the night.

He seemed to see the dark-blue glistening dress, the white neck bent, and the soft, shining coils of hair, long after the lady had left the room, and the husband had assailed his ear with confidences which, in their turn, he found unexpectedly interesting.

CHAPTER V

THE departure of the ladies is usually hailed by the coarser sex with relief as the signal for a more unrestrained feast of such reason and flow of such soul as the august assembly can command. When, however, Mrs. Crosmont left her husband and his two companions to their own devices, there fell upon the group a depressed silence, which was broken by the host, who, rising abruptly, suggested an adjournment to his own study. So he snatched up the lamp, which flared and smoked under his rough handling, and, followed by the other two, turned to the left along a wide and rambling passage, which led out of the hall to the servants' offices at the other extremity of the house. On their way they passed the principal staircase, a rather mean erection in light oak, opposite to the dining-room door, and two or three closed doors on either hand.

"This house is nothing better than a rabbit-warren," grumbled the master of it, raising the lamp at every other step to illustrate his words. "It's full of little holes that won't hold more than two people at a time, and there isn't a room of decent size in the whole place. You will laugh when you see what I call my study, Dr. Armathwaite."

They had reached a door at the end of the passage, and Mr. Crosmont explained that it was the back entrance of the house, and that it was the one by which he himself went in and out. On one side of it was a narrow staircase leading to the upper rooms and on the other another door, which led them into the study. Armathwaite had not expected to find himself in an apartment which breathed learning and leisure, but on the other hand he was not quite prepared for such a bold misapplication of the word "study," as the room, which was scarcely larger than a good-sized cupboard, betrayed. There was not a book in sight except "Ruff's Guide to the Turf" and two or three more works of a similar kind, which lay on an office table, strewn with papers, in one corner. There was a shabby carpet and a worn hearthrug. There were two large and comfortable easy chairs, a high office-stool, a straight-backed hall seat and an iron safe, on which stood a handsome punch-bowl. There were more whips and fishing-rods, another gun, and a tennis-bat. Over the mantelpiece was a trophy consisting of a hunting-crop, a cavalry sword, and a revolver, underneath which were scattered a collection of pipes, an almanack, a clock, a match-box, a tobacco-jar, and several pieces of billiard-chalk. On a nail behind the door hung a dear old lounging coat, threadbare, shiny at the seams, ragged at the cuffs; the sort of treasure a dutiful wife makes away with by stealth and bestows in charity, afterwards disclaiming all knowledge of the deed. Into this den Mr. Crosmont brought his companions, and the atmosphere of it had a speedy and wholesome effect upon his temper. He drew the chairs up to the huge, well banked-up fire which was burning in the grate, and producing a bottle of whisky and glasses from a cupboard in the wall, put a small kettle on the fire, and proceeded to slice a lemon, with the sweetest expression he had worn that evening.

Armathwaite, who had now lit a cigar, watched his host through the mellowing smoke with curiosity and interest. The man was seen to more advantage here in his own den than in his wife's presence in the more conventional dining-room. Even the dogs seemed to feel this, for having followed the gentlemen from the one room to the other, they now absorbed the warmest part of the hearthrug in a perfectly fearless manner. One little action, too, which would scarcely have been noticed except by very keen eyes, revealed a more attractive side to Mr. Crosmont's character than had yet been manifest. In passing the office table he knocked off the pile of sporting books, and out of one of them fell a photograph which, after examining it carefully to see that it had sustained no damage, he put, not into the book again, but into his pocket. Whether the portrait was of a man or a woman Armathwaite could not see; but he felt glad that he could not. Under the unromantic but soothing influences of punch and tobacco Edwin Crosmont became good-humoured and genial, and the talk turning upon the Englishman's fetich, the horse, the utmost harmony prevailed until his uncle suddenly asked him why he had sold Alma's horse, when riding was her chief pleasure. In an instant the young man's face clouded.

"I can't let her risk her neck riding about in the winter time along these slippery roads," he said in a tone which showed little of the affectionate solicitude his words implied. "When the Spring comes I'll get her a better horse. Grey Friar was getting old and was touched in the wind."

"She never complained of him. I think she misses her rides. She's not the woman she was six months ago," said his uncle abruptly.

Edwin Crosmont frowned. "She reads ghost stories, and talks about spiritualism and mesmerism and such nonsense, until she makes herself ill with her own fancies," he said irritably.

"I don't think she reads many ghost stories, and I never heard her mention spiritualism until to-night. And then I think it was Dr. Armathwaite who introduced the subject, not Alma."

"Yes, it was I, Mr. Crosmont. I think I was describing to your wife the nervous symptoms which are the result of dabbling with the forces we call mesmeric and hypnotic."

"I must beg you, Dr. Armathwaite, not to talk to her of them again. Of course you don't believe in them yourself, but there is no saying what a nervous and fanciful woman will get into her head."

"I will certainly not mention them to Mrs. Crosmont again, since you wish it ; but as to believing in the existence of those forces, I think it is a matter which has passed out of the realms of dispute."

"You believe in all that rubbish?"

"I believe in the existence of a power we call mesmeric, by which the possessors of it can control the wills of other persons, especially those of a highly nervous temperament."

"Then you are more credulous than the members of your profession usually are, doctor."

Annoyed by his blunt rudeness and ignorance, Armathwaite was about to cite some experiments which had been made in his own presence, when the elder Mr. Crosmont broke in very concisely :

"You have a short memory, Ned. You went to a course of lectures on this subject with me eight years ago, and you were much impressed by them."

"I was younger then," said Edwin shortly, while his face flushed and he glanced with a sort of suspicion at each of his companions. "I recognise now that it was mere quackery."

" These men are obliged to become quacks in the long run, because their powers are intermittent," said Armathwaite. "And they have to introduce the old stuff about messages from the spirits, because the mere controlling of one body by another, through an interesting but not supernatural physical gift, has really too little of the marvellous in it to afford a good living to the possessors of this gift."

"Controlling of the body, you say," broke in the elder Mr. Crosmont. "And how about the mind?"

"The two are so intimately connected that you cannot influence the one without effect upon the other. But that this mesmeric power is in its essence a physical gift is proved, I think, by the fact that people of comparatively coarse and feeble minds have been known to exercise it over persons who were undoubtedly their intellectual superiors."

"H'm; rather a dangerous power then, I should think."

"It might be, certainly, in unscrupulous hands."

Edwin Crosmont had dropped out of the conversation, and was busily choosing a cigar. Armathwaite fancied, however, that in spite of his scoffing, he was more interested than he wished to appear.

"I should think Alma would be a good medium; she has just the nervous, excitable temperament that is open to all influences," said the uncle.

"Well, I won't allow any experiments to be made upon my wife," said Crosmont abruptly. "It is quite bad enough for one doctor to have saddled me with a wife who was the daughter of a lunatic; I don't want another doctor to reduce her to the same state."

His hearers were both shocked—Armathwaite by this revelation, the elder man by the coarseness with which it was made.

"Ned, Ned, think what you're saying," said his uncle.

"Well, and why shouldn't I say it?" cried Edwin, whose face was by this time flushed and his manner reckless. "Why should I hide the way in which I have been hoodwinked into marrying a woman whose eyes tell everyone the horrible truth? Years ago, Dr. Armathwaite," he continued hotly, turning his back impatiently upon his uncle, "this house was a lunatic asylum, very private, very select, but none the less an asylum, in which there was a mad musician who dabbled in your mesmerism and your quackery as well. He was cured, or said to be cured ; at any rate he was discharged, and Dr. Peele, who was some relation of the proprietor of the place, took an interest in him which he extended to a daughter the man had. When the musician died, Dr. Peele was his executor and guardian to the child. For some reason or other he took it into his head to make a match between us, and when I, at that time suffering from a great disappointment, went to make a stay in London, he introduced me to this girl, who was then studying at the South Kensington Art Schools, and without telling me a word about her father's history, never rested till he had made a match of it. Was that what you or any man can call honest ? "

" On the face of it one hardly likes to answer. Did he offer no explanation ? "

" Oh, yes, he swore the father never was mad at all. But you have only to look into her eyes to see that it was a lie, and I don't care who knows it from my lips instead."

Armathwaite was appalled. On the one hand this seemed the only rational solution of the problem presented by Mrs. Crosmont's weird eyes and mysterious manner ; on the other, he was unwilling, even passionately unwilling, to believe that the strange, spiritual fascination this woman exercised over him, the atmosphere of refinement of person and of mind which seemed to surround her, proceeded from nothing but a weak or deranged intellect. But the lady had a stronger ally than he could dare to be. Rising from his seat, his kind blue eyes alight with feeling, the elder Mr. Crosmont laid his hand firmly on his nephew's shoulder and said in a solemn voice :

" You would see no madness in your wife's eyes, Ned, if you hadn't been bewitched by a pair that have no heart behind them."

There followed upon this direct speech a minute of excited silence, each man of the three waiting with loud-beating heart for what would come of the challenge. At last Ned Crosmont raised his head; his sallow skin looked grey in the lamp-light under the influence of some strong emotion, the lines seemed to have suddenly deepened in his face, and his light eyes to have grown bright and eloquent.

"Don't talk about things you don't understand, Uncle Hugh," he said in a husky voice. "What right have you to prate of the heart or no heart of a woman to whom you have only said 'How do you do' and 'Good day?' And if you can learn so much by a casual glance at a pair of blue eyes, why shouldn't I be able to learn something by daily looking into a pair of brown ones? I will listen to whatever you have to say in excuse for Alma, but not a word in blame of—anyone else."

Armathwaite kept very still, feeling the awkwardness of being present at this domestic skirmish, and recognising with astonishment and sympathy the tragic intensity of the passions that surged in the breast of each member of this quiet country household: the fierce and fervid devotion which the surly and coarse-mannered man felt for his old playfellow; the tender fatherly sympathy of the elder man for both rough husband and delicate wife; the yearning unrest of a disappointed heart which looked out from the sad eyes of the neglected wife. Ned Crosmont pulled himself together in a few moments and with a loud laugh said they were making a dull evening of it. He mixed more punch and drank himself more deeply than the rest, but the hilarity he wished to promote would not come. Uncle Hugh told some good stories, for he had been all over the world, first in the English and afterwards in the Turkish army, and had gained much strange experience and the art of recording it well: but through all his laughter, Ned looked harassed, and Armathwaite found the living drama, among the personages of which he had been suddenly cast, more interesting than any of the picturesque incidents of a roving life.

When the little clock on the mantelpiece struck twelve, Uncle Hugh, glancing at the nodding head of his nephew, who had for the last half-hour sunk into silence and moroseness, gave the signal for retirement, which Armathwaite, who could scarcely keep awake, had long been earnestly craving. Ned sprang up and angrily demanded what he meant by breaking up the party just when they were beginning to enjoy themselves; but his uncle merely said:

"I fancy after a day's hard travelling Dr. Armathwaite would enjoy himself more in bed."

Going out of the room he returned immediately with three candles, and lighting them deliberately without heeding his nephew's grumbling, he marched serenely out of the room, avoiding by a clever and nimble "duck" of his head, "Sport in the Reign of the Georges," which the dutiful Ned aimed at him with a parting benediction. Armathwaite seized the opportunity to wish his host good night, and was allowed to follow Uncle Hugh without molestation. Half-way along the passage the elder man halted for the younger to come up with him.

"He'll perhaps be there by himself half the night," he whispered. "He's making himself an old man before his time by this turning night into day and—and—other follies. If he has to make a short journey, to Liverpool or Edinburgh or anywhere else, as he has to do once or twice a month, on Lord Kildonan's business, he starts off at night, when there's no earthly reason why he shouldn't go by day. He says it's the night hours that are hardest to get through. Sometimes he makes poor Alma sit up in that little den all night with him when he's in the blues. Now I ask you is that a right state of things for a man with the constitution of a horse, leading a life which ought to be the healthiest in the world?"

"Certainly not. It's about as wrong as it can be. And is there *no one* with influence enough over him to induce him to alter it?"

"The only person who has the influence hasn't the will to care two straws what he does with himself when he is out of her sight. As long as he is at her beck and call by day, it's all the same to her whether he sleeps or drinks himself into frenzy at night. At least that is my impression. And for all that I don't believe there's any harm in her; I suppose no man could look at her and think there was. She's just a beautiful spoilt woman, and I don't suppose anybody could make her understand that she hasn't a heaven-born right to the worship and the submission and the dutiful reverence of every man who comes near her. You can't blame her: lots of ugly women think the same: only the ugly women can't get their rights, and she can. It's rough on Alma though, very."

"Can't her husband see that his treatment tends to bring about that very derangement of which he speaks? For he does not really believe in it, surely!"

"It is hard to say. One inclines so naturally to believe what would excuse one's own conduct."

"How long have they been married?"

"Eighteen months. Since the first six weeks of their marriage they have always lived here, and I have lived with them by their own desire. From the very first things have all tended the same way; no quarrelling, no discussion; but always the same estrangement, the same neglect, moroseness, and irritability on his side, the same silent submission on hers getting more and more marked as time goes on. It's a strange and unhappy state of things, and one wonders how it will end."

Armathwaite wondered still more how it had begun. That a man in all the freshness of the first weeks of married life should be indifferent to the grace and charm of such an attractive and interesting woman as Alma Crosmont seemed to him marvellous, in spite of the impression Lady Kildonan's more dazzling beauty had made upon him. They were absurdly ill-matched, evidently; this coarse, uncultivated man, with strong sensual inclinations, and few ideas beyond their gratification; and the nervous, sensitive woman, who seemed to quiver with repressed passion and sentiment even while, with pathetic wifeliness, she listened with dutifully-bent head to her husband's grumbling comments on his dinner, the weather, her dulness, the conspiracy of all things, animate and inanimate, against his comfort. And Lady Kildonan, did she know or care for the havoc she was working in her old playfellow's household? The question raised many others equally interesting, and

Armathwaite decided that he must at all hazards accept this lakeside siren's invitation to The Crags, as he easily could do on pretence of returning the twice-lost handkerchief; for whenever he inclined to the belief that she was acting in very wantonness, her sparkling face would rise up again in his memory as he had seen it smiling good-humouredly through the veil of falling snow, and he said to himself that it could not be: she was as fair as a rose, and it was no fault of hers if men would look upon her fairness until it shut out everything else from their sight. And with these reflections he found himself at the top of the staircase, exactly opposite to which was the door of his room.

Uncle Hugh opened the door for him, and said he hoped the wind wouldn't keep him awake.

"I don't fancy it will," he added, cheerfully. "You see this room is in exactly the centre of the front of the house. When it was an asylum," he continued in a low tone, "this was called the doctor's room, and was used by the principal; so it ought to be pretty comfortable. However, if you should be harassed by uneasy spirits or anything of that sort, my room is two doors off, to the left on the opposite side; you can come right in and jump upon me, or tilt the bedstead up, for I sleep like a log. Good-night."

He went away, shutting the door after him, and Armathwaite gave a glance round the apartment. It was a rather small room, plainly furnished with a high iron bedstead and a mahogany suite. No well-regulated phantom can be conceived as haunting a room in which there is not a four-poster with dark green or dark blue hangings; and as besides the young doctor's thoughts were still too fully occupied with the living for him to trouble himself about the spirits of the dead, he undressed, blew out the candles and got into bed without even the passing tribute of a smile at the reputed mysterious attributes of the room.

Infatuated husband, fascinating and neglected wife, dangerous beauty, were all, however, powerless against the effects of his long journey. Worn out by fatigue and excitement, in two minutes he was fast asleep.

CHAPTER VI.

INSTEAD of enjoying the dreamless slumber to which his day's work fully entitled him, Armathwaite had not been asleep more than a quarter of an hour when he was half-awakened by certain dull sounds in his ears which he heard at first drowsily, as if they had been part of a disturbing dream. But the sounds continued until his dulled faculties apprehended that he was listening to a woman's sighs. This became gradually clearer to him until, convinced that he was awake, he sat up and held his breath, on the alert for the least sound. The wind had gone down since the evening, but still from time to time a gust would sweep round the house, rattling the window-panes, rustling the ivy, and then dying away with a moan among the hills. He heard one such gust as he sat up, staring with sleepy eyes in the direction of the window, through which, however, there came as yet no light. Then, satisfied that his drowsy senses had deceived him, he lay down again with already closing eyes. No sooner had his head touched the pillow than once more, close to his ear, he seemed to feel rather than to hear, a long, quivering sigh. He put out his hands, feeling right and left in the darkness, but they encountered nothing but the cool linen sheet and the yielding surface of the eider-down quilt. He sat up again, and listening, heard nothing but the faint cracking noise of tree-branches blown together by the wind. Then once more as his head fell back upon the pillow he heard the strange sound which had disturbed him. The story connected with the room came back into his mind, and, as he was not a person of weak nerves, it quieted his curiosity instead of stimulating it.

"Ghost—wind in trees!" he murmured to himself; and as the sound continued at intervals it would speedily have lulled him again to sleep if the sighs had not given place to words which seemed to be whispered straight into his ears.

"Who is it?" he heard distinctly. Then, after a pause: "Come in." He was half-asleep now, he was sure ; and the weak but clear little whisper that buzzed on into his stupid ears was one of those odd dreams of partial consciousness which a touch of fever, consequent upon over-fatigue and excitement, sometimes brings. The tiny whisper went on ; he heard it quite clearly, though it bore him at first no great meaning.

"What is it ? Why have you come ? You frightened me !"

Then a different voice, thin, attenuated, but louder, said, "Frightened you, did I ? Well, you may be sure I sha'n't stop long. I want to know what you were telling that doctor-fellow while I was out of the room this evening, and what you meant by bringing him here, and where you got him from."

An odd dream this. Armathwaite turned his head on the pillow, but still the soft buzzing voices went on, the weaker one speaking now.

"I told him only what everybody can see—that I am growing stupid, nervous, ill."

"Ill ! Well, it is your own fault if you are. You won't go out. Only the other day you were invited to The Crags, and——"

"The Crags ! No. It would do me no good to go there. Let me go away. Oh, Ned, Ned, let me go away ! I am no comfort to you, only a burden to you. Try as I may, I am nothing to you. You will not treat me as a wife, or even as a sister. Oh, I have been trying for days and weeks to get courage to speak to you, to call back my old spirit, to insist on being treated fairly ; but my mind and my will seem to be ebbing away. I cannot tell what has happened to me, but I think I am—dying !"

The blood rushed suddenly to Armathwaite's brain as these words, weak and faint but clear as a bell, came to his ears. He was not dreaming ; he was listening to the plaintive outcry of a wife who felt, rightly or not, that she had been cruelly wronged. By what means this strange communication was being made to him he did not know, he had no leisure to guess. But he was convinced that by an accident which he did not hesitate to bless, he was hearing the appeal of a woman who, as he began to think, was the victim of something which looked suspiciously like foul play. He was on the alert at once, listening boldly with all his ears, not for an instant doubting now that by some agency he dared not name he had been brought to this house to use what wits nature had endowed him with on behalf of a creature who was being ill-used.

It was impossible to distinguish tones in the thread-like sounds which alone reached his ears. But the words told him that it was the man's voice he heard next.

"Dying! Stuff and nonsense! Don't for goodness' sake try to make yourself out a martyr to my cruelty. What on earth have you to complain of?"

The answer came very slowly, as if the words were dropped out one by one under the oppression of despair.

"What—have—I—to complain of?"

"Well, well, I don't pretend that you did not expect a different sort of life from the one we lead. But circumstances——"

"Circumstances! What circumstances can justify a man for treating a girl as you have done me? I must speak—I must speak; I will be quiet enough to-morrow, but to-night I am excited, my head feels strange and light—you must hear me now. I have something to ask you."

"Well, what is it?"

"Let me go and see Dr. Peele."

"Dr. Peele! What do you want to go and see him for? There is nothing the matter with you; if you think there is, you can consult this young fellow Armath-waite if you like. I'm sure he takes a deep interest in you, and will prescribe you whatever you have a fancy for; that's the sort of doctor you want, like all women; a good-looking fellow to feel your pulse, and look into your eyes, and vow yours is the most interesting case he has ever come across. I'll speak to him to-morrow."

"And I will go to-morrow and see Dr. Peele. I have not had a talk with him alone since the winter began."

"What do you want to have a talk with him alone

for ? It can be only for one thing that you want it—to grumble at the life you lead, or at me, or at something."

"Ned, you might trust me that it isn't for that. Why, if I had wanted to complain, shouldn't I have begun before ? Do you ever think what a strain upon me my life has been ever since the day I married you ? The moment I saw Lord and Lady Kildonan in the church that morning, and noticed the change in your face and the coldness of your hand as it touched mine, I knew that I had made a dreadful mistake, as clearly as I know it now."

"Nonsense—all nonsense ! I was nervous, naturally enough. I hadn't known they were in London, and I knew their coming meant that I must give my mind to some dry business or other, instead of to the pleasure a man naturally looks forward to on his wedding-day. Come, Alma, I swear I never expected to see them that morning—I swear it ! "

"I believe that ; I always have believed it."·

"And do you believe it was my fault that I was sent off to Moscow that very day on Lord Kildonan's business ? Do you think I should have married you at all if I had expected to have to go off like that at a moment's notice ? You know yourself how annoyed I was, and that I said things which no employer but Lord Kildonan would have overlooked."

"I know all that ; I remember quite well how they carried you away with them, and I am glad now to remember that I had the sense and spirit to hate Lady Kildonan for it."

"But you were hard and cold to me. You said bitter things. You would not even give me a wife's good-bye. If you had been kinder then, I should have hurried back to you, and everything would have been different."

"No, no, no ! How could I be tender and sweet to you when I saw that every light word this lady said moved you more than my tears ? It was not in human nature to bear that—and on one's wedding-day ! All the time you were away I was full of remorse that I had been hard, but I knew even then that you never thought about it.   If you had, would you have stayed in Paris three weeks after your business in Russia was done, with a bride waiting for you in England.   Of course not."

"But I was in Paris on business, you know that, with Lord Kildonan !"

"And Lady Kildonan.   Only the poor old fellow unluckily let slip, in talking to me afterwards, that it was some business of your own, and not his, which kept you so long in Paris !   But I don't want to go over the old ground of wearisome reproaches again.   When you all returned to England together, you took me on from London with them : we did not even travel by ourselves. You told me a relation of yours was going to live with us, and when we got here we found Uncle Hugh, who has been my good angel and my consolation ever since. I was wounded to the quick ; and I frankly own that all the love I had felt for you when you were kind to me in London and seemed so passionately, feverishly anxious to marry me, died away out of my heart and left me only bitterly hurt and disgusted.   But I was too proud to show it.   You remember how I received your shame-faced, apologetic attempt at an explanation that first evening, when poor Uncle Hugh, thinking he must be awfully in the way, left us in the drawing room to-gether."

"By Jove, I do !   If you hadn't treated me as if I had been a dog, if you had made one appeal to me as a wife to her husband, I should have taken you to my arms at once and told you, what I swear to you solemnly now, that there has never been between Lady Kildonan and me the——"

Armathwaite could imagine the dignity with which she interrupted him :

"There are some explanations to which a wife of years' standing may listen, which ought never to be needed to a bride."

"Well, you were old enough to know that you must take a man as you find him."

"How can you complain ?   I listened to you ; I made you the only promise which even at that moment you cared to ask—that I would not let Dr. Peele know the circumstances of our honeymoon. I have kept my promise, and your place in his will is quite safe."

"What rubbish are you talking? The doctor's will is nothing to me; he's got his own wife and daughter to provide for, and I'm quite independent of him or anybody. I only don't want to hurt the old man by letting him know we have made a failure of it."

"Yet you gave the expense as the reason for selling poor old Gray Friar!"

"Well, it looks ostentatious for you to be riding and driving about just like her ladyship; and besides, I want to save. And you are not strong enough to ride since you have taken to these nervous fits."

"You have forgotten, too, the dangers of the slippery roads!"

"Anyhow, I've sold him, and that's enough. No woman has a right to pester her husband with questions as to what he does with his own money: if he chooses to cut down any expense, or in fact whatever he chooses to do, she must accept the fact quietly as long as she is kept in comfort without having to work, and he does not treat her cruelly."

"That is really your view of married life?"

"Not under all circumstances, perhaps, though most men would even go so far as that, I can tell you. But there is something in the way you look at me, the way you have looked at me ever since we have been in this house, so repellent, so utterly different from what any man has a right to expect, that I can tell you I would pass the night in the snow on the top of Skiddaw rather than so much as look at you."

"I think the fault of that must lie in your own conscience and not in my eyes, Ned. For if you would look at them, you would see as much sorrow for you as for myself. You are not happy. For weeks past you have looked harassed and worried. It is not only my eyes you avoid, but Uncle Hugh's, Dr. Peele's, everybody's. Do you think I would have submitted all this time with scarcely a word to the humiliating position I occupy, not a wife and yet not a free woman, neglected and yet obedient to you, if I did not feel for you and pity you, and shrink from giving you the least annoyance? But we can't go on like this: I think my very presence exasperates you now. Let me go away—for my health; since I have grown so nervous and depressed it will be easy to say that. When you want *me*, not as a shadow to haunt the house, but as a woman to comfort or nurse you, if not as a wife to love you, I will come back—instantly. But I cannot bear the strain of this life any longer. I must go."

"No, no, you shall not, you must not." These words came so rapidly that Armathwaite could scarcely distinguish them. "Wait, wait a little while, and it will all come right. I will be kinder to you, you shall see Dr. Peele, you shall do anything you like; but you must not, shall not go away."

There was a pause. Then came the answer to this outburst in a very weak voice.

"Ned! Ned! What do you mean? You don't care for me—you almost hate me. Why do you want me to stay?"

"Why do you want to make a scandal? For you know it would be a scandal, whatever reason we might give. What would people—what would Lord Kildonan say?"

"Oh, Ned! For Heaven's sake don't let me think you only want to keep me here for—*that!*"

"Don't make a scene for goodness' sake, and fill the house with wails and groans in the middle of the night! I only want to keep you here because it's right and proper and better for a wife to remain in the same house with her husband, whatever their mutual relations may be. Nobody need know that we are not the most attached couple in the world, if you wouldn't go about sighing and making a long face like a heroine of opera. Look here; promise me you will stay here quietly until —until the winter's over, and then if we don't get on any better, and if you still think a change would do you good, you shall go away somewhere for a little while. There now, you've behaved beautifully all this time for the sake of Dr. Peele, that he might be satisfied you were happily married. Bear up to the end for his sake, if you won't for mine. I tell you you are quite wrong; it is not as you think; it is not to keep people from talking I want you to stay here; it is because I am harassed and over-worked and driven, and if I am left to myself here, the Lord knows what will become of me. For mercy's sake, Alma, stay till the Spring, and I will be a better husband to you, I swear it. Promise, Alma, promise."

There was a long pause, and another of those quivering sighs which had first roused Armathwaite from his sleep. Then a sound like a faint, heart-broken laugh came to the young doctor's ears.

"If I stay till the Spring I shall get my change for nothing, Ned. I—promise."

"There's a good girl. Now I know you must be dying to get to bed. You look awfully tired. Good night."

"Good night."

There was the sound of a brief, perfunctory kiss, and in a few minutes a man's steps came stealthily along the corridor past Armathwaite's room. Again the young doctor heard the long-drawn sighs of the lonely woman. But he could bear it no longer. Understanding by this time that a communication had been established between the two rooms to enable the late proprietor of the house to keep constant unseen watch over any one of his patients whose case rendered such a precaution desirable, he cut the communication off by transferring the pillows to the foot of the bed, where he passed the remainder of the night without further disturbance. But he had little more rest.

For to Armathwaite, who could not yet shake off the effect of the unaccustomed sensations and startling incidents of the previous day, this crowning experience of the night had a deeper significance than the actual words revealed to him. He believed, to begin with, with perfect sincerity that he had been drawn to this place by something more than a series of coincidences, to render service to a woman who was being unfairly used. In what this service was to consist, how it was to be performed he did not know; but the belief made him look for mountains where, if his judgment had been less biassed, he would have seen nothing but mole-hills. Therefore, instead of seeing in Lady Kildonan's determined and successful endeavour to keep husband and wife apart either a mad and jealous passion or a cruel and heartless caprice, he set about imagining what other motive she could have for what seemed to him to be on the face of it barbarity too inhuman or folly too outrageous to be conceived. If Lady Kildonan had been so frantically in love with Ned Crosmont that the idea of his marrying another woman was insupportable to her she would certainly, being clearly a lady of most determined will, have kicked over the traces of caste-prejudice and defiantly married him herself: therefore, since she had not done so, there must be some motive other than jealousy prompting her to this wicked and dangerous severance of husband and wife. On the other hand it seemed to Armathwaite a circumstance little short of marvellous that a woman of so much sense and spirit as Mrs. Crosmont should submit to the humiliation of living under the same roof with a man who not only denied her the rights of a wife even to the extent of treating her with open neglect and discourtesy before strangers, but who was also admittedly under the influence of another woman. Gentle and yielding as her nature might be, natural as her shrinking from the parade of her wrongs undoubtedly was, there was yet something unexplained in the meekness with which, while feeling the bitterness of her position with a passionate warmth, she had submitted almost too suddenly to the endurance of it for an indefinite time longer. Roused to chivalrous ardour on behalf of this lady, the young man refused to admit even so much of blame to her as a too ready submission would imply, and he insisted on seeking some fault in the husband to explain what looked like want of self-respect on the part of the wife.

In the midst of his reflections, however, he was overpowered by physical and mental fatigue, and fell into a disturbed sleep, from which he was roused at half-past eight o'clock by the knocking of a housemaid at the door of his room. He was careful to examine the bedstead, and found that it was fixed to the floor close to the wall; in the centre of the upright frame at the head of the bed was the usual small embossed iron ornament where the bars crossed; this was exactly on a level with the head of the sleeper. In the middle the ornament was hollow, and behind this hollow was a hole in the wall which proved, on careful inspection, to be covered with a grating of the finest wire. This, Armathwaite had no doubt, was the opening to a tube, or series of tubes which, in days dating before the telephone, formed an ingenious means of communication with another room. He had just resolved, without much need for deliberation, to keep his discovery to himself, when he heard another knock at his door, and the voice of Uncle Hugh asking if he was ready for breakfast.

"My nephew has to be out early, and so he breakfasts at eight." Mr. Crosmont explained as they went downstairs, while Armathwaite noticed on the way that the upper floor was constructed on the same principle as the lower, with an irregular corridor straight down the middle from end to end, upon which the rooms opened on each side. "The little one has nothing in particular to get up for, so she waits till the chill is off the morning, and generally breakfasts about nine. I divide my favours between the two, and have my chop with one and my toast and marmalade with the other. Ned rather wanted to have you pulled out for his breakfast, but I protested in the interests of humanity that you should be allowed to rest an hour longer."

As they came to the last step of the staircase, Mrs. Crosmont met them, coming along the corridor from the back of the house. She looked very fresh and sweet, and explained, as she took off a little shawl that was wrapped round her head and neck, that she had been to the stable to see Gray Friar."

"Ned's gone, I suppose?" asked Mr. Crosmont.

"Oh, yes, long ago! He's going to lunch at The Crags, and won't be home till dinner-time," she answered, as she led the way to the dining-room, where breakfast was laid.

With the morning glow, caused by her run through

the frosty air to visit her old favourite, still upon her cheeks, Mrs. Crosmont showed for a few moments what nature had meant her to be—a sweet-faced young English-woman with a healthy pink skin, clear eyes, that whole-some air of dainty neatness which is a special charm of the race, and a certain radiance, not only of hair and complexion, but of expression, which was like soft sun-shine. But Armathwaite had scarcely noted these things with admiration and surprise when the glow began to fade and the smile to disappear, and in a few minutes the dark rings of sleeplessness showed under her eyes, and the momentary vivacity died out of her manner. She was perfectly sweet and courteous to him, and affec-tionate to Uncle Hugh; but nothing could have em-phasized more strongly than did that little incident the difference between what she was and what gentle treat-ment would have made her.

Both uncle and niece questioned Armathwaite with much interest as to his adventures in the Dolly Varden room, and were disappointed by his assurance that he had met with none.

"I don't think I'm the sort of person even a well-authenticated ghost would care to visit," said the young doctor quietly, looking down upon his egg. "If they've been ever so much ill-used, there is nothing one can do for them. I would rather save up my sympathy and my service for those living people one sometimes meets, whose souls are all the more restless for being tied to a body which has no true home."

He was afraid to glance up immediately after this speech, lest Mrs. Crosmont should look coldly at him, conceiving it to be presumptuous. But when he did raise his eyes, while Uncle Hugh fulfilled his usual mission of making conversation when required, he again felt the magnetic attraction of her eyes drawing his to meet them, and by the solemn kindness with which she looked at him, he knew that she was not dis-pleased. As a matter of fact, there was already established between the three a sort of friendly free-masonry, Mrs. Crosmont and her uncle having made the visitor free of the guild of their own sympathy within a few minutes of his arrival on the preceding evening. They had left the breakfast-table and were standing at the window, looking through the straggling, thick-growing ivy, at the snow-laden evergreens, and at the hill on the opposite shore of the lake, when Uncle Hugh suddenly stopped in the middle of something he was saying to put his head on one side in a listening attitude.

"Bells!" he said ; then he added after a pause, during which a sort of dead calmness had fallen upon his niece : "Sleigh-bells."

Nobody spoke again for a moment, until the jangling of the bells had come quite near and stopped. "Hallo!" cried Uncle Hugh, in astonishment, "It's stopping here!"

"They are at the gate," said Alma quietly. Then in explanation she turned to her visitor : "It is Lady Kildonan—the wife of my husband's employer. You will be glad to see her—she is quite a celebrated beauty."

"I—I have seen her," stammered Armathwaite.

In spite of himself the blood had rushed up into his face. As Mrs. Crosmont looked at him he saw what seemed like a film of disappointment come over her soft eyes. The next moment she was leading the way to the door, glancing at the gentlemen to follow her.

"Come," she said, "Lady Kildonan is a queen, and likes a full court."

At that moment a maid entered and announced that "her ladyship" was in the drawing-room. They all filed out, Armathwaite feeling strangely excited at the thought of seeing these two women face to face. Alma walked first, and had reached the drawing-room, door, talking as she went, when her powers seemed suddenly to fail her, and falling abruptly into silence, she stood for a second looking with intent, imploring eyes, straight up into the young doctor's face. The next moment she resumed her self-command, and signed to him to open the door for her, as Lady Kildonan's bright voice, singing softly to herself, reached their ears.

CHAPTER VII.

IF the morning light improved Alma Crosmont, it did more for Lady Kildonan; it transformed her. Every brilliant tint of her skin, the silvery sheen on her yellow hair, the lustre of her blue eyes, and of the even teeth which she show'ed every other minute in light-hearted laughter, gained a new and more dazzling radiance in the brightness of the sun. She was kneeling on the floor, playing with two of the dogs like a merry child; and as she sprang up on the entrance of the mistress of the house, the retriever bounded and placed his fore-paws against her waist in the belief that her quick movement was but a ruse of the game. She was dressed as plainly as a man, in a tailor-made gown of dark-brown cloth, a hat to match, with a single straight feather, and an outer garment reaching almost to her feet, cut like a man's overcoat, and lined with dark sable. The coat was unbuttoned and thrown open, displaying the curves of a tall, slight figure in a perfectly-fitting dress. Her right hand, from which she had drawn the glove while playing with the dogs, was white and slim; the left was covered by a dogskin driving glove.

"Down, down, down, Lancer!" she said, as she came forward, brimming over with smiles. "You're a very nice and important person, but you can't expect to monopolize all one's attention. Oh, Mrs. Crosmont, where do you get these heart-breaking dresses from?" she cried, her tone suddenly changing to mock plaintiveness as she shook hands with Alma, and surveyed the ruby-coloured morning-gown that lady wore with hearty admiration. "You always look like a picture; but it's really too hard to bear one's husband always saying, 'Why don't you dress like Mrs. Crosmont?' He insists that you make your frocks yourself. That's what a man always thinks if one isn't covered with little bits of fringe and buttons and bows—isn't it, Uncle Hugh?"

And she turned to shake hands with Uncle Hugh, who was smiling upon her with the indulgent manner which

was the farthest departure from absolute adoration that
any man had the heart to show to her.

"I don't think *you* make your own frocks," he said,
shaking his head. "I don't believe you know one end
of a needle from the other."

"That is an insult. Will you withdraw it if I give
you a kiss ?"

"Certainly."

"There, then !"

She kissed him merrily on the forehead, and as she did
so she appeared to notice for the first time the presence
of a fourth person. Alma began to introduce the young
doctor, but Lady Kildonan held out her hand and looked
at him with arch demureness.

"Dr. Armathwaite has met me before, unluckily," she
said, with a mischievous laugh. "You won't soon forget
the discrimination I showed on our first meeting, will
you ?"

"I shall never forget any incident connected with
you," said he, bowing.

"I am sure that is meant to be a very pretty speech ;
but as about half the things I do are not much to my
credit, I fervently hope you will not keep your word."
Then she turned to Alma, and drawing that lady's arm
in her own, led her to the sofa. "I've called at this
unearthly hour to ask you something," she said, with
pretty seriousness, passing her own soft fingers caress-
ingly over the other lady's unwilling hand. "I've just
met Mr. Crosmont in the village, and he tells me you
are getting quite ill and depressed because you never go
out. And so I've come to ask you to let me take you
back to The Crags with me to luncheon. We've got a
few people there now, and though I can't plead that they
are highly interesting, still you'll have the satisfaction of
giving them pleasure, for they've all heard a great deal
about you, and are very anxious to know you. Now do
say you'll come, please. Your husband is going to lunch
with us, as you know ; and if only these gentlemen also
will honour us with their society, we shall be awfully
pleased to have them."

"Thank you, Lady Kildonan," said Alma, with coldness which could not fail to seem ungracious after the effusive warmth of the invitation. "It is very good of you to think of me, but I have a very great deal to do to-day, and cannot avail myself of your kindness."

"Oh, don't be so disagreeable!" cried Lady Kildonan, pouting like a spoilt child. "You never will come and see me. You are as formal as if we were two old dowagers. I wish you wouldn't be so dreadfully dignified. You remind me of what I ought to be with those regal airs of yours."

"My position is not the same as yours. If it were, I should not require regal airs either."

She tried to say this playfully, but Armathwaite, who knew more of the situation than anybody guessed, detected a heart-wrung break in her voice which brought a lump into his throat. Lady Kildonan, who seemed bent on conciliating the other lady, tried a different tone, and spoke again with a plaintive note in her voice too.

"Your position is, at any rate, a much happier one than mine," she said, looking straight in front of her, with child-like blue eyes, in a distracting manner. "You haven't got a husband who thinks of nothing but his books, and looks at you as if he thought it a pity you were not bound in half-calf!"

She turned her eyes languidly in the direction of the gentlemen, and seeing a smile on their faces, she fell to laughing outright herself.

"Nobody will believe I'm unhappy; and really perhaps things might be worse," she said, good-humouredly. "Only the way in which you glide about with mournful eyes gains everybody's sympathy, and makes me seem vulgar and bouncing."

"Would you care for the appearance of unhappiness at the price of being unhappy, then?" asked Alma, gravely.

"I'm not quite sure that I *could* be unhappy. Nothing seems worth the while. I can be cross when anyone thwarts me, but I suppose you won't allow that that is the same thing?"

A certain bright archness in her manner charmed the

gentlemen, but seemed to have a different effect upon her fellow-woman.

"It is a question of temperament," said Alma quietly, "and perhaps also of climate. This lake-country doesn't agree with me, and I'm going away shortly for change of air."

Armathwaite, who was talking to Mr. Crosmont, but with eyes and ears on the alert, saw a fierce light, like a flash struck from steel, dart out of Lady Kildonan's handsome blue eyes. For a moment she made no answer; then, with a bright laugh, she sprang up to go.

"Well, I know it is of no use for me to say anything to you. You gentle women with low voices and downcast eyes always will have your own way. But if only I could do anything to make the country endurable to you it would make both my husband and me so happy. But whenever you like to come up to The Crags, we will welcome you like the flowers in May."

Without meeting her eyes, she shook hands with Alma, who answered quietly, "Thank you, I am sure you will."

Lady Kildonan then turned to the gentlemen. "Uncle Hugh, I know it is of no use to ask you to come to luncheon without your 'little one.' I am disappointed of my prey for to-day at any rate. Dr. Armathwaite," she held out her hand to him, "you told me last night you had not five minutes to spare in Mereside. As I see you have found some attraction sufficiently strong to make you change your mind, I still hope to see you at The Crags in a day or two."

Armathwaite started, and stammered as he answered. For indeed Glasgow and his appointment there had been thrust out of his mind by the incidents of the night and morning.

"Thank you a hundred times," said he. "But at this very moment I ought to be on my way north. I was detained by an accident, and then by the kind hospitality of Mr. and Mrs. Crosmont. I was just going to ask for a Bradshaw."

Again his eyes felt impelled to meet those of Mrs. Crosmont, who said in a soft voice:

"And Dr. Peele?"

"You are going to see Dr. Peele?" broke in Lady Kildonan, brightly. "Then I can do you a service after all. I am going to Branksome now; I will drive you to the doctor's. Now, no excuses; I am in a benevolent mood this morning, and I absolutely must oblige somebody, either with their will or against it. Go and put on your ulster, and hey presto! we'll be gone, for I've kept my poor ponies waiting too long, and I can see that I've worn out Mrs. Crosmont's patience."

Armathwaite thanked her, made a courteous speech to his hostess, and went into the hall in search of his overcoat. A servant had taken it away on the preceding evening to shake the snow off, and as he looked for it among the coats which were hanging on the stand, one of the maids, a dark-eyed, bright-looking girl called Agnes, came rushing like a tornado down the passage to inform him that she would fetch it, and returned in a few moments, all smiles and friendly giggles, with the overcoat on her arm. Agnes was a coquette of renown, and would always contrive to be noticed by any man, high or low, who pleased her fancy. She helped him on with his coat, and took the opportunity to compliment him on his courage in sleeping in the haunted room.

"Well, Nanny and I—Nanny is the other housemaid, sir—we said we wouldn't have slept in that room, no, not if it was ever so!"

This rather vague assertion was emphasized as though it clinched the question.

"Why, you're not afraid of ghosts, surely!"

"Oh, well, I don't know but what I might snap my fingers at them in any other house; but in this one sees such funny things sometimes that I'm sure it's enough to make anybody turn in his grave, or even come out of it, to see the goings on!"

Agnes, delighted to have a chance of pouring forth such chatter as could not fail, she felt, to be interesting, was arranging his coat collar with great pains when another and shriller voice from the passage behind them made her start. Both she and Armathwaite turned, and found themselves confronted by Nanny, who was a tall and buxom blonde with a face like an overblown baby, and silky fair hair that curled in little natural tendrils round her pretty head. She held her arms akimbo, and her infantile features expressed much indignation.

"For shame, Agnes," she said hotly, but in a sufficiently subdued tone for her words to travel very little further than the person she was addressing, "to talk ill of your own mistress, and she as kind a lady as ever lived, and you a pretty one to talk, indeed! And a nice thing of you to be prating to strangers, and you just the first person who might be caught tripping yourself one of these days. And not even knowing whether it mayn't be all right, which I'm sure it is, too, and no business of yours if it wasn't. Telling tales on your own bread-and-butter, you serpent's tooth, you!"

Poor Nanny's well-meant if rather ambiguous eloquence had the one good effect of turning her companion's tongue from the dangerous subject ; for Agnes, while expressing her scorn of the interruption with ejaculations of wounded pride, seemed really ashamed of herself, and withdrew without further gossip. But on the other hand it roused Armathwaite to a maddening pitch of anxiety, for it strengthened his belief that there was some mystery about the treatment of Mrs. Crosmont which, if he was to be of any service to her, he must manage to solve. The two maids had scarcely disappeared, whispering, down the passage, when the drawing-room door opened, and the ladies came out, followed by Uncle Hugh, who accompanied Lady Kildonan to the gate, and helped her into the sleigh. Armathwaite got in beside her, and noticed, as he did so, the figure and walk of the groom, who was a little slim lad of seventeen or eighteen. This inspection caused him to decide that, although it was Ned Crosmont who had been driving when the lady dropped her handkerchief on the preceding evening, it was this young man who had taken his place when the sleigh stopped at old Peggy's cottage. Lady Kildonan was clever enough to perceive the look of curiosity in her companion's eyes.

"You look as if you thought you had discovered a secret," she said, laughing, as she took the reins and the

ponies began to descend the hill. "Doctors are men to
be trusted, we all know, so I don't mind confessing that
if I have to drive a long way after dusk, and want a more
muscular protector than poor little Martin could prove
in an emergency, I get Ned Crosmont to meet me at
Peggy's cottage, and he borrows Martin's coat and goes
with me, while the lad toasts his toes over a jug of beer
till we come back again. You see, in a place like this,
all the neighbours would be agape if poor Ned were
recognised driving me about, although we've been play-
fellows ever since we were mites in the nursery."

"But surely it's a great risk. It would be so much
worse if he were recognised in—in spite of everything."

"No fear of that. I'm independent of any arm but
my own as long as daylight lasts, and look at the pace my
little ponies go!"

"Then that lad—how can you dare trust to his discretion?"

She turned her head and made the young doctor meet
her eyes, which were sparkling with the serene consciousness of triumphant beauty.

"How can I? Ah! as you are not a woman, I'm
afraid I can't explain it to you."

There was something that jarred upon him in this
bold avowal of her condescending to use the power of
her brilliant beauty to cajole a servant into silence; but
at the same moment that upward gaze through the
golden brown lashes of her eyes set the tide in his own
blood running fast. You really couldn't be hard upon a
woman for getting by a look the obedience that money
wouldn't buy. She seemed to read a trace of disap-
proval in his silence, and when she spoke again it was
with some moving passion in her voice.

"It is so easy to be hard on a woman, and say she
ought to be as open as the day in every little thing, and
never deceive her husband about so much as the price of
a scrap of ribbon; and of course it would be much better
and pleasanter too if one could do like that. But if you
are married to a dear old Sobersides of a Scotchman—I
don't want to complain of him, for he's a very good, kind
old thing as long as one keeps off the bawbees, and

doesn't touch upon religion, and likes an evening spent in silent contemplation of the opposite wall—why, you must find some vent to your pent-up vitality, if it's only in taking a sleigh-drive to the other end of the estate, with a poor dash of romance in it in the shape of an old sweetheart disguised in a coat that doesn't belong to him! There, there, now I've made my confession. Look grave over it if you like!"

If Armathwaite had not remembered the neglected wife who suffered by these escapades, he could scarcely have felt inclined to look grave at all, so piteous even in imagination was the picture of this beautiful, brilliant woman tied to a dry-as-dust Scotchman thirty years her senior. But what on earth did she marry him for? The interest he naturally felt in this and kindred questions made him rather glad than otherwise when, after a drive of about half an hour, Lady Kildonan, pointing with her whip to a handsome modern, warm-looking, red-brick house, built in the Tudor style, standing half-way up a steep hill which they had just begun to ascend at a gallop, said :

"That, oh, stranger, is the pirate's lair! By which I mean only that instead of taking you direct to Branksome, I have brought you round the lake to The Crags to luncheon. And it is of no use to try to protest, because the deed is done."

Armathwaite didn't protest much : but he wondered where his wits could have been for his suspicions not to have been aroused by the fact that they had come through the outskirts of the village of Mereside and driven round the head of the lake instead of along the east side of it, according to the direction given him at the hotel the night before. Just before the sleigh reached the gates, an elderly woman came quickly out of the red-brick lodge, and, throwing them wide, stood smiling at the approach of her mistress. Lady Kildonan stopped and spoke to her in the most winning manner.

" Well, Mrs. Wheeler, and what has become of Tommy? We don't generally see you at the gate on washing morning."

"I wanted to ask, my lady, whether his lordship is any

better to-day. Mrs. Flint says he's been ailing for the last month, ever since that night he was took so bad ; and that his eyes seem queerer than ever."

Mrs. Wheeler was a sharp-featured woman, with an upturned, inquisitive nose, intelligent eyes, and quiet, pleasant manner. She looked her mistress straight in the face with a frank and kindly smile as she spoke.

Lady Kildonan answered in her usual bright voice, but with the least little touch of restiveness at the earnestness of these inquiries.

" Oh, yes, he's all right, thank you. People who stay indoors as much as he does are always rather inclined to exaggerate their ailments, you know. As for his sight, of course it never has been very good, and sitting up reading half the night doesn't improve it. But he has made no complaints lately."

" Complaints ! No, he never would complain if he was ever so bad. He's too afraid of worriting your ladyship. I'm glad to hear he's no worse, indeed, my lady."

And as her mistress wished her good morning and drove on, she shut the gates and retreated into the cottage.

" I think that is such a disagreeable woman," said Lady Kildonan with some irritation, as the sleigh wound round the curves of the snow-covered drive, between wide white lawns dotted with gnarled oaks and shaggy, black-fingered cedars. " She's an old servant—of course you could guess that from her impertinence. I hate old servants. I would have pensioned her off the premises long ago, but Lord Kildonan, who has a sympathy for fossils, and who besides has a national aversion to pensioning anybody who still has an hour's work left in his old bones, has installed her here."

" She seems a civil sort of body, and not so very old," suggested Armathwaite, who had been rather favourably impressed by the woman.

" Oh, civil in the *aigre doux* manner, yes. She doesn't dare to tell me quite to my face that I ought to sit indoors all day making poultices for my husband— which he'd be perfectly certain to eat in a fit of absence of mind—or reading to him in languages I don't understand, like Milton's daughters. Selfish old wretch Milton must have been : I feel quite glad he only got five pounds for 'Paradise Lost!' And I wonder, by the bye, whether Archibald would get five pounds for all the learned treatises he's always writing : I suppose there must be some other people in the world who like their literature dry. If he'd only turn out to be a genius one wouldn't mind so much !"

She didn't seem to mind much now, for already she was in high good humour again, laughing at the thought of the sensation she should create among the guests she had left to amuse themselves the whole morning without her, by her reappearance "with—er—well," and she looked at him with a saucy, bewitching uplook of her child-like blue eyes, "with a very presentable hostage from the savage tribes of the prairie."

"Lord Kildonan doesn't quite shut you up without any society then," said Armathwaite, who had imagined from her representations that her daring sleigh-drives were the only resource from a perpetual *tête-à-tête*.

She burst into a ringing laugh as she answered :

"Society ! Oh, no, when I tell him I want society he sends out invitations to a bevy of assorted bores ; and when I say I am dying for lack of excitement, he goes over to Liverpool and brings me back a bagatelle-board ! Luckily he took an old aunt of mine with the fixtures when my marriage brought him this house, and she's been a great success, cheap, never out of order, and a treasure who takes into her own hands all the trouble of the idiots whom my husband invites as companions for me. Shall I describe them to you, or will you wait to be dazzled by their united effulgence without any preparation ?"

"I would much rather hear your description."

"Well then, first comes Lady Greydon, with samples of her marriageable daughters, two hideous girls, and a third who has by some chance missed the family squint, and who is in consequence to be considered a beauty before whom Venus pales. You must be very careful, for if you meet Lady Greydon in the hall before you

have been introduced to her, you will certainly give her
your hat and ask her the way to the drawing-room. She
is extremely Low Church and very particular, so that the
girls are miserable and silent before her, and insufferably
indiscreet chatterboxes as soon as she goes out of the
room. Then there is Sydney Mason, who was christened
Samuel, but who slipped into a different name and an
effeminate manner as soon as his father, who was a dry-
salter, or a bill-sticker, or one of those things where you
begin with half-a-crown and end with half a million—
dropped the outer skin of trade and developed the wings
of the millionaire. That's quite a poetical bit, isn't it?"

"Charming. If you were to re-write your husband's
treatises with all that flow of popular imagery, there
would be a great future for those works."

"I feel sure of it myself. Then there's a plain young
man named South, who is said to be very clever and
rather fast, though he hasn't shown the cloven foot in
either instance yet. But he can make lots of things out
of an orange, and I can't find out any other reason for
my husband's asking him here. Of course he and
Sydney profess to be in love with me; perhaps my
husband considers that excitement enough. You shall
judge when you see them. Look! we are coming
to my favourite view."

Instead of driving straight up to the house, she had
taken a road to the right and made a tour of the park,
brushing under boughs bent down with the weight of
snow, which sometimes discharged their load on the occupants of the sleigh; an accident which Lady Kildonan
bore with undisturbed good-humour, on one occasion re-
questing the doctor to take her handkerchief out of her
coat-pocket and wipe the snow from her hat with it. He
obeyed very carefully, and then she held her face
towards him with perfect nonchalance. A little rivulet
of melted snow was trickling down slowly from her white
forehead. He wiped the pretty cheek rather awk-
wardly, for she was so very beautiful, and yet was so
straightforward and simple, that the action perturbed
him and made his own manner stiff and shy. Seen
thus quite close, her skin, one of those thick white skins

which appear so delicate and yet are the hardiest, affected by neither sun nor wind nor cold to any unbecoming redness or roughness, was bright as satin and soft as velvet, while a certain languishing droop of the outer corners of her eyelids proved at close quarters quite an intoxicating charm. But Lady Kildonan herself appeared to know none of these things. She thanked him briefly and simply, and pointed with her whip to a view which certainly merited her ecstatic praises.

They were on ground higher than the house, the tall red chimneys and gables of which rose to the left above bare trees from which the bright sun was dislodging the snow in a glittering shower. On the right the hill still rose above them, growing bare of trees towards the top, but picturesque and majestic in outline. Below them the ground sloped away, and gaps had been made in the plantation, so that peeps and stretches of the grey lake were visible, and the roofs and chimneys of Mereside on the opposite shore. In the flood of bright morning light Armathwaite, who had keen eyesight, even fancied that he could distinguish the square-built, ivy-mantled house which had been the scene of his adventures of the night. He strained his eyes in the endeavour to be sure of this, and Lady Kildonan noticed the direction of them.

"You can see Ned Crosmont's house from here," she said, watching him. "What a pretty woman Mrs. Crosmont is, isn't she?"

"Ye—es, I suppose she is," answered Armathwaite, who was not *naïf* enough to be led astray by a woman's praise into enthusiasm over another woman's beauty. "And more interesting than pretty."

"Yes, a little too interesting poor Ned has found her. I understand that some allowances must be made for the poor little woman, as she comes of an eccentric family. But it is a pity she doesn't put her fancy and originality into novels or poems or something of that sort, for a fanciful and original wife becomes rather trying sometimes. I'm sorry for old Ned. I have always been very fond of poor Ned," she continued frankly, turning to look into the young doctor's face with a smile. "If they had let me I think I would have married him once.

But papa wouldn't hear of it. He had great notions about the rights and duties of property, and other things I didn't care a straw about. So he ferretted out a steady-going gentleman of his own age, who might be supposed to look well after the family acres, and I was thrown in to close the contract. And so Ned married somebody else, and I'm dreadfully afraid he isn't happy, though to do him justice he never tells me so."

She told it very prettily, with just a note or a glance now and then to suggest a deeper feeling of sadness or regret than was betrayed by the words themselves. Armathwaite was touched. No man could have listened to her, watched her, and not felt that it was an infamous thing that these dazzling charms of youth, beauty, and brightness should be wasted on an avaricious and insensible man too old to please, and too much absorbed in his books to value her. But she was too happy by nature to indulge in sentiment long. With a flourish of her long whip and an encouraging word to her ponies she drove on again, and sweeping round the lower side of the park at a gallop, she pulled up before the door of the house in a very masterly style of coachmanship, flung the reins to the groom, and sprang to the ground as lightly as a bird, almost before Armathwaite had time to hold out his hand to help her.

"And now," she said, "for the enchanted palace of fogeydom, and a peep into the realms of dulness."

She ran up the steps with a laugh, and introduced him into the house with a deep curtsey. Armathwaite followed, full of interest and curiosity.

CHAPTER VIII.

From the very first step he made inside the outer hall, with its oaken nail-studded door, tesselated pavement, and diamond-paned windows, Armathwaite felt that the atmosphere of this spick and span mansion was as different from that of the desolate-looking, rambling old house in which he had passed the previous night as light from darkness. The inner hall was panelled and roofed with oak, the floor was of parqueterie, the walls were laden with trophies of elk-horns, boars' tusks, and unmistakably modern armour. A great fire burned in a high tiled fireplace, square brass lanterns hung from the roof, and the sunlight streamed through stained glass, and made the armour shine and the tiles of the fireplace glitter, until the incomer was dazzled whichever way he looked. Armathwaite was instantly and strongly conscious that he preferred the mouldy old hall at the Crosmont's house, with its faded, buff-coloured walls, and the untidy border of guns and coat-stands and fishing-rods, to this brand-new mediæval splendour; although the wide oak staircase, with its handsomely-carved banisters, and the woodwork round the doors, met with his approval, and some tapestry hangings, arranged curtainwise before one wide doorway—which were said to have belonged to Marie Antoinette, but the history of which did not become authentic until their arrival in Regent Street—gave a harmonious resting-place to the eye from the glittering brightness.

Lady Kildonan glanced at him doubtfully.

"You don't like this place, I see," she said with a dubious look at one particularly overpowering arrangement of weapons and banners crossed behind a huge brass shield. "Nor do I much, I think. My grandfather built this house, and filled it with mahogany chairs and tables that were neither old nor interesting. So I gave one of the big London upholstery firms *carte blanche*, and told them above all not to make it gloomy. They've overdone the Afghan guns, I think. It looks like a shooting gallery, three shots a penny."

But her disappointment was only a joke to her. She darted through the Marie Antoinette curtains with the graceful agility which recalled to Armathwaite's mind the movements of a greyhound, and leading him along a passage which was evidently a reproduction of a convent cloister, opened the door of one of the rooms with an arch pout of penitential demureness.

"For what we are about to receive——" she whispered, and sprang into the room like a ray of sunshine.

It was the morning-room, entirely in the taste of a
fashionable London room, with bent-wood furniture and
plush-betasselled cushions, Japanese vases and Japanese
screens, reed curtains and dried bulrushes, with an
"antique" cabinet, and a lot of little tiresome tables,
laden with objects of no value to the owner or to anybody
else.   Half a dozen figures sprang up like Jacks in the
box from different parts of the room as Lady Kildonan
came in, and Armathwaite recognised each individual by
the hasty sketch he had received.   Only the master of
the house and the accomplished artificer in oranges were
absent.   Mr. Mason, his fingers still encumbered with a
skein of wool which he had been obligingly assisting one
of the ladies to wind, ambled up to his hostess at once
in a burst of enthusiasm, told her that the morning air
had made her look "quite too lovely," and led the
feminine chorus of welcoming small-talk with the pre-
cision of a precentor.   He was a small washed-out
looking fair man with a large head; he wore a velvet
coat, a huge diamond ring round his tie, and another on
one of his fingers, and he spoke with an effeminate voice
and an affected manner.   Lady Kildonan cruelly told
him that he would have been better employed making
snowballs out of doors than winding wool in a hot room,
and after a few words to everybody, and a glance round
the room in apparent search for someone who was not
there, she threw her hat off, and carried the young people
off to tennis in a covered court at the end of the cloister.
This was a spacious place, sufficiently warmed by hot
pipes, with a high glass roof and a carpeted gallery at
one end, from which the non-players could watch the
players luxuriously in lounging chairs and low seats.
This gallery led into a conservatory which ran alongside the house on ground higher than the tennis-
court.

Lady Kildonan, who was a far better player than anybody present except Armathwaite, but a bad playmate
for the poor girls, as they looked ill-shaped and clumsy
beside her, ran up into the gallery to rest after about
half an hour's play, and calling the young doctor to her,
was chatting merrily with him when they both caught

sight of a man standing half-hidden by the plants in the conservatory.

"Ned!" cried Lady Kildonan, springing up with a flash of excitement.

Edwin Crosmont came forward, sullen and silent. She stood looking at him for one moment; then, with a hasty apology to Armathwaite and an anxious expression in her eyes, she joined the agent, and they walked away together, affecting to stop from time to time to gather a leaf or smell a flower, but evidently intent on some exciting subject of talk. Armathwaite, who was sitting at one corner of the gallery where he could look both into the conservatory and into the court below, saw them disappear together behind the central grove of camellias and other tall plants, and tried to interest himself in the game going on below. He was alone, for Lady Greydon had just descended from the gallery to join her daughters. Just as a little excitement was caused in the court below by the entrance of a tall man, very much wrapped up, and wearing blue spectacles, whom the rest greeted as "Lord Kildonan," he suddenly heard the voice of Lady Kildonan in tones of passionate excitement.

"I tell you you must insist upon her staying. Use any means you like, but make her stay Am I nobody? Are my wishes, is my life, nothing to you?"

Into Armathwaite's mind rushed the remembrance of the poor lady who had saved his life, as it seemed miraculously, the previous night; and even before he could argue with himself whether or not he should listen to this talk, which might prove to throw some light on the mystery of the unhappy wife's position, he heard, after a whispered answer in the man's voice, the lady's clearer, shriller tones.

"If you are tired of doing my pleasure, I can soon find somebody else to!"

Another short, angry, inaudible speech.

Then Lady Kildonan's voice again.

"Well, and haven't I made use of doctors before now? Answer me that!"

Crosmont said something, to which she replied in a whisper, having apparently been warned that she might be overheard ; and Armathwaite caught no word more, though faint tones of their voices came to him from time to time for the next few minutes. Presently they both joined him where he still sat watching the group below, and Lady Kildonan, who seemed already to have recovered her usual manner, except for a certain slight restlessness which betrayed that she had been yielding to some violent emotion, told the young doctor that he must come down and be introduced to her husband.

Instead of the cross-grained, withered-looking person he had been led by the description both of Lady Kildonan and the villager Haynes to expect, Armathwaite saw a tall, broad-shouldered, fresh-coloured man, with scant sandy hair, and a plain Scotch face, the features of which, however—small light eyes, short nose, long upper lip, high cheek bones and all—seemed to shine with an expression of mingled shrewdness and kindliness which made the whole face irresistibly attractive, and caused Armathwaite to say to himself that either this was one of Nature's most grandly-dowered hypocrites, or a good man. The genial manner in which he extended his hand to the young man, removing his blue spectacles, as he said, "to have a look at the new friend, once for all," confirmed this impression, and further observation during luncheon resulted in the discovery that Lord Kildonan, however much wrapped up in his books he might be, had a kindly interest in outside things, but especially in everything that in the remotest degree concerned his wife. Whenever he spoke to her he lowered his blue spectacles and looked over them, with the graceful implication that he appreciated her beauty too highly to regard it through any disfiguring medium ; and when she was speaking—she was very seldom silent—he would pause in his own talk to listen to her voice, or glance at her from time to time as if to assure her that though his words might be for somebody else, his thoughts all the while were with her. It was natural enough that this beautiful young woman, in the excitement of the discharge of her duties as hostess, should take small note of these things. But to Armathwaite, moved by the deep interest in this household which the

disclosures concerning its inner history had roused in
him, the husband's solicitude and the wife's indifference
were suggestive facts, with a bearing upon the mystery
which was detaining him against his interests and almost
against his will at Mereside.

When luncheon was over, Lord Kildonan affectionately asked his wife how she was going to amuse herself
during the afternoon, and whether she would drive him
as far as Plasmere, where he had some business.

"Oh, Archibald, I simply can't ! " she answered at
once. " I am expecting the Stanfords, and if I were to
be out when they came, Mrs. Stanford would cut me for
ever. Take Lady Greydon or Aunt Theresa—and
Bertie South to talk to you," she added in a low voice.

"No ; if you can't come with me, I'll put it off till to-
morrow," replied her husband. " It's not a very urgent
matter. And I will show Dr. Armathwaite my books,"
he added, evidently finding consolation in that prospect.

"Oh, my dear Archibald, you mustn't expect any
man under fifty to be as confirmed a bibliomaniac as
yourself," his wife cried, laughing.

Lord Kildonan smiled indulgently, but he winced, and
Armathwaite wondered how she could make so jarring a
speech. She turned to the doctor and told him that
when he had had enough books he was to come to the
drawing-room and let himself down to frivolity. Then
she flitted away to her other guests, and her husband,
gazing after her with a wistfully admiring expression on
his homely features, asked his companion :

"Are you a married man, Dr. Armathwaite ? "

" No, not yet ; in fact, I have no thoughts of getting
married at all."

" Ah, but that's bad. Those thoughts come to every
man sooner or later, and it's better for his happiness
that they should come soon than late. Not but what
you'll be a man more to a lady's fancy at fifty than I was
at five-and-twenty," he added, with a good-humoured
glance of admiration at the young fellow's well-propor-
tioned figure and handsome face. " But I wasn't such
an old fossil as I am now when I married, you understand ; I had a sort of seizure last autumn, and all this

winter I have been a recluse and a kind of invalid. I really don't mind so much for myself; I can always amuse myself with my books; but it makes me a duller companion than ever for a young wife."

He had led the way across the mediæval hall and up two steps into a narrow passage, at the end of which he opened a door on the right and invited Armathwaite into a large and lofty room, the two tall narrow windows of which were shaded by green blinds, which allowed only a subdued and gloomy light to penetrate into the apartment. On every side plain shelves, filled with books, reached from the ceiling to the floor; the furniture was of the barest and simplest kind; a couple of tables piled with books and papers, two or three step-ladders for reaching the books, and six library chairs.

"Here," said Lord Kildonan, looking round him in the gloom with a loving smile, "I spend nearly all my time now. Very often I sit up half the night with my work, which, by the bye, I must show you, if you are interested in philology."

"Very much," murmured the young man politely.

"I have a theory on the origin of language which I believe to be entirely new, and I am most anxious to bring it before the attention of philologists through the medium of a little book on which I am now engaged—of which, in fact, more than four volumes are already finished. My theory is that all languages have for their starting-point the vowel O, which is, you will have observed, the first sound emitted by the human infant, and the first cry of adult nature in pain, anger, or surprise, three sensations which throw the man back by their acuteness into his primitive state, in which, therefore, we may judge him as being under the influence of instinct alone. Starting from this fact——. But I will give you my first treatise on this subject; it is only a pamphlet, and will not take you long to run through, and it will prepare you thoroughly for my longer and more important works, if ever you care to read them."

"I shall be delighted," said Armathwaite, remembering something about a joke, a surgical operation and a Scotchman's head. But he felt the pathos of the old student's next speech.

"I have worked harder than ever lately. That is the great advantage of a love of study; it is such a resource if things go at all wrong in the world outside."

"I suppose it is," answered the young man gravely. "But I've never myself had the kind of trouble one can get away from like that. Not that I've had a particularly large share of troubles of any sort, except the struggles of a man to get a fair start in life."

"I am certain," said Lord Kildonan, looking at him with much interest in the gloom, "that you are the young fellow Dr. Peele once spoke to me about, as showing a perfect genius for investigation, so that when any malady was brought under your notice you never rested until you had found out not only a cause for it, but the right cause. He described your appearance to me, though he did not mention your name."

"I wonder Dr. Peele spoke so strongly as that," said the young doctor modestly, "for it is years since I was a student under him at Guy's. It is nothing to do with genius, but simply the most commonplace and plodding care, which all doctors are bound to take, not to pronounce an opinion until one has gathered as many of the facts of the case as one can possibly get hold of."

"Yes. Well, that is just what I want a doctor to do, but it is just what I can't get Dr. Peele to do. I wish you were staying in this neighbourhood; I should consult you, and put your talents to the test."

"About yourself, Lord Kildonan?"

"No, about my wife."

Armathwaite felt a shock, and held his breath; not indeed that he had the least idea of what the facts might be upon which Lord Kildonan wished to consult him, but he knew at once that the case would be a difficult and delicate one.

"On two occasions lately," Lord Kildonan continued gravely, "I have been taken suddenly ill from too close application to my studies, which I often pursue until far into the night. On each of these occasions Lady Kildonan has been entirely prostrated for a couple of days by her anxiety on my account, prostrated both in body and mind, and rendered so nervous and lifeless that I have felt the gravest apprehensions for her. You, who know what high spirits she generally has, can understand how great the change must be. Now it seems to me, although I am touched by it, that there is something gravely wrong when a bright young creature like that, who seems full of health and life, can be suddenly reduced to the inanimation of a statue by what most wives would only consider a trifling matter—the temporary indisposition of a not very lively husband."

Armathwaite assented. There was something gravely wrong, certainly.

"Now upon inquiry I find," Lord Kildonan's voice began to tremble, "that there have been cases in her family, remote certainly, but none the less real, of a malady which seems to me to correspond terribly well with the symptoms I have noticed in her : it is heart disease." His voice broke on the last word ; the peril it suggested was too horrible for calm consideration. After a pause he cleared his throat and went on again. "Now if this is so, the system I go upon with her—of allowing her every innocent excitement she loves—is not only wrong, but dangerous. A trifling accident to the ponies she drives, a little over-exertion at tennis, or a burst of excitement if she wins a game at billiards—any one of these things might be fatal to her. Now, on the face of this awful fear, is it possible for me to rest contented with Dr. Peele's assurances that it is all right, that there is no cause for alarm, that the cases of heart disease in her family are remote, and so on ? He has not even seen her at the times I speak of, for she, with a natural and brave desire not to make what she called 'a fuss about nothing,' refused absolutely to see him on both those occasions. But I cannot rest upon that. I——" He stopped, a gleam of gentle pleasure came into his face—he had laid down his glasses on entering the darkened room ; going to the door, with a nod of caution to the young doctor, he opened it and admitted Lady Kildonan, who glanced from the one to the other with a quick perception of the fact that they had been talking about her.

"Well, what have you been conspiring about so long?" she asked as her husband patted her affectionately on the shoulder. "You have been talking about me, I'm certain, and I will find out what the conspiracy is, or perish in the attempt. In the meantime I have come to ask you," and she turned to Dr. Armathwaite, "if you will go on to Dr. Peele's now with Ned Crosmont, who has his gig at the door to go to Branksome, or whether you will wait an hour till these people are gone, when I shall be able to drive you over myself."

Lord Kildonan laughed good-humouredly.

"See, Dr. Armathwaite, you are more honoured than I. Her imperial majesty would not condescend to drive me to Plasmere this afternoon."

" Well, I wasn't going that way," she said with a pretty pout.

"It is very good indeed of you, Lady Kildonan," said Armathwaite. " But I am sorry to say I shall not be able to avail myself of your kind offer to drive me, as I really must not delay one moment longer. I will ask Mr. Crosmont if he will take me."

He added his warm thanks to both, as they accompanied him to the hall, where Ned Crosmont was getting ready to start. The strongest impression left upon Armathwaite's mind, as, after shaking hands with both host and hostess and receiving their assurances that they expected to see him again before long, he got into the gig beside the agent, was that Lady Kildonan was greatly annoyed by his choosing to go now rather than wait to be driven by her, and that she would take some wicked little feminine vengeance upon him for thwarting her hospitable caprice, if ever she should have the opportunity.

- - -

CHAPTER IX.

FRANK ARMATHWAITE found the long *tête-à-tête* with Ned Crosmont, as they drove in the latter's gig from The

Crags to Branksome, rather an awkward thing to keep up satisfactorily, for more reasons than one.

"What a hospitable country this is !" he began, as they drove straight through the park towards the lodge gates. "It seems to me that I have never before met with so much kindness within so short a time from so many different people !"

Ned Crosmont looked out sullenly in front of him at the steep road outside the park gates, which the early-setting winter sun had already left in cold gloom.

"Lady Kildonan likes strangers—for a little while," said he gruffly.

"But everybody seems to like strangers here, at least to the extent of being awfully kind to them," pursued Armathwaite with persistent cheerfulness. "Lord Kildonan received me almost as if I had been an old friend. The very first minute I arrived at Conismere a villager who overheard me asking the distance to Branksome offered me a seat in his cart ; while you and your uncle and Mrs. Crosmont treated me, not like the vagabond on the tramp which England expects every wanderer without credentials to turn out to be, but as an honoured and welcome guest."

"Well, you don't look like a vagabond on the tramp," admitted Crosmont, glancing at him half-ungraciously out of the corners of his eyes. Then, as if he thought he had debased himself by being too civil, he added, "Every woman snatches at the chance of talking to any man who is not her husband."

"Even that does not account for the kindness of four people, yourself among the number, who, not being women, have done everything in their power to make my short visit pleasant to me."

"You are not going to stay here, then ?"

"Oh, no ! It looks now very much as if I should have to put off my journey north until to-morrow, but——"

Crosmont interrupted him by a rude grunt, and Armathwaite, beginning to feel a little nettled, stopped and turned to him for an explanation.

"No man at whom—at whom the Kildonans look twice, goes off like that," he said shortly.

"Oh, yes, but he does if he has more important affairs elsewhere," the doctor remarked in a rather constrained voice.

"Ah, well, we shall see," said Crosmont, with a disagreeable laugh. "I've known Lady Kildonan since she was a baby, and nobody's been able to thwart her wishes successfully yet. She's chosen to take a momentary fancy to you, and not all the attempts you may or you might make to leave this neighbourhood will be of the least use until her ladyship's caprice is worn out—which will be," he added tauntingly, with a savage glance at his companion's handsome face, "in about three days, I should say; four at the outside."

Armathwaite saw that the man was bent on insulting him, but he had already seen too deeply into the springs of the unhappy young fellow's strange conduct to be more than momentarily annoyed by this outburst of ill-temper. After a minute's silence he laughed good-humouredly.

"If there is any efficacy in absence, then, this fancy you say her ladyship has been condescending enough to take to me ought to grow into a very fair passion; for most certainly it will be months, and probably years, before I am so fortunate as to be within fifty miles of The Crags again," he said imperturbably.

Crosmont looked hard at him, still with a scowl upon his face.

"I suppose you belong to that class of London young men who set up for being indifferent to women, and let them run after you; the class we in this country call fops," he said presently.

"If by a fop you mean a man who doesn't run after other men's wives, I don't mind confessing I belong to it," Armathwaite answered, in such a very low and deep voice that his companion, perceiving that at last he was to be taken very seriously indeed, dropped the surly bluster of his own tone.

"I didn't mean anything offensive," he said quickly. "It would be out of the question anyhow in talking of her ladyship. Everybody worships her about here. I was only talking as a kind of joke, you know—of the

feeling we all have for her—and her—her husband.
They're royalties about this part, you know, and we are
jealous that they should have homage paid to them. We
expect a stranger's admiration as a kind of toll—do you
see?"

"Oh, yes, I understand," said Armathwaite, accepting
the clumsy apology readily. "I do admire them both
immensely. But if you really think the homage of a
stranger worth having, I will tell you frankly that there
is another lady I have met here to whom I should yield
a far handsomer tribute of admiration than even to Lady
Kildonan—and that is Mrs. Crosmont."

"My wife!" cried Ned in unfeigned astonishment;
adding quickly, "You don't mean it!"

"Indeed I do."

"Oh, but you can't! What, like a long face that
gives you the blues to look at better than one full of
smiles and laughter? Like a woman who depresses your
spirits better than one who raises them? It's all very
well to say that, but it's quite impossible for me to believe it, you know. There is one sort of beauty which
isn't a matter of opinion, but a matter of fact. You will
be saying next, I suppose, that Lady Kildonan isn't as
handsome as my wife."

"It is a different kind of beauty altogether."

"I should rather think it was."

"The one is beauty of the body merely; the other
seems to me, to speak in a rather sentimental manner,
to be beauty of the mind and spirit, which impresses its
own stamp upon form and feature, look and movement,
and makes every smallest word or action expressive,
significant and fascinating."

"Fascinating! Good lord, what a use for the word!"

"That is the impression Mrs. Crosmont made upon me."

"Of course, I know what you mean to imply; that
I'm too much of a clod to appreciate such a refined
style of beauty. But you are wrong. I know exactly
what it is you see in her, and when I first met her it
affected me in just the same way: a sort of odd look in
the eyes that made one want to know what she was
driving at. That's it, isn't it?"

He had not expressed himself in the words Armathwaite would have chosen, but the meaning was near enough for the doctor to assent.

"Well, that may be fascinating, as you call it, just at first," continued the agent, "but it precious soon grows repellent when—well, when it becomes a sort of ' nagging without words,' till I declare it gives me a creepy sensation up the back even to think she's looking at me. That may be fascination, but it's not my sort. Give me a pair of eyes that will laugh back at you, even if they go with a tongue that will shoot a shower of nasty little darts at you sometimes. One can deal with words ; a row now and then clears the air ; but those black looks are infernal."

"Do you think they are meant to be black ? " hazarded Armathwaite presently, in a very guarded manner. It was rather rash of him to pursue the subject, he felt, but as Mr. Crosmont was inclined to be so very communicative about his domestic affairs he thought he might make the venture. " To an outsider she looks merely sad, not in any way ill-tempered, or reproachful, or anything of that sort."

" Reproachful ! I should think not ! It's I should be reproachful if anybody is. But I never am ; I'm not such a brute. I dare say there may be faults on both sides. I don't say I'm a saint. But it's not for my wife to make me a miserable sinner."

Through all his scoffing talk there was an uneasiness in the man s manner which made Armathwaite think he was not below the grace of an occasional conscience-prick ; and this impression was considerably strengthened by a little incident which occurred when they reached Mereside. The winter sun was sinking fast by this time, and the village, lying snugly among the hills at the head of the lake, lost the red beams early, and looked, in the dusk, with its snow-covered roofs and snow-filled gardens, like a phantom hamlet of grey shadows. The gig stopped at the hotel where Armathwaite had dined the previous evening, to enable the young man to pay his bill and account for his failure to return with the horse he had hired.

The landlord had taken the matter very easily, however, and said he would send for Gray Friar in the course of a day or two.

"To tell the truth, sir," he said, good-humouredly, in a low voice, as Crosmont left them to have a glass of sherry at the bar, "I shall be glad of the excuse to leave the horse at Mr. Crosmont's for a day or two. He sold him to me a couple of months ago, and it quite goes to my heart to see the way Mrs. Crosmont comes here, and makes a pretext of going round to the stables to see how John the ostler is, when it's for nothing in this world but to get a peep at her old horse. I can't make out how Master Ned—Mr. Crosmont, I mean—could have the heart to sell the animal, with his wife so fond of him as that. It's no business of mine, of course, but I like to give the lady the little pleasure when I can."

The way to Branksome, when the dangerous junction of the higher and lower roads into Mereside was passed, was level and good, and they reached the little town before the last glow of the sunset had faded behind the hills. They took a turning to the left out of the town, and passed a number of pretty little villas, detached and semi-detached, on their way to the doctor's.

"We shall be there in two minutes now," said Crosmont, who had been morosely silent for some time. "I'll put you down just this side of the house if you don't mind, for I don't want to see any of them. The doctor bores one with his psychical research, his wife is too dictatorial to be borne, and his daughter is ugly enough to make one sick. On second thoughts, though," he went on dubiously, "I suppose I'd better call and leave inquiries."

He drew up at the garden gate of a rather pretty little semi-detached house, the tesselated pathway of which had been carefully cleared of snow. On the gate was a brass plate with the name "Dr. Peele." There was a fernery in the lower window and a birdcage hanging above it. Crosmont remained with his horse as Armathwaite went up to the door, which was open in spite of the weather, and rang the bell. In a few moments the door of the inner hall was opened, and Armathwaite found himself confronted by the plainest feminine person he remembered to have seen. She was very short, and of what may be irreverently termed a "squab" figure, with a round back and a head held too far forward. She had a bulging forehead, small round eyes, a nose that turned up so much that it seemed to draw her upper lip with it, exposing to constant view a row of prominent and uneven teeth ; and her complexion was of that sallow kind to which no exercise brings a becoming flush. In spite of all these disadvantages, Armathwaite, who guessed she was the ugly daughter referred to, felt that he should like the girl. Not that he held the copy-book maxim that beauty was no object as long as you were good ; but this plain little person had a kindly and good-humoured expression which promised all sorts of good qualities to anyone who should not be deterred by her ugliness from further acquaintance.

"Is Dr. Peele at home ? " asked he, raising his hat.

"Yes, but he's ill, and can't see anyone, I'm afraid. Isn't that Ned Crosmont out there ? " she asked in a louder voice, coming a step forward.

"Yes. How do, Nellie ? How's the doctor ? Dr. Armathwaite has come all the way from London to see him."

"Really ! " said she, looking up in surprise at the young fellow, who seemed a giant beside her.

"Not exactly that," he began, when a sharp, loud, and very authoritative voice from within the house broke in :

"Who is it, Amelia ? "

"I think you'd better come in if you will, and see mamma. She will tell you everything better than I can. Are you coming in too, Ned ? "

"Thanks, no ; I can't leave the mare. Just give them both my kind regards and Alma's love, and tell the doctor I hope we shall see him again soon."

"But when is Alma coming to see us ? Papa's always asking after her, and can't understand why she doesn't come."

"Oh, she's got a cold and a bad sore throat, and I don't dare let her come so far this weather," said Crosmont, taking up the reins to start.

Armathwaite heard this explanation with attention and surprise.

"Well, then, I suppose we sha'n't see each other again?" said Crosmont, turning to him. "You can join the main line from here as well as from Conismere, you know, if you're anxious to get on to Scotland without delay."

"Yes, that is what I had better do," said Armathwaite, as, after apologizing to Miss Peele, he ran back to shake hands with him. "Thank you again for your kind hospitality. I shall never forget the way in which I have been received here."

They wished each other good-bye, Crosmont warming at the last to some show of genuine cordiality. But as their eyes met before parting, each knew, the one with impatience and mistrust, the other with vague wonder, that they had not met for the last time.

Crosmont drove off, and Armathwaite hastened back to the door, where Miss Peele was waiting. She led the way into the house, and passing through a narrow little hall, ushered him into a small, simply-furnished, but cosy looking sitting-room, with closed folding-doors at one end. A lamp stood on the table, and by its light the visitor saw a lady of fifty, of matronly figure, sitting by the fire engaged in needlework of the plain and domestic kind. She looked up and displayed a face which might have been handsome in the majestic style before long years of dictatorship had made eagle eyes, hooked nose, and closely-shut mouth so overpoweringly fierce that Armathwaite almost blinked, and glanced in a meek and childlike way at little Miss Peele for protection.

"Here is a gentleman, mamma, who wants to see papa. His name is Dr. Armathwaite, and he has come all the way from London," said Millie, looking good-humouredly up at her big companion as if she understood his trepidation and enjoyed the joke of it.

Armathwaite smiled down at her: he already felt that he loved that girl. When her mother spoke the love increased.

"Dr. Peele is much too ill to see anybody at present,"

said Mrs. Peele in the voice with which she routed little boys like a clap of thunder.

"Well, mamma, let me go up and see what he says himself," suggested Millie.

Before her mother could say one word in opposition, the little person had slid behind Armathwaite with the most comical uplook of mischief into his face, and left him to bear the brunt of the elder lady's cool reception all by himself. From this point, however, her treatment of the visitor was so outrageously unconventional that it became a joke, and lost its terrors. She dropped her work in her lap, examined him from head to foot slowly and with a black scowl as if he had been a notorious rascal, and then said abruptly, in a deep tone:

"Sit down."

He accepted the invitation, scarcely able to resist a temptation to laugh.

"You come from London?" she asked inquisitorially.

"Yes, I—I come from London."

There was no other way of putting it, though this seemed rather crude.

"A bad place, London."

This was a little too much.

"There are some very nice people in it, quite as nice as any in the country."

"I dare say." This was said very defiantly, and then there was a pause before she went on. "Londoners are fond of sneering at us country people, as if we were not good enough to black their shoes."

Armathwaite did not contradict her. She might be a very estimable woman—he had heard she was; but he did not see any adequate reason for her presuming to ride rough-shod over him. So he looked placidly at her and then at his boots, and began to smooth the ends of his moustache for amusement. She prefaced her next remark with a disdainful cough.

"I have no patience," she began, "with people who think, simply because they have lived in a particular spot of the earth, that they ought to be bowed down to by the inhabitants of every other spot."

"Neither have I," said Armathwaite simply.

And each glared straightforwardly at the other as if they thought they had fought this round very satisfactorily. Before they could begin again, Millie came downstairs and brought a message of peace.

"Papa will be very pleased to see you at once, if you won't mind coming upstairs to his room," she said.

And, with a bow to Mrs. Peele, Armathwaite followed the girl out of the room. Millie stopped when she had mounted stairs enough for her face to be on a level with her visitor's, and turning round, she said in a low voice :

"You mustn't think anything of mamma's odd manner of receiving you. She's always like that to strangers, but she's perfectly easy to manage when you know het. I think she must have read too much about Napoleon the Great when she was a child."

This sly apology was rendered so funny by the twinkle in her eyes that Armathwaite with difficulty stifled his laughter as he followed his conductress into the doctor's room.

————

CHAPTER X.

THE events which had preceded this visit to Dr. Peele were of such a strange nature, that all inclination to mirth gave place to an awestruck feeling of interest and mystery in Armathwaite's mind as he passed into the presence of the sick man.

The weak daylight still showed faintly through the drawn blinds, and helped to give a mournful look to a room which dark mahogany furniture and a funereal four-post bedstead rendered already sufficiently gloomy. By the fire sat the doctor in a large arm-chair, sorting papers by the light of a couple of candles on a small table at his side. Armathwaite was startled by the look on his face as he raised his head and held out a thin hand in welcome. Having heard on all sides that the ailment which kept the doctor at home was nothing but a cold, the young man had not been prepared for the sunken eyes and ashy paleness which, to his observant vision, seemed the unmistakable heralds of death ; he

was so much changed that but for the keen and kindly
eyes, the weak and vacillating mouth, Frank would
scarcely have known him. The old man watched the
face of his visitor with great keenness as he told him,
gravely and without surprise, that he was glad he had
come, and bade his daughter bring a chair and place it
near him. He then with a gesture invited the young
man to sit down, and with very little preface, with the
grave manner of a man who felt that he had no time left
for trifling, asked him what had brought him.

"I have come here by the strangest accident,"
answered Armathwaite. "Or rather by an incident
which has already led to so many extraordinary adventures, that I hesitate to call it an accident at all."

Dr. Peele pushed back his grey hair with a gesture
peculiar to him when he was interested; and with a
touch of affectionate dismissal to his daughter, who was
standing lovingly beside his chair, he gravely bowed his
head to intimate that he was ready to listen. As soon
as they were alone, Armathwaite, as much impressed by
the manner of the doctor's reception as by any of the
previous events to which his strangely-interrupted journey
had given rise, related very simply the circumstances :
that he had met Alma Crosmont, passed the night, by
her husband's invitation, in their house, and that Lady
Kildonan had taken him to luncheon at The Crags.
Even narrated barely like this, without any hint of the
discoveries he had made concerning the inner life of the
two households, Armathwaite found that his story was
listened to with intense interest by the old doctor, who
considered his face in silence for some minutes after it
was finished.

"It is very strange," he said at last. "And perhaps
the strangest part of it all is that not many weeks ago
I mentioned you to Alma Crosmont as a man who, in
certain circumstances we were then imagining, would
be likely to have the skill and the courage to do her a
difficult and perhaps dangerous service."

"What was that service ? May I not know ?" asked
Armathwaite in a very low voice.

"Hardly—yet," answered the old doctor slowly.

"But if you will stay here a few days, I will talk to you again on this subject. Can you spare the time?"

"I will do so, if you have any strong reason for wishing me to stay. But if I may go up to Glasgow to-night and return to you, I should prefer it, as I have a chance of an appointment at the Infirmary there, and the candidates will be seen to-morrow."

"Let 'em be seen; I can give you something better. My wife and daughter think I shall be about again in a few days; but you and I know otherwise. I believe with Alma and with you, that it was no chance brought you to this place. Within a few hours of your arrival you have come face to face with the two cases which have been gnawing at my very life; for I warn you, you will have no easy post here; there are secrets which I will confide to you, if you care to take my place here, connected with certain of my patients, the knowledge of which will make your life an everlasting dance upon the edge of a volcano which must break out some day. You are young, energetic, honest, not over-emotional, with a head very well screwed on, though it's only on young shoulders. You may perhaps find a way to grapple successfully with difficulties which to an old man, weighed down by old recollections and sentiments bound up with the dead, have been like sleeping dogs allowed to lie. Stay here a few days; learn to know us; I will introduce you to my patients; if at the end of a week or a fortnight you decide to remain, you shall take up my practice, weighted with this one condition, that you look after my wife and daughter when I am gone. They will be provided for, but Millie is not handsome enough to marry, and she will need a guardian all her life : on you, therefore, if I give you this start in life, will devolve the responsibility, not of providing a home for her yourself, but of fulfilling a brother's duty towards her, and seeing that whatever home she chooses is a suitable and if possible a happy one. Now I have spoken to you very simply and very frankly, and perhaps you are startled by a proposal which comes upon you so suddenly. But my time is short, and my reasons for making this offer to you instead of to an older man are strong and clear. Think over what

I have said and study your new surroundings for the next few days, and when you have made up your mind, give me yes or no."

"I can give it you now, Dr. Peele. It is, with my heartiest thanks—yes."

"Well, you have still, until I tell you the secrets I spoke of, the power to retract. In the meantime, will you go downstairs and have tea with your new sister?"

He touched a bell by his side twice, and in a few moments Mrs. Peele appeared, her approach heralded by a tread like that of a man.

"Margaret," said her husband, "this is the young fellow of whom I once told you that if I had had a son I would have had that son like him. He will stay with us for the next few days, and you will make him welcome."

Armathwaite felt rather uneasy, after their encounter downstairs, as to how this exhortation would be taken. To his surprise and consternation she marched up to him, and just as he made an involuntary step back, half expecting that her intentions were pugilistic, she drew him down by the shoulder with a powerful hand, and printed on his coy cheek a martial kiss. Recovering quickly from his astonishment, he respectfully returned the salute, and having thus signed articles of peace, he hastened to obey her deep-voiced command to go down to tea. In the sitting-room he found Millie, now busy with the tea-things, and, as it seemed to him, rather absent and preoccupied. She was, however, such an extremely intelligent and agreeable person that Armathwaite soon found himself telling her of his newly-made acquaintance with the two lakeside beauties, suppressing, however, all details that savoured of the marvellous. Miss Peele listened with great attention, and was very anxious for his opinion of the two ladies. He gave it in a guarded and modified way, but the bias of it delighted her.

"Then you like Alma Crosmont best! I'm so glad. It's a good sign in a man to do that, I feel sure. I know," she continued hastily, "that Lady Kildonan is very bright and charming, and very good-tempered too,

I think, for such a beauty. But there's more in Alma than that, a great deal more ; and I often feel my hands tingling to box the ears of that husband of hers, when I see him——"

She stopped in confusion and hastened to put some coals on the fire ; but in the midst of this occupation she turned to Armathwaite with a genial laugh.

"It's of no use ; I've done it, and no artifice will cover it !" she cried. "I'm always getting myself into trouble by blurting out things that are better left unsaid. I haven't the least atom of tact or discretion. So I may as well finish what I was saying, and relieve my feelings."

"Especially as I know what you were going to say."

"Do you ?" Then her kind plain face grew grave. "Yes, it needs no conjurer to see that the poor little woman is thrown away on that great empty-headed fellow, who doesn't know the difference between gold and gilding. Papa made that match, you know : I think he's sorry for it now." And she looked into the fire again.

"You know Mrs. Crosmont intimately ?"

"I used to ; but she never comes here now. I believe it's her husband prevents her ; he's afraid papa will see and be angry about the alteration in her. I met her in Mereside about ten days ago, and I scarcely knew her ; she seems to be growing quite old and—and ghost like. Oh, it's a shame, it's a shame !"

Armathwaite warmed to this girl, with her open heart and straightforward speech.

"Yes, she is losing her health and growing old before her time. We must see what can be done," he said earnestly.

Millie looked up at him sharply. He was sitting in a chair before the fire, with his arms resting on his knees : and she was crouching, with a round back and protruded face, upon the hearthrug.

"Ah, I thought so. You're going to stay here," she said, with a nod of intelligence.

"For a few days, yes," said Armathwaite, taken aback.

"Oh, for more than that ! I know. You're going to

be papa's partner. It's of no use to try and hide it from me, because I'm personally interested, you know; and in anything which concerns oneself one gets to be abnormally clever. Oh, I knew what you'd come about the moment I saw you!"

"You knew a great deal more than I did then, for when I came here I hadn't the faintest notion that Dr. Peele wanted an assistant at all; and your father hadn't the faintest notion I was coming."

"Really! Well, it's the very strangest chance I ever heard, then. Because we knew very well that papa was finding the practice too much for him, and that it's dreadfully tiresome for him to be ill and to have nobody to do the work. And he wouldn't have an assistant since—well, since he had one a little while ago who didn't do very well. So the moment you appeared, I made up my mind that papa had been making arrangements without telling us, and that you were to be his partner. And mamma thought so too, and was very angry because she hadn't been consulted."

"Oh!" said Armathwaite, a light breaking in upon Mrs. Peele's strange reception.

"So you see you may confess without breach of confidence, because we know."

"But nothing is settled yet," said Armathwaite. "It is quite true that Dr. Peele has made some suggestion of the sort to me——"

"Ah, ha! I knew it."

"But these things are not arranged in such a hurry."

"You have a practice already?"

"Well, no, I have not."

"You are afraid of the dulness of a place like this?"

"Most certainly not."

"Ah, then I know the reason why you don't want to come!" She tossed her head, and looked again at the fire.

She was chuckling over some little secret all by herself, and was apparently in doubt whether she should communicate it to him. Armathwaite felt curious.

"Supposing I do want to come. What becomes of your reason then?"

"In that case we should have to form an alliance, defensive and, if necessary, offensive, against my mother and her evil machinations."

Armathwaite looked puzzled and rather alarmed, and Millie burst out laughing.

"I will be plain with you," she said, still struggling with her merriment. "I can't be anything but *plain* with anybody, you know," she added, putting her hands up to her face to emphasize her little joke, with a comical grimace. "No sooner will my mother know that there is a chance of your settling here, than she will begin the attack by informing you that the first thing necessary to a country doctor—before talent, before experience, before anything, in fact—is a wife. Next she will enlarge upon the fact that what you want in a wife is goodness, and a capacity for making the most excellent pastry; great accomplishments are a disadvantage, and good looks a positive disqualification. Then she will go on—Ha, ha! you guess what is coming!—she will go on to say that the very sum and substance of all the needful perfections is at hand in the person of *me*," and Millie embraced herself jubilantly. "Ugly face, complete ignorance of any art but darning and cooking, and all!"

"But really, Miss Peele, you are doing yourself the greatest injustice," began Armathwaite, rather embarrassed by her frankness, though her honesty and strong sense of fun amused and interested him.

"Oh, no, I'm not," said she, looking up into his face with smiling candour, which, though it did not make her beautiful, had a strong attraction of another kind. "You see, I've had some experience in these matters. About two years ago papa took a partner, and all went as merry as a marriage-bell until mamma began to hint at marriage-bells, when the unlucky young man, foreseeing his doom, promptly caught an affection of the lungs from a patient who had scarlatina, and ordered and carried out his own removal to a drier climate." Millie evidently enjoyed the recollection of this episode immensely. "I didn't like him, so I didn't interfere Then last summer came the assistant I told you of. He made a very valiant struggle; he got as far as giving me flowers and lending me a book of poetry. But then the violence of his emotions disturbed his brain, I suppose, and he got careless with his prescriptions, and very nearly poisoned two of the villagers. So he had to go, and all the flowers and poetry were thrown away. I was sorry for him when he had to leave like that, but he was a silly fellow, and he shouldn't have pretended to care for me when all the time he was crazy about somebody else."

"I think you were rather hard upon him. Why should you think he wasn't sincere?"

"Because, though I'm not at all a brilliant person, I have a little sense, and I know quite well that I may be the sort of girl a man would like for a sister, but I'm not the sort of girl he'd care to have for a wife."

This was so exactly Armathwaite's own impression of her, that an involuntary twinkle of appreciation in his face caught her sharp eyes.

"So I thought that I'd better put you on your guard," she continued brightly; "and if you don't want to have me flung at your head from morning till night, you will, if you haven't got one already, invent a *fiancée* to whom you are madly attached, with whom you correspond regularly, and whom you are only waiting for a favourable opportunity to instal here as your bride."

At this fiction they both laughed heartily; and with extravagant suggestions as to the devices to which they would be driven if Mrs. Peele should insist on inviting the *fiancée* to stay at Branksome, they cemented their friendship and closed a firm alliance Mrs. Peele, when she joined them a little later, had evidently received full instructions from her husband, and was majestically cordial; while the friendly relations established between the new-comer and her daughter, to the mischievous amusement of both, gave her undisguised pleasure. Armathwaite did not see the doctor again that night; but when he retired to the prim and neat little room which had been prepared for him, after an evening of pleasant, sympathetic talk, which to a sisterless man was full of charm, he felt that if he had spent days in imagining an ideal career, he could not have formed an opening more entirely to his taste than that which had sprung up under his feet by what seemed a series of miracles. As for the difficulties and dangers spoken of by Dr. Peele, it was natural enough that to a young man they should appear merely as fresh interests : and knowing as he did that the promised secrets concerned the two beautiful women who had filled his thoughts so entirely since he first saw them, he was madly eager for the doctor's disclosures, and hoped that he might be sent for by the invalid early on the following morning. But this hope was dispelled by an unexpected circumstance, which caused him to begin his professional duties with less delay than he had foreseen.

Next morning, breakfast was scarcely over, and Mrs. Peele, having bullied her visitor unmercifully for not eating marmalade, had only just marched from the room, armed with a clanking bunch of keys, to attend to her household duties, when a small groom drove up to the house in a dog-cart, and delivered a note for Dr. Peele. This note was sent down by the doctor to Armathwaite to read. It was from Lady Kildonan, and contained only a few lines to say that one of the housemaids had cut her hand badly, and if the doctor could not come himself he was to send Dr. Armathwaite. The young man read this, and his face flushed with a dozen different emotions. Millie, who was filling the seed-trough of her canary, looked at him furtively as he glanced through the note, which she herself had brought down to him.

"Have you read it?" he asked.

"Yes. Papa read it to me."

"And what did he say?"

"He said he supposed you must go."

"And what did you say?"

"I didn't say anything, but I thought——"

"What?"

"That she was beginning pretty soon."

Armathwaite burst out laughing.

"Oh, you ill-natured little thing! I shouldn't have thought it of you."

"Dr. Armathwaite, it is not in nature for a plain woman not to see the faults in a handsome one. It relieves my feelings, and makes no difference to yours. Lady Kildonan is a born coquette, fond of excitement, dying of *ennui* because her husband makes her live in the country. She looks upon every stranger that comes to the neighbourhood as her legitimate prey; she even condescended to turn the head of papa's unfortunate assistant, who couldn't hear her name mentioned without falling a-trembling. From gentleman to peasant, she won't be content till every man worships her, and you may be sure she won't let *you* off."

Millie gave him a sagacious nod, while Armathwaite buttoned up his coat gravely.

"I don't think I'm one of the worshipping sort," he said. "Lady Kildonan has my heartiest admiration, but I flatter myself it's not so easy to turn the head of a true-born Yorkshireman."

"Well, I hope not," said Millie doubtfully.

Armathwaite got into the dog-cart and drove off with a slight feeling of irritation towards Millie for her obstinate persistence in an injurious doubt. But he presently reflected that the girl could not possibly know the reasons he had for looking with suspicion and mistrust upon the beauty, nor the secret partisanship with which he regarded her sweeter rival, Alma Crosmont. He would let it be plainly seen this very morning that the doctor busy with professional duties of to-day was a very different person from the idle guest of the day before, and make her understand once for all that he was no ladies' physician, with hours to waste in listening to lisping accounts of trifling ailments, but a straightforward and practical man with his heart in the duties of his work.

It was another beautiful and bright morning, but the young man scarcely noticed how the snow sparkled in the sun and lay in patches of fantastic shape upon the hills. He was quite bristling with duty by the time he arrived at The Crags, dashed up the drive, jumped down from the dog-cart, rang the bell, and asked to be taken straight to the injured maid, as if each moment of his time had been a golden guinea. The hurt turned out to be a trifling one, as indeed he had expected. Having bound up the wounded hand and given the simple directions necessary, he was hurrying out of the house when a footman ran after him and requested him to stop, as her ladyship desired to speak to him. Armathwaite hesitated, inclined to offer an excuse, when Lady Kildonan's maid, a middle-aged and astute-looking person, fluttered down the hall and said she had been sent to show him up to her mistress's room.

"Is Lady Kildonan ill?" asked Armathwaite.

"Not very ill, but she thought she would like to see you, sir."

There was no choice left for him. He followed the woman up the wide staircase, along an oak-panelled gallery large enough and handsome enough for a ball-room, to a door at which she knocked softly.

"Come in," cried Lady Kildonan's voice, which was as bright as ever.

The next moment he found himself in a room the colouring and decoration of which suggested to him the inside of a sea-shell, adorned with hangings of pale satin, and carpeted with thick soft velvet which looked like sea-moss. The lace curtains, drawn close, were lined with pale rose-coloured silk, through which the bright sunlight came pleasantly subdued; in a tiny fire-place, tiled with paintings of flowers, burnt a small fire. Close to it, lying back in a large easy chair, her head resting on a satin cushion, was Lady Kildonan. The illness concerning which she had to consult the doctor was luckily not serious enough to dim the brightness of her eyes, or to render less dazzling the lustre of her brilliant complexion. On the other hand, it was grave enough to permit her to appear in a white cashmere wrapper, with her hair loosely knotted together and a black lace mantilla round her head, a costume beautifully suited to an invalid in perfect health, such as Armathwaite at once decided her to be.

Standing at the threshold of the door as the lady languidly beckoned him in, the young doctor, with a haze of memories and resolutions before his eyes, wished that he had not come.

CHAPTER XI.

IF Lady Kildonan did not look like an invalid, she knew how to assume the airs of one; and it was with the most affecting languor that she turned her pretty head on the cushion which supported it as the young doctor entered.

"Oh, Dr. Armathwaite, how do you do? I'm so glad you've come. What a lucky thing that you hadn't left Branksome before my messenger reached you!"

And, apparently exhausted by the effort of shaking hands and inviting him to a chair beside her, she drew a long sigh, and let her arms fall at her sides with the abandonment of utter lassitude.

"I feel just like that," said she, raising her blue eyes and dropping the white lids over them again immediately, to indicate the completeness of the physical prostration from which she was suffering.

He felt her pulse as a matter of form, and could almost have laughed at the barefaced nature of the fraud she was carrying on so beautifully. Luckily, he was sitting with his back to the light, which fell full on the lady, so that any indiscreet incredulity which might peep out in his face could not be noticed by his interesting patient.

"I see," he said, with becoming gravity. "Your case is very serious."

Neat little hypocrite as she was, this decision was too much for her equanimity. She opened her eyes to their full extent, and gazed at him with that childlike expression which only blue eyes have, and asked him in a soft tone of astonishment what he thought was the matter with her.

"That is what I want to know," he answered. "It must be mental trouble, and of some very acute kind, since it can prostrate you so entirely while your physical health is perfectly good."

"Perfectly good!" she echoed, in a disappointed tone. 'Don't you find me feverish?"

She offered him her wrist again, and, to satisfy her, he felt her pulse a second time. But he shook his head.

"You are a little excited, that is all."

"Isn't my tongue white?" asked she, as a last resource, displaying the tip of that organ, which proved, however, to be perfectly pink and healthy.

"No" He had almost added, "I am afraid it isn't," but stopped himself in time. "As I said before, the disturbance must be mental," he said, "and it preys upon you so much that you can't help thinking it must have some physical effects."

She lowered her eyes and sighed. "I have a great many worries, and troubles too," she said, "but, of course, I couldn't think of troubling a doctor with them. But when I feel conscious of a languor and lassitude which make the slightest exertion seem a fatigue to me—when I find my appetite is variable——Oh, I didn't tell you that! Yes; yesterday I ate three eggs for breakfast, and this morning I only ate one. That shows my appetite is failing, doesn't it?"

Armathwaite thought it showed chiefly that she had had an exceptionally good appetite yesterday, but he suggested gravely that if she would follow his advice, rouse herself, and take a long walk, he thought he could promise that she would be able to eat two eggs the next morning. She shook her head: never was invalid so anxious not to get well.

"You think, Dr. Armathwaite," she began, stretching one arm above her head to adjust the lace as it slipped off her golden hair, "because you saw me yesterday gay and lively, that that is my natural state, and that the listlessness I complain of to-day is only an imaginary ailment. Now confess that is so. Indeed, I am sure of it."

"At any rate, your gaiety became you so well that it is difficult to believe it was not natural to you."

"I won't tell you not to make pretty speeches, for really it is a treat to meet anyone in this wilderness who can string half a dozen words together in a civilized fashion. I believe that gaiety would be natural to me if

I were—happy." She paused, but as he said nothing she very soon went on again. "And I think it may be as you say, that it is unhappiness and not ill-health that is the matter with me."

He had not said this, and he certainly had not meant it, but as this was an opening which promised to lead to something definite, he was careful not to interrupt her.

"I suppose," she said, with a pretty mournfulness, "that some people think I have everything I can wish for: no doubt I have everything that some people could wish for. I have a great hideous house that some people might like, and a husband whom I made no objection to when they married me to him, and whom I've only one objection to now. But that one objection is fatal." A pause, during which Armathwaite still, while maintaining an attitude of respectful attention, asked no questions. She continued with a weary sigh. "He treats me like a child! I never have his confidence; I never have his trust."

Armathwaite was astonished. Remembering the way in which Lord Kildonan had spoken of her, had treated her; the friendly welcome he had extended to himself, a stray acquaintance whom Lady Kildonan had picked up in a particularly easy fashion; the kindness he had shown to the playfellow of her childhood; this charge seemed not only without foundation, but preposterous.

"I think," he said gently, but with some decision, "that here is an ailment I can remove. If one of your troubles is the belief that your husband does not trust you in the fullest manner, I can relieve your mind by assuring you of my own knowledge that for this particular fear there is not the slightest foundation."

"You don't understand," she said, turning in her chair so that her great blue eyes, which shone with a radiance that seemed to throw a liquid brightness round them, like stars on a summer night, looked full into his. "When I explain the peculiar circumstances of our marriage, you will see what I mean. I was an only child, and inherited all my father's property, which was considerable. Papa was naturally anxious to marry me to someone who could look after my interests, and see that the estates were managed properly: that was comprehensible enough. But when he decided on Lord Kildonan, who had no money, or scarcely any, of his own, for my husband, papa was so delighted to have found such a pearl among men, as he considered him to be, that he left the estates to him for life in trust for me and my children, if I should have any. So that, you see, I was made dependent on my husband for every penny of my own money."

"But surely Lord Kildonan lets you have everything you want."

"Yes, like a child for whom you buy a half-crown doll, though you won't let her have half-a-crown to buy a doll with. He has too much conscience to refuse to get me anything I want, but his Scotch instincts of carefulness over the siller will never allow him to put the money into my own hands and say, 'There, dear, buy what you have a fancy for.' Well, I dare say this sounds only like a trifling grievance after all, but it's galling, inexpressibly galling, when it goes on day after day, and month after month, over the smallest expenses, and when you know that after all it's your own money."

Armathwaite was obliged to admit that it was an irritating thing, and he saw by the puckers of annoyance and almost of shame in the lady's beautiful face that in her pampered life this restriction attained the importance of a grievous affliction.

"But there is one lucky thing," he said, consolingly, "and that is, that living up here as you do, the hardship of not being able to buy anything yourself cannot press very hardly upon you, as there is nothing to buy."

At last he had touched the mainspring of all this woe. She sprang up in her chair, the lace falling off on to her shoulders, and the golden hair loosened about her face, which had instantly become convulsed with excitement and indignation.

"No," she cried passionately, her bosom heaving and her eyes flashing. "Nothing to buy, nothing to see, nothing to do. And that is the life I am condemned to, chained to a man who doesn't understand that I am active, pleasure-loving, young. I can't read, I can't comfort myself with philology and all that stuff. I want life and movement round me, not this dreary lake and these stifling hills. I shall break away some day and become an actress, or a governess, or a telegraph-clerk; anything is better than this hateful stagnant existence. It is like being buried alive with a corpse."

She sat up, trembling and panting from the effects of her vehemence; no longer looking at him but staring before her with such fierce yearning in her eyes that it was evident she was agitated by a very genuine and consuming passion. Whether it was merely a vague longing for excitement or a more definite hankering after some particular pleasure was more difficult to decide; and Armathwaite, who had reason to doubt her absolute sincerity, watched her with wonder and curiosity as she sprang up from her chair, crossed the small room, drew aside the curtains, flung open the latticed window, and leaned out into the frosty air.

"Don't you know that is very unwise?" said Armathwaite, following her.

She turned sharply, and leaning back against the window-frame, so that her golden hair, disordered by the lace she had torn off, stood out round her head like the dishevelled mane of a bacchante, she fastened her fierce eyes upon him with a reckless and dare-devil fascination impossible to resist.

"If I am not ill, I will be ill," she said, in a fierce whisper. "Then your noble scruples will be satisfied, and you will tell my husband that he must take me away, or see me die."

She hissed out the last words with passionate abandonment. Never had her brilliant beauty looked more dazzling, more irresistible. The cold white winter sunshine could show no defect in her exquisite fairness, no fault in her graceful form. The state of violent excitement to which she had lashed herself made her eyes glitter and her cheeks burn; while the defiant attitude in which she stood, with the left arm stretched across the window to keep it open, and the right hand clutching the curtain high above her head, if a trifle unnecessarily dramatic, was unmistakably becoming. Armathwaite's face changed, and his breath began to come faster. Lady Kildonan, who had not lost control of herself so much as to be unable to note what effect she made, let her raised hand fall heavily to her side and her beautiful head sink, with a sudden change to inviting humility. The blood ran hot in the young man's veins, words as vehement as her own were on his lips, when suddenly, before he could speak, before he could move, there came a film over his eyes, and he saw, not the beautiful actress before him, with her fierce lamentations and sensational threats, but a pure young face worn before its time, tender eyes full of sweetness and sorrow, a mouth on the soft lips of which still lingered the trembling words : " Oh, Ned, I cannot bear this ; send me away ! " The vision faded at once, but it left him cold and calm, confronting Lady Kildonan with the gravest of faces, the driest of manners.

"What is the matter with you ? What are you looking at ? " asked she, impatiently, noting with surprise the great and sudden alteration in him.

He had turned away to the window.

" I am looking," he said, "at Mr. Crosmont; he is coming up to the house at this moment. And I was thinking how strangely unpopular this beautiful place is with you ladies, for Mrs. Crosmont seems quite as anxious to go away from it as you are, and certainly, to judge by her looks, with much greater reason."

Lady Kildonan shut the window with a very ferocious snap. He could see that she was furiously angry, and, feeling that his presence was by no means soothing to her, he picked up one of his gloves, which had fallen to the floor, and prepared to take his leave, satisfied, that she would not ask him to prescribe for imaginary ailments again. But she was too angry to be wise. Instead of letting him go with a few curt words, according to her first impulse, she stopped him when he was at the door by saying :

"You are a great admirer of Mrs. Crosmont's, I see."

" I was considering Mrs. Crosmont from the point of view of a doctor, rather than an acquaintance. She looks ill, unhappy."

"And I do not. So my troubles get no sympathy."

"From the doctor's point of view, no. But as a man who has been received by you and Lord Kildonan in the kindest manner, I——"

"Oh, yes, oh, yes, of course. You are overwhelmed with concern for Lord and Lady Kildonan's mutual happiness. But you would like to prescribe for Mrs. Crosmont."

"I should, indeed."

"And pray, as a doctor or as an acquaintance, would you see any fault in the stolid unconcern with which she bears her husband's difficulties, difficulties which drive me, who am merely his old friend, nearly mad with desperation to think that, with all the money which is nominally mine, I haven't so much as a five-pound note really my own, to help the poor boy out of his troubles?"

She was passionately in earnest, most sincerely and heartily distressed. Armathwaite was touched. She really did care for this man, then. "Stolid unconcern" were curious words to use in connection with Alma Crosmont ; but he let that pass.

"That's very hard, certainly," he said.

"You see, I daren't ask my husband for him, because if he thought his own agent was in money difficulties he would get info a dreadful state, and think poor Ned managed his affairs as badly as he has done his own."

"Yes, I suppose he would," said Armathwaite.

"And that's not true at all," continued she, taking up Crosmont's cause warmly. "He has speculated with his own money, I believe, but I know that he is even fanatically scrupulous about his employer's. Why, he won't even let me have a five-pound note if I beg for it when he's got the rents in his own hands ready to be paid into the bank at Liverpool !"

Armathwaite was rather puzzled. "One would have thought a man might be safe from the speculation-mania here," he said.

"Oh, people send round prospectuses of mines and companies and things, you know ; and then, I suppose, the poor boy gets seized with the idea that he can make his fortune in a week."

" But don't you use your influence to persuade him that it is foolish ? "

"Oh, my influence, what is it ?   I believe his wife encourages him in these things, and that, of course, weighs down the scale."

The young doctor began to look more incredulous than ever.   Lady Kildonan, who had not sat down again, but was wandering restlessly about the room, stopped and thrust out her hands before her.

" Look," she cried. " If I really had any influence over him, ought not this to be enough to restrain him—the fact that I have sold the very rings off my fingers to help him?   I tell my husband I don't care to wear jewellery—he thinks what trinkets I once had are locked up in my dressing-case.   But they are not.   They were sold, long ago, to pay Ned's debts."

" But how did you manage to dispose of them without your husband's knowledge ? "

" Oh, Ned goes to Liverpool once a month, som.times oftener, on my husband's business.   He sold them."

" To pay his own debts !   It was an infamous thing to do ! "

" Don't tell him I told you," she said, frightened by his tone.   "It is all right now.   I assure you it is all right now.   I only told you this to show that I am not the heartless creature you seemed to think me.   But now, now can't you understand how it is I want to get away, out of this wicked deceit I am forced to practise, this life of little lies and excuses, which make me ashamed to look my husband in the face?   In a few minutes he will be here.   He always comes to me before eleven to wish me good morning.   Can't you persuade him that if he would only take me away somewhere, to Paris or the south of France, he would get quite well and strong himself, and I should eat and sleep again as well as ever, and we could come together again, and end by being a regular Darby and Joan."

" If you can't persuade him to do what you wish, Lady Kildonan, I am afraid nobody can.   As for your husband's health, I seriously think you have the care of that in your own hands.   If you were to put a stop to his night studies, and were to take him with you on your long drives, it would not, as you fear, try him too much, but would, on the contrary, brace him up and tire him just sufficiently to make him too sleepy for that killing and unnecessary night-work he is so much attached to."

Lady Kildonan could not conceal her distaste to this proposal.

"Really," she said with irritation, "one would think I was to blame for his fancy to work at night!"

"Oh, no, I am merely showing you how to cure him of it. If you care—and I am sure you do care, Lady Kildonan—to begin the cure by taking your husband for a long drive every day—three hours at the least—I promise you I will do my best to induce him to finish his cure at some foreign springs."

She seemed to be balancing the future gain with the present sacrifice.

"Springs!" she echoed at last with a sigh. "You don't mean some place where there is just a pump and an inn? Because one might as well be here."

"No, I don't," said Armathwaite smiling. "I mean a place with big hotels, and bands, and balls, and a promenade which shows off pretty dresses and—their wearers."

"Agreed!" she said hastily, and she gave him her hand to close the bargain just as a slow rat-tat was heard on her door. She ran to open it herself, and received her husband with an effusiveness which, to judge by the flush it brought to his plain face, was as unusual as it was evidently welcome. She had prepared for his visit during the last few minutes by twisting up her disordered hair into a loose coil, which she deftly harpooned with a quantity of little gilt pins. He took off his spectacles as she led him forward, leaning on his arm with a lithe, half-caressing inclination which had the appearance of rendering him stiff and constrained, but which caused his grey eyes to glow with a tender light as he glanced shyly down upon her. To Armathwaite, as they advanced, they made a beautiful picture, until Lord Kildonan withdrew his right hand from his wife to shake hands with the doctor, and lightly patted her shoulder

with his left as he did so. At the affectionate touch
Lady Kildonan gave a slight but malicious grimace and
a shrug of the insulted shoulder, both directed to Armathwaite and unseen by her husband. In an instant the
young man's admiration turned to disgust and repulsion
as surely as if he himself had been the victim of the art-
less trick : all the falsehood that disloyal women can use
to their masters seemed to be embodied in that hypo-
critical caress, and he felt on the instant in arms for
his sex, the more that he felt inclined to doubt whether
a few minutes previously he himself had not had a narrow
escape. The rugged face of the elderly Scotchman,
beaming with honesty and kindliness, seemed to him,
in this new frame of mind, to show not only more attraction, but absolutely more beauty, than the fair features of
a wife who could be indifferent to so much affection.

Lord Kildonan's one thought, on finding the doctor
so early with his wife, was anxiety lest she should have
been ill without letting him know. She told him, sinking
again into her chair by the fire, that it was nothing more
serious than her old enemy, sleeplessness ; that she had
sent for Dr. Armathwaite as soon as she was up, for fear
he should be leaving Branksome, and that he had given
her a prescription which he said would do her good.

"At least, as much good as anything can do me until
you take me up to London to see one of the great physicians," she added with feminine persistency.

"If Dr. Armathwaite thinks it advisable, I will send
for Sir Henry Dove," said her husband at once.

Lady Kildonan moved petulantly. "No, of course I
don't want anyone to be sent for. It would cost fifty
times as much as our going up. However, I daresay I
shall get through the winter somehow," she continued,
with a little cough.

Armathwaite, who feared his interesting patient would
take advantage of his conditional promise to try to
extort from him a more thoroughgoing adhesion to her
pet plan, now for the second time prepared to take leave,
and succeeded in getting halfway down the corridor
when Lord Kildonan overtook him. This was just what
the doctor had expected and feared.

"She has sent me away," said Lord Kildonan rather ruefully; "I offered to read to her, when she jumped up and said she was going for a walk. She says my accent spoils any literature; and it's too late to get over that now. Come into my study, Dr. Armathwaite; I should like to speak to you."

Rather reluctantly the young man followed him down a narrow private staircase at the end of the corridor, and into his darkened room.

CHAPTER XII.

"Now, in the first place," said Lord Kildonan, as soon as he had closed the door, "did she, when she sent for you this morning, mention any symptoms which would support my idea about heart-disease?"

"Not one, Lord Kildonan, and I think you may safely dismiss the notion altogether from your mind. Lady Kildonan's physical health appears to me to be perfectly sound, and the only thing that seems to be wrong with her is a slight tendency to *ennui*, and a spirited craving for a little more excitement than life in the country can give her. I think a shopping expedition to Liverpool would make her all right again, or the trip to London she seems so anxious for."

"Did she say that to you right out, in so many words?"

"Well, yes, at last."

"Ah! It is generally her health, or my health, or something like that, and not 'Please take me away, I am dying of dulness.' And she is not dull. That is the strangest part of it. She is as gay as a lark, day after day, entering into all the pleasures of the country as if there were no others, and then suddenly there comes a change, and she gets one of these restless fits, in which nothing will please her but something she hasn't got and can't get. If you could tell me the reason of this, and how to cure her, you would do me the greatest service anyone has rendered me yet."

Armathwaite said he would do his best, and he thought there was no need for Lord Kildonan to worry himself over the natural caprices of a lady accustomed to the instant gratification of her wishes. But he remembered the flashes of fierce, feverish longing in her eyes, and thought of Dr. Peele and his secret. After listening to his assurances, Lord Kildonan said:

" Well, I should like to comfort myself with the belief that you are right. You will understand my fear better if I show you a letter I received from her father a few days before her marriage. There is only one passage I need trouble you with ; I have read it again and again."

There was little necessity for this explanation ; the letter itself betrayed the fact. Worn in the fold so that it scarcely held together, the old letter, which Lord Kildonan took from a case in his breast-pocket, showed evident signs of the number of times he had taken it out to pore over its meaning. The particular passage which he pointed out to the doctor ran thus:

" There are two injunctions which, before you marry Aphra, I wish particularly to impress upon you. The one is to let her live always in the country, an arrangement which will, I know, cause you no inconvenience, as it is directly in accordance with your own tastes. From her earliest childhood this has been impressed upon me by the medical men who have seen Aphra, for they point out to me that her buoyant health and spirits are not such a sign of a robust constitution as we should like to think, and that in the vitiated air and distracting excitement of a town, she would pine and die. I beseech you not to be coerced by her girl's craving for amusements into doing anything so hurtful to her as residing in a town would be, particularly a great city like London or Liverpool. The second thing I wish to impress upon you is said not in her interests, but in the interests of the estates which will after my death be in your care :— Buy her everything in the world she wants, in reason, but pay for it yourself. Do not let her have any command of money, for living in the country where there is nothing to buy, the reckless generosity of her nature will cause her to become the prey of every scamp and idle baggage who chooses to appeal to her, and encourage the pauperism which it has always been my endeavour to suppress. I earnestly enjoin you to follow my advice in these two things, as I believe you will do absolutely in consideration of the entire confidence I have placed in you, of the importance of the trust I make over to you, and of the happiness I feel in the knowledge that my dear child and everything else I care for in this world, will be in the charge of a man I respect and esteem as I do you."

"That is the passage," said Lord Kildonan, when Armathwaite had got as far as this. "I read it quite simply when I first received it. But since then the frequent recurrence of her fits of feverish melancholy has made me wonder whether there was not a deeper meaning in her father's words—whether, in fact, the delicacy to which he referred was not really a disease, which might carry off my wife at any moment if she were exposed to the strain of undue excitement. Now, doesn't it strike you in that light?"

"It is certainly a possible interpretation to put upon it. On the other hand, you must make allowance for the exaggerated sentiment of a father with one only child; especially as you see from the other clause, his far-fetched fear that a little indiscriminate charity would breed pauperism, to what wild ideas his morbid sensibility could lead him."

"Yes, yes, that is true; that notion is far-fetched, of course. Yes." After a pause he raised his head. "Dr. Armathwaite, you have given me great comfort. Young blood like yours is sanguine, and you see things in a truer, healthier light than we old fogeys, who croon over our real and imaginary troubles. Yes, yes; far-fetched, that's what it is—far-fetched. I might have had the sense to see that for myself."

"And now let me venture upon a word for yourself, Lord Kildonan. Get her ladyship to take you out with her on her long drives, and give up your night-work, and you will be a different man."

"A different man! Ah, it's too late—too late! And my night-work—I can't give up that! The night is the worst time ; one lies awake and thinks of one's grievances and one's follies. My studies keep me occupied ; I couldn't give them up."

"Not to please your wife ? "

His face changed, and he shook his head.

"If she wanted me to, yes—I would then. But how should she, poor child? She thinks they make me happy, and I would not for the world undeceive her. Since the seizure I had in the autumn, I can't bear the light and the buzz of talk in the drawing-room : so after dinner I come here and work until ten, when I take an hour's rest—on the sofa, in here."

He held aside a curtain, which hid the entrance to a small dark room, containing little besides a sofa and a low table with a water-bottle and a couple of books upon it. This tiny room led into a bedroom beyond, the door of which was open, displaying furniture of the same bare simplicity as that in the rest of the suite.

"At half-past ten, while I am resting in here, my wife comes and bids me good-night. I can hear the drawing-room door shut after her at the other end of the house when she is coming," he added, simply. "And she trips in and chatters for a little while, and trips out again, leaving a perfume of violets behind her. When the room has grown dark and cold again I get to my work, and generally write and study till about three, when I go to bed. But I'm a poor sleeper now, and I often get up and read until the morning."

"Ah, we must cure all that. Ask Lady Kildonan to take you out with her on her drive to-day, and you will sleep better to-night, I'm sure."

"But she finds me such a dull companion. She will be going with one of the girls, I expect."

"Ask her, and say I suggested your going. In fact, I spoke to her about it, and I think you will find she is delighted at the possibility of being able to give you pleasure and do you good at the same time."

"You spoke to her? Ah, I am glad. And she seemed pleased, did she? Well, that has done me good already," said Lord Kildonan, and his hand shook with pleasure as he held that of the young doctor in a farewell grip. "I wish you were going to stay in the neighbourhood," he continued. "I should like to see you again."

"I am quite at your service whenever you please, your lordship. Dr. Peele has asked me to stay here and assist him."

"He has? Well done. Then I shall see you again, and before very long. I think Peele sticks too much to the traditions—a little old-fashioned, you know. He never would make any pretence of listening to anything I said about my wife—always ran away, you know. Now, one likes to be listened to when one has anything on one's mind."

Lord Kildonan would have liked to be listened to all day on this subject, which was the one nearest his heart. He accompanied the young doctor to the front door, and let him go with great reluctance after another five minutes' monologue on the doorstep.

When Armathwaite reached Branksome, he had to pass the station on his way to Dr. Peele's; but no sooner had he done so than he retraced his steps, and going straight through to the platform, found himself face to face with Alma Crosmont. He raised his hat, but showed no surprise, and neither did she.

"Are you going away?" he asked, in a low voice, all thought of addressing her with commonplaces disappearing as he noted the utter sadness of her expression.

"No," she answered. "It is Uncle Hugh who is going. My husband has sent him away."

She could only just breathe out the last words, her voice failing her entirely, and her underlip pitifully quivering. Armathwaite flamed into wrath, and spluttered out indignant interjections half aloud. She looked up at him and laughed a little.

"We knew you would be sorry too," she said, holding out her hand to him. "Uncle Hugh pretends he doesn't care, and it's all right, and Ned and I shall get on better when he's away. But we sha'n't. He's just gone up to say good-bye to Millie. I'm rather jealous of Millie with him, you know."

And she looked mournfully away again. At that moment the elder Mr. Crosmont came out from the ticket office; he was ostentatiously cheerful, and resolutely bent on making the best of this new turn of affairs. He made Alma sit down to rest, while he carried off the young doctor for a drink and more particularly for a talk. Uncle Hugh was overjoyed to learn that Armathwaite thought of remaining in the neighbourhood, and began eagerly to explain to him the position of affairs.

"The fact is, Ned made up his mind to give me notice to quit a long time back," he said. "But I saw his little game, and was so lamb-like, for the little one's sake, that he didn't know where to have me till last night, when he came home in a villainous temper, and pitched into the poor child for being extravagant. Now you've seen a good way into the ins and outs of things up at Ned's, and I want you to be a friend, as far as you can, to the little one while I'm away, so it doesn't matter if I tell you a little more. I don't want to say a word against my nephew; he's as good a lad at heart as ever lived, but he hasn't been quite at his best of late, and he's taken to being so very close-fisted that it's all the little one can do to manage with what he gives her. She's never had a new dress since she was married; though, luckily, Dr. Peele gave her such a handsome *trousseau* that it doesn't matter. But though you can manage like that to dress on nothing, you can't keep a household going on nothing, and that is what Ned seems to be trying to train her to do. I've done what little I could, I needn't tell you; but I'm not a rich man, and the trifling driblets I've been able to pay have not been much good. And now it will be awfully hard for the child to fight the debts and the duns alone."

"And what does he do with his money? Surely he must get a decent salary from Lord Kildonan? He seems to have a lot more confidential work to do than a man in his position usually has."

"Well, he says his lordship has the defect of his

nation, and expects him to make a great show on very little."

"But it's enough to live upon, surely!"

"It ought to be. Look here, there's no denying the money goes somewhere where it oughtn't to go. And the question is—where? Is it betting, or speculation, or a woman?"

"Which do you think?"

"Well, from something I heard the other day in the town here, I think—the last."

Armathwaite was deeply interested, but he said nothing.

"There's a woman, well enough known in the place, who lives close by the station here. She has been noticed to go away by train on the last three occasions that Ned has gone to Liverpool."

"Are you sure of this?"

"Well, in point of fact it is I myself who have noticed it. It struck me as rather strange that since the winter has come on he always starts on his journeys after dusk. Therefore I have managed lately to be about the station and on the look-out. And I fancy Ned has either seen me or suspected me, and from that moment determined that I was in the way."

"You have not told him what you saw?"

"No, I haven't seen enough, and I'm not sure enough of what I did see. I'm afraid I make but a clumsy detective, for him to have found me out so soon. And now it's a pretty state of things, isn't it? A wife has to pinch and starve and worry for this wretched fellow to enjoy himself with a—— Heavens, it makes me hate Ned, that it does!"

"Why don't you speak to him?"

"I did try last night, and he flew into a rage, and said his wife's aversion and Lady Kildonan's cold coquetries drove him mad, and he must get a vent to his feelings his own way."

"Lady Kildonan's coquetries! He said that, did he?"

"Yes. I told him she ought to be ashamed of herself, and he grew suddenly quiet, as he always does if her name is mentioned, and he said she was an angel of goodness and purity, and had stood by him again and again. Well, I could only say she'd better have stood away from him, and after that we both spoke at once, and it was all up with argument; and the end was, I have to go."

"Well, but is it right? What will her life be without you?"

"Perhaps I've been with them too long. It doesn't do for a young wife to look for sympathy to someone else and not to her husband. I'm hoping that when I'm gone, and there's nobody to smooth over the breaks and the pauses, that they'll draw nearer together; else I would have made a longer fight of it."

The warning bell had already rung, and Alma was coming towards them, making a valiant effort not to cry. Uncle Hugh got into a smoking compartment, chattering to the very last, and making a great fuss over the disposal of his hat-box and rugs. But when the train was starting, and he had leaned out of the carriage window to give a last kiss to his little one, there was a tear on her veil which by its position could not have come from her eyes. And his last farewell was a very husky whisper.

When the train had crawled out of the station, Armathwaite spoke to Alma, who remained standing on the platform staring hopelessly after it.

"May I put you into a cab, Mrs. Crosmont?"

She started, and began to move hurriedly away.

"No, thank you; I shall walk back."

"I think you had better not," he ventured humbly. Indeed she looked too tired to stand. "Will you come to Dr. Peele's and see Miss Millie? She is so much distressed at not having seen you lately."

The suggestion seemed to frighten her; she declined at once, and bowing to him with a hasty "Good-morning," hurried out of the station. After a few moments' hesitation, Armathwaite followed. Standing at the outer door, he watched her as she started on her way back to Mereside, and saw at once she was quite unfit to walk the four miles alone. A few quick steps brought him up to her.

"I am going some distance in this direction, Mrs. Crosmont. May I have the pleasure of walking with you a little way?" he said very diffidently

She was glad: he saw it in her eyes. Accommodating his pace to hers he walked beside her, talking on indifferent subjects, and noting how her steps grew slower and more wavering until at last, before they had gone half the distance, she was fain to accept the support he offered. The moment he felt the touch of her hand within his arm his attempts to make conversation ceased, while at the same time his constraint disappeared. Perhaps it was the comfort of feeling that, in a humble and commonplace way, he was able to render her a little service; perhaps it was really, as he thought, that by the medium of physical contact the gentle spirit which shone through her soft eyes wrought with a soothing influence upon his own mind; at any rate they walked on silently, with the slow steps adapted to her weakness, until her house was in sight. Long before this Armathwaite had found out the cause of her refusal to drive back from Branksome. In striking contrast to the handsome fur-trimmed mantle and neat little velvet bonnet she wore were the shabby boots and well-mended but worn gloves which covered her feet and hands. The reason was plain; the mantle and bonnet were part of her wedding *trousseau*, and being only worn during one season of the year, they lasted well. But boots and gloves, perishable things in need of constant renewing, betrayed the secret that they also dated from the same period. She was absolutely penniless.

This fact, brought under his notice in such a striking manner, caused Armathwaite to ponder on the contrast between the two women who, if the facts which pointed that way were correct, had both been forced to make most humiliating sacrifices for a man whom the young Yorkshireman, in his indignation, was ready to pronounce a mere soulless clown. He supposed that old Mr. Dighton's injunction to Lord Kildonan, not to allow his wife any money, was the result of experience as to the quarter to which any money she might have would go; but the slight inconvenience which this deprivation caused the spoilt Lady Kildonan, and the sacrifice she said she had made of her jewels, seemed to him nothing compared with the life of constant self-denial and anxiety which the woman by his side endured without a word. Lady Kildonan's sacrifices might be the result of a headlong passion for a man she had not been allowed to marry ; but Alma Crosmont's existence was not even warmed by affection for the man for whose faults she had to suffer. Even if she stopped short of hatred, she could feel for him nothing but contempt.

As they drew near her house Mrs. Crosmont kept her eyes fixed upon it with a strange, expectant gaze, while the pink colour brought by the walk faded and left her cheeks white, and her steps grew slower than ever. Armathwaite thought that perhaps, as it was luncheon time, her husband might be waiting for her, and might be angry at sight of her escort. As, however, he attempted to withdraw his arm, she answered his thoughts, and shaking her head said sadly :

"No, there is no one to keep waiting now."

So he went with her to the gate, where the dogs rushed out upon her, and bounding about and running a little way down the road, seemed to be looking for someone else.

"No, Lancer, no Fidget, Uncle Hugh's gone away," she said piteously, though she tried to be cheerful over it.

Whether the retriever thought on hearing this, that a new friend is better than none, is not known. But he leapt up on Armathwaite's breast and licked him effusively. Mrs. Crosmont's face lighted up suddenly with a flash of excitement, and a ray of youth and sunshine beamed in her eyes.

"Ha, ha ! Lancer has found it out. Lancer knows it's all right. I've a friend left near me after all ! "

Armathwaite stammered something incoherently, but she scarcely listened.

"You are going to stay here," she said confidently.

"How did you know ? How did you guess ? " asked he.

The brightness died out of her eyes again, and she spoke in the old soft, muffled tones.

"The music told me," she said, dreamily ; and giving him her hand in a dulled and listless way, she smiled faintly as she bade him good-bye and thanked him, and disappeared through the heavy iron gates.

But he turned when he had gone a few steps away, and saw that she had come back, and was watching him. A miserable sense of the barriers of difficulty which stood between him and his powers of helping her came upon him, as he saw the gleam of her sad eyes through the iron grating.

CHAPTER XIII

FRANK ARMATHWAITE spent the first ten days after his arrival at Branksome in making the acquaintance of the various gouty old gentlemen and semi-invalid ladies whom the indisposition of Dr. Peele had left for some weeks without the comfort and excitement of a medical adviser's visits.

For ten days he saw nothing either of the Kildonans or of the Crosmonts. Then he received, towards the end of his second week at Branksome, a little note from Lady Kildonan, inviting him to a skating-party to be held on the lake on the following afternoon from two till five. There was a postscript, of course : " Mrs. Crosmont has been invited. I trust to the mutual attraction to bring you both."

Armathwaite wrote back, accepting the invitation, and wondered whether his walk back from the station with Mrs. Crosmont had reached Lady Kildonan's ears, and had been used by that imperious and spoilt beauty to irritate Crosmont against the man he chose to consider his rival. He had already discovered that life in this quiet town was an egg-dance, in which the slightest unguarded movement might have disastrous consequences.

As the incidents of his arrival, without fading from his memory, got pushed into the background of his mind by the rush of petty but necessary duties which now filled his everyday life, Armathwaite had begun to feel all sorts of doubts as to the sacred championship of an ill-used wife which at first he had believed himself called upon to take up. Cold common sense began to tell him that his coming was not the result of a mysterious attraction of an unknown woman who proved on acquaintance to be interesting enough to encourage such a belief, but a well-timed remembrance of Dr. Peele's vicinity, and of the fact that he was growing old, and might possibly have an opening for a young practitioner of whose talent he had always held a high opinion. He had already begun to take himself to task for daring to conceive the possibility of interfering between a young husband and wife, when on the afternoon of the day on which he had received Lady Kildonan's invitation, he was seized, while sitting quietly by the fire as Millie made the tea under her mother's directions, with an uncontrollable restlessness which seemed to make every limb quiver with the effort to keep still. After about ten minutes of this, during which he looked at the clock twenty or thirty times, Mrs. Peele fixed upon him glassy eyes of displeasure, and wanted to know what he was fidgeting for.

He jumped up, put down the cup of tea he had just received but scarcely tasted, and inventing a beautiful fiction on the spur of the moment, said he had just remembered that he had been particularly asked to call upon a patient whom he had quite forgotten until a few minutes ago.

"Well," said Mrs. Peele, lowering her head as she did when she felt suspicious, in the knowledge that the upward look of her black eyes made them particularly keen and penetrating. "You're a pretty doctor to forget an appointment so important that the thought of it makes you tremble and turn quite white like a girl!"

"Quite true," said he very quietly. "However, you will excuse me now I have remembered."

Without another word to her, but with a brotherly and significant glance at Millie, whose quick intelligence understood by it that there were no desperate issues at stake, he left the room, and putting on his hat, snatched up his overcoat and ran out of the house without waiting to draw it on. He felt all right again as soon as he got into the open air; nothing more terrible than an eager desire to get to Mereside troubled him, and obeying this impulse without question, he got over the ground at a great rate, thinking singularly little meanwhile of any possible result of his walk except this—he should see Alma Crosmont. The day was already darkening towards evening; the westward hills were quite black against the yellow light left in the sky; faint shouts of the boys on the ice-covered lake came to him over the intervening narrow stretch of land; here and there a bird, rendered tame by the bitter weather and the hunger it brought, chirped weakly from the hedge as he passed. Armathwaite neither saw nor heard anything very clearly, for the vision of the face by the fire came to him again, the bright blue eyes fading into the soft brown ones and re-appearing, the one face always pressing close to his, the other retiring before he could well distinguish it. They were no portrait pictures, to which he could give names; but there was enough individuality about them for him to recognise the types, to warm to the one, to feel alternately fascinated and repelled by the other. And so, in a strange, semi-ecstatic state, docile to the impulse which drove him, he walked on until he drew near the outskirts of Mereside, and stopped at the junction of the higher and lower roads.

But at sight of the square walls of the house on the hill he abruptly woke out of his hazy imaginings, and found the cold water of actuality quenching his visionary ardour. His unaccountable impulse seemed suddenly to have died of indulgence, and here he was, a young man with a career and a reputation in his hands, risking them both by as inexplicable an escapade as was ever perpetrated by one of the poor lunatics who had been the inmates of that house years ago. He stood for a moment irresolute, and then, firmly making up his mind to conquer the mad impulse which impelled him to call and see Mrs. Crosmont at all hazards, he walked up the hill with the intention of passing the house, gleaning what scant information he could from a careful inspection of the exterior, and then when he had reached the village itself, returning by the lower road. As he ascended the hill he found his pulses throbbing faster and his steps growing quicker until, having passed the iron gates and come under the high outer wall, he looked up and stood still with fear at the sight which met his eyes. Towards the north end of the house, where the ivy grew thickest, a sash-window had been thrown open ; and peering out of the heavy green mass Armathwaite saw the face of Alma Crosmont, staring across the lake at the hills opposite with unnaturally wide-open eyes, while her hands clutched the leaves which hung over the window, trying with feverish eagerness to tear them down. She did not see him ; she seemed to see nothing nearer than the tops of the distant hills. Without any further hesitation he went quickly back, passed through the iron gates up to the house, rang the bell, and asked for Mrs. Crosmont. It was the big and bonny Nanny who opened the door, and after saying that her mistress was lying down and could not be disturbed, considered the visitor attentively for a moment with her head on one side, and then added, with a sympathetic shake of the head :

" She isn't well."

Armathwaite instantly made up his mind for a bold stroke.

" No," said he, " I know that. That is why I have come. I have been sent for to see Mrs. Crosmont. I come from Dr. Peele. Will you ask her if she can see me ? "

Nanny looked puzzled and doubtful. Then she evidently deliberated with herself, and finally made up her mind with a rush.

"Come along," she cried. "If I lose this place I can get a better one any day."

And with a majestic defiance of fate in the carriage of her head, but an excusable feminine timidity in the corners of her blue eyes, she led the way up-stairs with subdued footsteps, and along the irregular corridor to the door of one of the front rooms near the north end. Here doubt and hesitation seemed again to assail her. She looked from the door to the doctor, and said, in the hissing and far-carrying whisper of the uneducated :

"She's locked in. Master was afraid of her getting about and tiring herself, so he's just turned the key."

Armathwaite's blood boiled.

"All right," he said, quietly; "I'll take upon myself the responsibility of unlocking it."

And he knocked at the door twice. At the second knock Alma's voice asked slowly:

"Who is it?"

"It is I, Dr. Armathwaite. I have come to see you. May I come in?"

A low sound, half like a sob and half like a stifled cry of joy, came through the door, which Armathwaite unlocked with a hand which all his manhood could not keep from trembling.

"You had better come in," he said to Nanny, who was heaving a great sob of pity mingled with fear. "I may have to send you for something."

She followed him hesitatingly into a bare little sitting-room, with mean, old-fashioned furniture, warmed by a small stove, near to which was drawn a narrow sofa. Alma was standing half-way between the stove and the open window, as still as a statue, with her hands clasped together.

"My gracious, ma'am, you didn't ought to have the window open; it's enough to give you your death of cold!" burst out Nanny, in a cheery, bawling voice, intended to wake the poor lady from her depression.

She was rushing across the room in a whirlwind of busy kindliness, when her mistress stopped her.

"No, don't shut it. I—I want to see out. And this room is stifling."

"You ought not to sit in such a small room, Mrs. Crosmont. With a stove like that it is absolutely dangerous," said Armathwaite, who had taken the lady's hand, led her gently to the sofa, and was feeling her pulse. "As a consequence, you are highly feverish."

"Well, it isn't master's fault about the room, sir," said Nanny, looking pityingly down on her mistress, and taking upon her to explain things as if the patient had been a child. "He wanted her to stay in her bedroom, or in the drawing-room. But this is where my mistress always likes to sit, and so she chose it, and Agnes and me put the stove in so it shouldn't be cold. I've been in a dozen times to keep it up, and every time till now my mistress has been lying here on the sofa."

"Well, go down and have some lemonade made. You know how: boiling water on the lemons, and put it to cool. That won't take long this weather. You are thirsty, aren't you?" he asked, turning to his patient.

"I don't know. Yes, I think I am," she said quietly.

"And bring some light," said Armathwaite.

Then Nanny disappeared, jubilant and rather proud of herself, now the daring deed was done. Doctor and patient were left sitting side by side, in the dusk. By the faint light of the stove, Armathwaite could see that Alma was quite calm now; there was a feverish glitter in her soft, brown eyes, but the restless agitation he had noticed in look and movement, as she stood at the open window, had given place to perfect peacefulness.

"What makes you choose this room?" he asked, in a low and kind, but authoritative tone.

She answered at once, without the least hesitation.

"Because it is the only room in the house in which I don't feel lonely, or, at least, in which I have not felt lonely until to-day. I hear music in this room," she continued, raising her eyes slowly, and watching his face, as if looking for the expression of incredulity she expected. "Very soft music which comforts me, and often gives me pleasant and beautiful thoughts. You think that strange, do you not?"

"Very strange. Do you hear music now?"

She was silent, and threw back her head for a few minutes in a listening attitude. Then in the red light of the stove, he saw a smile that was like a beam of soft light pass over her face.

"Yes," she said, "I hear it—but very faintly." She paused, and looking at him inquiringly, asked "Do you?"

He shook his head, and she looked rather disappointed.

"I know that nobody hears it but me," she said. "But I have never before been able to hear it myself, except when I was alone. So I thought that perhaps—"

She stopped, gazing at him gravely with the most touching confidence.

" Does anyone know that you hear this music, then ? "

" No, except Uncle Hugh. They would not believe me. They would say I had delusions. Now, would they not ? "

" Very likely."

She moved, so that she could look straight into his eyes.

" *You* do not think they are delusions, do you? You see that I am perfectly well—in the head, at any rate ? Tell me the truth ; I must have the truth from my friends."

Even as he frankly returned her gaze, Armathwaite felt the strangest, most unorthodox belief creep into his soul.

" I believe," he said, " that through some causes, of which I know only a very little, you have a nature so delicately sensitive as to be susceptible to impressions which would not in any way affect the ordinary, coarser-fibred mortal."

A change came over her mobile face at once, which Armathwaite, usually a sufficiently prosaic mortal, compared in his mind to the opening of a bud into a flower.

" Even dear old Uncle Hugh thought they were only fancies," she said softly. " And he tried to keep me from coming to this room, because he thought they were bad for me. But they are my great happiness now he is gone. Your face is changed," she went on, looking at him fixedly. " What is it ? "

He smiled at her quickness of perception, and answered :

" I fancy I may be able to find out something about your music, that is all."

He was thinking of Dr. Peele, and the fragments he had heard concerning her father.

" And now," he went on, looking at her gravely, " was it the music you were listening to at the window just now ? "

" No," in a very low voice.

" What was it ? "

A long pause. Then she answered in the same whisper :

"I felt restless, and could not keep still; I have felt so only the last few days; then I wander about the house and the garden and the road outside, waiting for——"

Her voice dropped altogether, and she put up one hand to her face as if in shame.

"Well, waiting for whom?"

He never thought of any indiscretion in his question. No thought, no feeling that was not utterly pure and good could dwell in this fair-souled woman. He had held this faith since the first moment when, by the light of her warning lantern, he had looked into her steadfast eyes, and every word, every glance he exchanged with her confirmed him in it.

"For——for my husband."

She breathed it out almost without sound. Armathwaite was startled, puzzled. There was fear, not love in her face and voice; there was truth, above all. She suddenly raised her head, and saw the expression on his face.

"You don't understand it! I don't understand it myself: I want you to try. He has been kind to me lately——all the winter, especially since Uncle Hugh went away. He comes and reads me to sleep at night, and is dreadfully distressed by these restless fits I have had the last few days. I believe, poor fellow, he thinks I am going out of my mind."

"And so, during these last few days, you have never been able to rest?"

"Not when Ned is away," she answered, in a low, bewildered voice. "I feel helpless and——and agitated when I am left by myself. I can't read or write, or work, or do anything steadily, even if I reason with myself and try hard."

These symptoms seemed all to point to a development of that weakening of the will of which she had complained on the first evening of his acquaintance with her, and Armathwaite began to take some pains to hide the alarm he felt. Fortunately at this point Nanny brought in a lamp, and diverted attention from his anxious face.

"I will see you again," he said, rather abruptly, after a few minutes' silence. "Your nerves are altogether unhinged, and I should like to consult Dr. Peele about you."

"Dr. Peele! No," said Alma, quickly.

But Armathwaite put his hand very gently on her arm. "You must trust in my discretion now, indeed, Mrs. Crosmont," he said, firmly. "Your state of health is really serious, and I have not had either the experience oi the acquaintance with your constitution which Dr. Peele has had. I will take care that he shall not blame —anybody; you may trust me, I assure you." She gave him one earnest look, and he went on, retaining his entire composure only by an effort, under the touching, pitiful confidence of her gaze.

Her eyes seemed to say: "You see I am all alone; I *must* trust you."

"One thing I must impress upon you," he said with unexpected severity of tone. "You must no longer expose yourself to the necessity of being shut up to keep you quiet. I believe you are going to Lady Kildonan's skating party to-morrow?"

She seemed to shrink into herself with an expression of disgust and repugnance.

"I don't wish to go," she murmured.

"But you *are* to go," he said, almost sternly, insisting on her raising her head to understand the importance of his admonition. "You must seize every chance of breaking the monotony of your life. Your husband wishes you to go, does he not?"

"Yes," in a reluctant whisper.

"Then I shall see you on the ice to-morrow. Until then—good-bye."

"*You* will be there?" she panted out with the eagerness of a child.

"Yes, I shall be there," answered Armathwaite, as magisterially as he could.

He held out his hand, which she clasped in both hers for a minute, looking into his face with a dim, sweet gratitude which almost unmanned him.

"I will go. Good-bye," she only said, in a very low voice.

He left her quickly, and was out in the road in a few

seconds. Looking up, he saw against the lamp-light in the room a hand waving to him out of the ivied window. But in the moment before he turned away to hurry down the road towards Branksome he seemed to see at least half a dozen hands in a blurred mist.

CHAPTER XIV

ON the following day a heavy sky and a keen, biting wind seemed to threaten the doom of the proposed skating party. Armathwaite, who was out early in the morning, hardly knew whether he most wished for or dreaded it. There was something uncanny and alarming in the influence by which she drew him to her presence without the least exertion of his own will, and something dangerous in the absolute reverence with which, once in her presence, he regarded her. While looking into her dreamy eyes he saw, not merely a young, beautiful, and good woman, but a being to whom he bowed down as to one who bore no stamp of common clay ; a creature who fascinated him, not by physical, or mental, or moral attractions, but by some subtile quality more alluring, more entrancing than all the beauty and intellect that ever enthralled or appalled the world. On the other hand, he might reasonably hope that the sight of her by daylight on the ice, as one of a crowd bent on pleasure, would lessen the mystery of the worshipful awe he felt for her. Even Minerva would look less imposing on skates.

Millie had been invited, and Mrs. Peele had been included in the invitation as a matter of courtesy; but to the unbounded horror of her daughter and of Armathwaite, the elder lady let down upon them like a bomb-shell at breakfast-time the announcement that she should go too. A cat in a brood of young chickens was not a more undesirable visitor than Mrs. Peele in any assemblage in which her word was not law and her frown held as sacred thunder.

"I'm afraid you'll find it rather dull, mamma, as you

don't skate," suggested Millie, in a gently dissuasive tone.

"If I find it dull, Amelia, I shall come away," answered her mother majestically. "Lady Kildonan would not have invited me if arrangements had not been made for my entertainment."

And Millie dared utter no further protest.

At a quarter past one, having gobbled down a cruelly hasty dinner, they were all in the pony-carriage, driving towards the meeting-place, which was the Mereside end of the lake, on the opposite shore, close underneath the hill on which The Crags stood. The wind had gone down; the sky was still heavy and threatening, and a feathery flake or two fell softly in a weak and wavering way as an earnest of what might be expected before many hours were over. A small marquee had been erected on the shore of the lake, close by the boat-house and landing-stage belonging to The Crags; under this shelter a couple of bright maid-servants, delighted with this tiny break in life's monotony, were making tea and coffee, and unpacking consignments of cake and sandwiches. On the shore outside, Lord and Lady Kildonan were receiving their friends as they drove up, while on the ice a long row of chairs were already filled with rosy-cheeked, smiling girls, having their skates put on. Ned Crosmont drove up with his wife just as the doctor's pony-carriage discharged its load. Mrs. Peele shook the husband by both hands, calling him sympathetically "My poor boy!" with a sidelong glance at his wife, whose wicked London-lady ways had brought such lines of worry and care into his face. She did not refuse to shake hands with Alma, but she presented her fingers coldly, tightening her lips as she glanced at the tailor-made, fur-trimmed dress of dark-green cloth which the agent's wife wore. As Alma passed on, Mrs. Peele said to her daughter, in a far-carrying undertone:

"I disapprove of those mannish things. The doctor should have let *me* choose her *trousseau*. I wonder at a man of his age allowing her to buy things he would certainly not let his wife or his daughter be seen in. Fancy either of us prancing about in a dress like that!"

"Well, mamma, you see those things only look well on a slim figure. And as for me, it's only throwing money away to dress me well; it would be like painting frescoes on a barn."

"Amelia, you forget yourself. In my young days it was a maxim that a well-dressed woman was one whose dress could excite no kind of remark. It is a good maxim still. Therefore you are well dressed."

"Very well, mamma," said Millie, good-humouredly. "Here comes Leonard to ask me to skate."

Frank Armathwaite, in the meantime, had been graciously commanded by Lady Kildonan to put on her skates for her and to be her first partner. She had told off Ned Crosmont to do duty at the feet of the Greydon girls, much to the disgust of their mother, who loathed him, and never spoke to him without affecting to have forgotten his name.

"We poor women shall be dreadfully short of partners to-day, so I mustn't monopolize you long," she said, as she held out a slim foot in a laced boot that fitted like a glove. "I have had a lot of disappointments, and Sydney Mason won't come out of doors to day at all. He fancies he has lost some money, and he is sitting up in his room to count it over and weep over the missing shillings, or half-crowns, or whatever it is. Thank you very much. Now put on your own skates, while I take a preliminary canter and feel my feet."

She wheeled about gracefully for a few moments, until he was ready to join her; then, giving him her hand, she glided away with him down the frozen surface of the lake, chattering and laughing gaily enough, though all the while she gave him the impression that she was in a state of high nervous excitement to which the active exercise gave a welcome vent. He was rather surprised that she said no word about her desire to get away from the country and its monotony, though her eyes burned with the same unnatural lustre as on the last occasion when he had seen her, and though her gloved fingers, as they skimmed over the ice hand in hand, were fiery hot and dry like burning wood.

"Faster—faster," she said, putting fresh energy into

every flying step, until the landscape on either side swam past in a blurred grey mass, and the keen air lashed their faces like a scourge. Her hot hand clasped his with a tighter grip, the movements of her lithe body showed more *abandon* at every step; and when she indicated with her disengaged hand a tiny bay on their right where the bare trees grew close down to the lake's edge and the untrodden snow still lay thick upon the ice, her eyes glowed with such a fierce lustre, the expression of her face was so instinct with some fiery unknown yearning as she slackened her speed and turned to her companion with a bright laugh and an affectation of being fatigued by her exertions, that Armathwaite thought she might have stood, with her golden hair disordered by the wind and her hungry luminous eyes, for a picture of the destroying angel bearing a plague-torch over some death-stricken city.

"Let us rest here," she said, languidly; "I am tired."

But the doctor saw no sign of physical fatigue in her blooming face, in her elastic movements; and his previous experience of the lady's wiles made him by no means anxious for another *tête-à-tête* with her. He shook his head in a gravely professional manner

"No," he said; "I cannot allow you to rest now. It would be absolutely dangerous after having come along so fast. We must return at a slower pace, and by the time you reach the marquee it will be safe for you to rest a little after your exertions."

He looked at her frankly as he spoke, while she examined his face on her side in astonishment mingled with anger. He could not say to her in so many words: "Lady Kildonan, I don't know what object you have in view, but I am not going to help to further it without knowing what it is;" but it was quite clear that he mistrusted her, and that her own feverish exhilaration had not infected him to the extent of making him lose his head. She laughed as it seemed to him rather malevolently, and then there came into her eyes, as she gave a last swift glance at him before taking his hand for the return journey, a momentary expression of paralyzed fear like that in the eyes of a shrew-mouse caught in the hand among the grass and brambles of a country hedge-row. Armathwaite's heart gave a leap of pity ; to see a woman, and a beautiful woman, look up at him with abject fear was so painful that, if she had but known it, the moment was come when it would have needed only a word, a sob, for her to have disarmed him for ever. Fortunately for his freedom of action, she did not know her opportunity, and the next moment her hypocrisy was emphasized by the fact that she started to return at exactly the pace at which they had come. They exchanged very few words as they sped over the ice on their way back to the marquee, where Lord Kildonan broke off in a kindly talk with Alma Crosmont, to fetch a warm velvet mantle which with his own hands he wrapped tenderly round his wife.

"I see you are quite a first-rate performer," he said to Armathwaite. "Now take Mrs. Crosmont a little way. She looks as if she wanted warming terribly. And then, when the snow comes down, which will be within ten minutes if I am a judge of the weather, you bring her up to The Crags whether she likes it or not—mind, I say whether she likes it or not."

"Oh, Mrs. Crosmont will not honour The Crags with her presence—at least, she will not for my asking," cried Lady Kildonan, with a high, cold voice. "It is of no use to try to persuade her, I assure you."

Again Armathwaite noted a look of fear in her face as she glanced at Alma. But this time it was fear that seemed, by the steely flash of her blue eyes, to be so nearly akin to hatred, that the impulse of pity it evoked in his heart was not for her but for Alma, who flushed at the hard tone without seeing the look which went with it.

"You ought to have skated with me first, for you will find me a very poor performer after Lady Kildonan," said she as they started.

She was weak and nervous at first, afraid to trust her own little feet ; but gradually the firm, helpful touch of his hand, the feeling that she was safe with him, gave her confidence, and by the time they had gone half the distance he had reached with his first partner, she looked as resh and as fair as an opening rose, and her soft brown eyes looked up at him with a plaintive yet innocent allurement, as she told him that he and Lord Kildonan and the skating had made her feel a different woman.

"Lord Kildonan commanded me to take you to The Crags as soon as the snow came," said Armathwaite, looking up and receiving on his face two or three of the flakes which now began to fall fast. "I think we had better be turning back that way now."

"No, no," said Alma quickly; "I don't want to go to The Crags. I never have been there, and I never will go."

He hesitated a few moments, and then suggested, diffidently :

"Don't you think, perhaps, it would be wise to go just once, even at the sacrifice of your own inclination? Forgive me for suggesting this, but you have been kind enough to treat me with so much confidence that I feel I may venture to advise you, in the absence of your older friend and counsellor. It is best to be conciliatory when one can."

"Conciliatory! Oh, you don't understand. I am more than conciliatory—I am broken-spirited," answered Alma bitterly. "Nobody wants me at The Crags but dear old Lord Kildonan."

"But is it not true that Lady Kildonan has often asked you there ? "

"Yes, because she knew I should not come. And I have more than a fancy—I have a conviction that there is nothing my husband desires less than that I should accept any of the numerous invitations I get to call there. I don't know his reason ; there is some mystery about it."

"Will you on this occasion sacrifice your own feelings, and brave displeasure by accepting the invitation ? My reason for asking you is simply this : if there is a mystery, it will be the best step you can take towards clearing it up."

She grew excited, nervous at the suggestion, and clung tremblingly to his hands as he guided her steps towards the marquee, in front of which the skaters were now busily taking off their skates before hurrying towards the private road which led by a gradual ascent to The Crags. It was quite a painful symptom of that weakening of her own will of which Alma had previously complained that, although her agitation went on increasing as they neared the shore, she uttered no single word in protest. It was difficult to pursue his plan in face of this silent, helpless suffering ; but Armathwaite felt sure that here was a coil which must be attacked boldly and at any open point, so he took off first her skates and then his own very quickly and quietly, and helped her along the plank which led to the shore without further discussion. By this time, however, all signs of outward agitation in her had given place to a lifeless, nerveless calm; her eyes had become dull, dreamy, and fixed, and the hand he took to assist her lay in his own clammy and cold through her glove like that of a dead person. Armathwaite thought she was going to faint, and, hastening her last two steps ashore, he put his arm under hers to support her. Scarcely seeming to notice his action, she turned to the left and began to walk on, drawing him with her.

"Come into the marquee and rest a little while. You are ill," he said gently.

She shook her head and still walked on.

"If you are going to The Crags you are going the wrong way," he suggested, glancing back at the few remaining guests, who were hurrying in the opposite direction, marshalled by Lord Kildonan, who stood at the foot of the private road and bade welcome to them all as they passed him.

Alma listened in a puzzled and dreamy way, and again shook her head.

"This is the way," she said quietly. "And I ought to know."

Something in her weak, faint tones, in her dull eyes, struck Armathwaite, and without another word he let her lead him where she would.

CHAPTER XV.

IT was already growing dusk under the shadow of the hills when Frank Armathwaite, impressed by Mrs. Crosmont's dreamy earnestness as she assured him she knew the way to The Crags, let her lead him along the road in the opposite direction to that in which the great body of the guests were streaming. The snow was now falling faster; already a thin white layer covered the broad space on the frozen lake which had been swept clear that morning. The hill on which The Crags stood frowned above them on their right, covered for the most part with coarse grass and bramble, with here and there a clump of small birch trees, or a tiny hollow in which the rain-water collected and made a little pool, now frozen and choked with snow.

When they had gone about fifty yards Alma released her companion's arm, crossed the road towards the right, pushed aside the snow-covered branches of some tall shrubs which grew at the foot of the hill, and beckoning to Armathwaite to come too, disappeared through them. He followed, and found her at the bottom of a steep and slippery path which, sheltered by overhanging shrubs from the snow, was wet, clayey, and as difficult to ascend as a glacier. After a few yards it appeared to end in another clump of bushes; but Alma, who kept ahead without uttering a word, bore to the right, skirted this growth through the snow, and emerged, keeping her foothold with some difficulty, on a little stone-paved resting-place on the higher side. From this point zigzag steps, roughly paved with stone and brick, led up the face of the hill, bearing still to the right, to a point from which they could see, about eighty or a hundred yards above them, one of the red, pointed gables of The Crags.

Armathwaite uttered a cry of surprise. Though certainly a very steep and, as it seemed, an unnecessarily difficult way, it brought one to the house in about a quarter of the time that it took to go by the road, and he was on the point of asking Alma how she came to know of this path, when he perceived that she had met with an unexpected obstacle. Before them was a high wooden gate, flanked on either side by a long paling, which reached on the right to an impassably steep slab of rock, and on the left to a somewhat distant thicket. Alma had approached the gate and mechanically pushed it as if expecting it to open at her touch. But it did not. She pushed it again with more force; then she shook it, but still without result. Armathwaite came up to her.

"It is locked, Mrs. Crosmont," he said, looking at her attentively.

"Locked!" she repeated in a low tone. "The gate is locked."

She paused, and again touched the wooden bars mechanically.

"We must go back again, and get to the house by the road."

"The road!" she echoed, in the same tone as before "I don't know the way."

"It is all right. I know that way," he said in a re-assuring tone; and without any comment on this strange adventure, every detail of which was stamping itself on his mind and awaking there many strange ideas, he helped her to descend the steps and the slippery path which followed, and hurried her back towards the more circuitous road, while he kept up some sort of idle talk about snowstorms and the long frost. She said very little, but he was glad to notice that the numbness which had fallen upon her mind and body wore off as they proceeded, so that by the time they came in full view of The Crags the colour had come back to her face, and she looked as well as usual.

"And so you have never been here before?" he said, as they walked up the winding drive.

"No, never," she answered, as she examined from end to end the long, be-turreted, be-gabled house, with its lights twinkling in every mullioned window. "It looks a pretty place; I didn't expect that from the way Lady Kildonan always speaks of it."

She was beginning again to feel a nervous fear as to her reception.

"I hope Ned won't be very angry," she sighed out plaintively, as a footman crossed the hall to open the door.

The whole house was full of movement, and life, and brightness. The brass lanterns which hung from the roof of the great hall shone on the armour trophies, and threw a pretty, subdued light upon groups of laughing girls and their admirers, and bevies of chattering chaperons, among whom Mrs. Peele stood conspicuous in severe majesty. Every other minute the Marie Antoinette curtains were lifted, and the buzz of voices and the pretty clatter of tea-cups and tea-spoons came through the cloister, as a couple went through to the morning-room or returned from it. Lord Kildonan, kindly and genial as ever, came forward with outstretched hands towards Mrs. Crosmont.

"Welcome, welcome, my dear child. You must forgive an old man for calling you 'my dear child,' but you are so subdued and shrinking that one forgets you are a full-grown woman. Bless me! Your dress is quite wet. Dear, dear! Come through," he continued, leading the way to the gallery at the back of the hall on the right hand. "There is a room here where there is no fireplace. You can shake the snow off there before it melts. William, a light here! Dr. Armathwaite, you come too."

Lord Kildonan went first, Alma followed, and Armathwaite brought up the rear. No sooner, however, had Mrs. Crosmont taken half-a-dozen steps along the corridor than she staggered, and, with a faint cry fell back against the young doctor, who supported her while Lord Kildonan, in great distress, sent the footman in search of his wife and of Ned Crosmont.

"It is all right," said Armathwaite reassuringly, as he lifted the lady in his arms, carried her into the room indicated, deftly unfastened her jacket and bodice, and kneeling down on the ground, laid her head back and watched her face. "The candle, please. Thank you."

He looked at Alma with lines of deep anxiety on his face.

"She has only fainted," he said, in a grave tone

Then looking up suddenly, with a very stern expression, he asked, "Where is her husband?"

Lord Kildonan, who in his perturbation and distress had upset a quantity of candle-grease on Alma's dress, and was now trying vigorously to rub it off with a silk pocket-handkerchief, looked at him apologetically.

"I have sent for him. William went just now. Shall I go? I will do anything——"

Armathwaite's face changed as he looked at him.

"I am sure you would," he said, with a depth of gentleness and sympathy which struck the old Scotchman with wonder. For he could not know the thoughts which were passing in the young man's mind. Here was a man, pondered the doctor, kind and loving, modest and generous-hearted; here was a woman who only wanted a little tenderness, a little love, to bloom into as sweet and as bright-witted a creature as ever warmed a good man's fireside. And they were both mated with, to say the least of it, as selfish and callous a pair of ingrates as ever rejected honest love and ruined honourable lives. The thought of it, and the weight of responsibility which he felt growing heavy upon him as mysterious fact after fact came to his knowledge, and suspicious doubt after doubt came into his mind, made his manner so solemn as to alarm his unsuspicious host.

"You think this illness is serious," he asked most anxiously.

"Not in itself. It may be a symptom of a serious illness. I must give that young fellow an admonition to look after his wife. In his attention to business he neglects her," he said, drily and briefly.

"Dear me, dear me. You make me feel that I am in fault. Of course it is not right that my affairs should take up so much of his time as to interfere with his domestic duties. I must speak to my wife. She is too exacting; she forgets he has a wife to think of, when she has him here to luncheon and tea and what not. Of course, of course it is not right."

Armathwaite began to be annoyed at this exaggerated loyalty and guilelessness which, however, he dared not disturb. Through the open door footsteps were now heard coming along the gallery, and Lady Kildonan's voice, talking in a high, offended tone.

"Of course he will want to make out that it's my fault—or yours; but I won't be talked down, and you must make a stand, too. I knew perfectly well there would be a scene of some sort if she came; I simply wash my hands of the consequences. They are in the study, I suppose. Of course——"

"She had passed the door of the bare, cold apartment in which the little group were waiting for her. Crosmont was with her; they could hear his voice, in the very lowest tones, entreating her to be careful, to be silent, while, with her usual wilfulness, she took no heed of his admonitions. Lord Kildonan went to the door and called her softly :

"Aphra, come here."

She turned with a start, and let him lead her into the room. The air of the unused and half-furnished chamber seemed to strike her with a chill, for she shivered as she entered. Armathwaite saw at a glance that she was excited and anxious. It might have been partly a result of the flickering and weak light of the candle, but it seemed to him that all her pretty colouring had changed to a livid grey.

"Shut the door," he called out suddenly in an imperative tone.

Lord Kildonan obeyed, peeping out into the gallery as he did so, with an apologetic word to Crosmont, who had hung back a little, and did not offer to come in.

Lady Kildonan turned and tried to stagger to the door, but Armathwaite stopped her by the decisive ring in his voice.

"One moment, your ladyship," he called, in clear tones. "You suffer from nervous attacks yourself; you will be able to help us."

She turned quickly, avoiding the sight of Alma with repugnance, which the doctor noticed.

"How can I help a doctor?" she asked in a hard tone, into which she in vain tried to put the old bright ring.

"Look for a moment at Mrs. Crosmont."

Lady Kildonan shivered, and, summoning all her self-command, gave a swift, sidelong glance at the prostrate figure, and asked, hoarsely:

"Is she—dead?"

"Not yet. But this looks like the beginning of an illness which may kill her."

"Well, well, it is no affair of mine; it is no fault of mine! How dare you talk as if Mrs. Crosmont's fainting-fits had anything to do with me? Everybody knows she was not quite right in her mind when Ned Crosmont married her; and really if I'm to be made responsible for the eccentricities of every hysterical woman in the parish—— Archibald," she burst out, turning to her husband, breathless with this rush of words, "are you going to allow me to be irritated and maligned like this? Don't you see this man is making out that I am not a good wife to you?"

This appeal—her touch—reached Lord Kildonan's heart in a moment.

"My dear," he said, very simply, very nobly, "neither this gentleman nor any other dare call you other than a good wife in my presence. Nothing was further from Dr. Armathwaite's thoughts, I am sure."

"Nothing, your lordship," echoed the doctor, giving her a very straight uplook into the eyes. "I only want you for your own sake—I know you are delicate also—to note the symptoms of this rather unusual case, and to listen while I try to elicit from this lady an explanation of her sudden seizure directly she got into this house."

"Had you not better call her husband? He is the proper person to listen to all this," said the lady huskily.

Armathwaite, who had risen and was now supporting the reviving woman against his left arm, had got, as if inadvertently, between Lady Kildonan and the door.

"In one moment," he said quietly.

Looking down again at his patient, he saw that she had opened her eyes, was breathing naturally, and trying to collect her thoughts. Lady Kildonan began chattering feverishly to her husband, with her ears well open to what went on, while Armathwaite helped Alma to remember the events which preceded her loss of consciousness.

"We were out in the snow——"

"Yes, yes."

"And you showed me a path——" He glanced at Lady Kildonan, who stopped dead for a moment in the midst of her talk.

A pause before Alma answered : "Yes."

"Then we came up to the house. You remember the lights in the window—and you went in—and Lord Kildonan received you—and brought you into a gallery with a light at the end——"

"Ah!" She stopped him, putting up her hand to her head.

Lady Kildonan, beginning to interrupt in a scoffing tone, was silenced by Armathwaite with a peremptory "Hush!"

"Then you fainted. What made you faint? Were you so cold?"

"No." A long pause. "When I got into the gallery I began to remember—that—I have been in this house before!"

She had hardly sighed out the last word in a faint, scarcely audible breath, when Lady Kildonan burst into a fit of hysterical laughter.

"Now," she said to her husband, in a whisper, the sense of which Armathwaite caught, "will he dare to say after this that she is perfectly sane?"

But Lord Kildonan was much distressed, and gently putting his wife aside, he crossed the room, bent over the recovering lady, took one of her limp hands in his, and, trying to chafe back the warmth into it, asked if she was better. The kindness of the touch affected the sensitive woman at once. With a grateful glance up at the doctor she moved away from him and stood without support, holding Lord Kildonan's hand, and smiling at him with dreamy eyes, which scarcely yet seemed well open to the ordinary realities of life.

"Yes, I am quite well now, thank you. I am sorry I have given so much trouble."

"Trouble! Stuff and nonsense, my dear Mrs. Crosmont! If you had to faint, I'm very glad you fainted here, so that we could know how delicate you are, and scold that husband of yours for not looking after you."

"Scold my husband! Oh, no, don't do that! He could not help——"

She stopped, as if trying to remember something. During the pause, Lady Kildonan, who had come step by step nearer to the group at the door, stole behind Armathwaite and left the room quickly, returning in a moment with Crosmont. Instead of being nervous and shaken as Lady Kildonan had been, and anxious to avoid the sight of his wife's face, the agent walked in stolidly, his features set with a sullen determination, which showed him under a new aspect, and revealed an unexpected will-power which, while partaking more of the doggedness of the brute than of the earnest purpose of the nobler side of man, was undeniably impressive and striking. He went straight up to his wife, who, instead of shrinking from him as Armathwaite had half expected, turned her eyes at once towards him on his entrance, kept them steadily fixed upon his, and held out her hand to take his with a cold, fascinated submission which set a freezing current running through the young doctor's veins. Lord Kildonan, on the other hand, whose purblind eyes and blue spectacles destroyed for him all niceties of expression, was charmed with this pretty little token of the strong sympathy which existed between husband and wife, and, with a gentle murmur of appreciation, was for leaving the loving young couple together. Some words from Ned Crosmont, uttered in a harsh, grating voice, arrested him.

"Well, how do you feel now? Are you better?"

"Yes, quite well."

"Are you ready to go home?"

"Yes, whenever you like."

"You won't soon forget your first visit to The Crags, will you?"

A pause. Then in a very soft voice:

"Is it my *first* visit, Ned?"

"Of course it is! What made you think it wasn't?

You have got some of those wild fancies in your head again."

She did not like this speech. Still holding his hand, she bent her head and made a slight, hardly perceptible movement, as if a faint, half-formed impulse to escape had stirred within her. Crosmont turned to Lord Kildonan confidently.

"This little head gets some astonishing ideas into it sometimes, your lordship. What do you think of her hearing harps, and violins, and trombones, and cornets played by invisible hands?"

"Dear me, dear me!"

But Alma gave a little moan of distress, and her husband went on quickly, with a significant glance at his employer.

"Well, well, we won't talk about that. What makes you think this is not your first visit, Alma?"

"I—I don't know. I seem to remember—some place —so like it."

"But you didn't remember the house when you came up to it."

"No-o! I remembered the gallery outside and——"

"And "—he took up her other hand as he spoke and held them both, gently and reassuringly stroking them— "don't you remember my describing to you part of the inside of this house, how the staircase was oak, and the galleries all wainscoted and hung with old tapestry curtains?"

"Yes, yes; I do remember all that—oh! and a great deal more. Yes, I recollect it all very clearly now, like a picture—the steep pathway, with steps, up the hill; the staircase that led upstairs; the——"

She looked before her dreamily as she described it in a soft, slow voice. Her husband dropped her hands and interrupted her.

"She takes the delight of a child in these descriptions, your lordship, and she never forgets a single detail. It is one of her great pleasures to hear a full, true, and particular account of where I have been and what I have been doing."

"And very pretty, too—very pretty, indeed," said Lord

Kildonan. "And in future I hope she will often come with you, and see what you are doing for herself."

"She will be delighted, I am sure," said Crosmont, answering for his wife, whose arm he had drawn through his to lead her from the room. "And now, if you will excuse us, I think she had better go home and change her damp dress before she takes cold."

"Oh! but she must stay to dinner! I'm sure we can find her some dry clothes; she won't mind not looking quite so coquettish as usual for once."

"I am afraid your lordship must really excuse her this evening. She has already been induced to-day to exert herself a great deal more than is good for her."

With a sullen and vicious glance at Armathwaite to emphasize this thrust at him, Crosmont took leave of his hosts, and, ignoring the doctor altogether, led his wife from the room.

"Run after them, Aphra, and persuade the little lady to come again," said guileless Lord Kildonan; and, inviting the doctor to accompany him, he led the way into his study, where a lamp with a green shade was burning, lighting up just a small spot where the table and chair of the student stood.

He gave a loving pat to the pile of papers on which he was at present working, and honoured his guest with a short sketch of his philological labours of the last fortnight; but presently he returned to the scene they had just witnessed, some details of which had made a deep and painful impression upon him.

"That poor little lady seems to have some strange notions, if what her husband says about her is true—eh, doctor?"

"Yes; she has a quite exceptionally sensitive organization, and is open to influences which do not affect the happier, coarser run of mortals."

"You don't think there's anything wrong up here, then?" And he touched his forehead.

"Indeed, I shouldn't like to think so."

"No, no!" A pause. "Did you hear her mention a steep path with steps up the hill?"

"Yes."

"Well, it was curious that her husband should have described that to her, because it's never used, and I didn't think anybody knew about it but Aphra and me. It leads to a little door on the ground-floor of the east wing. I had a gate made half-way up as soon as I came into the place, for I found some of the servants made use of it to slip in and out without leave; it has a complicated lock, and I keep the key. So it's curious he should have mentioned it to her, isn't it?"

"Lady Kildonan must have told him of it."

"That's it, of course." Quite satisfied with this explanation, he turned to another point. "Now do you think young Crosmont is altogether as kind as he might be to that pretty wife of his? I confess the tone in which he spoke to her grated on me."

"I suppose it is difficult for a strong, robust man like that to make enough allowance for a highly nervous and sensitive woman. He calls her fancies delusions. Now perhaps no one but a doctor would make the subtile distinction of calling them anything else."

"Well, but Dr. Armathwaite, supposing they were delusions, is that a reason for a man to speak harshly to the woman whose weakness he has sworn to protect, whose frailty looks to him for support? Why, my goodness, sir!" This was a very strong expression for the old Scotchman, who began fidgeting up and down to work off his excitement as he uttered it. "Do you think if my wife were ever to have delusions—which Heaven forbid!—that I should treat her less tenderly, or love her less fondly? Why, if my darling Aphra were to be haunted with the most horrible imaginings that ever drove men into madness, instead of pretty fancies about music and such things, I should have to go down on my knees every morning and night to pray God to keep me from the sin of finding some comfort in her affliction, since it would throw her closer into my arms, and make her lean on my affection, and trust herself to me, as in her bright health it is impossible that she can do."

His voice shook with emotion, and he stood for a few seconds with clasped hands and bent head, lost in those thoughts and wishes which were his daily companions. Then he looked up and laughed rather shyly.

"It's a subject I've thought a good deal about," he said, in a more commonplace tone. "I've had to make allowances, too, in my way. But I have always acted on this principle : if a woman satisfies you that she is true-hearted and worthy of trust, indulge her in every way, bear with her in everything. You can't do too much to show your appreciation of a good woman. Those are my opinions, doctor, and I think they're sound."

"Mr. Crosmont might adopt some of them with advantage, Lord Kildonan."

It was all the doctor could say. But even as the words dropped from his lips, he wished that the result of the different systems practised by the two husbands had preached a better moral.

CHAPTER XVI.

LORD KILDONAN and Armathwaite were still conversing when the first dinner-bell rang.

"Stay and dine with us—you must stay and dine with us," said the former, eagerly. "I like talking to you ; you have the active sympathy of the young and a touch of the silent discretion of older folk. And if I bore you, as I am afraid I do, you may at least flatter yourself that you are the only person I babble to at this rate. Come, you must stay."

"You are very kind, your lordship, but I am not dressed for dinner."

"Never mind. I won't dress either, and her ladyship must excuse us both together."

Armathwaite found, as he entered the drawing-room with his host, that all the guests of the afternoon were gone with the exception of himself, another young fellow, and Crosmont, who slipped in at the last moment just as they had all risen to go in to dinner.

At the dinner-table, when all had sat down, there was still a vacant chair, and cries arose of : "Where's

Sydney?" "What has become of Mason?" mingled with murmured jests and stifled laughter. Lord Kildonan was the only person present who knew nothing of the reason of the young fellow's absence; and his ingenuous inquiries after his missing guest produced a hush in the merriment, it having been generally agreed that Sydney's loss of his money should be concealed from the master of the house, on account of deep distress and annoyance it would cause him. A servant was dispatched in search of the young fellow, who appeared with pink-rimmed eyes and a more washed-out appearance than ever, took his seat with the air of a martyr opposite to Armathwaite, and answered all Lord Kildonan's questions by lisping out in lachrymose tones that he had a headache, which, being the sort of effeminate complaint he most affected, passed as sufficient reason for his languor and his lateness. But Armathwaite, who was on the alert, and inclined to look upon every unusual incident as a possible link in the chain of mystery, the scattered portions of which he was picking up so carefully, watched the pallid face with interest, and threw across the table a kindly remark on his want of appetite, which Mason received effusively amid the general inclination to make light of his trouble.

"He doesn't really deserve any pity," observed Armathwaite's right-hand neighbour, the brightest of the Greydon girls. "He is enormously rich, awfully mean, and is always boasting of his money, not in the manner of the millionaires of the comic papers, of course, but in lots of little indirect ways. So, of course, although it's an awkward and disagreeable thing to happen in a house, yet we can't help laughing at the fuss he makes about it. Look, he's got on an extra number of rings to console himself."

Armathwaite noticed that, besides the marquise ring of diamonds and sapphires which he generally wore, he had a big single brilliant on his little finger, at which he gazed furtively from time to time as if the sight of it really did afford him some consolation for his loss. The young doctor did not share the general politely suppressed amusement at his misfortune.

"I think you are all rather hard upon the little fellow,

he said in a low voice, turning to Miss Greydon, and meeting her eyes with a kind grave look. "He is perfectly sincere; his loss is for him as genuine a calamity as say temporary lameness would be to me, or as the loss of her beautiful hair"—Miss Greydon's abundant locks were one of her few "points"—"would be to a lady. One can see he hasn't the strength for what we call manly exercises; I doubt whether he has the brains for a student. You ladies won't have anything to say to him for the paradoxical reason that his tastes are too much like yours. What remains to him, then, but his little velvet coats and his perfumes and his toys and his trinkets, and the money which makes all his importance in the world? You are too hard, Miss Greydon, too hard."

"I'll forgive your censure for the sake of your eloquence. But I believe you will be as much disgusted with him as any of us when you have stood the ordeal of a conversation with him."

"Well, I am going to try this evening."

"Will you let me know the result?"

"Perhaps. Unless it should be too favourable to your own views."

"Then I foresee that I shall hear no more."

The ladies were rising to leave the table, and Armathwaite, who opened the door for them, took advantage of their departure to take a vacant seat beside the disconsolate Sydney. This move brought him within three seats of Ned Crosmont, who had been morose and silent during dinner, and who now greeted him with a black and undisguised scowl, which the young Yorkshireman resolved stolidly not to see.

"You were not on the ice this afternoon, I think?" began Armathwaite, as an opening.

"Oh no, I was not *nearly* well enough. And I hate ice and snow, and all those things."

"Well, I really think you would have looked better if you had put on a pair of skates and tried your luck on the lake to-day."

But Sydney's teeth almost chattered at the idea.

"Oh no, I shouldn't," he answered plaintively. "If

I catch cold I am always ill for weeks. Besides, I was too miserable to go out to-day, even if it had been fine and warm. I have had a great misfortune, Doctor Armathwaite ; it has upset me terribly. I think I shall cut short my visit here, and go up to town to consult Dr. Manville. The Grand Duchess of Schletterberg suffers in exactly the same way that I do, and she always goes to Dr. Manville."

The remembrance of this fact seemed to bring consolation to him ; he recovered sufficiently to eat a grape. Meanwhile Ned Crosmont, who was on the other side of him, drew his chair, as if inadvertently, near enough to hear their conversation, which was carried on in a subdued tone.

"Dr. Manville will only recommend you to come back again to country air, and to take as much of it as you can," suggested Armathwaite.

"I think you don't quite understand my case," lisped out Sydney in a languid tone, but with an obstinate expression on his unhealthy, suet-coloured face. "I suffer from the nerves ; any shock upsets me ; and I have had a great shock."

"Indeed !"

"Yes. You must know, Dr. Armathwaite, that I always carry about with me wherever I go an ebony and pearl dressing-case with silver-gilt fittings, which I had made for me exactly on the model of one the Marchioness of Stourbridge had given to her by her father on her wedding-day. Well, in the little drawer at the bottom I generally keep some money—not much, but a couple of hundred pounds or so, partly in gold and partly in silver. And in the trays and other compartments I keep my watches and a few articles of jewellery. I always put back at night whatever I have been wearing during the day, and as I do so, I sometimes look over the other things to see that they are all right. Well, last night——"

"Don't you think everybody has by this time heard enough of that story of yours ?" interrupted a harsh voice behind him. For in his excitement Sydney had turned his back upon the rest of the company, and was hanging on to the chair of the first listener who had shown deep and unmistakable interest in his misfortune. The sufferer jumped up as if he had been stabbed in the back.

"I think, Mr. Crosmont, that that is my own affair. And if you really believe, as you seem to imply, that my story is not true, I can soon settle that by going to Lord Kildonan and asking him to let me put the thing into the hands of the police."

Either of malicious purpose or through loss of self-control, Sydney had raised his voice so that its high effeminate tones carried his words from end to end of of the room ; and Lord Kildonan, who was in the midst of an argument about rare editions, hearing his name mentioned, stopped in his talk. Crosmont's dark face assumed in a moment a livid hue, and it was with an effort which caused the muscles of his mouth and eyes to twitch in convulsive hideousness that he burst into a constrained laugh, and slapping Sydney on the shoulder with a familiarity which the latter strongly resented, told him that he was too touchy, that he mustn't take offence at a joke ; then he added quickly in a much lower tone, while his eyes seemed to pierce right into the lad's shallow brain :

"*You* could never commit an act so unworthy of a gentleman as that."

He had struck the right chord. The word "gentleman" was a fetich to the heir of the advertisement contractor. Sydney gave him a faint and sickly smile of condescending truce, and was about to resume his talk with Armathwaite when the agent again interrupted him.

"You haven't told me all the details of the affair yet, Sydney. Seriously, I think, knowing this place as well as I do, I might be able to find a clue to the disappearance of the things, if anybody could."

At this moment Crosmont caught the eyes of the young doctor fixed upon him with great intentness. Sydney, offended at hearing his Christian name from the lips of the rough-mannered man he disliked, shrugged his shoulders and said languidly :

"You have heard all the details already, and I don't really see why you should be able to find out any more about it than Dr. Armathwaite can. Don't you agree with me?" and he turned to his other neighbour.

"Well, yes," answered the doctor. "I agree that Mr. Crosmont, having heard the details, knows much more about the affair than I do. And I also agree that by hearing them I shall find out a great deal that I don't know now."

"Perhaps you have a special faculty for discovering mares' nests?" said Crosmont rudely, choosing to take as an offence a speech which Armathwaite had uttered in a perfectly conciliatory manner.

"I have not yet had experience enough in hunting for them to know."

"Well, you won't be long in getting it at the rate you are going," said the agent in the same tone.

Armathwaite, who was exceedingly anxious, for Alma's sake, not to be led into a quarrel with her morose husband, affected not to catch these last words, and again begged Sydney Mason to let him hear the promised story.

"I was telling you," began the young fellow at once, "that I keep some money always by me in my dressing-case. And the key I keep on a steel ring with some others, which I always leave in the left-hand breast-pocket of a little velvet morning coat you may have seen me wear, garnet-coloured, and lined with silk of the same shade. I had it made from a pattern Lord Penistone gave me. Last night I went to the wardrobe and took the keys out of my coat (for they were there quite safely, as usual), opened my dressing-case, and found that all the gold, about sixty or seventy pounds, was gone, and worse than that—a diamond breast-pin which, Lady Shireoaks told me, had a finer stone in it than any in that celebrated tiara of hers. Now what do you think of that? The money's nothing, and, for the matter of that, the diamond's nothing, for I could buy plenty of others as large in Bond Street to-morrow; but it's the feeling that here, in a house where you are on intimate terms with the people, and do expect to be treated with some consideration, you should be as unprotected as if you were sleeping in a barn, and liable to be robbed and —who knows?—perhaps murdered, by any thief in the neighbourhood who takes it into his head, from your appearance or your manner, that you are a person worth plundering."

"But surely you can't blame Lord and Lady Kildonan? They would be awfully vexed if they heard of it."

"*He* would, but Lady Kildonan doesn't care. She was told about it, and she only said "—here his face began to pucker up almost as if he were going to cry— "that the little laddie must have been dreaming! What do you think of that? I call it shameful. When it appears too, that some unknown person really did get into the house not very long ago, for marks of feet that had been covered with clay were found in one of the galleries in the morning. The maid who discovered them told me so. She said it was hushed up for fear of alarming her ladyship, but I say it oughtn't to be hushed up, and the sooner a detective is sent for to watch for this thief who gets in and robs people, the better it will be for the reputation of the place. And I say Lord Kildonan ought to be told, and must be told, Dr. Armathwaite, and I am sure you will agree with me."

But Armathwaite was in no hurry to do so. He did, indeed, evidently take a most deep interest in the matter; but it was interest which expressed itself by almost tragic silence, and by a look of anger and fear in his blue eyes which puzzled Sydney by its intensity.

"Don't you agree with me," repeated the latter, in a fainter tone, "that Lord Kildonan ought to be told?"

Armathwaite looked at the little fellow as if he were something so small, so insignificant, as scarcely to be seen.

"No," he said, in a very low, hoarse voice; "I do not think Lord Kildonan ought to be told—yet."

With the last words he raised his head sharply and fixed his eyes very directly, not at the lad but at Crosmont, who had, he was sure, heard, if not every word, at least the purport of the conversation. Lord Kildonan, who always retired to his study after dinner, was rising and telling the rest that they had the drawing-room and the billiard-room to choose from. In the general move which followed, Armathwaite, whose brain seemed to be beating in his head like a steam-hammer, found himself side by side with Crosmont as they went along the gallery. The agent looked up into his face with a sullenly aggressive expression.

"Look here," he said, in a savage and dogged tone, which struck Armathwaite with a sudden and horrible sense of what its effect must be on the fragile and sensitive Alma, "you think yourself an uncommonly clever fellow, and you have taken it into your head that by playing the private detective—as you have been trying to do ever since you came here in one way or another—you may find some pickings which may not be beneath your notice. Now, I tell you, it won't do. There may be little disagreements in the families about here, just as there are in other places. But we like to keep them to ourselves; and we don't want any interfering stranger to come and take our linen abroad to be washed in spite of us. I heard of your sneaking visit to my wife yesterday, a thing which any gentleman would be ashamed of. I'm not a jealous husband; I chose my wife carefully, and I can trust her; but I'll allow no more visits, you understand. There's nothing the matter with her that you can cure. If you come near my house again—and if you do I shall hear of it, I promise you—or if I find you meddling in any way with matters which don't concern you, I shall go straight to Lord Kildonan and denounce you without more words as a prowler after other men's wives."

Armathwaite listened to this discourse, which was hissed into his ear with great virulence, in attentive silence; and when Crosmont ended and glared up at him in defiant expectation of an angry protest, he only said, in a perfectly calm voice:

"Will you come into the tennis-court at the end? We can talk better there."

The agent, taken by surprise, looked as if he would have liked to refuse. But, for all his bravado, he felt enough anxiety as to the doctor's attitude to be forced to give a reluctant and ungracious assent to the proposal. They walked in silence the short distance along the cloister which lay between the drawing-room door and the tennis-court, which, dimly lighted by oil-lamps in the conservatory and little gallery above, was now deserted, cold and silent. Armathwaite took out his cigarette-case, offered it to Crosmont, who curtly refused, and choosing a cigarette for himself, lit it, and throwing himself on one of the divans which were placed against the walls of the great bare apartment, began to smoke, looking up at the twinkling lights in the gallery with a thoughtful but imperturbed countenance. Crosmont began to feel angry and uncomfortable.

"I didn't come here to be made a fool of," he said brusquely.

"No, Mr. Crosmont; and I had no such thought in my mind when I asked you to come. But as you brought against me about the gravest charge you could bring against a medical man, and as at the same time it was too groundless for me to take too seriously, I thought the best thing we could do was to have our talk out quietly, so that I could remove the suspicion which exists in your mind, and you could remove the natural vexation which exists in mine."

"Well, the best way to remove my suspicion will be to remove yourself out of the neighbourhood, or at any rate to break off all connection with this house as well as with mine."

"That is, of course, asking too much. As a matter of fact, it would be impossible for me to do so, even if I wished it, as Lord Kildonan has consulted me upon a matter which will render it necessary for me to advise him frequently for some time to come."

Crosmont, who had taken out a cigar and done everything with it except light it, now threw it away in mistake for a match, which had gone out as soon as it ignited.

"I thought you were a lady's doctor," he said, trying to speak as coldly as Armathwaite himself, but throwing as much venom as he could into his tone.

But Armathwaite appeared to take the remark in perfect good faith.

"I think, on the whole, I have had more experience with men than with women," he answered. "But I admit that I have frequently found the latter cases the more interesting, for the reason that women, having feebler organizations, are more easily affected in health through their minds."

"Minds! I never met a woman who had a mind to speak of."

"Well, well, heart, spirit, soul—whatever you like that is not body. Your own wife, for instance, Mr. Crosmont,"—Armathwaite, feeling here that he was making a very bold stroke, had to keep a tight hold on the outward man to maintain his useful imperturbability—"is an excellent proof of this. So entirely is her physical well-being dependent upon moral causes that I have no hesitation in saying the only physician who could bring the colour back into her cheeks and a healthy brightness to her eyes, instead of the unnatural lustre which now shines in them, is her husband."

His voice quivered a little on the last words; he was in for it now, and desperately anxious to succeed in his bold pleading. Crosmont, greatly agitated, stamped on the ground, and asked him "what the —— he meant by his impertinence." Armathwaite jumped up, his handsome face aglow with passionate earnestness, and met the other man eye to eye.

"Look here," he said, in a ringing voice, "who are the persons who will benefit by the physic I want you to use? I? If I had the designs you affect to credit me with, I shouldn't be giving you this advice; it's contrary to reason. Your wife? Yes; she will become a different woman. But you—you most of all, for you will exchange anxiety that wears you, conscience that burns you—no, hear me, Mr. Crosmont, I am doing you justice—for peace and happiness, and honest ease."

"Curse you! What do you mean? You are drunk —mad——"

"No. I have learned a secret, and I am putting it to the most honest use I can."

"What secret? Speak out," said Crosmont, in a low voice, with the sudden calm of a desperate man.

"You are in difficulties. You are using unworthy means to free yourself from them."

"What means?" asked Crosmont, with a sudden subtile change in his voice which gave Armathwaite his first suspicion that he was somehow on the wrong tack, and must find out more before he ventured so far as he had intended to do.

"It is currently reported in the village that your economy is starving your wife. Of course it is an absurd exaggeration, but it shows what people think. You understand, Mr. Crosmont, that I acknowledge that my speaking out to you in this way would be an impertinence if it had not been for the direct charge you made against me at the outset."

But Crosmont was in no mood to be offended at anything, he was so evidently overjoyed at the levity of the charge which had been so portentously heralded.

"I see," he said mockingly, "you want me to look after my own wife so that you may have a better opportunity of paying court to someone else's."

Armathwaite took no notice of the taunt; his intended blow having been turned aside, he was only desirous of speedy and safe retreat without any present renewal of hostilities. Fortunately, a chattering group from the drawing-room at that moment made their appearance in the conservatory above, and gave them an excuse for breaking up the *tête-à-tête*. The rest of the evening was blurred to Armathwaite; he moved and spoke mechanically, wrapped in a maddening whirl of suspicions and conjectures. The only thing that remained on his mind afterwards was the sight of Crosmont talking apart to Lady Kildonan in a low, earnest voice, and glancing towards him with an expression of hatred and mistrust, which the lady accompanied by one of reckless defiance.

CHAPTER XVII.

FRANK ARMATHWAITE walked back to Branksome from The Crags that evening with his heart more moved and his mind more disturbed than they had ever yet been in the course of his life. A hundred questions tormented him, and at the end of his walk home he was as much perplexed as ever, and inclined to be utterly despondent as to his chance of saving Alma from the doom with which her husband's selfish cruelty was threatening her. That she herself would be able to make a successful stand against his treatment was now hopeless, such terrible progress had the weakening of her will made since the departure of Uncle Hugh. The appeal to the agent's feelings, to his best interests, having failed, Armathwaite's hope now lay in the pressure he could put upon him through his employer. Crosmont would do anything, it was certain, rather than lose the position which kept him near Lady Kildonan. If, after the warning he had received that night, he should still continue to exercise over his wife the power with which he was now crushing out her health both of body and mind, Armathwaite resolved that he would address himself, as discreetly as might be, to Lord Kildonan. In the meantime he would find some means of keeping a watch over the movements of the two households.

Next day the thaw set in; the roads were ankle-deep in mud and slush, varied by smooth and slippery slabs, on which it was hard to keep one's footing. Armathwaite, in waterproof gaiters, and aided by a sharp-pointed stick, got over the ground pretty fast; but it was long past mid-day before he reached the furthest point of his morning's round, a white-washed village inn, that stood in the midst of a straggling row of cottages, on the road between Mereside and Lakiston. The occupier of this inn, an old man named Blake, who had been for some time in declining health, had at last taken to his bed with unmistakable signs of a break-up. Armathwaite had already visited him twice, and had been much prepossessed by the old inn-keeper, an industrious and honest man who, having fallen upon evil days, was now in his last weeks of life harassed by the thought of the debts and difficulties he should leave for his wife and children to contend with. The rent, in particular, having been in arrears for some time, caused him much anxiety.

On this occasion, therefore, it was with the greatest pleasure that Armathwaite saw, as he tramped his way up through the slush to the inn, a high dog-cart standing at the door, with Lady Kildonan in it. But as he drew nearer and stood by, waiting for an opportunity to address Lady Kildonan without interrupting her, he was amazed to find that, instead of comforting the poor woman in her misfortunes, the mistress of The Crags was scolding, and even threatening her, for the non-payment of the rent which was due, while Mrs. Blake was meekly protesting that it was no fault of her good man's that he was behindhand, that trade had been bad, and his health sickly, and times had been very hard with them.

"Oh, yes ; of course, it's always the same story," said Lady Kildonan, not with any harshness, but flippantly, and with some impatience. "The times are not hard for you only. They would be hardest for us, if all our tenants were to decline to pay their rent because trade was slack. I might be inclined to let you off myself, perhaps, but his lordship simply won't hear of it. The house is a nice one, in a good position, and could, it appears, be let again and again to paying people, if only you were out of it. I'm sure you can't complain that we haven't given you grace. Mr. Crosmont has been really very kind to you. And now understand : you must find one quarter's rent—that's only half what you owe—by this evening, when Mr. Crosmont goes to Liverpool to pay the rents into the bank, or else you must have notice to quit. Now you understand, don't you ?"

But the woman, finding her tears unavailing, had wiped her eyes and plucked up a little spirit ; for to be trampled on and let off the payment of your rent, is a grievance that can be borne, but to be trampled on, and then threatened with notice to quit, is more than hard-working flesh and blood can bear.

"I understand your ladyship, and perhaps I understand better than you think," said Mrs. Blake, bitterly. "Lord Kildonan didn't use to be so hard ; no, nor Mr. Crosmont didn't threaten us with notice to quit, we that's been here all these years. It's like the times of your ladyship's grandfather back again, when, as I've heard tell, the poor folk was pressed and worrited to pay the last farthing for him to squander on his pleasures in foreign parts—that's what it's like, your ladyship, and may I never say no truer word. And if me and my good man and the children's turned out, why we'll go to his lordship himself, as the new young doctor—bless him, for he's got a heart, he has!—told us to do. And Mr. Crosmont's own poor lady, for all they say she's a bit strange in her ways, she's said the same to me. 'Mrs. Blake,' says she, 'go to his lordship yourself and tell him all about it.' And if he likes to turn us out, why, after all, he's not bred in these parts, and it's not as hard a thing for him to do as it is in you, my lady, what was reared here, and who we've looked up to as our own, for your father's and mother's sake."

And Mrs. Blake, overcome with her emotion, broke down and sobbed in earnest. Lady Kildonan, who had sat quite still while she listened to this outburst, answered, in a quiet, hard and cold tone :

"By all means go to his lordship. You can guess how pleasantly he will receive you when he hears you have insulted me."

She called the groom from the horse's head sharply, wheeled the dog-cart rapidly round, and, still with an angry and excited face, encountered Armathwaite, who was standing in the road. Though unable instantly to assume her usual gaiety, she stopped, wished him good-morning with great cordiality, offered to drive him back if he was going her way, and appeared annoyed by the excuse he made that he was going to see old Blake.

"Oh, he's all right. I've just been calling there," said she hastily. "By-the-bye, Dr. Armathwaite, I've a quarrel with you. I hear you have been encouraging them not to pay their rent, which is, I think, a little exceeding the duties of your profession."

"It would be, certainly, your ladyship. But I am quite innocent of ever having done such a thing."

"Of course you take their part ; you are not the loser by their obstinacy."

"I am by their poverty though, your ladyship. Where

are my fees to come from, do you think, unless you, for instance, beg me to remit them?"

"Oh, my influence would do nothing! Mrs. Crosmont had better use hers. No woman can now be in the right, either with my husband or you, but Mrs. Crosmont."

"Well, you see, no one seems to be so much in the wrong with her own husband."

His manner and look were so perfectly frank and ingenuous that Lady Kildonan examined his face with great curiosity as well as mistrust.

"Ah!" she said at last, bending down and speaking in a very low voice, so that the groom should not hear. "That is the man's view, of course. You think that a pretty lady, with gold-brown hair and soft eyes, must be a model of all the virtues, and a martyr into the bargain."

"Not quite that——" he began.

But she would not let him continue. "Something very like it, at any rate," she said. "Now I'm certain that yesterday you thought poor Ned was very harsh to her. But if you knew what he has to put up with, your pity would, I think, be for him and not for her. The fact of the matter is that she has delusions, and these delusions lead to escapades which put the poor fellow at his wits' end. She rambles about at night like a sleep-walker; she shuts herself up in unused rooms and fancies she hears music played without hands; and all the time that her erratic conduct is driving her husband mad she walks about with a long face and makes everybody thinks he ill-treats her! Now don't you think it is rather hard on him?"

"Why doesn't he try sending her somewhere for change of air, and scene, and association? I am going to get Dr. Peele to prescribe her going away at once for——"

Lady Kildonan's face clouded suddenly. She drew herself up and tightened the reins.

"You are more complaisant in your prescription for Mrs. Crosmont than you were for me," she said coldly.

And with a stiff and haughty little bow she drove off

and left him free to enter the little inn.　Here he had to listen to a doleful account of her ladyship's visit, and of her unexpected harshness.

"I dunno what's come over her ladyship of late," said Mrs. Blake, who had begun now to take heart a little, as Armathwaite assured her that the threat of eviction would certainly not be carried out.　"She was always high-spirited and a bit hasty-like, but it's only the last month or so she's been so cruel hard.　I suppose it's this Scotch husband her father gave her that's making her as close-fisted as himself.　Mr. Crosmont says he's awful sharp after the money, and when a man gets into arrears a bit is always for making him pay or go, and no grace given and no nothing."

"Oh, so Mr. Crosmont says his lordship is hard?"

There was quite a chorus of assent to this, and more lamentation over the deterioration in Lady Kildonan. At last the small voice of the eldest child, a thin-faced, thoughtful girl of sixteen, uttered a very suggestive remark.

"Mother, do ye mind t'other time her ladyship was so hard and excited-like was t' day before Mr Crosmont went to Liverpool, just same as to-day?　And three days after she met me quite calmed down and different-like, and said she was sorry she'd been a bit vexed.　Maybe she'll be sorry again in a day or two."

Armathwaite was a good deal struck by these words, and when he had left the inn with its occupants somewhat comforted, he turned them over in his mind, and decided to note carefully the symptoms to which they pointed.　In the meantime the moment had come when he must boldly invite the confidence of Dr. Peele.　He generally saw the doctor twice a day; for half an hour in the morning, before he started to visit the patients, and for an hour in the evening, after dinner, when the day's work was done.　It was with a loudly beating heart and a sense that he was on the threshold of a chamber of mysteries that the young man, at half-past seven that evening, knocked as usual at the door of the old doctor's room.

CHAPTER XVIII.

IT seemed as if Dr. Peele had some inkling in his mind of the fact that the evening visit of his young colleague was of deeper import than usual.

"I am afraid I am going to open a subject which distresses you, sir," Frank began respectfully. "But I have come, as I think you foresaw that I should do, to a point in my knowledge of certain cases within your practice, when my remaining ignorance becomes insupportable, and my mind is continually tortured and even distracted in my work by the thought of certain hideous wrongs, the object of which I can only guess at. You remember the words you used to me when I first came, concerning secrets which I was to learn if I decided to remain here. I do not wish to force your confidence, sir; but I shall be grateful to you if you will at least let me tell you what I have found out for myself, and advise me as to my future conduct in the matter."

"I advise you!" said the old man solemnly and bitterly. "I tell you, Armathwaite, it was my inability to move in any direction in this matter which broke me down, and made me take refuge between these four walls from evils I could not witness and could not cure." He glanced at a pile of papers which lay on the table at his left hand; some of them were neatly tied together, some unfolded, as if he had recently been handling them. These papers, at whatever time of the day Armathwaite saw him, were seldom absent from the old doctor's side, and it was easy to guess that they had reference to the subject which so deeply preyed upon his mind. "Aphra Kildonan's father," continued Dr. Peele, "gave me the start in life that I am giving you; and it was my sense of the weight, upon a man of honour, of such an obligation, which made me so desirous of fastening my own responsibility upon a man whom I could trust. Are you anxious, knowing so much as you do, to draw back from the post?"

"On the contrary," answered Armathwaite fervently, "I have conceived, rightly or wrongly, that I was brought

here for the express purpose of releasing Alma Crosmont
from the unhappy circumstances in which she is placed,
and I can honestly say it is the object I have at present
more at heart than anything in the world. Dr. Peele,
you must surely agree with me that her mind is in danger.
You have influence with Crosmont ; he is anxious to
retain your good opinion. Can you not induce him to
send his wife away for a time ? "

Dr. Peele looked at the young man with solemn,
plaintive earnestness, and shook his head.

"No," said he ; "to save her would be to put Aphra
in danger, and I am bound by oath to her father to stand
by her at all costs."

"To stand by Lady Kildonan ? "

"Yes."

"And the danger for her—what is that ? "

"Ah ! It is a secret which nobody in the world knows
except herself and me."

"Her husband. Doesn't he know—doesn't he suspect
it ? "

"No. You shall learn it in good time ; but we will
take the other story first—Alma's." He paused, arranging the materials of his narrative in his mind. Then he
began in a low, monotonous voice. " Twenty-two years
ago the house where Ned Crosmont and his wife live
was, as you know, a private lunatic asylum, where only a
few patients were kept, who paid very well, and were, I
can answer for it, treated very kindly. The house
belonged to a relation of mine, a doctor of reputation
and ability, who had given up a practice in London to
establish this place in which to try a new system of his
own. One result of his system certainly was that very
few of the people in the neighbourhood had any suspicion what the malady was from which his patients
suffered. I had already been established some years
in Branksome when he bought this house and started
this thing ; and as we had always been very good friends,
I now spent much of my time with him, and heard the
history of each one of the patients, about whose cases we
had frequent consultations. One man in particular roused
a deep interest in me. He was a musician and composer,

a wild-looking person, with wide-open blue eyes and madder manners than any lunatic I ever saw. In spite of this, however, I conceived the idea, very early in our acquaintance, that he was at least as sane as I. He fascinated me, and I spent hour after hour with him, listening to his playing—he played every instrument, and all equally well—or to his fiery, enthusiastic accounts of his researches in philosophy, in mystical religions, in mesmerism. He had travelled in every part of the world, he spoke eight languages, and the only sign of a delusion I could ever detect in him was an uncertainty as to what country had given him birth. Sometimes he would speak of himself as a Pole, at others as a Spaniard; he would say of a Hungarian air that it recalled his native land, and the next moment allude to his childhood as having been passed in Norway. Little by little I gained his entire confidence, and he told me, bit by bit, as it occurred to him, in his own wild, erratic fashion, all of his life that he considered worth the telling; that is to say, very few of the outward incidents which most men count as the waymarks of their lives, but his feelings, his researches, his discoveries in the regions of thought and emotion. The last study he had taken up, and to which he devoted himself with his usual fervour, was mesmerism. He looked upon it as the yet unrecognised power which would, in a score or two of years, regenerate the world. As he held forth on this subject to me, however, tossing back his long hair, looking out with glowing, enthusiast's eyes to the sky, I confess he seemed to me to talk no wilder nonsense than I have heard from many a pulpit and many a platform, while his kindly eyes shone with a faith in humanity and in his own pure wishes which would have excused many a futile harangue. Mesmeric force, he said, was the articulate voice of the soul, by which one spirit called to another with irresistible power, the strong spirit stimulated and upheld the weak, and by which, when it became recognised and developed, the whole world, rejoicing in its new awakening, should be permanently raised out of the slough of mere bodily desires and mind-knowledge, through the cultivation of that nobler part which each new religion as it sprang up could only stimulate for a time.

"It was at this point of his communications," continued the doctor, "that I asked my friend, the head of the establishment, the reason of the musician's detention in this place, since his fancies were of so harmless a kind. But then I learned that these fancies had resulted in experiments upon his wife, whom he had subjected to mesmeric influence until she lost all control over her own will; and her parents, who had regarded the marriage with distaste from the first, had never rested until they got the imprudent musician put under the mild restraint of my friend's establishment. The astonishing part of the whole affair was his entire comprehension of the situation, and his happy acquiescence in the arrangement.

"'They think I am mad,' he would say, shrugging his shoulders with the easiest good temper, 'so they put me away in this nice house, full of fresh, sweet air, where I can play—play and read—read from morning till night, with nobody to disturb me. I have known want, I have been without bread; here I live like a prince. I have been turned out of two stuffy rooms in London for playing my violin till four o'clock in the morning; here I play all night. They look in and say, smiling, "He plays all night. It will keep him from a paroxysm." In the meantime I write my opera, and I am not bothered by the people they call sane. Oh, oh! they may keep me here as long as they like. I shall not complain!'

"This opera was to be the great work of his life. He had had it in his mind for years; had written the libretto, and was now busy with the music. I heard many portions of it. I used to sit with him in a little front room on the first floor, where the ivy peeped in at the window,"—Armathwaite started, remembering Alma Crosmont and her dream music—"while he played me his beloved melodies on his violin or on an American organ which had been put up in this room specially for his use. Then he would tell me the story, dwelling lovingly on the character of his heroine, the most flawless creature that ever poet raved about, pure to unearthliness, sweet as morning on the mountains, fair with a soul-fairness that shone in her eyes and cast a veil of reverence between her beholder and her own loveliness, attractive with the attraction of a spirit that repelled creatures who had wilfully degraded their own souls. These words, or something like them, are not mine, I need scarcely say ; they are his."

Armathwaite was listening almost breathlessly ; he began to see the outcome of the story.

"The libretto of this famous opera," continued Dr. Peele, "was founded on a classical story, and was to be called 'Psyche.' The work was to be a revelation in art, musical and dramatic. The strains sung by the heroine while, persecuted and forlorn, she roamed the earth in search of Love, were to show the Divine gift of harmony, emancipated at last from the sensuous thraldom in which for ages it had been bound ; while the heroine herself, instead of being the conventional victim of commonplace passion and intrigue, was a type of ideal purity and innocence, in her sorrows unmarred by bitterness, always merciful, always holy. Men looking into her chaste eyes were attracted by something higher than themselves ; but if, by mean, sordid lives, by dishonour or by vice, they had stifled their own souls, and fallen far below themselves, then the attraction of the pure Psyche changed into fear and even into loathing, until their eyes would drop at her approach, and they would avoid meeting hers, as men avoid the piercing beams of the sun. And so she wandered over the world looking for Love, her lord, and not knowing under what form she should meet him, and exposed to all sorts of wounds from coarser creatures on account of the exquisite sensitiveness of her nature, like a nautilus without its shell."

"And the end—how did the story end—in this version ? " asked Armathwaite, in a low voice, as the doctor paused.

"Ah! he never reached the end while I knew him. Of course Psyche met Love, and she knew him from the fact that he alone of all men could always meet her eyes unflinchingly. A pretty story, but not dramatic, according to the received notions of such matters, as I told him. It was hardly to be expected that he would listen though, and, as a matter of fact, he did not. The story, and the music to which he set it, haunted him, and filled every cranny of his brain and heart."

"What became of him?"

"His wife's parents, who had sent him to Mereside, fetched him out again when they thought she was going to die. It was near the birth of her child, and whatever mischief her husband's mesmeric experiments had done was done beyond recall, for she pined and drooped, and had always on her lips a verse of the wandering Psyche's song:

> "'I hear my master's whisper
>   In the rush of the autumn wind;
> On dead leaves grown browner and crisper
>   The print of his feet I find.
> The sea-surf that breaks on my shoulders
>   Sweeps soft as my lord's own wing,
> And echo rings out from the boulders:
>   "Thou shalt see thy love's face in the spring."'

"So as I say," continued Dr. Peele, "they sent for him, and I lost sight of him for some years; and when I did see him again, poor fellow, he was in a rapid decline, and had by that time worked and worried himself into a state a good deal nearer to lunacy than any he had passed through when in the asylum. His wife was dead; he was in very bad circumstances. There was no more talk of the opera, and I did not even dare to mention it, not knowing whether it might not arouse painful recollections of failure and disappointment. But he had a tiny girl, born, so he told me, while her mother was in a mesmeric trance; in her name, Alma, I perceived a connection with that of the heroine of the famous opera, and in her eyes I liked to fancy—and so, I am sure, did her father—that I saw something of the look we had imagined in the ideal Psyche. At any rate I was deeply interested in the little creature; and when her father, a few weeks later, was on his death-bed, I willingly undertook to become her guardian. Both father and daughter were living in London, in the house of some relations of his late wife. These people were fond of the child, and after her father's death they desired that she might still remain with them. So she grew up, and the tendency to dreaminess seemed to die out of her as she advanced towards womanhood. I made her study at the South Kensington Art Schools to develop her marked taste for drawing, and on my occasional visits to town I found her a bright, healthy, active, intelligent girl, affectionate, sweet, beautiful, well-educated—in fact, everything that a girl should be. I wanted to take her home, but my wife would not hear of it—'it would interfere with Millie's prospects;' of course good old Millie was not consulted. I was determined to have my dear new child near me, however, and I hit upon the idea of marrying her to young Ned Crosmont, an honest, good-hearted fellow, as I thought, who only wanted a nice wife to make him steady down into as good a husband as a girl could wish for."

The old man paused, and seemed for a few moments to be buried in the gloom of his disappointed hopes. When he resumed, his voice sounded weaker, and it was evidently with a great effort that he uttered the few closing words of his story.

"I knew that Ned and Aphra Dighton had been boy-and-girl sweethearts, but I could not conceive that he would have the audacity to think seriously of her when they had grown out of childhood, still less that when she was once married "—the doctor paused and went on with bowed head, in a slower voice—" he would forget his honour and duty for her. Understand, Dr. Armathwaite "—and suddenly he raised his head, and spoke with decision and authority—"that I am casting no slur on Aphra Kildonan's character. Aphra is like a voluptuous goddess on canvas, rousing men's passions by looks which express emotions she does not feel ; at least, that has always been my opinion of her, and I have watched her grow up from a child. But the consequences to Alma have been more disastrous than if Lady Kildonan had done her a greater wrong. I know all this, you see, and can, unluckily for me, watch this drama as well from the four walls of this room as I could when I saw its scenes with my own eyes. But I can do nothing."

He stopped. The story was over. But there was another which Armathwaite was still more anxious to hear.

"You said, sir," he began at last diffidently, "during the first interview you gave me, that it might be possible for a new-comer to move more freely in this matter than you could do. If you will only put me on the right tack, and give me the benefit of your discretion, I will answer for it I shall not want for energy."

"I am sure of that," said Dr. Peele. "But I begin to fear the time for action has gone by ; to interfere would only increase the danger for Aphra Kildonan, without improving the circumstances of Alma Crosmont."

"May I know what the danger for Lady Kildonan is ? "

"Not to-night," answered the old doctor, hurriedly, drawing himself together with an instinctive demonstration of reluctance to part with his secret, which filled Armathwaite with the fear that he might perhaps never disclose it to him after all. "I am really tired ; I cannot talk more to night. I will see you again to-morrow —yes, to-morrow."

But as the young man shook hands with him, and wished him good-night, he saw a look on the old doctor's face which suddenly drove all thoughts of the secret out of his head, and made him very gentle and solicitous, and almost reverent, so that he retreated from the room reluctantly, with the soft steps and measured tread of one who leaves a solemn presence-chamber, turning at the door for one long look at the man who had received him so generously, and conferred upon him so great a trust.

"I am glad, more glad every day, every hour, of your coming," Dr. Peele said, in a weak voice. "I can rest now I know that I am leaving a head behind me when I am gone. I have left you this writing-table with the papers it contains. They will tell you all you wish to know ; you will keep them under lock and key as I have done. Good-night, God bless you, Armathwaite ! "

With a long, earnest gaze into each other's face, the men parted ; and it was with a new and solemn sense of duty and responsibility, shadowed by a grave fear, that the younger closed the door of the sick-room behind him. His mind, his heart, his whole being were absorbed by the last solemn words he had just heard from the doctor's lips; they rang in his ears as he went downstairs, they echoed in his brain as he stood, hesitating and cold with a new sensation, in the dimly-lighted and tiny hall. Then, with quick but not hurried movements, he took his hat and coat from the stand, and went out of the house in the direction of Mereside. He had felt again the prick of the mysterious monitor which had twice directed his steps against his will to Alma Crosmont's side. On this third occasion, with the romance of her strange story strongly upon him, he started off without a doubt, without a pause.

It was a cold and starless night, with a mist in the air and a drizzling mixture of rain and sleet falling; the roads were silent and deserted. It was not until he had tramped fully two of the four miles which lay between Branksome and Mereside that he bethought him of the exceeding awkwardness of his position, on the way to visit a married lady against the express wishes of her husband. And then came a recollection which made him pause and slacken his steps. It was the night of Ned Crosmont's journey to Liverpool. With a flash of discretion and of remembrance of the conventionalities, Armathwaite decided that it was impossible for him to go to the house in the absence of the master, who had positively forbidden him to approach his wife again. He turned back, and began to retrace his steps at a run. But then in the misty air before him, as the sleet drove into his eyes, he saw Alma's face, white and wan, with the jaw drawn down and the eyes fixed and staring, while her voice seemed to whisper in his ears as the wind and the snow and the rain hissed past him:

"Come, come, do not fail me now!"

He turned again, and the wind seemed to cease and the air to grow clearer. Full of solemn dread and passionate anxiety, he strode along in the direction of Mereside without another moment's pause.

CHAPTER XIX.

THE mist had thickened, and the sleet had given place to a fine, penetrating rain, before Frank Armathwaite reached the thicket of trees where he had first met Alma Crosmont, at the junction of the higher with the lower road. He glanced up the hill to the right, and saw the sharp angles of Ned Crosmont's house standing out black in the darkness, without a ray of light from any of the windows to indicate that there was life within. And yet it was not ten o'clock. The drawing-room, the dining-room, Alma's bedroom, and the little chamber with the ivy-covered window where she shut herself in to listen to the dream-music which comforted her, were all on the same side of the house, and the faintest gleam of light in any of them would have been visible to him from the spot where he stood, staring up at the blank, cheerless building with intent eyes. He did not attempt to approach it; the attraction which had drawn him so far seemed to have suddenly ceased, and given place, exactly as it had done on the two previous occasions when he had been under its power, to commonplace reflections on his own idiotcy in giving way to it. His reason had resumed its full sway; and while he was sur-prised at the discovery that Alma, who by all analogy should have been a bad sleeper, afraid of the darkness and prone to long night-watches, had evidently retired to rest exceedingly early, it was quite plain to him that he had come on a fool's errand, and that it would be the height of indiscretion to go a yard nearer and risk being caught prowling round the house when all folk of honest intentions were supposed to be safely in their homes.

So he turned his back on the house, and retraced the few steps he had taken up the hill. But when he reached the bottom, and faced the thicket of trees growing by the water-side, he became conscious of a sighing wind that came through the branches and over the lake, and he heard the little waves splash up against the shore, and the boughs rustle and crack over his head, and in each sound there was a low wail that pierced his heart, and made him cold and sick with a vague fear. For he knew that it was no physical human voice that was calling to him, and that these noises of the night, which now seemed to bear a human message of pain and prayer to him, were only such as he had heard a thousand times before and taken no note of.

After standing a few moments longer in a state of hazy stupefaction, his reasoning faculties in vain trying to get the mastery over the wayward fancies which began to run riot in his brain, it seemed to him that the faint, wailing note which formed the accompaniment to every sound he heard came from the opposite shore of the lake. At the same moment the restless fever to go forward seized him again : why should he not make the tour of the lower and the higher roads, and thus passing close under the walls of the Crosmonts' house on his way back, try to discover an explanation of the impulse which had driven him forth in the mud and the rain on a miserable February night. By the time he got to the point where the higher road again joined the lower near the entrance of the village, however, his thoughts had wandered away to Dr. Peele and his story, and to the connection between the opera written by the so-called mad composer in the little front room, and the dream-music which his own daughter, twenty-two years later, heard within the same walls. Had not the dreams of the mesmerist-musician been realized? Did not the poetical creation of his heart and mind stand embodied in Alma, whose pure and sensitive soul shone out of her brown eyes as that of the imaginary " Psyche " had done in his inspired fancy ? Through Armathwaite's excited brain there flashed reminiscences of the old Greek legend of the beautiful maiden condemned to marry a monster, and persecuted by Venus for her innocent rivalry ; and mingled with these scraps of legend came vivid pictures of the realities among which he lived, of Lady Kildonan in her splendid beauty coaxing him, commanding Crosmont; of the simple and kindly middle-aged husband who could think no ill of the wife he loved ; of the old doctor, dying oppressed by the burden of a secret which weighed upon him night and day ; of a fair, sweet woman in whom the life and reason were being sapped out at the will of a rival who was something worse than heartless.

This last picture stood out in his mind with striking vividness, and remained there clear as a material picture, long after the rest had faded out of his brain. Through the mist, through the soft rain, he seemed to see her bodily presence, with a faint dusky outline indeed, but unmistakable, irresistibly pathetic, a mournful, darkly-clothed figure, the folds of whose drapery seemed absolutely to change and shift before his eyes, as if the very wind which buffeted him were playing with the garments of the image in his mind. Still, as he walked, the figure remained before him, until the idea crossed his brain that it might be really the physical presence, and not merely a mental image, of the woman who occupied his thoughts that he was following. He now perceived for the first time that he had left Mereside behind him, and was skirting the head of the lake, always in the wake of the dim figure which, lost from time to time either in the physical darkness or in the confusion of his mind, constantly reappeared and led the way with a steadiness and swiftness which seemed incompatible with the possibility of its proving to be Mrs. Crosmont in the flesh. He was walking at his best pace, but yet he failed to make the slightest appreciable difference in the distance between them. When for a few minutes he broke into a run, he lost sight of the figure altogether, and it was not until he had stopped and peered about on all sides in the gloom that he at last discerned the object of which he was in search, fainter than ever against the bare trees at the bottom of the hill on which the residence of Lady Kildonan stood. The Crags! Armathwaite's heart beat faster as the conviction stole upon him that it was no phantom of an excited imagination that he was following. The figure glided along under the steep cliff, passing by the winding roadway which led to the house, and seeming to pause for an instant, as he had expected, before the group of damp and straggling bushes that blocked the secret path up the hill.

He redoubled his pace, and reached the clump of

bushes while the branches were still swinging. Brushing his way through them in his turn, he began the
ascent of the hill; this was by no means easy, for the
rain had made the clayey soil loose and slippery. On
close inspection he discerned in the darkness long,
smooth lines made by the sliding back of smaller feet
than his, but he saw no sign of the figure he was following. When he had reached the point where the rough
steps began, however, he heard a sharp " click," like the
snap of a lock; he hastened his pace, but on arriving at
the gate which had barred his passage before, he found
it securely shut and impassable, while a last glimpse that
he caught of fluttering drapery far above him among the
trees on the brow of the hill was seen so faintly and
passed so swiftly that it might almost have been the
flight of a wide-winged bat through the gloom. Armathwaite stood for a few moments at the gate, and
speedily decided on his course of action. He descended
the hill, pushed his way out into the road, and drawing
his pipe from his pocket, proceeded to fill and light it;
then buttoning his coat and turning up his collar, he
began to march up and down between the entrance to
the private path and the foot of the drive, keeping a
sharp watch on both points. For four hours he paced
up and down in the darkness, without sight or sound of
a living creature. By midnight the drizzle had ceased,
and the wind had gone down; the moon, hung with a
rainy haze, shone out over the black hills, and threw
silver-grayish lines upon the lake, on which the mist still
hovered. The dark tufts and patches of trees and
brushwood which fringed its shores broke up the outline
of the water with a blurred and ragged belt, and here
and there a white villa gleamed out, looking from the
opposite shore like a tombstone in a valley of shadows.
To a man in Armathwaite's present mood the scene was
unspeakably gloomy and depressing. He felt, as he
glanced from the turrets of The Crags, just visible from
one point of the road below, to the corner where Crosmont's house stood on the opposite shore of the lake, as
if, instead of keeping watch for the living, he were
guarding the homes of the dead. So strong a hold,

indeed, had these sombre fancies taken upon him when, after four hours' dreary pacing up and down, he looked at his watch and found that it was just past two o'clock, that as he approached the entrance to the private path and found himself face to face with a woman who was forcing her way out through the bushes, he uttered a short, hoarse cry, as if he had been confronted by a corpse.

It was Alma Crosmont. In the weak white moonlight she looked haggard and death-like, with deep, dark furrows under her eyes which stared out before them and saw nothing, dry lips slightly parted, and a dull expression which never changed. She appeared neither to see nor hear the man standing in front of her, but came straight on with her hands held a little in front of her, as if groping to find her way. When quite close to him she took a step aside to avoid his person, and as she passed at a flying pace he noticed that her breathing was heavy and stertorous, like that of a person in a deep, unrestful sleep. He turned and followed her, calling to her by name. She made no answer, but hastened on with the same rapid, yet striding steps, as if her feet, quickly as they moved, were heavy, and could not rise well from the ground. Her pace never varied as she skirted the head of the lake, and glided up the hill towards her house without a pause or a look behind. It was a walk of quite two miles, the roads and paths were deep in mud, and Armathwaite, who was splashed and bespattered to the knees long before the end, wondered at the febrile strength which enabled the fragile woman to accomplish her mysterious task. She went in by the back door of the house, which was on the latch for her, and Armathwaite, having waited in vain for a light to appear at any of the windows, tramped rapidly back to Branksome, tormented by indignation and anxiety, but convinced that he had made one important step towards the discovery of the mystery of The Crags.

The next morning, tired out by his night's patrol, Frank slept late, and woke oppressed. As soon as breakfast was over he went to see Dr. Peele, who had not risen, but who caused himself to be propped up in bed to listen to the night-adventure the younger man had to relate. He then said, with a grave and troubled face, that he would send Armathwaite to The Crags with a note for Lady Kildonan.

"If you will kindly hand me that writing-case and a pencil, I will send the note down to you," he added.

So Frank took leave of him, and went down to the dining-room, where he found Mil'ie, who was in the highest spirits this morning, rushing to the window-recess to bend, in a loving manner, over some treasure which she had concealed in her work-basket under the canary's cage. Armathwaite was fond enough of this girl to be interested in all her interest, and they were already on terms of such brotherly and sisterly intimacy that he could ask for her confidence without indiscretion.

"What have you got in there?" he asked in a low voice, coming behind her just as she shut the basket.

"It's a letter."

"A letter! Oh, and who is it from?"

"Really, sir, don't you think you are rather presumptuous?"

"But you always read your letters aloud."

"But I shan't read this one aloud," said Millie, demurely.

The downward look with which she said this took Frank's breath away.

"You don't mean to say it's a love-letter, Millie!" he said with mingled reproach, disdain and disappointment.

"And why not? Is it a sort of thing that has never come under your notice before?"

"Oh, I know that silly girls have them, but I thought you had more sense."

"My dear Frank, you can't gauge my measure of sense without seeing my answer."

"Well, I hope you don't mean to say 'yes.' If you do, you will let yourself down in my esteem to an extent you may perhaps never recover."

"Dear me, you make me hesitate."

"I must beg you to do more than that, Miss Peele; I must beg you to reject this person's advances without further delay. I don't wish to speak of my feelings, which are frightfully lacerated at the mere thought of a rival; but I must make one little stipulation; if you do go away and marry this ruffian, you must live near enough to drop over here every morning to breakfast, for I simply won't submit to have my coffee made by Mrs. Peele. She gets angry over it, and joggles it up and makes it thick; besides, she never gives me enough sugar. You don't mind my mentioning this?"

"Not at all. What you say is very reasonable, and shows a lot of forethought."

"Yes. It's better than having to forbid the banns. May I know the name of the wretched miscreant?"

"I don't like to tell you. We reigning beauties have to be careful. I always avoid bloodshed in these affairs if I can."

"Then I will decimate the neighbourhood. You little know of what blood are the Armathwaites."

"Would you go so far as to decimate London?"

"H'm, well, that is a matter for my consideration. Then the hated one is a degraded cockney?"

"To the extent of having had lodgings for a week in Bedford Square, yes."

"Bedford Square!" echoed Frank slowly, while a faint smile twinkled at the corners of his mouth and grew broader and broader as Millie's face assumed a deeper and deeper tint of not unbecoming pink. "You don't mean to say, Millie, that it's——"

"Well, and why not?" said she, laughing shyly. Then she grew suddenly serious. "To tell you the truth, I'm overwhelmed myself with the honour," she said very simply. "I—I never minded being plain before. But now when I think that I may some day be Mr. Hugh Crosmont's wife, I do really wish something could be done to my nose. It is so very 'tip-tilted,' and yet without in the least suggesting 'the petal of a flower'!"

"It's a very good nose, Millie, and it's in a very good face, and the face belongs to a very good and sweet girl.

"H'm, yes. I suppose it's something even to be good, in these hard times. But I hadn't thought the quality was a showy enough one to be brought to market."

"It's an out-of-the-way fruit, Millie, that it takes a connoisseur to find out and appreciate. But I say, isn't dear old Uncle Hugh rather old for you ?"

"No. *I'm* a connoisseur too, and I don't like my fruit green."

"When is he coming to see you ?"

"Oh, dear me ! we haven't got as far as that yet. I only received the letter this morning. I shan't answer it to-day, and I shall try and hold out over to-morrow. I don't want to seem to jump at him : on the other hand, it won't do to be too haughty, or he might see someone with a better nose ! "

She was brimming over with fun, but there was a tenderness in her eyes, a joyful tremor in her voice, which told that her heart was really touched.

"Did you ever ask a girl to marry you, Frank ?" she asked after a pause.

"Oh, yes ; three are four times, perhaps more, certainly three or four."

"And always the same girl ? "

"No, always different girls."

"Oh, Frank, you must be a flirt ! "

"No ; it was the girls who were flirts. There are some girls—lots of girls—whom one always asks to marry one when one has known them long enough. They seem to expect it, and one drops into it as a matter of course. Then you are engaged—for they never refuse you—until some other fellow turns up, and you are not exactly shelved, you know, only you come in and find your *fiancée* kissing him, and you feel a little out of it, and you don't call so often ; and then some other girl turns up, and you don't call at all."

"But that is very frivolous. It seems strange to me. I never thought I should have much to do with them, but love and marriage have always seemed to me such solemn things."

"Some people take them that way."

"Come, Frank, I've spoken very openly to you. You might be more honest with me. Surely there must be some love which means more than that to a man like you ! ”

Armathwaite started. The girl had suddenly put so much energy and penetration into her look and tone that she could not again be answered by mere badinage, the more so that a new and most unwelcome consciousness began to steal over him at her question.

“ We all love seriously at one time or another, I suppose,” he said evasively.

He began tapping his riding-gaiter with his whip, and looking through the window at the cob, which had just been brought round, instead of going out to mount. Millie played with her work-basket, and looked out too.

“ What made you say that to me, Millie ? ” he asked abruptly, without looking down at her.

“ Oh, I oughtn't to have said it at all, I dare say,” said she.

“ Yes, yes, but what did you mean by it ? ”

She paused for a moment because Mrs. Peele, who was delivering a long monologue to the housemaid at the fireplace, had talked herself out of breath, and had to recruit her forces by a short silence. As soon as her sonorous voice resounded again through the room, her daughter began her reply very softly and shyly.

“ For the last week you have been silent and restless, and — I fancied — unhappy. Twice — last night and another time—you have gone out very suddenly, with a strange look on your face, as if you saw something invisible to anybody else——”

“ Last night ! How did you know that ? ”

“ I had run round to see Mrs. Lennox next door, and I passed you on my way back as you rushed out.”

“ I did not see you.”

“ No, you would not have seen anybody, I think.” A pause. Then she went on in a lower tone than ever : “ I waited up to see you when you came home.” The fair skin of Armathwaite's face flushed as he listened. But she paused again. “ You did not come back, so I went to my room—very late. But first I drew back the bolt of the front door so that you could let yourself in.”

"Thank you, Millie."

"I heard you come in—very much later than that. I had been asleep, and it startled me to hear sounds in the house in the middle of the night. I ran to my door, and opened it a very little way. The light was just beginning to come through the staircase window, and I saw your face as you came softly up the stairs. It was all lined and old, as if you had gone through some terrible anxiety. I was so sorry I nearly cried; I was sure you were very unhappy. I thought I would speak to you and tell you so; I don't know whether I am right."

"You are always right—dear, good old Millie," said Frank, huskily. "That escapade is a secret, of course; but it is not a discreditable one, believe me."

Millie was very sweet and sympathetic, but she was not guileless enough to be satisfied like that.

"I *hope* it is not," she said, with emphasis.

"Won't you believe me ?"

"I don't know much about secrets," she answered, dubiously; "but I have my theories. I incline to think that a woman's secrets are generally not much to her credit, and that a man's are still less to his. And that when a man and a woman have the same secret, it's very much to the discredit of both of them."

"And if there is no woman in the case ? "

"If there were not, I should not be troubling you now."

"Miss Peele, you are doing me the greatest injustice."

"Indeed, I hope that nobody else may. But I am afraid you will find that I am not more censorious than my neighbours."

Armathwaite turned ashy white. The thought that he might have been seen following Alma Crosmont on her midnight walk, and of the hideous construction which would be put upon such an incident, unnerved him completely.

"Millie, Millie, this is not like you !" he said at last, in a very low voice.

"Indeed, Frank, I had hoped it was not like you."

"And do you mean to say you think it impossible for

any man, even in whom you had the greatest confidence, to have a secret connected with a woman in which there was nothing but what was honourable to both?"

"It depends on the woman," said she, rather curtly.

"What with such a woman as———"

He stopped just in time, but his tone of hot indignation was eloquent enough. Millie's face relaxed into a smile. She came a step nearer to him and whispered apologetically, and, at the same time, with great relief:

"That's all right! Oh, Frank, I was so dreadfully afraid it was—somebody else."

It was now Armathwaite's turn to be cold, for he saw that he had been tricked.

"I hadn't given you credit for so much ingenuity, Miss Peele," he said, getting very red.

"Oh, I couldn't help it, Frank! Let me explain, and then perhaps, you won't be so angry," she entreated, detaining him as he turned to walk away. "Sit down here and listen to me for two minutes." He obeyed very reluctantly, taking his place beside her in the window-seat, to the great delight of poor Mrs. Peele, who had heard nothing yet about the love-letter, and who still fondly cherished the hope of "settling" Millie by marrying her to the man who was to be her father's successor. The girl then went on: "There are living here two women so pretty and attractive that a man can't know them both and be insensible to both unless he is restrained by some other strong attraction. Though they are both married, they are only the more dangerous, as neither is married happily. You came here quite free, and a good deal inclined to be bored by your surroundings. From the very first evening I, knowing all this, knowing how strangely you had met both ladies on your arrival, and guessing that they influenced you in your decision to stay, couldn't help watching for some result of it all. Some little things I noticed very soon. Any allusion to The Crags or to Ned Crosmont's interested and excited you; you grew every day more abstracted and indifferent to other things, more on the alert to those two. I grew desperately anxious to know which of the two had the greatest interest for you. First I thought the one, then I feared the other; I could never be sure; and when—when you went out—at night—I was afraid."

Her voice had sunk to a timid whisper, and she hung her head.

After a few moments' silence, during which he caressed her head affectionately, she spoke again, looking him full in the eyes with earnest frankness.

"You must not think me bold in speaking to you like this, Frank. I have never had a brother, and you seemed to become one to me directly, and I felt as I should have felt if you had been a sailor out on the sea in a great storm. You might have the chance to do something so brave, so noble, that I should be proud of it all my life; but you might, on the other hand, be swept overboard without being able to make an effort to save yourself. And so I was afraid."

"And you are satisfied now?" asked Armathwaite rather puzzled.

"Yes."

"But you know very little more than you did before!"

"I know this, that it is the good influence, and not the bad, which is over you."

"I see, then, you look upon me as a mere shuttle-cock, good or bad according to the hands it is played with!"

"Well, you know, many a brave man has been in the same case."

"Millie, you are too abominably clever. I'm glad you're going to get married. It will tone you down. And so you are not worried about my secret any longer?"

"No; there's no harm in any secret that concerns Alma."

She said this very softly and gravely, and Armathwaite felt a tremor run through him as she pronounced the name. He rose hastily, and gave her hand a warm grip as he said good-bye.

"God bless you, Millie," he said; "there won't be much harm in any secret of mine while my little sister keeps watch over me!"

"And you don't think me impertinent and interfering?"

"No.   But understand, you must be satisfied for the present, and not ask any more questions."

"All right.   I'll endeavour to be good.   But you mustn't try me too hard!   Those midnight excursions, Frank, to a daughter of Eve, are——"

"Secrets.   Good-bye."

And without giving her time for another word he turned away, just as the housemaid entered with the note for Lady Kildonan, and this message from the doctor :—

"My master says, sir, there is no need to hurry with the note, and you'd better deliver it this afternoon, when you will be going that way to see Mr. Sanderson—and wait for an answer."

Armathwaite took the letter and started off for his visits.

———

CHAPTER XX.

THE morning passed uneventfully ; but Frank began his afternoon round in a state of strong excitement and expectancy.   It was a cold, raw day, sunless and dreary, with banks of dull cloud hanging over the hill-tops, and a rainy mist travelling towards the lake.   It was hard that day for the young man to keep his thoughts fixed on the maladies of his respective patients even while in their presence ; and when he was standing by the bedside of Mr. Sanderson, who lived in a small house not two hundred yards from Ned Crosmont's residence, he could scarcely keep his attention to the lumbago which was the subject in hand for thought of the more interesting case a few steps away.

On coming out of the villa, however, he was surprised to find Crosmont waiting for him.

"Oh, I say," he began, in his usual, abrupt, sullen manner, "I wanted to speak to you a moment.   Where were you going ?"

"To The Crags ; I have a letter to give Lady Kildonan from Dr. Peele."

"From Dr. Peele !"   Crosmont appeared half-anxious, half-relieved. "Oh!" He looked down on the ground and twisted his moustache. "Well, you go on there now. You won't stay, I suppose?"

"No. I have only to wait for an answer to this."

"Well, and then, if you will, just call here on your way back. Can you do that?"

"Certainly."

Armathwaite had no thought of bearing malice for the agent's injurious speeches at their last meeting; but Crosmont seemed to feel that some word of conciliation might be desirable.

"It's all right about the other night, isn't it? You're not nursing up any ill-feeling because of anything I said? You see you knew that my wife was ill, when I, not being a doctor myself, didn't see there was anything the matter with her. And there isn't anything the matter with her now—only temper. But—but, of course, that's a thing that only gets worse with a husband, and a few words from anybody else, and a powder or a mixture every three hours just to humour them, does wonders. So if you will come I shall be obliged to you."

Armathwaite promised that he would, and rode off in much anxiety. Such civility from the churlish Crosmont to a man he hated and even feared was an unmistakable sign that he was seriously alarmed by the condition to which his infamous treatment had reduced his wife.

On arriving at The Crags, he refused to dismount until Lord Kildonan, learning that he had come, sent an urgent message that he wished to see him.

The old Scotchman was lying on the sofa in the small room which divided his library from his sleeping apartment. He raised himself to a sitting posture as the doctor came in, and held out a cold, clammy hand to him.

"How are you?" he said in a weak voice. "I'm very glad to see you. I have been so very seedy that I almost thought of sending for you, only it seemed scarcely worth while. But as you're here, perhaps you can find out what is the matter with me."

The doctor went to the window, drew up the dark green blind, and let in the daylight upon the patient's face.

"Yes," he said, "you certainly don't look your best, Lord Kildonan. What have you been doing? I think I can guess already."

"Well, it's more than I can. I have done nothing that I haven't been doing every day of my life for the last two years."

"Are you in the habit of taking sleeping-draughts, then?"

"Never did such a thing in my life."

"Ah! well, then, I'm on the wrong tack. Will you tell me when and how you first began to feel indisposed?"

"It was last night. I was not feeling much inclined for work—so I found when I set about it. It has sometimes happened to me lately to feel heavy and stupid at night—I'm growing old, I suppose—and I'm afraid of spoiling my book by writing when I'm not in the vein. You see, Dr. Armathwaite, you can't expect to put anything but your best, your most matured work, before the notice of the men of science whom I want to catch for my public."

"No; I quite see that," said Armathwaite gravely.

"So when I had had my whisky and water and my biscuit—I generally take a glass of whisky toddy at about half-past nine—I find it rather helps my work than not——"

"Quite so," said Armathwaite, as the last remark was made with a suggestion of apology.

"I did very little writing before I took my usual rest, feeling rather drowsy."

"And you went to sleep?"

"No, no. I didn't go to sleep."

"Ah, but I think you did, Lord Kildonan!" said Armathwaite, whose hand, as he felt the pulse of his patient, had begun unaccountably to shake, as if with a rush of sudden excitement. "Now, you don't remember your wife coming in as usual last night?"

"Oh, but I do, though; I remember it perfectly," he

answered promptly. "I was lying like this, with my hand over my eyes, when she fluttered in, like a dancing butterfly, as usual, and took my hands away from my eyes and kissed me, and waited a few minutes as usual, and then flitted away again. Oh, yes! I am never too drowsy to remember my wife's coming."

"Well, and then?"

"Then presently I began to work; but I couldn't do much, for I felt dizzy and shivery, and before long I was violently sick."

"You sent for Lady Kildonan then, I suppose?"

"What, wake the poor child out of her sleep to wait upon me! No, I was very indignant when Johnson suggested it. He grew alarmed about me, poor fellow, and thought I was going to die, I believe. After a few very unpleasant hours, I managed to fall asleep, and this morning I have nothing worse than a headache."

"You have had these attacks before, you say?"

"Yes, the last bad one was about a month ago. I have had two slight touches of it since, but nothing to speak of."

"Well, Lord Kildonan," said Armathwaite, in a curiously constrained voice, after a short pause, "I believe I can prevent your having these attacks again. When I see the next one coming on, I shall ask your permission to spend the night with you."

"When you see it coming on!" echoed the patient in surprise.

"Yes; I believe, by a calculation I can make, if you give me the approximate dates of the previous attacks, I can find out when the next will be due."

"Dear me, dear me, that is very clever!" cried Lord Kildonan, in astonishment and admiration.

"Oh, not when one has studied these things," said the young doctor modestly, as he rose to go. "Of course, I may be wrong. In any case I strongly advise you not to mention your indisposition to Lady Kildonan until we have found a complete cure for it."

"Most certainly I shall not," said the patient, still overwhelmed by the young man's sagacity. "I always avoid giving her the least trouble or uneasiness she can possibly be spared. It is the least I can do when the child is the very light of my life."

Armathwaite murmured some commonplace in acquiescence.

"Are you going to see her?" asked Lord Kildonan. "I have only been with her for a few minutes to-day, because I was so limp myself that I knew I could not be a very cheerful companion, and I was afraid, too, that my yellow face would frighten her. But I think I should like you to see her. It struck me that she seemed rather depressed and nervous this morning."

"You are unnecessarily anxious about her health, I am sure, your lordship. If you were as well as she is, you would not trouble yourself so much."

"Ah, well, well, perhaps not. Remember me kindly to Dr. Peele."

Armathwaite left him, returned along the gallery, and had raised the curtain which divided it from the hall, when he came suddenly face to face with Lady Kildonan. She wore a hat and a long circular cloak, and was leaning back against a high carved cabinet with an expression of sleepy languor in her face and attitude which made her even more strikingly attractive than usual. As Armathwaite stopped short at sight of her, she pressed one hand to her eyes, let it fall limply, and then held it out towards him with a sleepy, good humoured smile.

"Been to see my husband?" she asked. Then, without waiting for an answer, she went on in the same lazy tone. "You brought a letter from Dr. Peele, didn't you? I'm sure I don't know what I've done with it. However, he wants to see me, and says he's very ill. So, I suppose, I'd better go. Will you drive me? I'm awfully tired to-day; I had a bad night, and I've been asleep nearly all the afternoon to make up for it, so I feel too demoralized for any active exertion."

There was nothing for it but to put himself at her service; and while they waited for the phaeton to be brought round, Lady Kildonan slipped into a large chair by the fire-place, and leaning her head against one of the carved oak figures which supported the mantelpiece, conversed about Mrs. Peele, and Millie, and the doctor in a pleasantly subdued and sleepy tone, which, while forming a great contrast to the high-spirited gaiety, the hungry restlessness, and the hard irritability of the moods in which he had previously seen her, was infinitely more charming than any of them. For the first time during his acquaintance with her he saw in the lady the one quality in which her buoyant nature had been conspicuously, almost painfully, lacking—repose. For the first time, also, the tints of her complexion had lost their almost startling brilliancy, her eyes their fierce brightness ; while in place of these temporarily dimmed attractions, her face had acquired that subtle quality, suggestive of storms past and passions lulled, which we call "interesting." She rose and strolled languidly to the door when the phaeton was announced, shivered at the first breath of the chilly air of the late afternoon, and insisted on having the hood up. At first she lay back placidly in the corner of the carriage, without any attempt at conversation, even without apparent consciousness of her companion's presence. But as they came in sight of Crosmont's house, and Armathwaite said he had been asked to call and see Mrs. Crosmont, Lady Kildonan flushed and gave him a glance of half-irritable, half-womanly, entreaty.

"Not now," she said. "When you have left me at Dr. Peele's, you can come back."

They drove on, but he gave one wistful glance towards the gloomy-looking house ; she noticed his expression, and made a first restless movement of her hands.

"I am sorry for her," she said in a low voice, more to herself than to him. There was a faint remorse in her tone. "But then those passionless women cannot suffer —at least not like others."

There was a fascination in the characteristic recklessness with which she made this half-confession. Armathwaite reddened as he answered her.

"Do you think not ? " he said. "I am afraid that is a rash conclusion. Then, again, it is difficult to say what you mean by passionless. You don't mean unemotional, doughy, like the ladies Greydon."

"Surely you don't want me to give you a definition of the passions? By a passion—a real passion—one means, if one means anything, an impulse that cannot be resisted, that begins by being nothing but a little trouble, a little restlessness, which grows and grows until it becomes a gnawing pain, which eats into you, and drives you, and cries and craves to be satisfied—till the whole world round you seems aching with it, and you yourself to be burning night and day with a fire nothing can put out. That is what I call passion. What else do you mean by it?"

"Well, whatever I might mean by it, I shouldn't have thought of meaning that," said Armathwaite, simply. "I am a commonplace and unemotional sort of Briton, I admit; but if I were troubled with any feelings of the kind you describe, I would certainly never rest till I got them under."

"There is only one way to do that."

"The best way would be to encourage and stimulate healthier ones."

"No, no; to wear out the stronger ones."

"A very dangerous attempt. One would wear out so much besides—perhaps one's life itself."

"And what is the use of life if it is to be one long struggle with the strongest part of one?"

"Not much to oneself, perhaps, but sometimes we have the chance of making it so much to others that the sacrifice proves well worth the making."

"Ah! it is so easy to preach. But you see I have been spoilt. Instead of having to live for others, I have found others too ready to live for me."

"Why don't you show them they have done you injustice? You have spirit enough for anything. It will be a new interest, a new excitement."

"One talks about these things, you know, and has one's fits of remorse, when 'the world is hollow, and one's doll is stuffed with sawdust,' but it doesn't last."

And she laughed languidly, and leaned back more comfortably in her seat.

"At least, while it does last, let it do some good. The

love that seems worth so little now, may seem worth so much some day."

He spoke in a very low, earnest tone, and bent his handsome face near to hers as he did so. She looked into his eyes, and smiled with voluptuous sweetness, and leaned a little nearer to him.

"Perhaps it seems worth more than you think now," she said softly.

Armathwaite was repelled, disgusted. He saw that he must be more explicit, but he found a difficulty in keeping his tone from becoming suddenly colder.

"It would be strange if it did not to *you !* Your husband does indeed live only to love you."

She covered her surprise at this turn in the conversation very well. Drawing herself a little away from him, as if to look him more fully in the face, she said languidly, with a laugh of genuine scorn :

"Love ! Love is such a poor thing. I don't know much about it."

He was surprised in his turn. He did not indeed think that the tumultuous and turbulent passion she had described deserved to be called love, but could she be so cynical as to think the same? At any rate, she had thrown him quite off his balance, and he ventured on nothing more but commonplaces till they reached Branksome.

An evil foreboding seized upon Armathwaite as soon as they came in sight of the doctor's house. The outer door, which always stood open till late at night, had been shut; a curtain of the bay window in the lower room had been drawn aside, and not pulled back into its place. These things, which would have seemed unimportant at any other time, gained a portentous weight when there lay in the house a man who would never again leave it alive. He glanced with an anxious face at Lady Kildonan, who, when they drew up at the garden-gate, was still leaning back without having made any attempt to alight.

"I think I had better go in and—and make inquiries," he said, in a solemn voice. "And perhaps—I think you had better prepare to hear that the doctor is very ill."

"Ah, yes; he said so in his letter," she answered at once.

Her mind seemed to be wandering off to something else. Armathwaite got down, went slowly up the path, and into the house. He was afraid of what he should learn there. When the housemaid came scurrying along the passage towards him with a scared, tear-swollen face, he stopped her, knowing at once what had happened.

"Oh, sir," she began, in a heart-broken whisper, "the poor dear doctor! He's gone! He would get up, because he expected Lady Kildonan. He said he could not receive her ladyship in bed ; for her father's sake he must do her honour. I heard him say it, sir, in his very own words. And he was all in a quiver expecting her, when suddenly—me, and Mrs. Peele, and Miss Millie were all there, sir—he said he felt faint-like, and asked to be taken to the window. And we took him to a chair, and he looked out along the road. There was a look in his eyes made us know what was coming. And he had the window opened, all in the cold and dark as it was ; and it was too dark to see, and so he listened. But he couldn't hear anything, nor we couldn't, though we all stood quiet as mice. And presently he fell back in his chair and said, 'Alma—give my love to Alma. But Aphra, tell her I thought of her last of all, and with my dying breath begged her——' Those were the last words he said, sir. Then he drew a deep, long breath, and he struggled to breathe a little while, and we laid him down. But it was no use. And he just held Miss Millie's hand, and like that he died."

The girl burst out crying, and Armathwaite led her gently into the sitting-room, which was empty, and with a few kind words left her there, and hurried back to Lady Kildonan.

"What's the matter," she asked, rather querulously. "Am I not to get out ? "

Armathwaite hesitated, remembering her confession about the uncontrollable violence of her feelings. The shock to a woman of impetuous and passionate temperament, who had prepared herself for an important interview with her oldest friend, would, on learning his sudden death, be great and terrible.

"Well, well, what is it?" she repeated, sitting up and looking down into his face in the dusk with some eagerness.

"I had better drive you home, Lady Kildonan," said Armathwaite, very gently. "The doctor cannot see you —just now."

"Not now! Can't see me now!" she repeated, excitedly. "Speak plainly. Do you mean that he's dead?"

He only answered by a look; he was himself deeply moved.

"He *is* dead, then?" she persisted.

"Yes, Lady Kildonan. The last words he said were——"

But she interrupted him in an unmistakably relieved tone.

"Well, then, it's of no use for me to go in. I should only be in the way. Will you drive me home?"

Armathwaite drew back in infinite disgust.

"I think I must ask you to excuse me, Lady Kildonan. The groom can drive, can he not?"

"Oh, yes, if you don't want to come!" she answered, in an offended tone. She was busily turning something over in her own mind. As the groom left the horses' heads to take Armathwaite's place beside her, she beckoned the doctor towards her, and said, in a low voice:

"You won't mind my asking you—I know you were in the doctor's confidence—do you know anything about the provisions of his will?"

"No, your ladyship; I am very sorry that I cannot satisfy—your anxiety."

"Oh, I only wanted to know if the poor ladies were provided for, and his *protégée*, Alma, not forgotten! Good night. Tell Mrs. Peele and Millie how dreadfully sorry I am."

These words were uttered in the softest and sweetest tones of condolence, but to Armathwaite they might as well have been jeers and curses. If there had been more daylight, or if the lady's usually keen wits had not been so entirely lulled by a reckless and indifferent languor, she would have seen an expression on the young man's face, as he raised his hat, more dangerous than any that had ever yet menaced her selfish enjoyment.

"She has saved me a pang of remorse, and freed me from my last scruple," said he to himself. "I thought it was a case of woman against woman; it is angel against fiend."

With slow steps and a heavy heart he went back into the silent house of mourning.

CHAPTER XXI.

DR. PEELE'S death had been expected, towards the end, by everyone but his wife, who, although she had been gently warned both by him and by Frank Armathwaite, had been unable to recognise the possibility that the husband who had always been submissive to her every wish, should flatly assert his authority, after all these years, by dying without her permission. When Armathwaite re-entered the house, after the departure of Lady Kildonan, he found Millie crying very quietly by herself in the dining-room, while Mrs. Peele, her grief struggling with a strong sense of injury, looked in from time to time to upbraid her. Millie raised her head as he entered the room, and came slowly towards him in the dusk.

"I suppose you've heard?" she said, giving him her hand.

"Yes," he said. "Poor Millie! My dear, how cold you are. You have let the fire out. You mustn't sit here in the dark and the cold."

"Hush! Never mind, Frank. Sarah is upstairs, and you mustn't call her or you'll bring mamma down, and when she is unhappy mamma is better by herself."

"Well, let me light the fire for you, and bring in the lamp?"

Millie's strength of mind had broken down; she was very limp and miserable, and mistrustful of the proffered help.

"Oh, Frank, no. *You* can't light a fire," she said, hopelessly, while her teeth chattered.

But this is one of the little domestic accomplishments which every man believes himself to possess, chuckling to himself as he does daily at the ineptitude of the housemaid, with her hazy notions as to the value of a " draught," and her wasteful and futile expenditure of paper and wood. Frank was quite as certain as any of his sex that he could perform the whole work of the feminine household far more efficiently than they in a quarter of the time they used, on scientific principles. So he gently pushed Millie into an armchair, and wrapped her up in the long woollen antimacassar, which was stretched over the never-used sofa to hide its shabbiness, and dived into the back premises, returning shortly with a lamp, and materials for lighting a fire. Millie left off crying to watch him, sure that in a few moments her feminine genius would be called upon to save him from the perpetration of some horrid blunder. But, apparently, the Providence that watches over fools and drunken men held out a kindly hand to him, for in a few moments the fire began to burn at least as well as if laid by Sarah's practised hand. Meanwhile, Millie felt that she was already warmer, for the very back of his fair head, as he knelt down on the hearthrug to his humble occupation, seemed to her to beam with sympathy and kindliness. As the flames shot up from the crackling wood, she slid down on the floor beside him, and looked up gratefully into his face.

"You'll soon feel warmer now," he said gently.

"I'm not cold any longer," she answered presently; adding impulsively, " Frank, you're an old dear."

"Well, I don't know about that, but I flatter myself I'm a decent domestic servant at a pinch. Now, I'm going to make you some tea."

"Oh, no, don't, there's a good fellow. Sarah gets *so* cross if her kitchen is upset."

"I see you mistrust me still. Well, I'll convert you yet."

He gave her a gentle shake to stop her protests and disappeared again. He was longer away this time, so that when he reappeared the fire was red and bright, and by its beams, rather than by the light of the lamp, Millie was deciphering once more the already well-known lines of her love-letter for companionship and comfort. Frank had a tray in his hand, and when he had poured Millie out a cup of tea, he took the tray up again, and went towards the door.

"You shall have some more when I come back," he said, nodding to her as he left the room. "I'm going to take some to Mrs. Peele and Sarah."

"Oh, you'd better not. Mamma will think it unfeeling!" cried she anxiously.

But he strode off serenely with his tea-tray, and Millie, listening in perturbation at the door, heard his mellow voice comforting Sarah, and persuading her to take his offered refreshment, then a portentous "Sh-sh-sh" in her mother's voice, followed by a low-voiced discussion. Presently Frank came down again, with the cups gone from his tray, and an expression of calm satisfaction on his face.

"Wasn't she angry?" asked Millie.

"Well, she was unhappy, of course. I met Sarah, who looked very tired and white, so I gave her some tea, and Mrs. Peele came out and told me she had caught me in the very act, and I was a disgrace and a profanation, and a pretty doctor, and a lot more things. Of course I knew she was unhappy, so I told her I would go right out of the house at once, and never come back, as soon as she had taken a cup of tea. And after a little while she took it, and she really got better—morally, physically, every way. Many people, when a great grief comes, try to persuade themselves that the ordinary rules of life are broken, and that they can live upon their sorrow, and a great many things of that kind. But it's childish, you know, and wrong. Mrs. Peele had given herself a bad headache, and perhaps a pain in the jaw, just because she thought it right to talk to poor Sarah about"—Armathwaite lowered his voice, and spoke more softly than ever—"about the dear friend we are all mourning, when it would have been better to remember those she has around her still. And it was silly to jibe at me as a pretty doctor, when my tea proved to be just the medicine you all wanted."

Millie listened to his gently-delivered sermon with a softened expression, and shook her head when he had finished.

"It wasn't the tea, Frank," she said gratefully, with a faint smile in her tearful eyes. "It all lies in—in the way it's poured out!"

"There may be something in that," he admitted. "And now, dear child, if you think you feel better, I have to go out for an hour. You won't make yourself too unhappy, will you?"

He left her with a brotherly caress, and in a few minutes was well on his way to Mereside.

It was Crosmont himself who opened the door of the big house on the hill in answer to Armathwaite's ring. The agent looked by this time absolutely ill; his sallow face was flushed, while the lines and furrows in it had grown so deep that they seemed to be a dark grey colour; his eyes were sunken and glassy, and his movements restless and nervous; his whole appearance and manner seemed to suggest that he had been drinking.

"You have been a long time," he said. "I thought you were not coming." He was leading the way along the hall. At the foot of the staircase he turned and said hurriedly, "And so the old doctor is dead. Lady Kildonan has just called to say so."

"Oh," said Armathwaite; then, not that he meant it, but that he had to say something, he added: "It must have been a great shock to her."

"Not a bit of it," said Crosmont roughly. "She didn't care! What does she ever care for anybody? Where is the man, woman or child who ever drew a genuine sigh or tear from that pretty piece of flesh and blood? You think I'm heartless, I believe; measure me by her and I'm all softness and tenderness. I'm——" He stopped short, and standing on the stairs, with his hand moving nervously up and down the handrail of the banisters, he seemed suddenly to be overcome by a strong revulsion of feeling, and he shook from head to foot as he went on, in a hoarse, shame-faced voice : "I'm out of sorts to-day; I hardly know what I'm saying. Come upstairs."

The young doctor followed him to the south end of the corridor, and they stopped before the door of Alma's room. Crosmont turned in a hesitating manner.

"She's in a kind of stupor," he said ; "and nothing will rouse her. I've tried in every way, and I can't. The servants tell me she s been like this all day. When I came back from Liverpool four hours ago she was lying just as she is now. I don't know what to do. Perhaps you can do something."

He opened the door, and they entered together. The room was full of light ; for the faithful Nannie, who now hung over the bed where her mistress lay, calling to her in loud but kindly accents, had conceived the idea that the darkness could but favour the dangerous slumber, and had placed lamps and candles of all sorts and sizes in every corner. Even at this moment she was passing a candle rapidly to and fro before her mistress's closed eyes.

Alma was lying on the bed fully dressed, except that she wore a dressing-gown, the upper part of which Nanny had thrown open to dash water upon her face and neck. She was very pale, and her limbs were cold; she breathed naturally as if in sleep, though rather heavily ; and her pulse was weak and faint. With one scrutinizing glance Armathwaite took in the fact that the edges of her skirts, just visible under the dressing-gown, were bedraggled with mud and clay, and he understood that the unfortunate lady had thrown herself at once on the bed on her return from her midnight walk, and had not moved since. He dismissed the good-hearted maid on some errand, and glanced from his patient to the guilty husband, who stood at a little distance with his head turned away, tapping the floor impatiently with his foot.

"You have called me in to attend your wife, therefore we can be frank with one another, for we meet no longer as man and man, but as doctor and patient, and secrets are sacred between us."

Crosmont started, and flashed a savage look across at him, while the flush on his face grew deeper.

"Secrets!" he began. "What the—— "

"Your wife, Mr. Crosmont," continued Armathwaite, looking at him steadily, "is not in a natural sleep, but in a trance, brought on by long and persistent subjection to mesmeric influences. It is for you to decide whether this indisputable fact is or is not a secret."

Crosmont leaned against the door, panting, and with glaring eyes. Then suddenly, with an abrupt change of manner, he rushed across the room, and seizing the doctor by the arm, began to whisper in his ear with hot breath and a thick and shaking voice.

"Yes, well I did it. She was restless, and I used to soothe her that way and make her sleep. I did it in kindness, mind—in kindness. I found out I had that power over her—the power of affection, pure affection, long ago, and I used it for her good, you understand— for her good," he repeated, with feverish emphasis. "And I could wake her when I pleased until to-day. She has never slept so long before. I don't know why. I don't know what has happened. But I have lost the power—lost it; it has gone from me, do you see? Quite gone."

He stared into the doctor's eyes in deadly earnest, the moisture standing in beads on his forehead, his hands tightly clenched as if he were struggling to call up the lost power. Armathwaite laid a calm hand on his shoulder, and returned his gaze steadily and gravely. He knew he must get this man's confidence before he could hope to be allowed perfect freedom in dealing with the illness of his wife.

"Yes; I see what has happened, and I can explain to you the cause. In exercising over a highly sensitive and nervous woman this strong will-power which you un-doubtedly possess, you have established over her mind and body such an ascendancy, that whatever harm you do to yourself re-acts upon her. You have lived lately in a state of high nervous tension, torn alternately by brooding anxiety and by unnatural excitement." Cros-mont tried to interrupt him, with a brutal and lowering expression of face. But Armathwaite, still keeping his hand on his shoulder, and looking down frankly and steadily into his shifting eyes, insisted with the authority of a calm mind over a distracted one. "This has affected your own system, your nerves are shattered, your health is seriously threatened, if not already broken. By the sympathy your will has established between yourself and your wife—a ghastly sympathy into which affection and inclination do not enter—the harm you have done to yourself is reflected in her with this additional result: that being a woman in whom the intellectual and imaginative faculties are exceedingly strong, and the physical organisation comparatively delicate, it is on the intellectual side that she is most seriously threatened."

"I quite understand. I've got no mind, so my mind can't suffer. My interesting wife, being all mind and soul and the rest of it, is in danger of losing it. I thought doctors were all materialists, and concerned themselves chiefly with the body."

"Look, then," said Armathwaite, turning the sullen and morose man so that he could survey himself at length in the glass of the wardrobe door, "at this body; consider the strength of its muscles and sinews, the activity and energy of its movements, the little sleep necessary for the carrying on of its daily work with vigour, even after a severe and exciting strain; compare it with the body lying here."

Making two steps back, Armathwaite showed the motionless figure on the bed, with its waxen face and nerveless fingers limply curved. The agent glanced at it and shuddered; then turned his back and said hoarsely:

"Finish your lecture, and—and do something."

Then, as there was a moment's silence, he faced the doctor again, moving with a heavy tread, as he asked, abruptly:

"Can you do anything?"

But he stopped and stood quite still as he saw that Armathwaite was bending to look down intently into Alma's white face. After a few moments the doctor raised his head, and met the haggard eyes of the other man with confidence as he answered:

"I think so, Mr. Crosmont."

Ned drew a long breath of relief; then, indicating his wife almost without glancing in her direction, he said :

"Well, make her open her eyes—make her speak."

"I want to impose a condition upon you first."

"What is it ?"

"That if I restore Mrs. Crosmont to consciousness immediately, you will put her under my charge until her recovery is complete, and in the meantime give me your word of honour as a gentleman that you will discontinue the—the interesting scientific experiments to which your wife has so nearly become a victim."

Crosmont swaggered forward to the bedside in a blus-tering and defiant manner.

"Certainly not," he said, in a loud voice. "You have no business to make conditions to me. She is my wife, and my relations with her are my own affair."

But as he spoke, by a restless movement of his arms he threw down and extinguished a pair of candles that stood on a table at the foot of the bed, and the noise made him start and tremble nervously. He was in no state of mind or body to exercise his dogged will effectu-ally, and as the doctor remained stolid and immovable, and looked at him with the expressionless imperturba-bility of a block of wood, he wavered and seemed to shrink into himself. His next words were spoken in an uncertain voice.

"She will wake up in a few minutes without your assistance."

He fancied he had detected a quivering of his wife's lips and eyelids, and he bent over her and called her by her name in a low, authoritative tone. Armathwaite meanwhile was making his way without hurry, but with-out hesitation, to the door.

"Stop!" thundered Crosmont, in a voice which made the room ring, though it produced no effect upon his unconscious wife. "I will promise you what you like; only wake her—for Heaven's sake wake her!"

He was cruel, brutal, but not altogether without heart, and the failure of his latest attempt to rouse her woke not only anxiety for his wife, but for himself. For who could tell how this numb sleep would end? The doctor came back and held out his hand.

"You desire me to attend your wife until she has completely recovered her normal health, and you pledge your word to me you will make no more experiments upon her in the meantime?"

He was holding Crosmont's reluctantly-given hand in a grasp as unyielding as if his own fingers had been steel.

"Yes," muttered the agent shortly, hardly forming the word.

But for all that the making of the promise seemed to give him relief, and as he withdrew his hand he raised his head and looked the doctor for the first time more steadily in the face. He disliked and feared Armathwaite, but a doggedness surpassing even his own inspired him with respect, and he had brought himself to a point where his own will was absolutely powerless, and he had to seek the assistance of a stronger one as helplessly as a child. He seemed to breathe more freely as, retreating to the furthest window, he stood watching the movements of the other man with fascinated eyes. Armathwaite, cool and stolid as he looked, was at least as much excited as Crosmont himself; but, instead of being shattered and unhinged by months of wearing passion and anxiety, he was in complete command of his healthy faculties, and full of purpose so earnest, so devoted, that he felt strung up to a pitch of force and energy he had never known before as he looked down upon the unconscious woman who had drawn him to her rescue, and whose destiny had been in this unexpected manner thrown into his hands. He had no fear for the result, no fear but that the loyal and chivalrous devotion he felt for this helpless woman would be a force strong enough to bring her back to life and health and perhaps happiness. No obstacle, not even the mad passion for another woman of a selfish and cruel husband, seemed, at that moment, sufficiently serious to stand in the way of his energy and his hopes.

It was with a look on his face which would have become the priest as well as the doctor that he took both the livid, listless hands in his left, while he passed his right palm several times swiftly and firmly down her arms from shoulder to wrist. She was sensitive to the very first touch. When, after a few moments, he asked in a low voice, "Are you awake?" she opened her eyes and smiled feebly at him in answer, keeping her gaze fixed on his face with scarcely more apparent recognition than a lost child shows to a stranger who is kind to it. Crosmont, who was watching the proceedings intently from the window, burst into a loud expression of relief as he came forward. But at the sound of his voice, of his noisy tread, Alma sprang up into a sitting posture, with the old look of gloom and sadness in her eyes.

"I thought I was dead," she murmured, in a weak and broken voice. Then, with a shudder, she closed her eyes and sank back again.

"Well, you're a d——d ungrateful woman!" burst out Crosmont sullenly, and, with a half-angry, half-contemptuous nod to the doctor, he swung himself out of the room, banging the door with a violence which made the corridor echo and the windows rattle.

The noise seemed to rack his wife's frame. She twisted her neck and curved her limbs in acute pain, and it was not until after the last faint sound of his heavy tread had died away in the distance that the contracted muscles of her face relaxed, and that, in silence and absolute stillness, the sensation of suffering subsided and gradually gave place to feelings of curiosity and surprise. Armathwaite still held her hands, and now tried to chafe some warmth into them; but he said nothing, being anxious to let her collect her thoughts undisturbed, so that he might presently find out how much she remembered of the incidents of her long sleep. The expression of her face grew gradually puzzled and troubled. At last she asked in the same weak voice as before:

"Why are you here? Have I been ill?"

"No, but you have been asleep so long that your husband got anxious."

She laughed, not bitterly, but with the involuntary amusement produced by incongruous ideas.

"So he asked me to come in and see you."

" He asked you to come ? "

" Yes."

This fact seemed surprising enough to require lengthy digestion.

" You didn't come of your own accord, then ? "

" No. I was coming out of a house a few doors off when Mr. Crosmont met me and asked me to call."

" That is strange. In my dreams you seemed to be with me, following me—oh! a long time. It made me feel safe."

" You had dreams ? "

" Yes, a long, strange dream—that I have had before, I think. Yes, I am sure I have had it before, twice, I think, or three times——"

" Well ? "

" I seemed to be flying through thick clouds. I had to cut my way through them, and then I went up—up, and the clouds slipped away from under my feet, and it was dark and cold. And then—oh, but it is silly to try to remember dreams !" she cried, breaking off suddenly, while there passed over her face a flush so slight that it scarcely stained for a moment the waxen pallor of her cheeks.

" But go on," said Armathwaite, still chafing her hands.

She was perfectly docile, and though she spoke with lowered voice, she continued at once :

" Then I thought I kissed—someone."

" Who was it ? "

But she did not know. With a puzzled expression she said : " I suppose it must have been my husband. I did not want to do it, but I did it, as I do many things now, without wishing, against my will. That is all I remember."

Her head fell back, tired, on the pillow. Armathwaite pulled the bell, and then, before it was answered, he crossed the floor to the corner by the fireplace, the cosiest in the room, where there stood an easy-chair and a reading-table. In the wall behind these a fine wire gauze, about two feet square, painted a greyish white to correspond with the paper, attracted his attention. When Nanny entered the room in answer to the bell, he was still considering this with interest, and she hastened to inform him that it was a ventilator. But he himself had better information, and did not doubt that the gauze covered the mouths of the tubes through which he had learned so many of the secrets of this gloomy household. As he was turning away from the wall with a nod of discreet acquiescence in the maid's view, she drew a deep sonorous breath that was almost a cry on discovering that her mistress was awake at last. Then she looked gratefully at the doctor, who stopped her before she could break out into voluble thanksgivings.

"Yes, Nanny, your mistress is better. My work is nearly over, and yours is just going to begin. You've brought the beef-tea? Right."

He took it from her, returned to Alma, and helping her to raise herself, insisted on her taking the food, which she did with the plaintive, reluctant docility that marked her every movement.

"And now," said he, when she had finished it, "you begin to look better, and I can safely leave you with this good nurse. Nanny," and he turned to the flattered and delighted girl, "you will have to answer for the condition of my patient to-morrow morning. You must leave the room as little as you can, and when you do, get one of the other servants to take your place—not the one that chatters, though. You are to sleep in this room to-night; you can make up a bed on that sofa. I will send some medicine, and you will see that your mistress takes it. Don't forget."

Nanny was not likely to forget; she was treasuring up each direction, delighted to be of use to the mistress whom, with a mingling of pity and admiration, she worshipped. Sure that his injunctions would be implicitly carried out, Armathwaite took leave of his patient, who clung to his hand with a helpless and pitiful reluctance to let him go.

"Good-bye," he said, while he felt a tremor run through him at the clutch of the weak fingers. "You must not allow yourself to get depressed, but must let me see you looking bright and cheerful when I call to-morrow morning."

"You will come to-morrow?" she said eagerly, while a soft light of hope beamed for a moment in her face, to disappear instantly. "Ah, no, you will not come again! He will not let you," she added, forming the words with her lips, but not speaking them.

"Yes, I shall, though. Mr. Crosmont wishes me to attend you until you are well—quite well."

"Till I am quite well!" she repeated, incredulously. "Oh, he won't let you come as long as that. If he did I should *never* get well."

It was an ambiguous compliment to pay a doctor, perhaps, but Armathwaite was so much affected by it that he could not speak to her again, but held her hand a moment longer, and then left her quickly and in silence.

Crosmont was at the door of the dining-room, half in, half out, as if he were hesitating as to whether he should or should not wait for and speak to the doctor. As the latter came slowly downstairs, however, the agent seemed suddenly to make up his mind that he would not meet him; and slinking back into the room, with a kick at one of the dogs who tried to run past him into the hall, he allowed Armathwaite to pass out of the house in silence.

CHAPTER XXII.

MUCH to the astonishment of his wife, and a little to the surprise of Armathwaite himself, Ned Crosmont kept his word to the latter most faithfully. Day after day the young doctor called on Alma without hindrance, and under his care her mind began rapidly and surely to recover its tone. She scarcely saw her husband now, she said. Instead of coming to her room at night to read her to sleep, as he had done sometimes before Uncle Hugh's departure, and frequently since, he now never even wished her good-night, but marched off to his study as soon as he had finished dinner, slammed the door, and was seen no more by her until the following evening, as, no matter how early she might get up, he was always out before she came downstairs. Armathwaite, who felt a good deal of sympathy for the agent, whom he looked upon more as a victim than as an evilly-disposed tyrant, was trying gradually to turn Alma's fear of her husband into pure pity, though, naturally enough, he met at first with little success. At the same time, he was beginning to feel as much loathing for Lady Kildonan, the heartless cause of all this mischief, as if she had been a vampire or a loup-garou ; and on his frequent visits to her husband, who, if the truth must be told, was creating in him a morbid distaste for philology, he found an ever-increasing difficulty in concealing his aversion from her.

Her conduct at the reading of Dr. Peele's will strengthened this feeling. The death of this old friend had been a great shock to Alma, but it had had a good effect in diverting her attention from her own trouble to that of the widow and her daughter. When she came humbly and shyly to see them, however, and to take a last look at the dead face of her old guardian, she found that there was but one lady to comfort, for Mrs. Peele was only sentimental in short, sharp gusts, and, moreover, the cause of her most pressing grievance was the would-be comforter herself. For not only had the disgusted lady found that her hope of marrying Armathwaite to Millie had proved fruitless, but she had learned from her late husband's solicitor that by a codicil executed a few days before his death, Dr. Peele had left a handsome legacy to Alma Crosmont, and appointed Armathwaite her trustee. The agent's unfortunate wife being quite ignorant of this provision for her, was bewildered by the violence of Mrs. Peele's attacks on "the new race of married women, who set themselves up in rivalry with the single ones, and prevent men from proposing." She beat a retreat as soon as she could, and it was not until after the funeral that she, together with Lady Kildonan, who was present by her own desire, and in a state of strong suppressed excitement, Millie, Ned Crosmont, and Armathwaite himself, learned that the old doctor, who was known to have been much better off than his humble manner of living betrayed, had left to Alma Crosmont a sum of about two thousand pounds, and had appointed Armathwaite, with expressions of great confidence, her trustee. His wife and daughter he left well provided for. To Armathwaite he bequeathed a legacy of five hundred pounds, and his writing-table, with all the papers it contained. To Lady Kildonan he left a letter, which was delivered to her by the solicitor, and opened by her immediately with quivering fingers. A look of the deepest and most angry disappointment convulsed her features when she found that it contained no enclosure of any kind, and after glancing at the closely-written pages she crushed them up in her muff.

Interested in the fate of that letter, which he guessed to be a last effort of advice and warning from the dead friend, Armathwaite kept Lady Kildonan in sight as long as she remained in the house, and not much to his surprise he saw her, when she was standing near the dining-room fire, with no one very near her but the agent, who looked more ill, more harassed than ever, withdraw the sheets of crumpled paper from her muff, and, without another glance at them, without even pausing in her talk, throw them viciously into the fire. She seldom took any pains to hide whatever thought might be passing through her mind, and she did not think it worth while to lower her voice while she expressed both astonishment and irritation at the provisions of the will.

"That young Yorkshireman must have worked pretty hard, Ned, to worm himself like that into the doctor's confidence in such a short time," she said, with her head held back in an offended way which was exceedingly piquant and becoming. "It seems you can't be trusted to look after your own wife so well as this stranger."

"Well, and he wasn't far wrong," said Crosmont, sullenly.

He had avoided Lady Kildonan as much as he could all the afternoon, and now he stood by her, morose and restless, with his eyes on the ground, wearing a sulky air of being detained against his will.

"Oh, I see he has your confidence, too. That is charming. I suppose, then, it is to this new friend of the family that I am indebted for the fact that you never

come to see me now.   Perhaps he disapproves.   In that
case, of course, it is not for me to complain that my
evenings are lonely now that there is no one staying
at The Crags, and that my old friends have deserted
me."

She had lowered her voice a little, and her softened
tones passed for the effect of her grief for the death of
Dr. Peele.   Crosmont shifted uneasily from one leg to
the other.

"Don't talk such nonsense, Aphra," he said, in a
husky murmur.   "I've been busy—very busy; I've
been out early and late.   I would have come to see you
if you had wanted me really.   But Alma has been ill—
seriously ill.   You must allow a man some heart, some
conscience."

"As much as ever you please," answered the lady,
with a charming bend of the neck.   "Only it is rather
late in the day to prate about those little things, isn't
it?" She paused, insisting that he should meet her eyes
and subject himself to the influence of such witchery of
lustrous blue and white, and slyly curved golden lashes,
as no man who had once felt their power could resist.
"But just as you please, of course.   I suppose it is Dr.
Armathwaite who has opened your eyes to the fact that
your wife is a pretty woman."

She could never mention Dr. Armathwaite without
a discernible tone of spiteful pique.

"I never see her," said Crosmont shortly.   "I am
ashamed—I don't suppose you know what that feeling is
—and I am doing my best to atone for what I have done
by never seeing her."

"Never seeing her!" hissed out Lady Kildonan, in
angry dismay.   "Never seeing your wife! Then—your
influence over her—you must be losing it—losing it every
day!"

She shook with her sudden excitement till all the jet
beads that hung on her dress rattled and glittered in the
firelight.

"Yes," answered Crosmont, doggedly, "I am losing
it, and I mean to lose it.   But whether I do or not, I
never mean to use it again.   And I've set that Yorkshire-

man to save me from becoming a greater blackguard than
I am."

Though he uttered these words in a whisper full of
savage, sullen determination, even while he spoke he
listened with anxiety to her panting breath, and looked
up with a sidelong glance of yearning and entreaty at
her beautiful, angry face. She drew a deep breath of
fear at his last words.

"You have told him—everything?"

"How dare you ask me such a thing! A woman's
secret! *Your* secret! You might hang me first!"

For a moment she stood more quietly, relieved from a
great dread. Then she turned to him with a hungry
fever in her blue eyes.

"And Liverpool—Liverpool!" she panted out under
her breath. "How, then, do you propose to do it—
next time?"

"I propose—never to do it again."

She stood quite still, glaring at him like a tigress behind
iron bars.

"And what shall I do? Do you know? Do you
care?"

"You will be reasonable, you will be wise. You will
see that I have done all I can—I have ruined myself
body and soul—for I will never face it, Aphra, I
warn you that," he whispered, incoherently. "I have
risked everything, lost everything to please you. Remember, I have borne the brunt of it all—risk, anxiety,
fatigue, infamy; for I wasn't born a rogue. I have
stopped at nothing. But it has broken me, Aphra. I
am on fire all night as I sit up in my study; I don't
know what sleep is, or rest, or happiness. And all the
time I know I have done you only harm, harm. God
knows I will never face the end—never see you dis-
graced. Aphra, break with it, even if you break with
me."

There were other conversations going on in the room,
mostly in whispers also, so that Crosmont's appeal,
breathed out in a low, broken, husky voice, passed unnoticed, unheard, except by the lady to whom it was
addressed. She listened very quietly, glancing at his face

scrutinizingly from time to time in the firelight ; and when he had ended she began in a very persuasive, good-humoured voice, having assured herself that her influence was as strong as ever.

" Look here, Neddy, you're making a great fuss about nothing," she cooed out softly. " Don't let us talk about this any more. But come up and see me to-morrow, and we'll have a nice talk all by ourselves, out of reach of old Tabby Peele and her ugly duckling—I mean daughter."

Crosmont refused promptly and bluntly ; hesitation would have been fatal. But even resolution was of little avail against her. She began to cry, or look as if she was crying. Crosmont got up, walked away, and, of course, came back again.

" What's the matter with you ? " he said roughly, under his breath.

She did not answer. Although he knew in the depths of his heart that she was shamming, the mere attitude of grief in her was enough to set him on fire with self-reproach, remorse, yearning.

He bent down and whispered : " Leave off—leave off, I tell you. I'll come—just for a minute."

And the tears, real or simulated, were stayed.

Although after this Crosmont resumed his visits to The Crags, he saw no more of his wife than before, and he encouraged the attendance of Armathwaite, between whom and himself there was gradually growing up an odd, shy, reticent goodwill, founded on respect on the one side, and pity on the other. When Armathwaite murmured a deprecating word of surprise at Dr. Peele's choice of himself as a trustee for Alma, for instance, the agent nodded and said, in an off-hand tone :

" Oh, it's not in bad hands."

And though he rushed off immediately without giving time for further comment, it was evident that he did not disapprove of the arrangement.

Alma, on her side, was gradually learning, under her doctor's influence, to lose her fear of, and cultivate her sympathy with, her husband. Ten days after Dr. Peele's funeral, when she had been under treatment a little more than a fortnight, Armathwaite was congratulating himself on the improvement in his patient, when, on calling one morning to see her at the usual time, he found her in the old limp, cowed, and yet excitable state, with dazed eyes and heavy limbs. He set to work to find out the reason, and after a few questions succeeded.

"Lady Kildonan came to see me yesterday—late in the afternoon," said Alma, in a dull constrained voice.

"Indeed! To ask if you were better?"

"No. She wanted me to do something. It seemed a strange thing for her to ask. But I don't know. I was frightened, anxious; it made my head swim when I tried to think."

"Well, and what did she want you to do?"

"She said "—Alma's face began to look heavy, bewildered, and miserable, and her eyes fastened in helpless reliance on the doctor's face—"she said that Ned was in difficulties—great, serious, dreadful difficulties—and that I ought to ask you to let me have money to help him."

"Is that all? Dear me, that's soon settled! I will speak to your husband about it."

"Will you? Won't you be afraid?"

"No. If you daren't speak to him, I must. You want to help him if you can, don't you?"

"Oh, yes—oh, yes!"

"Very well, then, that's settled, and you needn't trouble your head any more about it."

"But——"

"Well?"

"Lady Kildonan—she frightened me by the way she spoke, looked at me. It was almost as if I had the money about me, and she wished to tear it away."

"Oh, you are not quite well yet! You are still nervous, fanciful. You must not let yourself be frightend so easily."

He calmed her excitement with reassuring words, and did not leave until he had restored her to a healthier and brighter mood.

That evening, when, as he knew, Crosmont would have retired to his study, Armathwaite called at the house again and asked if he could see him. He would not go into the drawing-room, where Mrs. Crosmont was sitting, Agnes said, but waited in the hall until the maid returned and requested him to come to the study.

The agent was alone. Not even a dog lay on the hearthrug this evening. He was standing with his back to the narrow wooden mantel-piece, staring at the decanters and glasses which stood on the table in front of him. Remembering the former occasion when he had visited the room, Armathwaite was struck by the change for the worse which a few weeks had made in its owner. The furrows in his face had deepened, his glance had become more restless, his manner was less doggedly determined, his fits of violence were more frequent. One cause of his deterioration, Armathwaite thought, could be traced to the insidious comforter the agent had chosen in his embarrassments ; the others were not far to seek.

"I have come to speak to you on a delicate matter, Mr. Crosmont," said the doctor, when he had been invited to sit down.

The agent looked at him out of the corners of his eyes.

"Well, go on," he said gruffly.

"I won't apologize for interfering in the matter, for I believe you will agree with me that I can't help myself."

"I hate apologies. Get to the point."

"Lady Kildonan "—the usual change came upon Crosmont at the name; he became preternaturally quiet— "called upon Mrs. Crosmont yesterday——"

"The d—— she did ! " muttered Crosmont.

"Told her you were in want of money, but did not like to ask her for it."

"And what did my wife say ? Said she wouldn't give it me, if she had any sense."

"She asked me to speak to you about it, and to ask if it was true."

"With the object——"

"Of getting you out of your difficulties, if you were in any."

Crosmont began to walk up and down the small space

at his command, with his usual heavy tread, hanging his head, and evidently much disturbed.

"What shall I tell her?" Armathwaite asked at last.

"Tell her she's a fool," said Crosmont roughly; but even in his coarse words and tone there were signs of a kindlier emotion. "No, tell her," he said, stopping short and lowering his voice, "that if I were in difficulties her money would get me out of, I'd take it. No, no, better tell her nothing," he added in a harder voice. "No good to get spooney on her now."

And again he began to march up and down the little room with a reckless air. Armathwaite rose, much moved, and leaned against the mantel-piece in his turn.

"Why is it no good?" he asked, in a low, mellow voice. "I should say it was good, very good, to take the first opportunity to get right when one has somehow got wrong. You mustn't mind my preaching— the doctor and the parson have to get their vocations a little mixed up sometimes, because they both see so much into the province of the other. Look here; there's a woman not a hundred miles away sickening for want of kindness—real kindness. And here are you, quite as much in want of sympathy as she, pulling yourself all to pieces, and all for what? No good to yourself or to anybody. You'll be a wreck before you know where you are at the rate you're going."

"I am a wreck," said Crosmont shortly, stopping to frown at him. "I'm not going to abuse you. I don't believe you're a bad fellow. But you must mind your own business. And I think that—after to-day"—he seemed to get the words out with difficulty—"you had better discontinue your visits for the present. Only for the present, mind. I—I am going to take your advice, and be doctor myself to my wife. I—I am obliged to you for your services, though, very much obliged. And I shall send for you again before long."

He had opened the door, and was already leading the way along the corridor. Armathwaite was forced to follow, but he felt that as he passed the drawing-room door his heart ached and throbbed with a sudden, passionate impulse which seemed to make him giddy and sick, and filled him with a wild fear that Crosmont had penetrated into depths of his being unknown even to himself. He recovered himself, and got back to saner thoughts, however, when he took the hand the agent held out, and read shame and not suspicion in his look.

On consideration of this scene with the agent and its result, Armathwaite resolved to go up to the Crags next day, and try to learn there the reason of his abrupt dismissal. On the following afternoon, therefore, he made a pretext to call at the great house, and see the philologist. After a few minutes' conversation with Lord Kildonan, who was always much delighted by a visit from his favourite, he fancied he had made a discovery. For the old Scotchman, while commenting with some anxiety upon the appearance of a work on words which seemed to have usurped some of his own ground, said that he would get Ned Crosmont to obtain it for him in Liverpool, as he was going up there that evening. Whereupon Armathwaite grew suddenly silent, stupid, and unsympathetic upon the subject of philology, looked at his watch, and presently took his leave with some abruptness.

It was half-past four o'clock. Crosmont never started on his journey to Liverpool until after dark. The only two late trains from Branksome were the 6.10 and the 7.40, therefore it would be by one of these that he would go.

"I may be in time to give him a warning word," thought Frank, as he hurried along the road towards Mereside.

CHAPTER XXIII.

WHILE Frank Armathwaite was absorbed in anxiety about his interesting patient, Alma herself was going through an experience as strange as the return of a dead person to life. Her husband's mesmeric experiments upon her for months past had been so cleverly conducted that she herself was uncertain of the nature of the heavy sleep into which night after night he had succeeded in casting her ; and while she felt day by day her own will weakening under the influence of his, and knew dimly that this was unnatural and strange, the meaning of it all seemed to escape her struggling reason like a will-o'-the-wisp, and the feeble efforts she made to free herself from the mysterious thraldom died out gradually ; so that on the night when her husband had found himself forced to call in Armathwaite to the assistance of his own shaken powers, she had reached a point of helplessness and weakness at which both mind and body seemed to have relaxed their hold on life itself.

If the young doctor had merely broken off Crosmont's hold upon his wife, and left the helpless mind to struggle back to health unaided, it is doubtful whether Alma would ever have entirely recovered from the unnatural strain to which she had been subjected. But Armathwaite was not content with that. He had had ample means of understanding her peculiar temperament, and the circumstances which had affected it; he took the most loyal and earnest interest in her recovery. With heart and mind strenuously devoted to restoring her to the health and happiness she had, through no fault of her own, so completely missed, he easily gained such an influence over the sensitive woman, that one look into his honest and kindly eyes as he entered the room on his morning visit would restore the confidence and hope in her which a sleepness night had broken. Thus, in little more than a fortnight, he had not indeed completely neutralised the harm her husband's treatment had done her, but put her on the high road to perfect recovery, both of body and mind. He had even succeeded in lessening her fear of her husband, and in replacing it, in some measure, by pity. This was the less difficult, as the usual relations of husband and wife had never existed between them. To establish those relations was the final aim of Armathwaite's endeavour. He knew that there was no chance of permanent happiness, scarcely even of peace, between Ned Crosmont and Alma until the former was released from the infatuation in which an unprincipled woman held him bound, and his eyes opened to the womanly charms of the wife he had so long neglected and ill-used. As for the apparent incompatibility of the two natures, that difficulty appears in fifty marriages out of every hundred, and though it might prove an obstacle to ideal felicity, it need not prevent a reasonable domestic peace. So Armathwaite argued with himself, sparing no pains to bring about the difficult consummation.

When, therefore, on the morning after his visit to Crosmont, Frank Armathwaite failed to make his usual call, Alma, at first greatly disturbed by this breach of custom, and thrown into a state of nervous excitement in which clear thought was impossible, decided, as soon as she grew calmer, to apply to her husband for an explanation of the circumstance. He would not be at home until the afternoon, she knew; for he was going to lunch at The Crags. Armathwaite encouraged her to make up her mind decidedly in little matters, and then unswervingly to carry out her purpose, however insignificant. So, like a docile child, she decided that at four o'clock, by which time Ned would certainly be at home, she would knock at his study door. Through the intermediate hours she kept her mind, through many vacillations of will and feeble desires to draw back, steadily to the point, and wandered restlessly about her pretty, faded old-world drawing-room, now tending the hyacinths in the narrow conservatory, now setting herself resolutely to accomplish little tasks in her needlework, each one of which she would finish with fingers trembling and eyes aching from the strain.

So she whiled away the time, excited, unhappy, unable to rest, certain only of one thing—that it was by her husband's mandate that the doctor had stayed away. Oh, she would beg Ned to let him come back, if only for a day or two, until she felt stronger, calmer, more like the old self that she seemed already to espy again fitfully as if in dreams—the light-hearted girl who had been touched by Ned Crosmont's show of passionate affection, and had never guessed what a mockery his professions of love would prove to be. Dr. Armathwaite, whose judgment she accepted as final, said she must not condemn Ned too harshly; that his roughness, his rudeness, his neglect were more the result of remorse than of hardness of heart; that she herself must work to subdue her fear of him. When four o'clock came therefore, and she crept along the hall and knocked timidly at the study door, she tried to conquer herself, to be brave and calm, to subdue the excitement which made her quiver from head to foot at the sound of her husband's rough voice as he said:

"Come in."

She turned the handle with difficulty; her fingers were clammy, and for a moment strength and resolution seemed alike to fail her. When she entered and stood before her husband she was quite white, and so cold that she shivered even in the warm, close atmosphere of the little room. The afternoon sunlight came in upon her through the small window, which looked to the west; it made her gold-brown hair glisten, and threw her pale face into strong relief above the dark dress she wore. Ned Crosmont, who was sitting in a plain office-chair before the fire, with his legs stretched out and crossed in front of him, and his head bent on his chest, started up with a muttered oath on seeing her, and looked at least as much afraid of her as she did of him. The poor creature had come, if she could only have known it, at the worst possible moment. Ned had just returned from The Crags, more intoxicated than ever by Lady Kildonan's brilliant beauty and daring witchery, pledged moreover to fulfil a promise wrung from him in the face of some struggles with conscience and with fear.

"What do you want?" he asked, in a thick, hoarse voice, holding the back of the chair he had just occupied, and turning away towards the window, so that she could see nothing of his face.

"I am not disturbing you, am I, Ned?" she asked, in a faint, meek voice, full of persuasive sweetness.

Her soft eyes tried to meet his with a plaintive entreaty which, as he dared not allow it to move him, made his voice harsher and his words more brutal.

"Get on with what you have to say; I want to work," he said, stamping the chair he held down upon the ground.

Alma was struggling valiantly with her fear of him,

struggling too against the old numbness which his very presence seemed to cast upon her.

"I have seen so little of you for the last fortnight, Ned," she began.

"And you're panting to see more of me again, I suppose?" said he, grimly. "Very wifely and natural. Well, that's it, isn't it?" he added, with rough jocoseness, as she did not answer.

"No, Ned; I wish I could say it was that, but it isn't," she said, in a low voice, tremulous with feeling. "I can't wish to see more of you till it is a pleasure—to you—to be—with me, and it can't be that until I'm more like myself again—more like the girl at Kensington—you used to come—and say—you loved," she ended in a whisper.

"Did you come in here to tell me all this?" he asked, passionately, striding away, and refusing to look at her.

"No, Ned, no! Don't be angry with me," she said gently, trying to keep her voice firm, lest its breaking should annoy him. "I have been tiresome lately, I know—full of fancies, and difficult to manage."

"By Jove, you have!"

"Well, and now under Dr. Armathwaite's care I am getting better every day——"

"Dr. Armathwaite! D—— Dr. Armathwaite. I suppose he put you up to bothering me in this way?"

"Oh, no. Only he didn't come this morning, and I came to ask you why."

Crosmont stopped short in his pacing about. He did not care a straw for his wife, but he felt nettled on learning that her intrusion was on account of another man.

"Oh, that was all, was it? Your flirtation cut short just as it began to grow interesting!"

A pink flush appeared in Alma's cheeks and died away again, but she did not answer.

"That was it, wasn't it? Answer me. Don't give yourself these airs."

She raised her eyes to his face very simply, with the unaffected dignity of the most perfect and confident innocence.

"There is no need for me to answer that," she said, quite gently, "for you know you don't accuse me in earnest."

There was silence for a few minutes, during which Crosmont fidgeted with the fire and with his papers, and Alma stood quite still with one hand clutching the wooden mantel-piece and the other pressed tightly against her breast.

"Well, what are you waiting for," he asked at last.

"I don't like to leave you quite like this, Ned, when at last I've found the courage to come and speak to you myself."

"Why do you mind? I'm sure I don't."

"That's just it, Ned,"—she turned imploring eyes towards him and spoke in a whisper—"I do so wish— you did ! "

He was moved at last in spite of himself. Turning abruptly to the window he looked out, with a troubled, scowling face, but with a lump in his throat, as a sudden consciousness came upon him of the fair days he was missing, of the sweet peace and the charm of life he was foregoing—and all for what? Well, he knew the value of it if anybody did. He felt like a man in a burning fever who suddenly sees before him a cool, shaded river into which he would fain plunge up to his thirsty lips. But between him and the shining water there is a barrier of fire. Ignorant of the tumult and the struggle raging in her husband's breast, feeling only that she had touched him a little, since he neither scoffed at nor scolded her, she drew a little nearer to him. He felt the air stirred behind him as she moved quickly forward and stopped.

"Ned," she whispered, " Ned, I'm going to ask such a little thing. I don't want you to be kind to me ; only let me be kind to you. Don't make me afraid of you, so that I daren't look at your face for fear of shrinking, and so offending you more. I am so lonely, Ned. It is so horrible to be moved only by one feeling—dread ; to know that you have done no harm, and wished no ill to anyone in the world, and yet to feel always afraid—so that the shadow of the ivy over the window frightens me if the wind moves it, and when I hear your voice and try to be glad, I can't, for I know you will frown at me and turn away, as if there were something poisonous in my very look."

"The old story—you want to go away, I suppose?"

"I did, a little while ago. And after that, after Uncle Hugh had gone, I grew not to care for anything, to feel as if I was never awake, that I was looking at you, at everything, through a veil. But the last few days that has passed off, and I see things. I see that you are un-happy. Oh, don't tell me you are not, for I know. If you have ever been so unhappy as I have you can always tell. Well, and I am so sorry, I can't help thinking it would do you good if you knew how sorry I am. For I see that you would never have chosen that things should be as they are between us. It's not possible. Nobody chooses to live miserably, and when you used to come and see me at Kensington, and rest your head upon my shoulder and look into my eyes, and implore me to marry you soon, soon, you never meant to make me miserable then."

"What's the good of looking back? Marriages are just as often failures as not, with nobody to blame. I'm not blaming you. Only for goodness' sake don't be sentimental. Marriage is like tooth-ache. When you are once in for it there you are, and it's got to be borne."

"But, Ned, there's always a best or a worst to be made of it, and we're not making the best—now, are we?"

"I don't see my way to making anything better of it."

"Don't you? Won't you try?"

"What do you want? What do you expect me to do?" he asked, with an impatient movement. "To spend my evenings sitting looking at you while you make crochet, as Uncle Hugh was contented to do? Or to do crochet myself?"

Although he spoke roughly, he was not yet unkind. Alma was encouraged to answer steadily, though in the low, pleading tones she had used throughout the inter-view:

"I want you to look me in the face—not only when you wish to compel me to do things, but always. Then you will presently see in my eyes something besides fear. I want you to speak to me as to a woman, and not to a dog, and then presently you will see in me more than the dumb obedience of a dog. I want you to eat two meals during the day with me, and you will presently find that a face which is the brighter for seeing you is a sauce that goes well with everything. That is all I want at first, Ned; in a few weeks it will be for you to ask more."

Ned, half turning, stole a look at her, and he was not too insensible to the charms of her delicate beauty, and the sweet, modest pleading of her face, to think that perhaps she was right.

"Will you dine with me this evening?" she asked, venturing to place one hand upon his arm. "You are not busy to-day. You might easily be home in time."

But these words made him start violently, for they recalled him to the facts of his night's journey and the promise it involved. It cost him an effort at first to resume his roughest, most brutal manner, but the next moment this very fact served to increase his savagery, and Alma's pale face, drawn and contorted in an instant with the old horror, irritated him almost to frenzy.

"That's enough of this sentimentalism," he said, with a black scowl, as he shook her hand roughly from his arm. "You're excited, that's what it is. This precious Dr. Armathwaite's prescriptions don't agree with you. I'm a better doctor than he any day. Come here."

Alma had shrunk back, and was retreating towards the door. At his imperative command, she turned slowly with a stony face, but did not come nearer to him. She was struggling against the power he had exercised over her for so long.

"Come here!" he repeated.

She hesitated, fighting against the benumbing force of his will for a moment longer, clenching her hands, forcing her eyes to look down, away, anywhere but at him, and crying out in her heart to be delivered from the tyranny which was tightening over her again. But she had been in subjection too long and too recently for her weak efforts to be of any avail; against her wish, against her will, the heavy eyelids were slowly raised, and the long sweet brown eyes, now wide with despair, met those of her husband, and remained fixed, with dilated pupils, in a fascinated gaze. Hitherto her fall into the heavy hypnotic sleep had been managed so neatly by Crosmont, with such an adroit preparation of placing her on a sofa and reading to her, that it had been easy enough to deceive her into doubting whether there was anything unnatural in her slumber. But now, for the first time, he was reckless, careless; while she, with her faculties the keener for the rest and kindness of the past fortnight, saw, dimly and stupidly indeed, but none the less with dogged certainty, that the stupor which was coming over her like a suffocating pall, creeping up her limbs, dimming her sight, and forcing a crowd of confused sights and sounds in upon her dulled brain, was not a swoon, but was the strange undreamt-of result of the steady gaze into hers of eyes which seemed to grow large, lurid, and blurred even as she looked and felt her senses failing her.

She shivered as his hands touched her arms and passed rapidly down from shoulder to wrist. She heard her own voice, which seemed to come from some far-off hill like a faint echo, as she said, "Don't, Ned—don't let me have those dreams." Then the voice died away, and the hill seemed to grow larger and larger until it shut out all sight, and no further sound came to her but a muffled sigh, as her limbs died one by one to all feeling. Then the confused murmur in her head ceased suddenly, and she lost the last gleam of consciousness.

CHAPTER XXIV

THE sun had set before Frank Armathwaite reached Mereside, and a leaden February day was ending in a raw, wet evening by the time he stood at the door of Ned Crosmont's house.

The bell was answered, not, as he had hoped, by the warm-hearted and trustworthy Nanny, but by the loquacious little scandal-monger, Agnes, who started so violently on seeing him that it was evident his coming had some special interest for her. Her constrained answer to his first question made it clear that she had been carefully drilled.

"Is Mr. Crosmont at home?"

"No, sir." And Agnes blushed violently.

"Do you know when he will be in?"

"I can't say at all, sir."

"How is Mrs. Crosmont to-day?"

"Quite well, sir. She is writing now in her own room, and gave orders that she was not to be disturbed," giving off the message with the glibness of a lesson.

Armathwaite reddened.

"That is all right," he said, stiffly. "Please let her know that I called, and am glad to hear she is better."

He turned and went down the steps, too anxious to feel much mortified by his reception, which had justified his worst fears. He thought it wiser not to linger a moment in the neighbourhood, as it was plain that Crosmont would not see him, and very desirable that the agent should not suspect that he was being watched. He therefore rode straight back to Branksome, and did not leave home again until he learned by the clock that the 7.40 train had steamed out of the station. Then he got up from the chair in which he had been forcing himself to sit very quietly, and telling Mrs. Peele that he was going to pass the night at The Crags by Lord Kildonan's desire, he left the ladies to their astonishment without giving them time for comment.

Frank Armathwaite had entirely got the upper hand of Mrs. Peele since the day after the doctor's funeral, when, on opening the writing-table which was such an important part of his legacy, he discovered that it contained no papers bearing in any way upon the secret. Knowing into whose hands the doctor's keys had fallen after his death, Armathwaite had no hesitation in deciding by whom the documents had been taken; he therefore went to Mrs. Peele, told her that some important papers had been abstracted, adding that unless they were quickly restored he should put the matter into the hands of the late doctor's solicitor. "You see, Mrs. Peele," he had said to her, gravely and pointedly, "these papers concern a secret which has passed from your husband's keeping into mine." He saw through the stolid expression she maintained that this statement startled her. "They are in fact only necessary to confirm what I already know. I shall be sorry if I have to make a disturbance about them, as I certainly shall do if they are not soon restored."

"It is not very becoming in a young man to be so mightily interested in the secrets of married women," said the widow, icily.

"It can't be helped sometimes," he answered, in the same tone.

And so the conference had ended, and ever since that day Mrs. Peele had shown an unwonted deference to the young doctor, although she had not yet restored the papers. These were, however, as he had said, comparatively unimportant now; for he felt sure that he was well on the track of Lady Kildonan's secret, and desperately near to that dilemma which had hastened the old doctor's death.

From Branksome to The Crags was a walk of nearly seven miles, and it was nine o'clock before Frank reached the big red house, and asked if Lord Kildonan could see him. He had not long to wait: before he had stood two minutes in front of the great log fire which it was her ladyship's pleasure to keep always burning in the wide hall fireplace, the old Scotchman came trotting down the gallery from his study with outstretched hand. He wore his blue spectacles, a black skull-cap, and a loose alpaca coat, and looked in this get-up, with his awkward, ambling gait, rather like a good-humoured monkey of extra size.

"Dear me, dear me! I thought they must have made a mistake. It is good of you to come and see me like this in the evening, when I know how tired you must be after your day's work. Now I wonder——"

He paused for a few seconds, and looked well at his

visitor from head to foot, and back again with a mysterious, curious, and rather puzzled expression.

Armathwaite noticed then that, as the first flush of surprise and welcome passed from his face, Lord Kildonan looked worried, careworn, and anxious—quite a different man from the excited and earnest student he had left that afternoon. The young man almost felt his heart stand still with a great fear, and at the same moment it suddenly became clear to him that he was deeply fond of this kind and courteous gentleman, and that to give him a terrible shock would be a task impossible in its cruelty. And what if he had some inkling of the truth already? The doctor felt as nervous as a girl until, his silent and grave inspection completed, Lord Kildonan spoke again.

"I wonder," he said slowly, peering over his blue spectacles into Armathwaite's face. "You know we northerners believe in second sight, and all that sort of thing: do you?"

"I—I've never studied it—never had an opportunity," murmured Armathwaite, feeling that his voice was playing tricks with him.

"Ah! I was wondering—and I'm no so sure that I'm wrong yet—whether perhaps ye had come up to-night because ye had a kind of inkling that I was lonesome, and thought ye would come to bear me company."

"No-o," stammered Armathwaite; "I don't think it was altogether that. I thought—I took it into my head this afternoon that you did not look well, and might perhaps be threatened to-night with another attack like that one you had three weeks ago. So I came to ask your permission to pass the night here, and see for myself how you got on."

"Well, that is very kind of you; but it's strange, too, for I have not felt at all unwell. But, now I remember, I felt no premonitory symptoms of my last attack. Well, you're welcome, at all events, and I hope your foreboding may not prove well founded. Come to my study, come; and I'll show you some notes I've taken since you were here this afternoon."

He led the way back along the gallery, and Armathwaite followed, feeling sure that there was something as yet unaccounted for in his host's manner, and fearing that he might be forced into an embarrassing position if Lord Kildonan chose to question him. When they reached the study, and sitting down to the table began, the one to read aloud and the other to listen, both men felt conscious of a little inattention, a little reticence on the part of the other. This was the more astonishing in the elder man, as it was the first time Armathwaite had seen him falter in his allegiance to his hobby. It was quite clear now, however, that there was some object occupying his mind before which even philology paled in interest.

"I don't think," he said, presently, with less enthusiasm and less confidence than usual, "that this new man can have gone on quite so far as I have in this view. It may be so, of course, but I don't think it's likely."

"Not at all likely," said Armathwaite, quite meaning what he said. "At any rate, you will know to-morrow, when Crosmont brings you his book."

At this, the first mention of his agent's name, Lord Kildonan's face changed; and Armathwaite, who had never before seen him in any mood but one of homely, good-humoured, kindly concern for others, or regretful, yearning affection for his wife, was astonished at the stern and hard expression which his rugged features instantly assumed.

"I did not ask him to bring it," he said, in a dry tone.

Armathwaite made no comment, but affected to pore over some of the loose sheets of paper, closely covered with the student's professional scribble, with which the table was well strewn. Lord Kildonan picked up a note-book, but the thread of his interest was irretrievably broken, and he slapped it down again with a violence which was so unexpected in a person of his even temperament that Armathwaite started and looked into his face with grave apprehension.

"I think I've trusted that young man too far," he said, with the strongest Scotch accent Armathwaite had ever heard him use.

As it was impossible to differ from him in this opinion, the young doctor kept silence, waiting anxiously to learn how far his knowledge or his suspicion went. The old Scotchman neither thought nor spoke quickly, and it was not until after a long pause that he went on :

"It's varra deefficult to be always richt, and a young mon's a young mon, and apt maybe to use more zeal than discretion in a post of responsibility. Dr. Arma thwaite, ye're a mon of discretion, though ye're young yourself, so ye'll no be a bad judge of the case."

Frank decided from this opening that whatever Lord Kildonan had discovered, it was not so bad as what he had not discovered. Nevertheless, he felt the strongest reluctance to be a judge at all in a case of which he knew far too much. He attempted some protest; but his host silenced him, holding up his hand with so much imperious dignity that Frank began to feel more and more sure that there was a side to the Scotchman's character which wrong-doers would find some difficulty in reckoning with.

"Ye must know," he said, taking off his spectacles, and leaning on his elbow on the table so that he could shield his eyes with his hand from the lamp-light, as he looked intently at the doctor's face, "that this young fellow has a great deal to do, and that he shows plenty of energy in his work. I don't know much about business myself, or the management of a large estate, but I studied the subject a good bit when I first became trustee for my wife's property, and I saw varra soon that I had for my right hand, in Edwin Crosmont, a sharp young fellow, whose head was worth ten times what mine was. He seemed to me honest, I knew he was hard-working, and I thocht the business was better in his hands than in mine. But now I have found out, quite by chance, by a word or two to a puir body I met down by the Conismere road, that he's been too hard on the tenants that had a deefficulty wi' their rent, and that they tak' me for a hard-fisted skinflint that wad turn them oot like dogs in the road if they were a bit late wi' the money. Now, what do ye think o' that? What do ye think o' that? I turn a puir mon oot o' his little home in the winter for want o' a few dirty shillings! Now, an agent may be energetic, he may work like a horse, he may run aboot like a hare, but he suldna get me such a character as that!"

Armathwaite felt greatly relieved. Crosmont would get a severe reprimand; the fear of further investigations would frighten him into discretion, and Frank's own task of saving the agent's unfortunate wife would be the easier. He agreed with Lord Kildonan, but without extreme heartiness, having no wish to increase his host's wrath.

"Ye're too soft," said the old Scotchman, looking at him keenly. "There are some things one suldna pardon, and to be hard on puir folk is one o' them."

And his straight, thin-lipped mouth closed in a narrow, inflexible line. Armathwaite could not keep his deep concern entirely out of his countenance, so strong was the impression this new view of Lord Kildonan's character gave him. The elder man naturally misunderstood the reason of this, and thought that he was moved solely by compassion.

"However," he went on, as the doctor said nothing, "I shall not be too hard upon him, if it were only for the sake of his puir little wife. Besides, it would break Aphra's heart to think that her old playfellow and *protégé* had done any wrong. After all, nae doot he thinks it's his duty to mak' them pay up, and if he's over hard, it's for me, and not for himsel'."

Armathwaite made no comment on this last reflection, but asked:

"I suppose you haven't mentioned the matter to her ladyship, Lord Kildonan?"

"No, I'm afraid it would pain her too much. I did think of it, but I changed my mind."

"I should advise you to tell her. There is no fear of a lady being too hard. On the other hand, she has so much spirit, she would see the thing quite in its proper light."

"Well, I can't tell her till to-morrow now, for she went to her own room very early this evening, with a bad headache."

"Oh, then you will not see her again to-night?" said Armathwaite, very distinctly.

The young man's eyes, as he put this question, had suddenly become aglow with strong excitement.

"Only for a moment, when she comes to bid me good-night," answered Lord Kildonan. "I should not worry her with little tiresome troubles then," he added, his mouth softening as he spoke of her. "She only flits in and flits out again. I insist upon that always. Then I know she is all right, and I sleep better for knowing it. It's all selfishness, you see."

And he turned to the doctor with his old, good-humoured smile.

"Does she never fail you?"

"Never!" answered the elder man, with some surprise.

"And what would you do if she didn't come?" Armathwaite asked with a smile.

"Do! I should go and find out what was the matter with her, of course. But that has never happened—never! What makes you ask?"

"I was wondering why she had not come," answered the young man, after a moment's hesitation.

"Oh, it is too early yet. She does not come till after ten—nearly three-quarters of an hour." And he glanced at his watch as he rose from his chair, and opened a little cellaret which stood unlocked on a shelf in the wall. "You take whisky, doctor? I generally take a glass of whisky and water about this time in the evening; you won't let me take it alone, will you?"

"I don't think I shall let you take it at all, Lord Kildonan," said Armathwaite, as he took up a tumbler, into which the elder man had poured some of the spirit, and examined it narrowly. "I am here as your medical adviser, you know, and you must allow me to taste this."

"Certainly," said Lord Kildonan, who thought this was a joke.

Armathwaite raised the glass to his lips.

"They've put it into the wrong decanter," he said, calmly, though his eyes were bright with excitement; "or, no,"—he tasted the spirit again—"they've put it

into a decanter that hadn't been properly rinsed. What
is it they use for washing these things? Vinegar and
sand, or something of that sort, isn't it? I can taste the
vinegar; it spoils the flavour completely."

Lord Kildonan took up the tumbler, and tasted the
contents in his turn.

"There is a peculiar flavour in it; I've noticed the
same thing before. Vinegar, do you say? It doesn't
taste like vinegar to me."

"In any case, you had better not drink it. It might
make you sick. Have a fresh bottle opened, Lord Kildonan, and don't have it decanted at all."

Lord Kildonan rang the bell, and after some delay the
under-footman appeared. It was a most unusual circumstance for the master of the house, who was a man of the
simplest habits, to require any attendance so late, and
the lad seemed very much alarmed by the summons.
The butler had gone to bed, he said, and the keys of the
cellar were locked up in his pantry. Lord Kildonan, who
would not have broken a dog's sleep for his own pleasure,
looked ruefluly at the condemned decanter, and would
most certainly have contented himself with the deterior-
ated spirit but for the presence of the doctor, who, with
some astute knowledge of men and manners, said:

"You know where the butler keeps that bottle of
whisky for his own drinking?"

"Oh, yes, sir," answered the lad readily, and immediately fell to blushing furiously as both the gentlemen
smiled.

"Well, bring it, there's a good lad, just as it is."

And the young fellow disappeared without delay.

"I'm afraid Webster will think we're taking a liberty,"
said Webster's master doubtfully.

"If he does, Lord Kildonan, you may be sure he'll not
rest till he has taken ample compensation."

When the servant reappeared with the whisky, and
having put it softly down upon the table, took himself off
as noiselessly and unostentatiously as possible, Armathwaite mixed two tumblerfuls, the first very strong and
the second very weak, and having given the former to his
host, took the latter for himself.

"Eh, but this is stiff," said the old Scotchman, tasting the preparation without disfavour. "You have mixed this for a professor of medicine, and not for a student o' philology, doctor. If I were to drink off this, and then lie down for an hour as ma custom is, I should do na more work to-night, and there'd be some precious hours wasted. An' wi' these little whipper-snapper pretenders to science yapping a' round us, it ill becomes a man wi' any pretensions to learning to gie his time to whisky toddy and na to word-roots."

"Oh, I'll see that you don't sleep too long, Lord Kildonan. After that excitement about Crosmont and the tenants, you will work better when you've had a sleep to calm your nerves."

"There's something in that," said the student, not unwilling to be convinced. And while keeping up a conversation upon his favourite studies which was little more than a monologue on his side varied by exclamations of assent from his companion, he gradually emptied the tumbler, and being, as he had predicted, by that time well disposed for his usual hour's repose, he excused himself to the doctor, and retired to lie down on the hard little sofa in the antechamber.

As soon as the curtain between the two rooms fell behind his host's retiring figure, Armathwaite seemed to become a different man. Looking at his watch, he discovered that it was seventeen minutes past ten; and springing up lightly in a state of high excitement, which there was no longer any need to conceal, he turned up the lamp and paced the room from end to end with a soft tread, his ears on the alert for any sound. When he came close to the outer door, or to the curtain which hung in the doorway of the inner room, he would stop and listen; and as, at last, peeping behind the curtain, he saw Lord Kildonan lying with closed eyes, he stepped softly in and blew out the two candles that were burning on the table at the foot of the sofa. But the elder man was not asleep; he opened his eyes and said:

"What's that?"

"That light tries your eyes, Lord Kildonan."

"Oh, very well," he answered docilely.

And the doctor retreated into the next room. It was now twenty-five minutes past ten. Faint night-noises, unnoticed by day, but rendered startling in the silence of the dark hours, assailed the listening ear on all sides. The chirp of a cricket, the cracking of the woodwork, the scurrying of mice, each of these sounds came with almost deafening distinctness to Armathwaite as he stood by the door, hearing the drawing of his own breath and feeling interested in it, as if it had been that of a patient. At last in the distance he heard something which no nearer sound could stifle—the creak of a board under a human tread, followed presently by soft slow footfalls along the uncarpeted gallery outside. He drew back from the door. In the bare room there were neither curtains nor screens behind which he could retreat. On the other hand the lamp, with its dark green shade, cast only a small circle of bright light on the table, and a still smaller one on the ceiling above. He withdrew into the darkest corner of the room and waited, standing upright and as still as a statue.

The door-handle rattled and turned, and the door itself was pushed open so very slowly that Armathwaite had to battle with an impulse to take three strides forward, pull it towards him, and look round it at the intruder. At last a figure appeared, looking hardly more solid than a shadow in the gloom that filled every corner of the apartment beyond the little ring of the lamp's light—a woman's figure, moving slowly and lightly over the floor towards the inner room. Armathwaite remained motionless until she had drawn the curtain aside on its rings and passed through; then he stepped out from his corner and passed to the other side of the room. As he did so he saw in the gloom the lady bend down over the head of the sofa and kiss the forehead of the recumbent man.

"Good night, my darling," he heard Lord Kildonan murmur. And then followed a soft woman's whisper: "Good night." A moment later the curtain moved again, and the lady returned, passing close by where he stood without turning her head. She crossed the room, opened the door, and went out into the gallery, and it

was not until her footsteps had died away that Arma
thwaite began to breathe naturally again. He was still
standing with his face turned in the direction of the
closed door when he was startled to hear Lord Kildonan's
voice behind him. The doctor confronted the elder
man with an expression of deep, unmistakable alarm.

"Why, what ails ye?" asked the old Scotchman, and
coming closer he peered into the young man's face.
"Ye look as scared as a lass, and your face is wet and
your hands are cold, and altogether ye look as if ye'd
seen a ghost. Did ye fall asleep, maybe, and tak' my
wife for a ghost?"

"No, indeed, I did not! I was afraid finding me here
might frighten her ladyship, that was all," answered
Armathwaite, with a smile which was rather forced,
though he looked much relieved. "You had better not
go out into the draughty passages now, Lord Kildonan,"
he continued, as the elder man made his way to the door.
"If you want to send a message to her ladyship, let me
take it."

Lord Kildonan looked rather surprised, but he turned
back again, rubbing his eyes and yawning as he shook
his head.

"No, no; I've nothing to say to her that won't keep
till to-morrow, and to-night I'm so sleepy myself I'm
fearing I shall na keep awake much longer—if, indeed,
I'm quite awake noo," he said dreamily, as he sat down
in his large chair at the table, and rested his head on his
hand. "There was something so sweet in the touch of
her lips on my face to-night, something so tender, so
gentle," he murmured aloud—but to himself, not to the
doctor—"that I thocht maybe she felt kinder to me, and
began to feel——" After a pause, he tossed his head
up suddenly, and passed his hands over his head. "Ah,
I'm an old fule, and it's all the whisky, na doot! But,
young man, I wish ye were here to mix my whisky every
night, for ye've given me the sweetest dream I've had
for months past, though it did but last for a minute!"

Armathwaite shivered as he took the hand Lord
Kildonan held out to him, gently helped him to rise, and
led him to his bedroom door. Then the doctor disposed

himself for a little rest on the sofa, but not to sleep. Sometimes in his host's little suite of rooms, sometimes softly pacing the galleries and corridors of the big house, he kept watch until the morning. Standing like a sentinel under the great armour trophies in the hall, upon which a floating oil-lamp cast, through the hours of the night, a faint and murky light; mounting the wide staircase in the shadow of ponderous and doubtful old masters; creeping, with the soft steps of a cat, along the carpeted corridors of the upper floor; and finally gazing with straining eyes, as the struggling morning began to dawn, through a small window which commanded a view of the steep hill and the entrance to the secret pathway; Armathwaite passed a night so fraught with excitement, with doubt and fear, with anger and yearning pity, that when the morning broke fully, and found him lying in an uneasy sleep on the little sofa, old Lord Kildonan, trotting in to look at him and find out how he had slept, was shocked at his appearance.

"Bless me!" he murmured to himself, as without disturbing Frank he crept back again with ungainly, cautious steps. "That young man works too hard at his profession, or else he has not so clear a conscience as I should have thought. In the morning light he looks as old as I do myself, though I'm bound to say he doesn't look as ugly."

But he could not know that he was seeing the effect of his own wrongs on another man's face.

CHAPTER XXV.

IT was with a start and a confused sense of having been in some frightful danger that Frank Armathwaite woke and stared about him on the morning after his exciting vigil. Very little of the morning light came through the green blind that hung before the window; he had to grope his way across the room to distinguish the hands on his watch. He had scarcely stirred when Lord Kildonan, in his dressing-gown, came in from the study with a disturbed face.　Armathwaite had just discovered that it was twenty minutes to eight.

"You've had a bad night, I'm afraid," said the old Scotchman, in rather a hard voice.

The doctor felt it was needless to pretend that his rest had been as undisturbed on a hard little sofa as it would have been in bed.　So he only said he had had plenty of worse ones.　He was wide awake by this time, for there was something in his host's manner which roused his curiosity and his apprehensions.　He was not kept long in suspense; for on asking Lord Kildonan how he felt, he received the following answer :

"I feel very well in my body, and very ill in my mind, Dr. Armathwaite, and I'm not sure that I don't attribute both those circumstances to you, and I'm still less sure that I'm grateful to ye for either of them."

"Surely to be well in body is a gain, at all events, your lordship," suggested Frank, very deferentially.

"I'm no sae sure of that, I'm no sae sure of that.　It all depends upon what it costs, and when a heaven for the body is gained at the expense of a hell for the mind, why, then your physic is too dearly paid for."

"Tell me what you mean, Lord Kildonan.　Give me a chance of redeeming my character as a physician."

"I can't tell you what I mean; I hardly know myself. But I think you must have doctored that whisky wi' something to make a man's thoughts run wild, for the ideas that have passed through my head this night might well have made a sane man think he was going daft. And then this morning I wake up and remember I did not go as usual to my wife's room last night just to knock at her door and bid her good night."

"To knock at her door!" repeated Armathwaite, as if to himself.

Lord Kildonan looked at him over his spectacles.　"I always try the door ; if it is locked she is awake, and I call out good night, and she calls back.　If it is unlocked she is in bed, and I open the door and look in.　Then I am satisfied she is all right.　But I was telling you about this morning.　I went just now to her room ; but she was not there.　It is early for her to be up.　I am full of all sorts of fears about her. Her manner has been different lately; she seems dissatisfied and restless. She is never happy indoors. I don't like the thought of her wandering about out of doors at this early hour; it is not safe, it is not right for a lady to do so. The country people would think her mad."

"But why think she was out of doors?" said Armathwaite, in a clear, reassuring voice. "Is it not more likely that she had run into her boudoir to fetch a novel?"

"No, it is not so, unfortunately. I was so uneasy that I took a bold step, and opened the wardrobe where her shawls hang. Now every trifle which concerns my wife is of so much importance in my eyes that I could make a catalogue from memory of everything she has ever worn in my presence. I missed a shawl—a cloak I think she calls it—with fur inside. I am much disturbed about it. In the country the slightest eccentricity is thought so much of."

Frank could not feel sure whether these remarks were all as ingenuous as they appeared, or whether the old Scotchman was trying to penetrate into the depths of his thoughts. He made cautious answers to the questions put to him concerning Lady Kildonan's health and spirits, and tried to divert his host's thoughts to his studies. These, however, had this morning lost their fascination. After an unpleasant interview of a little more than half-an-hour, during which the conversation straggled on, while over both speakers there seemed to hang a dread of something to come, Lord Kildonan rose hastily from his chair, and, with a muttered apology, left the room. He returned in ten minutes with an expression of face in which bewilderment and doubt perceptibly struggled.

"Well, Lord Kildonan, I think I was right," said Armathwaite, with a shrewd guess at the cause of his companion's mystification. "You found her ladyship safe in bed, did you not, reading a novel?"

"She was safe in bed certainly—asleep, I think, but she had been oot and aboot, Dr. Armathwaite, as I told ye; for there was her dress lying on a chair that had been

empty when I went in for the first time.   Ah, well, I've
na doobt we shall have an explanation presently," said the
old Scotchman, who had relapsed into a broad North-
country accent as he grew excited.   " The servants will be
about by this, and I ken ye're dying for your tub."

He rang the bell, and Armathwaite, conducted by a
servant to a large ash-panelled bedroom with a wide view
from the windows of lawn and lake, saw no more of his
host till midday.   But in the meantime he had a little
self-appointed task to perform.   After a *tête-à-tête* breakfast in a huge room with the useful and inoffensive Aunt
Theresa, there being no other guests in the house, he made
his way to the study again, and found that his host was
still in his bedroom.   Frank went straight to the cellaret,
and had his hand upon it when he heard a faint noise of
light and hurried footsteps in the gallery.   He paused,
and made no sound as the footsteps came near, and there
was a very soft tap at the door.   The next moment
Lady Kildonan entered, and uttered a smothered cry
at sight of him.   He on his side was startled by her
appearance.   Her face was pale, her eyes were heavy: her
golden hair, rough and disordered, hung down untidily
about her ears.   A loose light wrapper was folded round
her, and held in place by one of her white arms, while
her feet were bare but for the slippers into which they
had been hastily thrust.   She staggered back a step like
a person roused suddenly from sleep, whose senses are
not yet quite clear ; then her heavy eyes travelled to the
decanter on which Armathwaite's hand still rested, and her
face changed ; the stupor that oppressed her faculties
broke up, a look of fear passed over her features, and
gave place immediately to one of stubborn recklessness.

" You are an early visitor, Dr. Armathwaite," she said
coolly.   " I did not expect to find any one in my
husband's room at this hour."

" I have spent the night here, your ladyship.   Do you
not remember seeing me when you came to wish your
husband good night ? "

She was standing in front of him, erect as an empress,
her commanding figure enabling her to appear dignified
in spite of her negligent attire.   As Frank put this

question to her distinctly and with studied emphasis, looking attentively at her all the time with exasperatingly calm blue eyes, he saw a doubt and then a flash of devilry in her handsome face.

"I saw you last night, certainly, when you appeared to be trying to hide from me. But I had heard nothing of your intention to instal yourself here, and therefore I repeat that I was surprised to find you still here this morning."

Frank said nothing. Strong as his suspicions—nay, more, his convictions—were concerning this lady's conduct, her ready wit and her daring struck him absolutely dumb with admiration. She waved her left hand in the direction of the *portière* with curt peremptoriness.

"I see you are chamberlain here. Be kind enough to ask whether my husband can see me."

A woman who can keep her head has much the advantage of a man in an encounter of this kind. His manliness calls out to him to put on at least the appearance of mercy. Frank, who had come as near to hating this woman as her superb beauty allowed him to do, felt both admiration and pity for her as he watched the splendid front she was putting on this dangerous affair. He raised the curtain, went through into the ante-chamber, and knocked at the bed-room door. Before he could receive an answer, however, he heard the sound of one of the study windows being thrown open. Lord Kildonan came out, having heard his wife's voice, and Armathwaite followed him back to the study. Lady Kildonan, with the magic art of a handsome woman who knows the value of her beauty and has spared no pains on its education, had already by a few deft touches restored an appearance of gracefully mitigated disorder to her hair and dress, and was leaning back in her husband's arm-chair in a charming attitude of repose. Frank had no eyes for her; he looked at the cellaret. It was open, as he had left it. The whisky decanter containing the spirit which he had rejected last night was a little out of its place, and was now empty. Then he glanced at the window, met her eyes, fixed upon him with an expression half furtive, half defiant, and smiled. Rather taken aback by this, Lady Kildonan stopped short for an instant in something she was saying to her husband, and regained the thread of her remarks with an effort. She was telling him, in answer to his questions, that she had had a restless night, and had been down in the morning-room hunting for a book she had left there when he looked into her room.

"Ah, Lord Kildonan, that was just what I suggested to you," said Frank.

She shot him an inquiring and rather venomous look as she went on:

"I feel so utterly tired out now that I shall sleep for the rest of the morning. I came in just to ask you not to come, or send to disturb me, Archibald." She rose as she spoke, and turned to Frank in a proud and defiant manner. "I suppose I shall see you at luncheon, Dr. Armathwaite?"

"No, your ladyship; I am on the point of starting on my visits to my patients."

"Indeed! Then I will see you off myself."

And she moved towards the door.

"Dr. Armathwaite is in no hurry, Aphra," said Lord Kildonan, who was still unusually grave.

"Neither am I," said she, with deep and deferential mock-sweetness, as she leaned languidly against the door with her fingers on the handle, while there burned in her eyes the determination not to leave the doctor for one moment alone with her husband. Her mind on this subject was so clearly made up that Frank saw that even if he had earnestly wished for another *tête-à-tête* with Lord Kildonan, it was out of the question now. So he shook hands with his host, who looked him straight in the eyes with a peculiar confidence and kindness, and was forced by the lady to precede her out of the room.

On arriving at the end of the gallery, he raised the heavy Marie Antoinette curtain which shut it off from the hall, and, turning, held it aside for her to pass under. As he thus let the streaming daylight upon her, he saw more than in the darkened study he had been able to notice. She was not only pallid, heavy of eye, leaden of foot; the excitement of the last few minutes having already in great measure subsided, she was rapidly becoming lethargic, and while she stared before her in an abstracted manner, her lips moved, as if she was repeating something mechanically to herself. Frank felt suddenly cold as he looked at her, and was struck with pity and horror. He took one of her hands, the palm of which was hot and dry, and said, in a low voice, bending over her with a kindly yearning to save a reckless creature from the threatening ruin her own fault had brought about :

"Lady Kildonan, listen to me. I am not your enemy, as you think. I would save you if I could. I can even now if you are ready to save yourself. But you must work against yourself, and let the good self conquer the evil now, at once, or it will be too late. One more step in the wrong direction, and no power on earth can save you. Try, I implore you ; I conjure you, try ! "

He hissed out these words with almost fiery earnestness close to her indifferent ear. When he had finished, she drew back her head and looked at him with languid recklessness, which had a most unhappy fascination.

"I am not in the mood for great efforts, doctor ; neither am I in the mood to be detained while you whisper sweet nothings in my ear. Your patients must be waiting. I have come to see you off. Pray let me have that pleasure."

She leaned back against a carved cabinet, just as she had leaned once before for an exciting little *tête-à-tête* with him. Whether her indifference was real or feigned, or the result of utter fatigue of mind and body, she seemed to have at the moment no objects in life more serious than his departure and her consequent freedom to go and rest. With one long, hopeless, fascinated look at her, Frank, attracted and repelled, pitying and yet profoundly disgusted, bowed, left her, and crossed the hall to the door. Just before he closed it behind him he gave one glance back, saw her throw her arms wide as if to shake off some benumbing, unwelcome influence, and disappear behind the curtains which hung before the entrance to the staircase.

It was past four o'clock when Frank, who had done the day's work on foot, set his face homewards.   He felt an inexplicably strong longing to reach home quickly, and when at last he opened the door of the sitting-room and saw Alma sitting by Millie's side, it was without the least surprise that he came forward and held out his hand to her.

"Aren't you surprised to see her?" asked Millie, jubilantly.

She was in high spirits, having a three-sheet letter on her lap, covered thickly with a man's handwriting.

"No," answered Frank, simply, without thought. Then he corrected himself, seeing astonishment on Millie's face and inquiry on Alma's.   "I mean I'm more pleased than anything else."

Mrs. Crosmont looked pale and sad, but there was a determination in her face which reminded him oddly of the expression he had seen on Lord Kildonan's face when he spoke of the discovery of his agent's harshness to the tenants.   He was prepared, therefore, for another disclosure; and when Millie, who believed, or affected to believe, that Alma had come for a consultation with Armathwaite as her medical adviser, left them together, he encouraged her to come at once to the point by assuring her that he guessed about what subject she was going to consult him.

"It is about my husband!" said she.

"Go on!" said Armathwaite.

CHAPTER XXVI.

It was not easy for Alma to go on with her story.   Ned Crosmont had been a husband to her only in name; but the very word forms a claim upon a pure-hearted woman, who remembers the hopes and affection with which she looked forward to a life with the man of her choice, long after those feelings have given place to doubt and despair.   So she hesitated to make the confession which laid bare the mockery her married life had been; and, at last, after a pause, Frank Armathwaite asked her if she had slept well the night before.

A deep blush rose to her face as she raised her eyes to his.

"I slept a long time," she said, in a broken voice. "And I had the dreadful dreams again. When I woke up it was very early in the morning, and I was out-of-doors, walking towards the house."

"And when did you go to sleep?"

"In the afternoon. I was in my husband's study. He sent me to sleep; I had suspected it before; I suppose you knew."

"Yes."

There was a long pause. Then she changed her seat for one nearer to him, and spoke in a frightened whisper.

"Do you know why he sends me to sleep? And what those dreams mean? I hardly dare to ask."

"I think you had better not trouble yourself any more about this, and you must think about it as little as you possibly can help, for I can tell you this: you need not fear that you will have that sleep or those dreams again."

"Not have them again?" she repeated, in a low voice. Then she asked fearfully, "What is going to happen? Is it something dreadful—dreadful for Ned? Uncle Hugh has written both to Millie and to me, saying that I am to keep a good heart, for everything will be all right soon. But if it will be all right for me, it will be all wrong for Ned, won't it? I feel that it will. And I must tell you—I get more and more sorry for him every day. As he gets harder and more irritable, I can feel that it is his trouble that makes him so; but I cannot comfort him; he will not let me. And I am afraid to think what it is that Uncle Hugh means to say to him."

Armathwaite was silent for a little while, considering this message of Uncle Hugh's, and shrewdly suspecting that what he had to say would be said not to his nephew, but to Lord Kildonan. He asked if he might see the letter. Alma produced it from her pocket, and he read it through. Uncle Hugh mentioned that he had heard of his "little one's" ever-increasing lassitude from Millie, and he spoke in very harsh terms of Ned, and said he wanted a lesson, and recommended Alma to leave him.

"I have written to tell him not to be hard on Ned, since he is unhappy and overworked," said Alma, as she took back the letter. "As for leaving him while he is miserable, and even ill, I shouldn't think of doing it. For though I cannot comfort him now, still I may some day. A fancy has come into my head—I am full of fancies, you know," she added, smiling sadly—"that before long he will want me, though he does not treat me very well now. This fancy has only come to me this morning, when I remembered his face as he talked to me yesterday. But it has quite taken away my fear of him."

"You can't care for him still, surely?" burst out Frank, in spite of himself rather indignantly.

Again her face flushed as she answered :

"I'm afraid I don't very much, especially when I feel afraid. But I want to."

The feeling of duty, a natural yearning affectionateness, and perhaps the pretty feminine fancy for taming a brute, all conduced to make her, as Frank thought, almost ridiculously forgiving and meek.

"You see," she continued, noting a little impatience in her companion's face and attitude, "it would be silly of me to be afraid when I have such good friends near," with a little uplook of the most innocent and yet alluring coquetry to assure him that she was not ungrateful.

"How did you come here?" asked Frank, after a pause. "Surely you did not walk the whole way?"

"I came part of the distance in the carrier's cart from Conismere. I had spent the morning in my room, feeling very, very heavy and tired, as I always do after those —sleeps, and I heard the outer bell ring, and Lady Kildonan's voice downstairs. She went straight to Ned's study." A shadow came over Alma's face and a reserve into her manner as she mentioned the lady's name. "The sound of her voice roused me, made me feel bitter and angry ; all my thoughts seemed to whirl in my head in confusion, then I thought I would come and see you. I could not stay in the house while she was there!"

Alma's eyes flashed, and her cheeks burned. Frank was pleased at this show of spirit.

"I have been invited to go with Ned to dine there on Monday, at The Crags; but I don't want to go; I hate the thought of going. I shall make an excuse to stay away."

Frank made no attempt to combat her determination, and at that moment Millie peeped into the room and broke an awkward pause by enquiring whether the consultation was over.

Alma had been lucky enough to call upon a day when Mrs. Peele was performing a weekly pilgrimage to her husband's grave at Plasmere, from which she did not return until half-past six o'clock.

As there was still half-an-hour to spare before the widow's martial tread might be expected to resound in the little stone-paved hall outside, Millie pushed Mrs. Crosmont back into her chair as she rose to go.

"No," she said. "It is my turn for a consultation now, and I've something very serious to say to you, Mrs. Crosmont, which will have all the more weight from the presence of a witness. Listen, and perpend, Dr. Armathwaite, if a man *can* do the first, and knows what the second means."

"I am all attention, Miss Peele. I have even a note-book ready. When I have duly perpended, or weighed in my mind, your valuable utterances, down they shall go here in masterly shorthand."

"That will do. You are to listen, not to talk, since Heaven has spared me the trial of being one of your patients. Well, then, Mrs. Crosmont, you are aware that I am about to marry Mr. Hugh Crosmont."

"You mustn't expect to see him the blithesome creature he went away, after a long course of this young person's letters," said Frank to Alma in a loud aside, which Millie affected to ignore.

"Now I have a very strong suspicion," pursued Millie, "that if he had been allowed to remain quietly at Ned Crosmont's, he would have remained so wrapt up in his 'little one' that he would have had never a thought to spare for poor me. So I should like it to be understood," continued the girl merrily, but with a certain under-current of good-humoured determination in her tone, "that for the future his little one is myself, and that he must not think that he will be allowed to philander, however paternally, around a lady who, I am not in a position to deny, rejoices in a much straighter nose than my good but plain visage can boast."

"Oh, Millie, how can you be so unkind! Are you going to make dear old Uncle Hugh dislike me?" cried poor Alma, in really plaintive accents.

"I don't know, madam. It depends a good deal upon your own conduct. For I must tell you that he is no longer to be 'dear old Uncle Hugh;' I am going to make a dashing young fellow of him, to put a little more romance into the thing. So if you will remember this, and treat him, not as a kind old fogey-friend to be kissed and petted, but as a 'gay young Lutherian' like my neighbour on the left,"—and she gave a laughing glance at Armathwaite—"why, then, I will spare you, and write you out an order to view my property, and say nothing worse of you than that you are a good creature enough, but frivolous. That's the trump card of us plain women you know," said Millie. "Everyone who is better-looking is eaten up by frivolity. So now I have put you on your guard."

They all laughed, and Frank affected much sympathy for the bridegroom of such a jealous termagant, and they kept up a lively chatter, which cheered Alma, until within a few minutes of the time of Mrs. Peele's return. Frank insisted on putting Alma into a fly for her return journey. As he led her down the garden-path towards it, he heard her breathe a little sigh, and when he had helped her into the vehicle, he stayed a moment by the door to beg her not to be unhappy, and to ask what troubled her. After a little hesitation she said:

"That—that Millie said just now, about Uncle Hugh —she can't have meant it, could she?"

"I—I almost think she did—a little," he answered reluctantly. "You see, poor, dear, good old Millie

knows she isn't handsome, and—and you are a dangerous rival, even as a daughter, Mrs. Crosmont."

"But Uncle Hugh! Uncle Hugh is the only person
in all the world who loves me," murmured the poor
lady in a broken, scarcely audible voice.

This was too much for Armathwaite; he felt his very
heart wrung. He thrust a strong, warm hand into the
carriage, and arrested hers on its way to dry her eyes.

"Oh, I shouldn't think that—I shouldn't trouble
about that!" he whispered gruffly. "If you haven't
got an uncle, why—why there are brothers about, you
know, lots of brothers, good brothers, who would—who
would punch a man's head, or do anything kind; they
would, indeed. Don't cry. Promise to—hold up, and
—and—and—things will all come right—they will
indeed."

Alma squeezed his hand violently, and gave him a
grateful look out of tearful eyes. He smiled back at
her, biting his lip, and shut up the window for her very
softly, as if he had been packing some fragile toy. He
stood for a moment watching the fly as it drove off.

"I wish they wouldn't look like that," he said to
himself, in a vexed tone—"I do wish they wouldn't.
It makes a fool of a man. If she does it again, I—I shall
have to go away. It's quite as much as I can do not to
be a confounded ass now—quite."

And he re-entered the house briskly, trying valiantly
to shake off that odd, unwelcome sensation.

For the next two days, Saturday and Sunday, Frank
saw nothing either of the Crosmonts or of the inmates
of The Crags; but on the third, the day of the dinner-
party, he was shocked and surprised to see Lord Kildonan's phaeton stopping before the house of the
woman who, according to Uncle Hugh, was in the
habit of going to Liverpool in the train by which Ned
Crosmont travelled. Lord Kildonan was quite alone,
having dispensed with the services of a groom. He
was descending from the carriage at the moment when
he caught sight of the young doctor, and waiting for
him to come up, he asked if he had a few minutes to
spare.

"Yes, I am quite at your service," said Frank, very much impressed by the marked alteration he noticed in the old lord's manner.

"Will you get into the phaeton, then, and when I have made a call, which won't take me long, we will drive a little way together."

Frank agreed, and watched the old Scotchman attentively as he knocked at the door of the house, which was opened by a tall, respectable-looking woman, with a hard, mean face. Lord Kildonan seemed to have grown suddenly older; his head was more bent, his step was slower, but his gait had lost all its usual ambling awkwardness, and his face and manner, while missing much of the old easy good-humour, had gained an unsuspected dignity. Frank waited for his reappearance with much anxiety and curiosity as to the means by which this change had been brought about; but he did not learn the whole truth until much later.

The fact was that Mr. Hugh Crosmont, growing more and more indignant as the news he received from the Lake side showed that his nephew was getting day by day more harassed and morose, while his wife, under his treatment, lost daily more of life and energy, made up his mind, since advice and warnings to Ned were alike useless, to communicate to Lord Kildonan himself his surmises that all was not right with the young agent. He had a very high opinion of the old Scotchman's rectitude and sense of justice, and believed that he would judge the indiscretions of youth with mildness. Uncle Hugh was not without doubts whether, if he investigated deeply, Lord Kildonan might not find errors in the agent's accounts; but he felt certain that these would only become graver by delay, and that the sooner the growing evil was stopped, the better it would be for landlord, tenants, the agent's wife and the agent himself. So he wrote a careful and guarded letter to Lord Kildonan, reminding him that he had done a rather incautious thing in putting so much responsibility upon such inexperienced shoulders as Ned's, expressing a fear that the young fellow had got under the influence of injudiciously-chosen companions, and recording the fact, for what it was worth, that he had seen a woman, whose address Uncle Hugh gave, go up in the same train with him on his journeys to Liverpool. He recommended his nephew to merciful consideration, not only on account of his youth and of his undoubted industry and energy, but because of the deep depression and anxiety from which it was evident that he was suffering, a depression so great that it was affecting his bodily health. It was altogether a kind and manly letter; and Lord Kildonan, who received it on the Saturday morning, was moved by it, not merely into emotion, but into action.

Forgetting the extreme feebleness of his health, in which he had been encouraged to believe, he spent that day in driving about the estate, personally collecting details as to the treatment of the tenants, and the next, after asking for a dispensation for such employment of the Sabbath, in collating such information as he had obtained, as a preliminary to asking Ned Crosmont for the books, as he intended to do in such a manner as to allay suspicion. On the Monday morning he telegraphed to two banks at Liverpool where he kept a drawing account, and where he kept various securities, for a statement of his affairs with them. By return telegram came information which left him in no doubt that certain of the securities had been withdrawn without his knowledge, a ridiculously easy matter, since Lord Kildonan had allowed them to be entered in his agent's name. It was at this point of his investigations that Lord Kildonan, already much shaken by his discoveries, had availed himself of the information given by Uncle Hugh to visit the woman who, it might be presumed, had influenced Ned in his misdeeds. He was in the house altogether about twenty minutes, during which Frank Armathwaite waited in the phaeton with much impatience and anxiety.

When at last the house-door opened and Lord Kildonan appeared, after the first glance Frank scarcely dared to look at him. If he had looked changed that morning, now he seemed to be transformed. Hardly a trace of the Lord Kildonan of a week ago was left in this erect, determined old man, with hard, cold eyes, and mouth shut like a hasp. Behind him stood the woman, holding the door wide open with great obsequiousness, and looking extremely well satisfied with the result of the interview. She even followed her visitor politely a few steps down the path, and the doctor noticed that she limped in her walk. Lord Kildonan mounted into his seat with scarcely any assistance from the doctor's hand, and said very quietly, but in a dry, rasping voice: "Drive a little way through the town. I wish to speak to you."

Frank took up the reins, and obeyed. Even if he had objected to do so, there was no disobedience possible to the old lord this morning.

"It is true, I believe, that Dr. Peele put the greatest confidence in you?"

"Yes, I think I may say that he did."

"He told you all particulars of the cases under his care?"

"Yes, that I might take them up in place of him."

"He was a great friend of my—of the late Mr. Dighton; he was the family physician, and knew all the secrets of the family, as such men must do."

"I dare say he did, your lordship."

"You *know* he did," snapped Lord Kildonan in a grating voice, turning to look at him with cold, penetrating eyes.

"Yes, I know that he did."

"And such secrets also passed to you?"

"No, Lord Kildonan." Armathwaite looked at him back with perfectly candid eyes. "They were to have passed to me, but they never reached me."

"How was that?"

"He left his writing-table to me, and stated in his will that all the papers it contained were to come to me also. But when it came into my hands, there were no documents in it of the least importance. Either Dr. Peele changed his mind at the last, and destroyed them, or—they had been abstracted before the table reached my hands."

"By whom?"

"Well, presumably by some person who believed in a prior right to the doctor's effects."

Lord Kildonan's lips tightened still more. "Women are the breed of h——" he muttered. Then, in a louder voice, he said : "Drive to the doctor's house; we must have those papers."

Frank could only obey. When they reached the garden-gate of the little house they both got out of the phaeton, and leaving the old horse, who was as quiet as a lamb, they went up the garden-path, and Lord Kildonan rang the bell and asked for Mrs. Peele.

Yes, she was at home, the maid said. So the gentlemen walked into the chilly little drawing-room, and after an audible rustling about the next room and a sepulchral whispering in a deep voice, the widow entered the room, and extended her hand to Lord Kildonan, all dignity and graciousness. But he was no longer the man whom she was prepared to welcome. He touched her majestic hand with the tips of his fingers and said :

"Good morning, madam. I have come on business."

Mrs. Peele looked astonished, but indicated a chair with a stately wave of her hand. Lord Kildonan, with a cold, hard dignity which shrivelled up into barrenness her ponderous majesty, declined.

"I would rather stand, madam, thank you. I have only a few minutes to spare."

The widow, under all her airs, began to look rather uneasy. Frank remained in the background, a silent spectator of the encounter. Lord Kildonan turned towards him.

"This gentleman, I understand, had all your husband's documents and papers bequeathed to him."

Mrs. Peele started and changed colour as if a cannon ball had fallen at her feet.

"Really, your lordship, that is no affair of mine," she said as soon as she had recovered herself a little.

"I am sorry to be forced to disagree with you, madam. Certain important papers were abstracted from among the rest between the time of your husband's death and his funeral. You see I am in full possession of the circumstances ; as no person interested in the matter had access to the room at that time except yourself, it is matter not for surmise but certainty that it was you who took them. I have come to request—to insist—that you give them up immediately to the person to whom they were left by your husband."

The widow, with an angry glance at Armathwaite, murmured something about their having been destroyed.

"No, madam, that is an act you did not dare commit," said Lord Kildonan, solemnly. "I beg you not to force me to take extreme measures, but to deliver up the documents at once."

But Mrs. Peele flushed and then grew pallid, while in her eyes there shone an abject, furtive fear.

"I dare not," she whispered, and her deep voice was hoarse and thick. "Not before you, my lord—not before you."

There was a moment's dead silence. Then the voice of Lord Kildonan, hard, but with a quiver in it, spoke again in tones of command such as there was no disobeying.

"I command you, fetch them, and give them, not to me, but to the person to whom they belong."

Mrs. Peele drew a gasping breath, gave one furtive, terror-stricken look at her guest's stern face, and slowly turned towards the door. Before she could reach it, Lord Kildonan was there, holding it open for her to pass out.

"You understand," he said, putting a thin bony hand imperatively on her arm. "*All* the papers, with nothing kept back."

"Yes, your lordship," she whispered like a lamb as she went out.

The two men awaited her return in absolute silence. This was no meeting in which the pauses could be filled by small talk. Frank Armathwaite found himself counting her footsteps when, after a very few moments, Mrs. Peele was heard coming down the stairs. He opened the door for her, impatient of a second's delay. As she came in he saw at a glance that the bundle of papers she held in her hand was that with which he had seen Dr. Peele, in the last days of his life, so often occupied.

The widow seemed even at that moment to wish to keep
them back, as he stood holding out his hand to receive
them.

" Restore them," said Lord Kildonan, coldly.

"Don't, don't give them up," murmured the widow,
huskily, as she put the packet with trembling fingers
into Armathwaite's hand.

But there was a stronger will than hers at work. As
soon as the papers rustled in the doctor's nervous clutch,
the old Scotchman held out his own long, lean hand with
a look half-piteous, half-commanding, which Frank could
not resist.

" For God's sake give them up to me ! " he said with
dry lips, in a rattling voice. " For I know that they
concern—my wife ! "

Armathwaite yielded them up without a word, and
Lord Kildonan, with steps that for a moment tottered,
passed, with a cold inclination to the lady, out of the
house.

CHAPTER XXVII.

WHEN Lord Kildonan left Mrs. Peele's house with the
late doctor's papers clasped tightly in his hand, Frank
Armathwaite followed him, fearing what effect the reading of the documents might have upon him. But the
old Scotchman had self-command enough to put off
examining them until he should have reached the solitude
of his own rooms. Hearing footsteps behind him, he
turned when he came to the garden-gate, and stretched
his mouth to a little withered smile as he noted the deferential sympathy in the young man's face.

" Have no fear for me," he said, kindly, as he laid his
hand on Frank's shoulder and moved on towards the
carriage with him. " Because I've been an old fule for
so long, it doesn't follow that I've no wits about me
when occasion calls for them. You understand,
Frank," he added, in a graver tone, calling the young
fellow by his Christian name for the first time, "that all
you have seen and heard this morning is a sealed secret

between you and me. And mind, laddie, whatever happens this evening, you will look upon in the same way. If you hear words you didn't expect to hear, you winna look up or tak' notice of them ; nothing will surprise you, and whatever your kind heart may prompt ye to, you will not by so much as a look warn others that are not so keen as yersel'."

Frank promised with a heavy heart. The time for warning the victims of their own guilty folly was indeed past now.

"Remember, you will be with us this evening to dine."

Frank had forgotten the dinner party at The Crags, and he now wished he could get out of it. Sitting in the presence of Ned Crosmont and Lady Kildonan, he would feel like a conspirator. However, there was no help for it ; the old lord was determined he should come. So he assured him that he would certainly not forget, and then offered to drive him home, as he was afraid of the effect of so much unusual exertion upon a frame already tried by a terrible excitement. His offer was accepted, and they drove almost in silence back to The Crags, and separated with a grave farewell.

At seven o'clock, Frank Armathwaite found himself again at the great house. He was feeling so guiltily nervous under the consciousness of some awful catastrophe pending over the inmates, that it scarcely seemed to him possible that Lady Kildonan, who sprang up from a sofa in the drawing-room as he was announced, could fail to detect the guilty knowledge which seemed to Frank to be inscribed all over him. He was the first guest to arrive, and such a strong dread seized him of the few minutes' *tête-à-tête* which might be before him, that he stopped short in the middle of the room as if lightning-struck, watching the lady with fascinated eyes as she bounded across the carpet towards him with the lissom, rapid, greyhound movements peculiar to her. She looked more brilliantly beautiful than he had ever before seen her ; dressed in pearly-white silk embroidered with gold, a little more handsomely, without doubt, than most ladies who give dinner-parties in the country, she looked more like an idealized picture of a queen than a flesh-and-blood provincial beauty. Armathwaite felt, as he looked at her, that he could not stand by and see this lovely woman run her dainty head into a noose, even if it were prepared by the most cruelly deceived husband in the world, without an effort to make her avoid her danger. He hoped with all his heart, as she ran towards him, that she was going to overwhelm him with accusations, reproaches, to tell him that she had discovered that a trap had been set for her, and to taunt him with being concerned in it.

He was disappointed, ashamed, miserable, when she reached him in an atmosphere of faint perfume from the azaleas on her breast, and thrust both her hands into his with a laughing welcome.

"I am glad you have come first. I told you a quarter of an hour earlier than the others that you might be here first, because I want to talk to you. Sit here."

She half swung him round, being nearly as muscular as she was graceful, on to the sofa where she had been sitting, and placed herself beside him.

"Now," she said, "don't you think I am sweet to you, considering that you spend your time persuading my husband that I want to poison him, and inventing all sorts of other accusations against me quite as baseless?"

But she did not look sweet; she looked reckless and fiercely defiant, and her hands burned with fever, while on this close inspection in the candle-light Armathwaite saw that the brilliant glow of her eyes and cheeks was hectic and unwholesome.

"I have never brought an accusation of any kind against you, Lady Kildonan." Then he added, boldly, looking her straight in the face, "Nobody accuses you ; but your own acts do."

"What acts ?—what acts ? I don't understand you," she said, restively, curving her white throat with a proud bend.

"Oh, Lady Kildonan, you are too clever to misunderstand me !"

"Indeed, you overrate my intelligence as much as you undervalue both my integrity and my humility. For I am not a woman to be lectured. And, to tell you the truth, lectures are thrown away upon me. I am not like other women ; upon them, like harps, you can produce, with a little skill, any air you will. I am like an Æolian lyre—wild, irresponsible, that sounds only to the music of the winds. And perhaps the worst wind, the fiercest, the most destructive, plays the best upon me. I tell you, I don't care ; I must live my life as I will, or as the winds will. Do you understand ? "

She rose, and looked down upon him with wilful, imperial haughtiness, leaning with her hand upon the high carved white marble mantel-piece.

" I wish I did not," said Frank, gravely.

" And now," she went on, more lightly, without a moment's heed of the solemnity and anxiety of his manner, " are you or are you not curious to know why I wanted to see you ? "

" I should be very glad to know," said Frank, rising too, that he might look down instead of up at her.

" Well, then, I want to see you as a patient. I am really ill at last. I cannot sleep, or when I do I have frightful dreams. My hands always burn like this." She laid a hot palm on the back of his hand. " My head is always hot and heavy, and I cannot keep still. I seem just for these last few days to be on fire day and night too. I feel as if something would burst in my head. Now that can't be right, and it is what your beautiful peaceful country life has brought me to. I tell you, the *ennui* of it is so great that I don't care what happens to change it, as my husband will find some day, and before very long, too, if he doesn't take care. Do you believe me now when I tell you I must go away, I must have a change, and that if he won't take me I——"

Armathwaite interrupted her.

" Yes, yes ; don't go on or you will say more than you mean. Listen. I see that you are not well, that the life you are leading is not good for you. But whose fault is that ? "

" Yours—my husband's—my father's—the fault of everyone who wishes or has wished to keep me in this stagnant place ! " burst out the lady with passion.

"No, Lady Kildonan ; it is your own. I can't talk platitudes to you now. You have made excitements for yourself of the most dangerous kind."

She started, and turned in a moment quite white.

"What—what do you know ? No—what do you mean ?" she stammered, drawing her breath heavily. "How dare you ?"

"I am only daring to tell you the truth. You are ruining your health, your happiness. You know that. You are doing harm and wrong not only to yourself but to others. All the pleasure has gone out of your life ; you are being drawn nearer and nearer to a whirlpool that will at last suck you down. You must stop ; you must calm yourself, and be wise in time. Lady Kildonan, if I, in my capacity of physician, give my whole energies to curing you, saving you, will you give me your word you will try with your whole might to resist temptation and to save yourself ?"

She looked impressed, frightened. Her large blue eyes were glittering, and her fingers moved restlessly.

"I—I don't know. If I do what you want what will you do ?"

"I will do my best to persuade your husband to take you away at once."

"You will ? Oh !"

She clasped his hands impulsively, as if she had been drowning, and a life-buoy had been thrown to her.

Her horrible, half-hysterical earnestness made Armathwaite shiver. She stood clutching his hands for several moments, and the doctor had to draw them away, and recall her to herself as voices sounded outside the door heralding the approach of some more of her guests. She had scarcely recovered herself, when the door was thrown open, and there entered three members of one of the "best" families of the neighbourhood, plump father, plumper mother, and round-backed daughter dressed in white piqué, with a taste for abstruse branches of learning. They were by no means the sort of people who are "easily entertained," and Lady Kildonan was not in the mood to work very hard to entertain them

Frank did his best to make conversation with the round-backed daughter, who happened to be seated the nearest to him, and he was rewarded for his pains by glances of open and simple-minded anxiety from mamma, fearful of the ineligible charms of the handsome doctor. On the whole, social intercourse languished, and when the door opened again, this time to admit Lord Kildonan, everybody felt relieved except his wife, who gave a careless glance at him, and remained as indifferent as ever, restlessly tapping her foot on the floor, and playing fiercely with the azaleas on her dress, the heads of which she snapped off one by one, crushed between her fingers, and threw away.

Frank watched his host narrowly, and it seemed to him scarcely credible that Lady Kildonan, excited and preoccupied as she was, could fail to notice the great change in her husband, which, instead of wearing off, seemed to have intensified since the morning. The rest of his guests noticed it, and their surprise at meeting a cold, stern old man, instead of the kindly, genial friend to whom they were accustomed, caused a hush to fall upon the party, now grown larger by fresh arrivals. The last to enter was Ned Crosmont, his face looking more drawn and harassed than ever: his eyes were sunken and his sallow skin looked sickly and pallid. Whether it was on account of his unhealthy looks, or whether the stories about him had been whispered more widely of late, his appearance was certainly the cause of an increased depression and silence in the assembly, of which Lord Kildonan seemed, with unusual keenness, to be the first to be conscious. Crosmont was at once absorbed in watching Lady Kildonan, and he seemed to have hardly enough self-control left to veil the fact.

As for the lady herself, she scarcely seemed to notice him, to notice anything. The significant circumstance, which spoke volumes to the watchful Armathwaite, that her husband, usually unable to keep his loving eyes from straying to her face, now studiously refrained from a single look in her direction, was quite unmarked by her. Never having cared which way his glances went, she was not likely to know now. She and Crosmont, absorbed in their own cares, were the only persons in the room who saw no alteration in the master of the house. The agent, to do him justice, would probably have been more clear-sighted, but that Lord Kildonan carefully kept out of his way.

A rather imperious old gentleman among the guests, who, dimly perceiving that something was wrong, made a bad guess at the cause, presently took Lord Kildonan's arm, and, looking at Aphra, with much assumption of acumen, said:

"Now I daresay many people would think just because your wife looks flushed and as handsome as ever, that she is in the best of health. But I knew better in a moment. And if I hadn't known it by looking at her, why I should have learnt it by looking at you. One can see you are as anxious as possible; bless you, I could tell by your face in a minute that something was wrong, and then I discovered in a twinkling that it was because you were worried about her. Now wasn't it?"

This astute gentleman was standing between the husband and the wife, and he took care to turn from the one to the other, that his extraordinary perspicacity should not be lost upon either of them. Lady Kildonan, who was talking idly, and without much effort to be coherent or entertaining, turned to listen to him. Something in the tone of her husband's voice as he answered, did, at last, strike her as unusual, and she glanced at him, and stopped to hear what he had to say.

"Yes," he said, in a grating voice, turning his face in his wife's direction, but looking over her head at a painting on the wall, "I quite agree with you, Sir Bernard, she does not look well. And I fear it is my fault, too. She leaves a nice warm room every evening to come down a long, cold, draughty gallery to visit me at my work. It is a kind imprudence that I am not going to suffer any longer." Lady Kildonan looked astonished, and her surprise increased as he went on, addressing her: "Aphra," he said, in the same dry voice, but with great courtesy, "you must no longer pay me that visit at night during my work. I have been most selfish to exact it, and I will do so no more. You have caught cold by it, and it has made you feverish, I can see. You understand that for the future I shall not expect it."

She rose slowly during this speech, examining his face, at first evidently somewhat puzzled. But as he went on she became gradually convinced that he was in earnest; and when he glanced quickly at her as he uttered his closing words, he saw upon her face a look of feverish relief and satisfaction.

At that moment dinner was announced. To Armathwaite—who talked mechanically to the lady by his side, and could not remember afterwards who she was—the meal was like a banquet of Royalists during the Reign of Terror. The heavy scent of the blossoming plants with which Lady Kildonan, in her love for all bright things, caused the table to be loaded from end to end, until it appeared to be spread for a feast of flowers, seemed to him deadly, poisonous; the candles, in tall gold-plated candlesticks that sprang up among the banks of foliage and bright blossoms, reminded him of the lights round a coffin; the talk that buzzed about him rang hollow in his ears, and the beautiful woman in her robe of white and gold, who sat at the head of the table, seemed to his excited fancy to be simply the victim of a gorgeous sacrifice, to which lights, flowers, and laughter were but weird accompaniments. For, before the second course was over, Lord Kildonan had uttered words which, bearing a deep significance to Armathwaite only, told him that Lady Kildonan's doom was fixed as surely as if, following out his fancy, she had been summoned to the guillotine. This was all the old Scotchman had said, in a quiet, almost indifferent tone, that bore no trace of suspicion:

"I want you to go up to Liverpool again to-morrow, Crosmont, to see about some business that I forgot when you went up the other day. You won't mind going, will you?" he added, with his usual courtesy.

"I am quite at your service, your lordship," answered the agent, while Lady Kildonan, from the other end of the table, watched and listened with kindling eyes.

Armathwaite involuntarily found himself casting intense, almost imploring glances, first at Crosmont and then at Lady Kildonan. Neither of them noticed him ; but as he turned his head away from the lady he met the gaze of her husband, peremptory, stony, reminding him of his promise. The rest of the dinner was torture to to the young man; he saw that a trap had been laid for the guilty couple, into which both were ready to fall, and that ruin and misery not only to them but to those nearest to them would surely be the result.

When the gentlemen followed the ladies into the drawing-room, Lord Kildonan, breaking through his usual custom, went too. Armathwaite waited for an opportunity of speaking to him apart, and was glad, when a few minutes after their return to the drawing-room, his host came straight to the corner where he was standing by himself, watching Crosmont and Lady Kildonan as they conversed under cover of a "brilliant" fantasia which a young lady was performing on the piano. Under the clever affectation of trifling conversation, which Lady Kildonan knew how to assume, Frank thought he could detect that she was urging Crosmont to some course against which the agent was protesting. Lord Kildonan followed the direction of the doctor's eyes as he came up.

"Have you anything important to do to-morrow evening ? " he asked, laying his hand with more of command than affection on the young man's shoulder.

"Nothing whatever, Lord Kildonan."

"Then you will come up here some time between six and half-past ? You need not say anything about it, I think, to anybody. Bring your ulster."

Having received a somewhat reluctant assent, he was moving away, when Frank detained him, saying, in a very deferential but earnest voice :

"I beg your pardon, Lord Kildonan. I have something very important to tell you, and to suggest to you. You will allow me to speak frankly, will you not ? "

"With as much frankness as you can, if you please. It is a virtue which needs encouragement in this part of the world."

"I had a talk, on my arrival, with Lady Kildonan. She is ill, very seriously ill, in spite of her brilliant appearance. Lord Kildonan, I beg you, don't treat her harshly just now. A shock, a sudden disturbance of any kind, might have the most dangerous effects upon her. She is in a highly excited and excitable state, and the very least harm you might anticipate from a shock would be the complete unhinging of her mind."

Lord Kildonan listened quite coldly, with his mouth set in a straight hard line, and without a moment's softening of the eyes.

Armathwaite continued : " Put off your investigations ; make them unnecessary. Take your wife away ; give her change of air, and scene, and amusement. Then when her mind has recovered its usual tone, you can make what accusations or reproaches you will, and spare yourself the remorse you will feel if you attack her when she is weakest—with the consequences I foresee. Remember her wishes, her caprices have been indulged all her life until she is utterly unable to fight against them. Is it not fair that those who have helped to do her this harm, although it was done in kindness, should judge her lightly ? "

But during this appeal the Scotchman's face remained quite unmoved. The only sign of agitation he betrayed was the Gaelic accent which appeared in his next words.

"Judgment, Dr. Armathwaite," he said, drily, "should be in proportion to the offence, or it is not justice. At present, the matter in hand is to ascertain the measure of the offence. Judgment should come afterwards. In your case, unless your knowledge is greater than mine, which I doubt, judgment seems to have been severe and premature. If you have no confidence either in my justice or my judgment, I will release you from your appointment to-morrow night."

Even when thus challenged, Frank would not pledge himself to approval of the harsh determination he saw stamped on Lord Kildonan's face.

" If you want me, your lordship, of course I am at your service," he said, simply.

And his host, instead of letting him off, repeated : " Between six o'clock and half-past, then," and left him.

Soon after, Armathwaite took his leave. As he took the hot hand Lady Kildonan held out to him, and looking at her face, saw that her blue eyes scarcely noted a detail of the scene before her, and that her mind was busy with far-away thoughts and calculations, he knew that no further warning he could give, consistently with keeping his promise to her husband, could save her now. He glanced back at her from the door. She was crossing the room, with her white and gold train sweeping behind her. Like a queen she looked, he thought, as he watched her with irrepressible yearning sorrow and admiration—but a queen on the last night of her reign.

CHAPTER XXVIII.

On the following afternoon, at a quarter past six, Frank Armathwaite came back to The Crags, and was shown straight into the study where Lord Kildonan, with a long, dark travelling-cloak on the table beside him, was waiting. He greeted the young man with a warm grip of the hand and a rather grim smile.

"Ah, so you have not decided to desert me, after all," he said in a subdued voice, with a sort of cheerless satisfaction. "Are you prepared to take a journey with me?"

"I am prepared to do whatever you please, Lord Kildonan."

"Then you will have to be eyes and perhaps limbs for me to-night, for I am going to do without my spectacles ; and if I should want an arm to lean on—as, Heaven help me ! perhaps I may—I shall depend on yours."

At that moment a servant appeared, and informed his master that the phaeton was at the door. He rose, and signed to Armathwaite to pass out before him. The young man hesitated.

"My lord, forgive me," he said at last, in a choking voice, "but this journey will be the ruin of us all. It will be a black stain on our memories that nothing will

ever wash out.　　Better be content with what you know—
what you guess."

But Lord Kildonan put his hand through the young
man's arm and led him towards the door.

"There are some things, Dr. Armathwaite, that only
our own eyes can persuade us of.　　There are some forms
of deceit which, like a virulent poison, create in one a
thirst even for the poison itself."

They went along the gallery, crossed the hall, and got
into the phaeton in perfect silence.　　It came into Armathwaite's mind as they drove along rapidly in the darkness that this mournful and mysterious journey was like
a pilgrimage to fetch home the dead.　　They skirted the
head of the lake and went fast along the other side.
Frank scarcely dared to glance up at Crosmont's house,
standing out square and black from the side of the hill;
this gloomy errand, which was to lay bare the misdoings
of Alma's husband, would wring the poor lady's gentle
heart, and make Frank himself feel like a guilty wretch
when next he stood in her presence.

It was a cold night, but very clear.　　Frank's eyesight
was good enough for him to make out that a vehicle
some distance ahead of them, and going in the same
direction, was Crosmont's Norfolk cart.　　It stopped with
a very sudden pull up, to allow a figure that seemed to
spring suddenly up from the wayside to get in.　　Frank
told Lord Kildonan in a low voice what he saw, and
obeyed his direction to drive more slowly.　　The pause
made by the vehicle in front was the shortest possible;
still, acting under Lord Kildonan's instructions, Frank
allowed the distance between them to increase until the
Norfolk cart was undistinguishable in the gloom.　　On the
outskirts of Branksome, just where the first few straggling
houses began, there was a bend in the road, round which
the cart disappeared altogether.　　When the phaeton had
passed the bend in its turn, it was much closer to the
cart, which had apparently stopped to allow the temporary passenger to descend, for the driver was again alone.
Slackening pace, Frank drove on, following the cart,
which stopped at a little inn.　　Here the driver got out
and went indoors, while another man took his place, and

turned the cart round to drive back to Mereside : as the phaeton drove past, Frank saw that it was Crosmont's groom.

Always acting in accordance with Lord Kildonan's suggestions, the young doctor whipped up the horses, drove past the station, and stopped. The two gentlemen then alighted ; and after having given directions to the groom, a fellow-Northerner, in whose discretion his master had confidence, to drive straight back to The Crags without any stoppage, Lord Kildonan led the way into the station by a private entrance, and went straight to the station-master's room, where they could wait without fear of being seen. From time to time Frank, filled with the most gloomy apprehensions for the issue of this journey, cast a glance at the elder man full of warning and solemn entreaty. But Lord Kildonan sat looking at the huge fire which blazed in the rusty grate with a cast-iron face, on which the dancing flames threw ugly shadows, while not by a word or a movement did he encourage his companion to speak, or even seem conscious of his presence. Frank went to the door, and looked through the glass of the upper panels at the groups of passengers gathering on the platform as the Liverpool train was brought alongside. Crosmont was there among the earliest arrivals, pacing up and down, not with the sauntering tread of the ordinary traveller, but with the restless strides of a man whose journey is a flight. The station-master himself had brought Lord Kildonan two tickets, and had reserved a compartment for him and his companion exactly opposite to the room where they were waiting. Frank, still watching at the door, saw Crosmont stop suddenly short in his walk, and, looking along the platform in the direction of the agent's gaze, he saw a tall woman, shabbily dressed, with a limp in her gait, cross the platform hurriedly from the booking-office and get into a compartment by herself. Frank's heart seemed to leap up as he recognised the figure. Lady Kildonan must have got wind of her husband's intended pursuit, and invented an ingenious trick as a reward for him. Crosmont stood still until the woman closed the door of the compartment upon herself, then made straight for the nearest first-class carriage and got in. The guard was crying, " Take your seats ! " The doctor felt Lord Kildonan's hand upon his shoulder, and in a few moments they too had taken their places.

The journey to Liverpool occupied four hours and a half. During the first four hours the two men scarcely interchanged a dozen words. The elder sat so still that three or four times the younger disturbed him on some slight pretext, having been seized with a vivid fear that the prolonged horror of this night expedition had killed him. But each time he raised his head and met Frank's solicitous gaze with stony eyes that bade sympathy stand off and be silent, and sank back into his old attitude, his head a little on one side, as if listening intently to some ghastly story told by the rattle and the roar of the train. At a station where they had to change trains, Frank saw that Crosmont and the woman with the limping gait got silently, and with no sign of recognition, into the same carriage. They had but a few minutes to wait, and then on they went again, pursuers and pursued, all enduring the maddening bumpety-bump, bumpety-bump, of a slow train, that strives by an extra amount of jolting and rattling and pursy effort to delude the passengers into the belief that they are going at a more than blackberry-gathering pace. Frank found himself counting the revolutions of the wheels, making calculations about them, getting frantically into unmanageable millions and billions, all to a horrible wordless dirge, in which every engine-shriek, every rush of another train as it passed them, made a note of weird and mournful melody. When he found by his watch, and by a sudden increase of speed in the rate of travel, that they were drawing near Liverpool, his excitement reached a point at which he found it difficult to keep still. It was with a shock that he heard Lord Kildonan's voice addressing him in harsh and strident tones :

" You know that we shall soon be in now ? "

" Yes, your lordship."

" You know my errand there is not a pleasant one ?"

" Yes, I know that."

"Would you prefer to wait for me at the station, or will you accompany me?"

"I will accompany you."

"Are you prepared for what you will see?" asked Lord Kildonan, after a pause, fixing upon him his light grey gimlet eyes.

Frank hesitated. "I think so, Lord Kildonan. I have a strong hope also that your suspicions will prove to be worse, far worse, than the truth," he said at last, in a low voice.

Lord Kildonan gave a short, grating laugh.

"Oh, no, not worse than the truth; I will answer for that. You will come with me to the end, then?"

"Yes, my lord, if I may."

"May?" he echoed grimly, yet with a plaintive note in his voice. "Oh, yes, you may bear part of my griefs if you will; I am not selfish."

And he said no more until the train drew in at the Lime Street Station. Knowing in what part of the train the two persons on whose track they were had travelled, they found it easy to watch them into a close cab, and then, without being seen, to take a hansom themselves and direct the driver to follow at a little distance. As the woman crossed the platform, Frank watched her narrowly, and his spirits rose higher and higher as he noticed again the slight limp in her gait, and grew every moment more certain that Lord Kildonan, for his own happiness, for everyone's happiness, had been tricked, and was following the wrong woman. Should he prepare him now? Frank thought, as they got into the cab.

"Lord Kildonan," he began, with some diffidence, "are you quite certain of the identity of both the people we are following?"

But his suggestion received no encouragement, for his companion answered very drily:

"Quite certain."

And Frank saw that he must leave events to enlighten him.

They were driving down towards the docks, through a low part of Liverpool, along dark streets lined with small narrow houses, of evil aspect and evil name.

There was little traffic in these unsavoury byways of a city which is the very capital of vulgarity and ugliness; the few foot-passengers they passed in this silent quarter seemed to shuffle by cautiously in the darkness, or else to glide along the ill-paved streets with suspicious haste. More and more certain grew Armathwaite every moment that it was not the brilliant, dainty Lady Kildonan they were following. Whatever the errand might be which brought her on mysterious night visits to Liverpool, it would not be to this noisome labyrinth of narrow, close-smelling streets and shabby houses, with secrets of sin and wretchedness stamped on their physiognomy, that the luxurious lady would come. The cab, which was some distance in front of them, stopped in a street as dark and narrow as the rest, but in which a few houses, larger than the others, with doorways that had once been imposing and handsome, told that they had formerly occupied a better position in the world. Frank noted that the man and the woman they were following, after dismissing the cab which had brought them, walked slowly on and began to glance behind them from time to time.

"They suspect they are being followed?" whispered Frank, with excitement.

Lord Kildonan shook his head. "Suspicion is a habit with the people who frequent this quarter," he answered, in the same tone.

With his stick he directed the driver to turn the next corner, and then he and Armathwaite got out.

"Wait here for us," said Lord Kildonan. "We may be some time."

The man looked down at him scrutinizingly by the light of his lamp, and shook his head.

"I'd rather be paid my fare now, sir, if it's the same to you," he said. "I've driven parties hereabouts before, that have stayed some time, and when they come out they didn't always happen to have the money for a fare about them. No offence to you, gentlemen; but, you see, I know Liverpool, and I know the house you want, though you do get me to stop in the next street. I knows 'em by the quality, and when I bring reg'lar swell tip-toppers this way, it's always 82, Blank Street, they wants, though it's only the young 'uns as gives the address."

"I'll take your number, and give you a sovereign as a retaining fee," said Lord Kildonan, quietly. "That will restore your confidence, will it not? When I return, I will give you another sovereign to drive me back to Lime Street. Are you ready to wait?"

"Well, yes, sir, under those circumstances, certainly."

This colloquy took two or three minutes, and when Lord Kildonan and Armathwaite returned to Blank Street, the persons whom they were pursuing had disappeared. They walked the whole length of the street looking for No. 82, as the cabman had luckily given them an address which Lord Kildonan assumed to be the one of which they were in search. For a long time they looked in vain. Such houses as still retained traces of figures on their shabby doors, seemed to have been numbered and then re-numbered at random. There were lights in a few windows, but there was nothing to guide them in their search. At last they heard footsteps coming quickly along the street on the opposite side of the way—a man who seemed, by the glimpse they caught of him, to be well-dressed, and of the so-called "respectable" class, crossed the road, almost brushing past them, and went up a narrow court or passage which divided one of the small houses of the street from one of the largest. In the windows of the large house there was not a single light. Lord Kildonan gripped his companion's arm, not with nervous excitability, but with the satisfaction of discovery, and led him up the court in the rear of the stranger. The latter was so far ahead of them already that they had only time to see him pull a bell, which gave a faint, single sound, like that of a small gong, and, turning the handle of a door in the wall of the big house, disappear through it rapidly and without noise.

Lord Kildonan and Armathwaite came up to the door. By a ray of moonlight which pierced into the narrow court, and showed the woodwork to be shabby and unpretentious, they saw to the left of the door a small barred window with no light in it, which suggested a watchful eye behind, and under the bell the number 82 in very small figures. Lord Kildonan pulled the bell, opened the door, and walked in confidently, Armathwaite following, with a sense that all his youthful nerve did not enable him to put on so bold a front as the old Scotchman seemed to wear with ease. They were in a small, bare, stone-paved passage, with nothing to distinguish it from the kitchen entrance of an ordinary private house. There was a knife-cleaning machine against the white-washed wall to the right, a child's hoop, a broom, and two or three flower-pots containing half-dead plants, in various corners; all this was dimly visible by the light of a small oil-lamp that flared on a bracket to the left. Straight in front of the door was a passage, down which Lord Kildonan promptly proceeded to make his way. Armathwaite, who was following, heard a step behind him, and a man's voice saying: "I beg your pardon, sir." Turning, both gentlemen saw a little man, with a baize apron on, innocently occupied in brushing boots. Nothing could have seemed more genuine than this diligent man-servant's surprise at the intrusion of two strangers, but for a certain look of shrewd inquiry in his little black eyes, which the visitors did not fail to note. Armathwaite would have been completely disconcerted but for Lord Kildonan, who, tossing the man a sovereign, said briefly, "Members!" and turned again to walk on. Armathwaite remembered, with a flash of intelligence suddenly grown keener, a suspicion which had occurred to him before; by the time they had reached the end of the long, dark passage, he knew into what kind of house they had come, and was prepared for the sight which met their eyes when, directed by the sound of voices which broke upon their ears when they pulled open a baize-covered swing door on the left at the end of the passage, they entered a room, the atmosphere of which was almost unbearably close, containing four or five small card-tables. These were occupied by men, for the most part respectably but not well dressed, some quiet, some noisy, some speaking with the distinct utterance of the well-educated,

some with the brogue and the bur-r of farmers and
cattle-dealers, but almost all showing, either by open
and eager excitement, or by the equally unmistakable
self-restraint betrayed by straightened lips and steadily-
glowing eyes, the absorption of the genuine gambler.

So marked was this, that at the entrance of the new-
comers scarcely a man at the tables looked up. A few
among the onlookers, especially one or two of the over-
dressed and bold-faced women who hung about, but got,
while the play went on, but little attention, glanced at
them curiously, or watched them with hungry interest,
while Lord Kildonan glanced keenly round the room
with a wooden face, of which no muscle quivered. He
turned to Armathwaite, and putting his arm through
that of the young man, asked, in a low tone, which to an
outsider would have seemed one of indifference :

"You must come to the help of my poor old eyes.
Do you see anyone you know here? The truth—if you
please."

Armathwaite looked round, shaking with apprehension.
Then, after scouring every corner with a searching
glance, he said, with a long-drawn breath of so much
relief that his emphatic tone made some even among the
gamblers look up at him :

"No."

Lord Kildonan's face never changed. Without releasing the young man's arm, and with a courteous reply
to one of the women, who offered to find a table for
them, he crossed the room to a doorway, before which
hung a thick curtain. Raising this, they passed through
together.

The apartment they now entered was much larger
than the first. In addition to small tables in two of the
corners, it contained one long table, upon which the
deepest interest of the assembly was evidently concentrated. The players, in two long lines of coldly keen or
restlessly eager faces, sat on either side, and staked their
money, won or lost, in almost unbroken silence. The
game was baccarat, and the stakes were for the most part
high, as the new-comers could see by a glance at the
little piles of gold and notes that chinked and rustled on

the table.   A constantly-shifting but quiet crowd moved about, taking their places at the table or watching the play, with steady and almost silent interest.   If a young man, in a lively after-dinner mood, began to disturb with unwelcome hilarity the absorbed attention of the players, he would be led off with little delay to a third room, in which, by the sounds of vacuous and discordant laughter and the popping of champagne corks, which came upon the ears with a loud burst when the communicating door was open, it might be judged that less austerity prevailed.

Slowly and steadily, examining the players on the opposite side face by face, Lord Kildonan, his hand leaning a little more heavily on Armathwaite's as moment by moment passed and yet he made no discovery, worked his way through the crowd, always a little in the background, until they had nearly completed the circuit of the table.   There were but few women among the players.   Armathwaite's eyes noted each one with passionate hope that there might be none among them whom he could recognise.   On the first side of the table that they scanned there was no face, man's or woman's, that he knew.   As they drew slowly to the opposite side of the room he scarcely dared to look. The first hasty scrutiny reassured him.   An old woman, lean-faced, hideous, with faded eyes that saw nothing fair or good; a stout woman, whose age was not clear; and a third, insignificantly dressed, who wore mittens and had no other salient point about her, were the only exceptions to the row of male players.   The two younger women wore short veils, thick enough to hide the upper part of the face pretty completely.   Unutterably relieved, Armathwaite let Lord Kildonan lead him on, beginning at last to feel with some certainty that they had happily got on the wrong tack, when suddenly he felt the elder man's grip tighten on his arm.   He looked up quickly, and felt as if he had been turned to ice. Following the direction of the old man's eyes, he saw Crosmont, his face set and livid with sullen anxiety and despair, standing among the onlookers on the opposite side of the room, watching, not the cards, but the insignificantly-dressed woman. She was sitting next but one to the dealer, staking her money, watching the game, with the stolid steadiness of an old hand. Through the thickness of her veil, as Armathwaite watched, he saw two steel-bright eyes flash like sparks of light; underneath the thick black edge he saw two coral-red lips tightly set. In spite of his suspicions, in spite of his fears, it was he who staggered, and not the older man by his side, when he recognised in the one person in the crowded room whom on careful inspection he would have chosen as the ideal representative of the passion for play, the well-disguised but unmistakable face and form of Lady Kildonan.

The secret was out; she was a gambler; not from pleasure, not from choice, but because it was in her blood, bred by generations of spendthrift, fast living ancestors, whom nothing but laws of entail, and the occasional happy accident of a possessor of the estates who was free from the family vice, had stopped in the race of ruin. Her father's strange injunctions; her feverish anxiety to go abroad; her exhausted calm after the visits to Liverpool; all was explained. As she sat with her brilliant eyes incapable of seeing anything but the cards, all the passion of her ardent, energetic animal nature concentrated in the one absorbing pursuit, so that in the very presence of her husband, her judge, she remained as unmoved, as unconscious, as if he had been a statue, the pity and the horror of it all—for the deceived husband—for the guilty but ill-starred wife—struck Armathwaite with a force that turned him giddy, and sick, and trembling.

Lord Kildonan looked at him, meeting his grief-stricken eyes with cold grey ones.

" The room is ower warm for ye," he said, in a low voice, with a strong accent.

And they made their way quite quietly, disturbing nobody, exciting no remark, into the first room.

CHAPTER XXIX.

THREE long hours of waiting, watching, in wearisome suspense, in feverish excitement, Frank Armathwaite passed that night in the gambling-hell by the side of his older, calmer friend. Lord Kildonan seemed to the younger man to carry his immovable stolidity to a point at which it was difficult to distinguish it from absolute apathy; and Frank wondered, as he glanced furtively from time to time at the steely eyes and hard mouth of his companion, whether the discovery of his wife's treachery, the confirmation of it by the evidence of his own eyes, had killed all his feeling for her outright, so that all that remained to be done was to cut her off, to cast her adrift without a quiver, without a pang. She had deserved it—there was no denying that ; but Frank felt, as he looked at the Scotchman's cast-iron face, and shuddered at the deadly patience which made him wait, wait to carry out some plan he had set himself, that the cold justice the injured husband was preparing to mete out was something unworthy in its harshness of his better, kinder self.

Frank's momentary pity for the woman had given place to utter disgust as her face grew more and more flushed with the gambler's fever as the night wore on, until even under her veil the beautiful features seemed to lose all their charm, and the unsexing passion to change her fairness into a lurid glow of boldness and daring almost diabolical. Lord Kildonan had sat down with his companion at one of the small tables in the *baccarat* saloon, from which they could watch both his wife and Crosmont. To avoid exciting attention they played *écarté*, the older man holding his cards as steadily and playing as carefully as if he had been in his own house, while the hands of the younger shook, his mind wandered, and the hot air seemed to raise films of steaming vapour between his straining eyes and the cards.

"You have bad nerves," said Lord Kildonan, glancing at him with a cold smile, and then turning his eyes, without the least apparent effort, to the woman and the man he was watching.

If they could know, those fools—if they had the sense to direct their eyes to the obscure corner where their judge, their master, sat, holding them with a penetrating gaze that froze Armathwaite's blood by its pitilessness! But they were blind, blind as moths—she intent on the game, and he on her. She was losing heavily. From time to time she would turn, with a fierce, imperious movement, to hold out hungry, clutching fingers towards Crosmont, and to hiss out an angry, hoarse exclamation of impatience if he uttered a low word of protest, or delayed in putting into her hot, dry hands the money she wanted. At last, when it seemed to Armathwaite as if the night must have dragged itself far into the next day, Crosmont put his hand upon her shoulder just as the stake had been swept in by the dealer, and she was turning ravenously for more money.

"It is a quarter to three," Armathwaite heard him say. "You must come."

"Just one more—one more deal!" she panted, hoarsely.

"I have no more money. Come!" said he.

She uttered an impatient exclamation, got up with a spring, and tottered, intoxicated by the furious excitement of the past three hours. Lord Kildonan was watching her with the same stony face. But as she staggered up from her chair, she fell against another woman, an over-dressed woman, with a face of staring pink and white, who pushed her roughly away. At that sight the stolid Scotchman shuddered, and he rose quickly, with an outstretched hand and a fleeting look of the old yearning kindness in his eyes; it faded away instantly, and left him as frigid as before, but Armathwaite felt a shiver of relief pass over him as he noted the humanizing look and movement. Crosmont and Lady Kildonan passed through the crowd, one or two faces turning to watch them with a passing interest.

"Been here before, hasn't she?" asked one man.

"Oh, yes; a regular d——l at it—would play away her soul, if she has one," was the coarse answer.

These and similar comments fell on the ears of Lord Kildonan and his companion, as, allowing Crosmont and the lady time to get away without danger of a premature meeting, they followed them out of the house. The air of the narrow court was cold, refreshing, exhilarating as a draught of iced wine after the stifling atmosphere, the evil, heated faces, the low-voiced oaths, the pestilential sights and sounds of the place they had left; but the recollection of it all seemed to Armathwaite to hang about him like a haunting noxious vapour, poisoning the night. At the end of the court they stopped, hearing voices.

"If you had only let me go on, I should have won it all back," Lady Kildonan was saying, in a broken, husky voice of fretful complaint.

"Well, you couldn't stay. The train goes at three. You have only just time to catch it now," said Crosmont's voice, harshly.

"What do I care about the train? I don't care if I never get back! I won't go back! I'm sick of it all! I can't lead the life any longer; I've done with it— I've——"

But Crosmont was leading her gradually along in the direction of the station, and her querulous words became inaudible as he induced her, little by little, partly by persuasion and partly by force, to quicken her pace. Lord Kildonan turned Armathwaite's steps in the opposite direction, towards the side street in which they had left the cab. The driver had kept faith, and was waiting, beguiling the time away, however, with a sleep inside his vehicle. He woke up with a start, not having expected them so soon. In two moments they were on their way to Lime Street Station. The gentlemen did not exchange a word on the way; the younger did not dare—the elder did not care to break a silence which lasted even when, having arrived at their destination, and paid the cabman, they walked up and down the platform waiting for the two persons they had pursued. Armathwaite knew, without asking a question, that the moment was approaching when Lord Kildonan proposed to meet the guilty couple face to face. With his nerves strained to the utmost tension of torturing, apprehensive expectancy, he accompanied the elder man up and down, up and down, starting like a girl at the occasional sounds that echoed loudly in the huge, empty station, where the lights were turned down low, and the night mists still hung in the dim corners, and the air was raw and cold. Suddenly, before any sign of life or movement had begun to herald the starting of a train—before the porters, with their lanterns glowing yellow in the mist, had begun to swarm out from remote corners to their short spell of activity, before disappearing again like underground elves when the engine had puffed, with a shriek and a hiss, slowly out of the station, there broke upon the intently-listening ears of the two gentlemen the sound of wheels rattling over the stones.

"There they are," said Lord Kildonan quietly. "I thought they would have come on foot."

He paused in his walk to say this, and, as soon as the words were out of his mouth, he went on again. He was walking with Armathwaite on the very platform from which the Branksome train would start, and he gave a glance at his watch to see exactly how long they would have to wait.

"The train does not start for twelve minutes," he said, still walking on, but listening to the rattle of the wheels as the cab drove up nearer and nearer to them.

It stopped, and as he heard his wife's voice, speaking in petulant tones, Lord Kildonan drew the doctor behind a pile of empty baskets which stood on the platform at that point, and waited. They heard the cab slowly turn and drive away ; they heard the lady's voice, again crying out in peevish accents that she was tired—tired to death ; that she must rest, or she should cry ; that she could not take the long journey to The Crags to-night— that it would kill her !

"Come back with me, Ned ; I can't go alone ; I won't go alone ! I tell you I have a feeling that it is all coming out, and I don't care, I don't care ! I am worn out ; my head swims ; I can't go alone !"

Crosmont reasoned with her, earnestly, angrily, anxiously. He told her she must go back ; that she had no walking to do; Anne Matthews would drive her back as usual in her little cart, and she would slip up to the house as usual by the entrance nobody knew of, and no one would see her—no one.

But upon the feverish excitement of play there had followed a reaction, stronger than usual because of the restless and uneasy state of mind in which, since her last night-expedition, she had lived. The craving satisfied, she broke down, and became limp, nervous, hysterical. In vain Crosmont reasoned with her fears, told her that she must not lose her courage, her high spirit now; she must bear up for his sake, and remember that he had borne this risk again for her though he was himself ill— so ill that it was pain to him to stand, pain to speak. She did not heed him, though Armathwaite, diverted by these words from the woman to the man, was struck by the unhealthy, hectic light that shone out like a marsh-fire from the agent's sunken eyes, and by the unhealthy flush that had replaced the habitual pallor of his drawn and sallow face. He had only time for one glance when the man and woman together—so much absorbed, she in herself and he in her, that they saw nothing in the gloom before them to warn them, to silence them—came suddenly, arm linked in arm, upon the two motionless figures awaiting them.

Lord Kildonan stepped forward and confronted them, the sickly light of a flickering gas-lamp high above falling on his figure, on what could be seen of his face. The words froze on their guilty lips; the blood leaped up, and then seemed to stagnate in their veins as the cold eyes pierced them. Crosmont stopped, and stared up, as still as a dead man, shattered, confounded, without a word, without a cry. Lady Kildonan, with a hoarse and broken shriek that rang in hideous echoes through the huge bare station, staggered back, back, with starting eyes and struggling breath, until, before they could stop her, before they had even time to realize the danger she was in, she reached the edge of the platform, and with a last fatal backward step, fell with a moan on the metals. Lord Kildonan sprang down like a young man, lifted her in his arms, stared into her face. When Armathwaite joined him, the old Scotchman's face was all broken up with passionate anxiety, his voice was broken and weak like a child's.

"I have not killed her, Frank, have I? Speak, boy, speak!" he said in a husky whisper, as he lifted the head that hung limp and powerless on his shoulder.

Armathwaite, whose professional instinct had given him back all his calm at the moment of the accident, looked at her, touched her.

"No!" he said, briefly; "she is not dead. We must get her on to the platform! Crosmont!"

This call to the young man, who was still standing like a statue with dull eyes and leaden limbs, woke him to life and action. He would have helped to raise the prostrate woman, but Lord Kildonan, in his coldest, harshest tone, forbade him to touch her. The latter, with the assistance of Armathwaite, lifted her on to the platform just as the Branksome train steamed slowly up towards them. Frank suggested that she ought to remain in Liverpool that night—that it would be dangerous for her to travel. Her head had fallen on the metals; no one could tell yet what injury she had sustained. Lord Kildonan was immovable.

"She must go home!" he said, briefly.

"And if it should kill her, my lord?"

"We can still perhaps save her reputation," said Lord Kildonan in his coldest tone.

But he was deeply moved. He never took his eyes off his wife's white face as they carried her into a compartment and laid her on the seat. Crosmont still stood on the platform, and Armathwaite went back to him, and laid his hand on his arm.

The agent was shivering like a man with ague.

"Come," said Armathwaite, "you must come back with us."

"No, no," said Crosmont, hoarsely.

"What, would you leave the woman to bear the brunt of it alone? You couldn't do that, Crosmont. Come."

He dared not leave the man, in his miserable state, to pass the night alone. When this fit of benumbed stupor had passed off, he would be desperate, dangerous. He must come. After some few moments' appeal, warning him that Lady Kildonan was perhaps dying, the doctor induced him to take his place in the next compartment to that in which the husband and wife, weirdly reunited, were travelling. Then, after exacting a promise from the agent that he would not try to escape, he rejoined Lord Kildonan and the unconscious woman.

It was a terrible return journey. During all the four cold, monotonous hours Lady Kildonan lay almost without movement, from time to time muttering a few words to herself incoherently, or opening her eyes with the blank stare of a doll, only to close them again automatically without having taken in any impression. The cold, grey morning broke gradually, showing bare, desolate hills and moors on either side of the line through a chilling veil of fine rain. The air grew keener as the night passed away, and Lady Kildonan began to shiver in the cheap cashmere cloak, lined with poor fur, which she was in the habit of borrowing from Anne Matthews to complete her disguise. The two men wrapped their own overcoats round her, each protesting against the sacrifice on the part of the other. He looked so old, so grey, so full of grief and remorse, this kindly-natured old Scotchman, whose indiscreet wedding of a young wife had brought him so bitter a punishment, that the heart of the younger man bled for him, and yearned for words to express the sympathy he felt. This very longing fulfilled itself, for Lord Kildonan, withdrawing his poor, blurred, distraught eyes for a moment from the cold, unconscious face, which had assumed with the calm of stupor the pale beauty of the dead, met a look which went straight into his heart. The rigidity of his rugged face broke up.

"My boy, don't ye look so miserable," he said, gently. "Ye're too soft-hearted. When the wheels of the world have gone over ye a little longer, ye'll be wiser and harder, and ye'll see that, for the Almighty's inscrutable reasons, folly gets punished worse than sin."

Frank listened with feeling and respect, although he

knew that the preacher's years had made him neither hard nor wise. Lord Kildonan went on :

"I've been a fule, and you see what my folly has done to others. To that miserable lad whom I weighted with work he was too young for. To "—he gazed down at the unconscious woman with a look in his eyes like that of a remorseful father over a child whom his indulgence has ruined—" to this poor lassie," he whispered, brokenly. "Her father—God forgive him !—and I— and God forgive me ! both meaning the best, have done the worst for her we could do. He thought a middle-aged man would be father and husband both, and save her from herself. But he should have confided in me. And what attraction could there be in a man like me to be stronger than an hereditary passion? Poor lass !"

And he looked down again, watching the white face solicitously, and said no more until, at seven o'clock on the raw February morning, the train steamed into Branksome Station. The stoppage roused Lady Kildonan ; she struggled up and looked vacantly about her, muttering incoherently that it was getting light—that she should be late—but without noticing her companions. Frank put her veil over her face and fastened it for her, to which she made no opposition. And she accepted his suggestion to take his arm, and allowed him to lead her through the station, apparently unconscious that it was her husband who was supporting her tottering foot-steps on the other side. She turned instinctively in the direction of the house where Anne Matthews lived, and at the opening of the little street they found a small covered cart waiting, with the woman who had been her treacherous accomplice inside it. Armathwaite recognised her at once, and saw first that she looked a little ashamed of herself, and secondly that she was seriously alarmed and remorseful when she saw how ill the lady looked. They lifted her into the cart ; Lord Kildonan took his place beside her, and insisted on Armathwaite's coming with them, that he might prescribe for her in his medical capacity on reaching The Crags.

They drove fast along the road by the lake. The springs of the vehicle were good, and the horse went well in spite of his heavy load. They passed Crosmont, walking with heavy feet, and his head bent between his shoulders ; he glanced up as the cart went by, and in the grey morning his face looked so wan and fierce, his eyes so wild, that the young doctor had his thoughts diverted from his patient by an ugly misgiving concerning her unhappy victim. Anne Matthews, who drove herself, stopped at the bottom of the private path to The Crags, as was her custom ; and the two gentlemen led Lady Kildonan, who was now growing excited and feverish, up the hill, through the private gate, which was open, and into the house by that entrance of which Lord Kildonan had fancied that he alone had a key. It opened upon a narrow private staircase, with another locked door at the top, by which they were able to reach Lady Kildonan's apartments unobserved by anybody except her ladyship's maid, an astute middle-aged woman, whom the unfortunate and guilty lady had always believed to be her dupe, but who had not only had the acumen to find out part of her mistress's secret and keep it to herself, but had seized the very moment when she saw that Lord Kildonan's suspicions were roused to make a clean breast to him of the lady's fraud, pretending that she herself had only recently discovered it.

With the assistance of this woman, Lady Kildonan was put to bed, much against her will, for she was by this time seized with the idea that she was starting for Liverpool instead of returning from it. But she was utterly feeble and dazed and stupid, and could only express the fancy which possessed her by weak incoherent mutterings. Armathwaite told Lord Kildonan that she was suffering from concussion of the brain, and after remaining with her about an hour, at the end of which time she had sunk into a wordless stupor, he left her to the care of her husband and the maid, and promising to return in a couple of hours, walked back quickly towards Mereside. He was anxious about Crosmont, anxious also to find out how this terrible event would affect the agent's wife. His thoughts about Alma had a separate and reserved corner in his mind, vague and crossed with all sorts of indefinite fears and longings as they were.

By the time he reached the agent's house it was half-past nine; the rain of the night had ceased, and it was a sunny morning. Frank walked once or twice past the house, his mind filled with misgivings which nothing in the appearance of the dwelling seemed to justify. One of the maids was talking to the bird in the dining-room window; the voice of another could be heard cheerfully calling the chickens to come and be fed. He returned to the gate, entered, and rang the bell. Nanny appeared, fresh and smiling, and looked at him with quite a welcoming face. He asked for Mr. Crosmont in an unsteady voice.

"He's gone to Liverpool, sir; he won't be back till this afternoon," said Nanny.

Armathwaite changed colour.

"Let me come in, Nanny," he said, in a hoarse voice; then, as he was passing her, he stopped and asked: "Where is Mrs. Crosmont?"

"She's just had breakfast, sir, and gone into the drawing-room."

But at that moment Alma appeared, having heard the doctor's voice and come out eagerly to meet him. She dropped her outstretched hand at sight of his face.

"What is the matter?" she faltered.

"Can I speak to you for one moment?"

She led the way into the drawing-room, and he followed quickly, feeling that he had not a moment to lose.

"Ned!" she cried at once, in a low voice, clasping her hands together against her waist. "Something has happened to him!"

"Something very serious for him has happened, and it will affect him very deeply. He went to Liverpool yesterday; I have reason to know that he has returned. But the servants have not seen him."

Alma interrupted him; she was very quiet, and grave, and calm.

"He lets himself in with his own key," said she. "He may be in his study. Come with me."

They went out together, going by some instinct so silently, so softly, that their footsteps, their movements scarcely made a sound as they went from end to end of the old house. At the study door they stopped, and, with a loud-beating heart, Alma knocked. There was no answer. She did not knock a second time, but looked at the handle with a pale, frightened face, as if she did not dare to touch it. Armathwaite came forward and tried the door. It was locked.

"He locks it when he goes away," said Alma, with faltering lips.

"You had better go back into the drawing-room and wait for me," said he to the lady very quietly. "He may be angry at being disturbed."

But she knew the thought in his mind, and shared it; and without taking any notice of his suggestion, she said, in a low tone: "There is a duplicate key in his room upstairs. Wait here; I will fetch it. We must get in, and without disturbance."

He waited at the door, listening with intent ears. He had heard no sound inside the room when, in a very few moments, Alma returned and put the key into his hand. They entered together.

The blinds were still drawn down, but the morning light was bright in the room; every object in it could be discerned clearly. There was the writing-table, with his inkstand and papers; the centre table, with a whip and riding-gloves conspicuous across a pile of other things; there was the fireplace, and the rough armchair he usually sat in; and there, sitting before the grate, which was littered with scraps of a torn letter, and in which the grey ashes of the previous night's fire yet remained, sat Ned Crosmont, his legs stretched out, his head on his breast, his arms hanging loose at his sides. Alma had often seen him almost in that attitude, and it reassured her. She came further into the room, calling softly, "Ned!" He did not answer, he did not move. Armathwaite thought she knew the truth. But having been prepared for some sight unusual, shocking, it had not yet occurred to Alma that death could come so suddenly and yet so quietly. She came close to him with rapid steps, thinking that he was lost in miserable brooding, put her arm round his shoulders, and tried to draw him to her, kindly, comfortingly. His head rolled heavily against her breast.

"Ned, Ned, never mind," she whispered, feeling, with a thrill through her gentle heart, that at last the moment she had expected had come, when he did not repulse her, when he was glad of her sympathy; "I'll comfort you, Ned—I'll console you. Never mind what it is, I'm sorry."

She put up her hand to touch his cheek, and found it cold; then, drawing a deep breath, she stood for a moment quite still, benumbed by a rush of thoughts so strange and feelings so acute that she seemed to herself to be in actual bodily pain. At last Frank gently touched her arm to draw her away.

"He is dead," she said, solemnly, raising her eyes to the doctor's face.

Then the tears began to gather in her eyes, and, bending over the dead man, she put her lips to his forehead, not in sorrowing love, but in pity and forgiveness.

"Come, come away," whispered Frank, who saw that the struggling emotions of horror and womanly regret and irrepressible relief were trying the sensitive lady beyond her strength.

She let him lead her out at the door, which Frank closed softly behind them ; but before she had made three steps along the passage she suddenly drew away her hand from his arm, put it up to her head, and, with a low cry as of a prisoner who sees the dungeon doors flung suddenly open, she reeled and fell to the ground. Frank gathered her up in his arms and carried her to the drawing-room. There he did not put her down, but seating himself in an arm-chair by the window in the full blaze of the morning sunlight, he rocked her for a few moments tenderly in his arms, as if she had been a child, while his blue eyes shone with hope and pity and yearning love.

"Poor little one," he whispered into her deaf ears. "You are no widow; you have never been a wife. I am wronging no man's memory in telling you I love you.

The gods will make you happy, Psyche, for you have found your love at last."

As she was still absolutely motionless and silent, he snatched a passionate kiss ; but the instant his lips touched hers, the colour flowed back into her face, and her brown eyes met his with a long look that told of the wakening of a sleeping soul. From that moment each had a secret, known only to themselves and to each other. Withdrawing his eyes from her face, Frank raised her to her feet, and gently withdrawing the support of his arm, said gravely and formally :

" I think you are better now, madam. If you will allow me to advise you, I would suggest your remaining here, while I will tell the servants what is necessary for them to know, and prevent their disturbing you."

" Thank you. You are very kind," said she frigidly, with her eyes on the ground.

With a cold bow, and without another look at her, Frank left the room. But as he paused for a moment outside, with glowing eyes and a yearning heart, he heard the swift rustle of a woman's dress across the room, and her panting breath close to the door. So they stood for a moment, each conscious that the other was there, each almost able to hear the beating of the heart of the other. But there was only a thin plank of wood between them now, where there had been a barrier as wide as the whole world. And so he went softly away to his work and his duty, and she to the woman's part of patiently waiting and perhaps weeping. For peace had come to her, not with a glad song of praise, but with a solemn requiem.

CHAPTER XXX.

FRANK ARMATHWAITE did not see Alma again for several days ; he even took some pains to avoid her, for he was in no anxiety concerning her future now, and he felt a delicacy about meeting her.

Ned Crosmont had been of late in such a critical state of health, and his looks had betrayed the fact so unmistakably, that the doctor, while he guessed at once that death had been accelerated by the man's own act, had reason to hope that the suddenness of it would cause little surprise or scandal. A search and an examination proved that death was the result of a small dose of laudanum upon a weak heart. But as the quantity taken was proved to be insufficient to kill a man in ordinary health, and as the history of the events which preceded Crosmont's death did not become generally known, it never grew to be more than a doubt whether he took the laudanum as a sedative or as a poison.

Frank had little difficulty in surmising how he came by the drug, since it was the same that Lady Kildonan used to stupefy her husband on the occasion of her nocturnal visits to Liverpool, in order that he might be the less likely to detect the substitution of another woman for herself.

Frank found, and carefully collected out of the fireplace before he let anyone into the study, a quantity of torn fragments of note-paper, which proved to contain the beginning of an unfinished letter addressed to Lord Kildonan, written in deep, fierce, defiant distress of mind, the few lines of which were inexpressibly painful to read. Frank kept these fragments, after some consideration, securely locked up in his own possession ; but, after watching the course of events for the next few weeks, he burned them without ever communicating their contents to anyone. On the person of the dead man he found a portrait of Lady Kildonan, and a packet of short, feverish notes from her. All these had been cherished close to his breast, and the disorder of his dress proved that they had been thrust hastily back into their place there by a hand on which death was already closing Frank took them out; but four days later, just before the coffin was nailed down, he contrived to replace both the letters and the portrait unseen on the dead man's breast. He had decided from the first that he would do this, but he had thought about it and puzzled over it a good deal during those four days in which he had carried the notes about with him. Such a feverish, desperate, devoted passion as that which had consumed the dead man, and laid his energy, his strong will, and his very life at the feet of a brilliant but almost heartless woman, was something so foreign to his own more placid nature, that it bewildered him, filled him with pity and perplexity, and gave him much food for thought. With all his errors, this dogged brute-nature must be judged with mercy ; and as he had lived and died for his terrible loyalty, his poor treasures, ill-gotten as they were, might well be allowed to lie with him. So Frank thought as he restored the packet, and almost wished that it were in him to dare as much.

In the meantime Lady Kildonan was lying utterly unconscious both of the death of her accomplice and victim and of her condemnation, pronounced by her own lips a hundred times in the delirium of brain-fever. Her husband, who during these long days and nights was scarcely ever absent from her bedside, used to sit listening to her and watching her with a grave, intent face, which expressed no sentiment harsher than the deepest pity. He would allow no one else to approach his wife except her old aunt and Armathwaite ; by means of this precaution, his own unremitting devotion, and a story which he himself laboriously concocted to account for her illness, Lord Kildonan managed to preserve her reputation, though he could not silence all the whispers. When the crisis of the fever was past, and the sick woman's bodily health began slowly to mend, it dawned upon both her husband and the young doctor, who had never exchanged a word since the night of the accident except upon the medical aspect of the case, that her mental recovery was not proportionately rapid. She would lie for hours together awake and quite still, with her eyes fixed upon her husband in a sort of vague surprise at his presence, with which mingled no shame, no annoyance, no deep interest. Yet she knew who he was, and replied to his questions in a voice which grew stronger every day, but which acquired no deeper meaning as the time went on.

At last she was well enough to get up, and to sit in her boudoir by the window, watching the birds flying from bough to bough of the still leafless trees in the park outside, the little clouds sailing slowly across the sky, and a hundred other sights of the narrow stretch of wintry landscape which she had never before noticed. Lord Kildonan, at first rather pleased by the new interest she showed in the nature about her, began after a few days to feel anxious concerning the meaning of the change.

"She doesn't seem at all the same woman yet," he observed to the doctor one morning, when his wife had been babbling in a childish way, as if she had no recollection of the terrible scenes through which she had lately passed. "Or is it a clever device of hers to bridge over the awkwardness of our intercourse, until she is well enough for me to accuse her and come to an arrangement?"

"I don't think it is that, Lord Kildonan," said Armathwaite, gravely. "And I must strongly advise you to give up all thoughts of coming to a clear understanding with her yet."

The old Scotchman's face, which seemed to have aged recently at the rate of a year for every day, wrinkled up with anxiety and apprehension.

"Ye mean that her mind has not recovered its full powers yet?" he said in a low voice.

"Yes. You can see what power it is that is still wanting—memory."

There was a long pause, Lord Kildonan staring before him, while emotions of fear and hope and doubt and wonder struggled within him. At last he asked in a low voice:

"You think it will come back?"

"It is impossible to say. In the meantime——"

"In the meantime," broke in Lord Kildonan, solemnly and with relief in his tone, "she is just a child again— my poor headstrong, over-indulged, spoilt child. Then I—I must not tease her with questions just yet."

In spite of himself, he felt that a great weight was taken off his mind by this discovery. During the hours when he had watched by his wife's bedside, and pondered with full knowledge on the circumstances of the deception she had practised upon him, his natural bent towards mercy had been increased by reflections on his own disadvantages as a husband to a young girl, and his own folly in marrying her, in spoiling her, and in observing too little vigilance over a young wife on the one hand, and an inexperienced man of business on the other.

Into all the counts against the dead man Lord Kildonan declined to go. He examined the late agent's papers and went through his books, and whatever errors he found he took the blame of, as indeed he felt bound to do when he discovered that Crosmont had in no way enriched himself by his breach of trust. Every penny he could spare from his own salary, or squeeze out of supposed insolvent tenants, or abstract by any means from any source, had been squandered by Lady Kildonan at the gambling-table in the half-dozen clandestine visits she had paid to Liverpool during the course of the winter.

There were graver accusations than these whispered against the late agent, and there were half a score of tongues about which a word from the master would now have set going. But not a word would Lord Kildonan hear. The dead man could not answer, and therefore he must not be accused. As for the living partner of the wrong he had done, she should be arraigned when her health permitted; but she could not be questioned upon facts which for the present had passed out of her mind, leaving nothing but a blank behind.

As the days passed on, however, and still, while her limbs regained some of their vigour, and her face much of its beauty, Lady Kildonan remained mentally in exactly the same state of childish oblivion of everything but the occupation of the moment, both her husband and the doctor agreed, reluctantly enough, that some attempt must be made to bring her back to reason and remembrance. Armathwaite, therefore, on the occasion of one of his visits about three weeks after the accident, led the conversation in such a manner as to introduce the name of Ned Crosmont.

"Oh, yes," she said, smiling, "I haven't seen Ned to-day. But he is going to drive me into Branksome this afternoon to get some new tennis balls."

Armathwaite laid his hand upon her arm. "Listen to me, Lady Kildonan," he said, very gravely, foreseeing already that his words would have little effect; "I have something very sad to tell you about Mr. Crosmont. He is ill, seriously ill."

She looked with a child-like stare into his face and shook her head.

"Oh, no, you have been misinformed," she said confidently, as if after a moment's thought. "I saw him yesterday—no, this morning—at any rate, quite recently, though I can't remember for the moment exactly when it was," she added, holding her hand to her forehead and looking rather puzzled. "But he's quite well, I know."

He made a few more efforts to bring her memory back, but quite in vain; the terrible events which had had such fatal consequences both to her and to Crosmont had faded out of her mind so utterly that not even a vague sense as of an evil dream remained behind.

Then Lord Kildonan sent for two eminent physicians, who came down from town to consult upon her case. But there was nothing to be done, and they could hold out little hope of a cure. Both brain and spine were affected, and the once active and lithe-limbed Lady Kildonan was now reduced, by the shock to mind and body, to the condition of a lame child. She could walk about the house, but it was with fatigue and difficulty which quickly became pain, and gradually she grew used to depending upon her husband's arm for support, and to allowing him to drive her about the country in her little pony-carriage. The old Scotchman was as patient with her, as tender, as watchful, as a mother over a weakly babe. No caprice could irritate, no petulance weary him. He was no longer the yearning, timid, over indulgent husband; he was the kind, wise, devoted father of an invalid child. She had so completely lost her memory that her lameness was wholly unaccountable to her, and caused her the plaintive bewilderment of an animal that has got injured in a trap. But when a cloud came over her face on finding that, after a few steps, she was tired and must rest, the assurance from her husband that she would be "all right in a few days" would always bring the smiles back to her face again.

So her punishment, tragic as it seemed to the on-lookers, fell lightly upon her. Her buoyant animal nature, shaken free, by the shock she had sustained, of the vice which had been her ruin, helped her to bear her affliction with the resignation of a lame dog, who, forgetting quickly the sensations of the old days when he scoured the fields after rabbits, and leaped up joyously as high as his master's shoulders, takes quietly to the peaceful joys of the warm hearth and the sunny door-step, and dozes the remainder of his life away in comfortable content.

The little quiet old lady, Aunt Theresa, took the whole matter so undemonstratively as to suggest a deeper acquaintance with the family secrets than she had been given credit for. She made no comments, no inquiries, listened tranquilly to Aphra's ravings, and tended her on her recovery with the unselfish devotion which the unornamental feminine members of a family so often lavish upon their more brilliant relations.

Frank Armathwaite never saw again the papers which Dr. Peele had left to him, neither did he ever learn their contents, though he could make a pretty shrewd guess what they were. They consisted for the most part of a sort of intermittent diary kept by the late doctor for the sake of recording the facts of Lady Kildonan's case as they became known to him, his own efforts to warn her of the consequences of her conduct, and his suspicions concerning Crosmont's application to his wife of the secrets of mesmerism and hypnotism which he had learnt in Paris years before. This was supplemented by letters from Aphra's father to the doctor, which revealed not only Mr. Dighton's devoted love for his daughter, but also his knowledge that she had inherited the curse of the family, and his passionate wish that, at all cost, it might be checked and concealed. Every line of the diary proved how deeply the doctor, a man of kindly but vacillating nature, had suffered between his affection for Alma, the daughter of his old friend, and his devotion to Aphra, the child of the man to whom he owed all his prosperity. To his warnings and entreaties, Aphra had replied by the threat that if she were interfered with, she should leave her home and husband altogether. So the doctor, bound by his promise of secresy to her father, and fearing the consequences of opposition on her reckless nature, had never dared to take active steps to check her, and had found relief in passing on the burden of his life and of his secret to another and a less irresolute man.

The person on whom the shock of Ned Crosmont's death fell the heaviest was Uncle Hugh. When the tidings reached him, together with an account of Lady Kildonan's rather mysterious illness, he came back to Branksome in the greatest anxiety and remorse, believing that his own letter to Lord Kildonan had been the cause of both misfortunes. The old Scotchman, who received him very kindly, assured him that his suspicions had been roused long before the letter reached him, and advised him to turn his attention to comforting the young widow. But there were difficulties in the way of this. He would have taken her back with him to her friends in London, away from the scenes of her short, but unhappy married life; but Alma, once so anxious to go away, now raised unexpected obstacles to this course. It would make public the fact that her marriage had been a failure, she said. Besides, she must wait until his affairs were settled, and she preferred seclusion for a little while before facing the curious inquiries of her old friends. So Uncle Hugh, disappointed in his wish to carry off his "little one," and resolved not to have his journey for nothing, obtained a promise from Millie that she would marry him within two months, on condition that the wedding should be a very quiet one.

This promise, at the end of the appointed time, she faithfully carried out; and Mrs. Peele, who had never held up her head with her old majesty since Lord Kildonan put her to the humiliation of having to give up the stolen papers, soon after made up her mind to leave Branksome for London, in order to be near her daughter.

Armathwaite was thus left alone in the little house;

but though he missed Millie, of whose sisterly companionship he had grown very fond, he was not dull, for he had taken it into his head to refurnish and decorate the place according to certain ideas of his own, and this occupation, to a man of limited income and fastidious taste, afforded amusement and interest for some time. The purchase of a horse, too, besides the late doctor's cob, was an extravagance which required deliberation; but there was an animal in the neighbourhood which Frank was bent on possessing, and after a few weeks the coveted beast held a place in his stable.

These little acquisitions, quietly and cautiously as he made them, attracted the suspicious attention of the old Viscount, who occasionally visited him now that he lived alone, and who was struck one day towards the end of May, when he was calling at the doctor's house, by certain changes which had recently been wrought in the drawing-room.

"A conservatory now! And so you're making yourself a little conservatory here?" he exclaimed, with some surprise.

"Yes," Frank mumbled something about being fond of flowers.

But Lord Kildonan's thoughts flew off at a tangent on another subject.

"I met our little widow the other day by old Peggy's cottage," he said, while Frank blushed furiously. "Those horrid black garments seem to suit her; I thought she looked younger and handsomer than I have ever seen her do. But you know it's too soon for her to look young and handsome yet."

"I think it's too soon for her to look old and ugly yet."

"Ah, well, we're not looking at her from the same point of view. By the bye, I don't want to say anything unpleasant, but don't forget that the same woman who has been a good wife to a bad husband, may prove a bad wife to a good one."

"If I should see any chance of that I should only have to jump upon her to reverse the position," said Frank, looking very sweet-tempered and happy.

"Well," said the old Scotchman, rather sadly, "you may tak' it as a joke, but the treatment, if one only had self-control enough for it, has its good points. It might be bad for us, but ye may depend upon it, it would be good for them."

Frank, however, was undaunted by these suggestions of a bitter experience, and all through the early summer he continued his leisurely occupation of transforming the prim house with its hideous mahogany and horse-hair to a very dainty little nest indeed, "much too pretty for a bachelor," as all the ladies said who ever had a peep inside. Of course the doctor was going to marry; there could be no doubt of that when Mrs. Peele, having expressed a desire to have the dining-room and drawing-room furniture in her new home in London, the young doctor joyfully packed it up and sent it off, and replaced it by something both prettier and more comfortable; for Mrs. Peele had a taste for stiff and slippery upholstery which mortified the flesh. None of the ladies of Branksome, deeply interested as they were in the matter, felt any certainty as to whether the handsome young doctor's choice was already made, for he naturally felt a great delicacy about approaching Alma, in the most ordinary way, during the first months of her widowhood, being far less sure of himself with her than he had been while there was a barrier between them. It happened, therefore, that, the lady feeling also shy on her side, they did not exchange a single word through the whole of the spring and the greater part of the summer, and limited their intercourse to the stiffest little bows at any chance meeting. So rigorous were they that the Lakeside girls and their mammas and chaperons were happy to believe that "poor Edwin Crosmont's widow" had put herself, by her stiff ways, completely out of the running.

It was the beginning of August when Alma, who with the recovery of her health and spirits began to feel her natural feminine coquetry awakening, decided that the first ice of their decorous estrangement might now be broken. One scorching afternoon, when Armathwaite returned home, tired and dusty from his day's work, he was informed by the servant that a little girl was waiting to see him in the surgery, and that Mrs. Crosmont was with her.　Frank's heart leaped up.　He seized a clothes-brush and began to brush himself violently, as much to gain time to conquer this horrible choking nervousness as because he was reluctant to enter her presence with the workaday dust of the roads upon him.　When he entered the surgery he was particularly calm and sedate, with "rising young medical practitioner with a character to keep up" writ large all over him.

Alma was sweet, and grave, and tranquil, but she had a brighter colour in her cheeks than Frank had ever before seen there, and in the front of her dress she wore a white rose, which the young man chose fatuously to think was a very good sign.　She had brought one of the village children to have a scalded arm dressed, and as the child screamed and struggled, and took up all their attention until the operation was successfully accomplished, the first part of the interview passed off without any feeling of awkwardness on either side.　As soon, however, as the girl found her arm bandaged and released, she darted to the door and made her escape like a wild thing, without a word of thanks to either of her benefactors.　They looked at each other and laughed.

"Poor little thing!　She isn't much tamer than a squirrel.　She was rushing about the road crying, and it was a hard task to persuade her to come with me at all," said Alma, moving in her turn towards the door.

But Frank stepped hurriedly across the room before her.

"I wish, Mrs. Crosmont, now that you are here, you would do me the pleasure of looking into the drawing-room.　I have made some changes there.　I should so much like to hear what you think about them."

Alma hesitated and then turned back with a smile.

"I will see it certainly, if you wish," she said, gently.

So Frank led the way into the drawing-room, which had been indeed transformed.　The violent colours, the tatting antimacassars, the wax flowers under glass shades of Mrs Peele's *régime*, had disappeared, while in their place were harmonious tints and soft fabrics, and bowls full of freshly-cut flowers.

"Why, Dr. Armathwaite, I am hurt for the credit of my sex. It looks as if some woman must have helped you," said Alma, as she looked with admiration round the pretty room.

"Some woman has helped me," said he, in a meek small voice.

She was not curious, or perhaps she didn't hear.

"And do you always have the place filled with these beautiful flowers ? "

"Always."

"Ah, you pass your evenings here, of course ? "

"Never. I scarcely sit here an hour in the week."

" Then why all this extravagance with beautiful flowers, which only get wasted ? Are they for visitors ? "

" For one visitor. I wanted the room to be always ready for that one whenever—she—should—come."

Alma said nothing to this, but began a rapid inspection of the water-colours on the wall with critical and appreciative comments, and then prepared to go. Frank interrupted her courteous words of farewell.

" I should like you, if you would, to come and see a horse I have bought," said he, rather nervously.

The colour rushed to Alma's face.

"A horse ! " she echoed in a low voice.

" Yes. Will you come ? "

She hesitated. He saw that she had made a good guess, and he hung with undisguised anxiety on her answer. At last she moved slowly down the passage with him in the direction of the stable. Frank, much excited, dared not trust himself to speak. When they reached the door of the loose box where the horse was, he, absorbed in doubt and hope, was beginning to lose his head, and fumbled nervously with the fastening of the door. Alma, much more self-possessed, smiled up at him very sweetly, and said perhaps she could manage it better. So he made way for her, and she opened the door, and peeped in with a face radiant with delight, while Gray Friar, seeing his old mistress, arched his neck for her caress.

" I think you guessed what horse it was, didn't you ? " asked Frank, very demurely, over Gray Friar's back.

" Well, I wondered whether——" she began.

" Would you like to have him again ? " he asked, after a pause.

" Oh, no ! I am sure he is quite happy with you ! "

" I am glad you think that he can be quite happy with me.   Of course, it's easy to make a horse happy."

" Yes, of course it is ! "

" And if you will only come and see him sometimes——"

" Oh, yes, I will."

Armathwaite was stroking the horse on one side, and Alma on the other.   But the fingers of both began to twitch and to tremble so nervously that Gray Friar, feeling that this sort of thing was a dozen times worse than flies, suddenly backed and threw up his head, and the caressing hands met.   Alma blushed, and Frank felt fired with sudden courage.

" If ever you should change your mind, and want to have him for your own again——"

" Oh, no ; I could never take him away from you ! "

" Well, you might have him without that—if you would !   Don't say no—don't say no !   I know I oughtn't to have spoken yet, but I—I couldn't help it.   Try to forget that I have spoken, and give me another chance later—I implore you ! "   burst out Frank, seeing that she turned away from him, and in a terrible state of dread that he had offended her.

" I—I wasn't going to say no."

" God bless you ! "

Oh, they were so quiet about it—as quiet as mice— she with her tremulous whisper, and he with his husky ejaculation.   Gray Friar scarcely knew that anything had happened, except that a few minutes later they both stood on the same side of him, and caressed him in unison.   For wasn't it old Gray Friar who had brought him to her on that winter night down by the lake's edge, when, by some power she did not herself understand, she had drawn him to her side at the time she felt most in need of a strong arm and a strong heart ?

Frank asked her, as he took her home in the tempered heat of the early evening, what Dr. Peele had said which

had made her desire his presence; for that it was her
wish which had brought him they were tacitly convinced.
Then she told him that early in the autumn she had gone
to Dr. Peele, told him of her husband's new custom of
reading her to sleep at night, and complained of the
strange heaviness and drowsiness from which she always
suffered on the following morning. This, as Armathwaite guessed, was the period when Crosmont first
began his experiments upon his wife. Dr. Peele, so
Alma said, had at first appeared much interested and
puzzled by her story, but on her next visit—a month
later—he had changed altogether, and instead of listening with attention to her account of the gradual
weakening of her will, he had tried to make light of it;
and when she persisted that her ailment was not an
imaginary one, he had told her that he was too old and
too ill to study her case with the necessary minuteness;
and in answer to the questions with which she plied him,
he had named Frank Armathwaite as one among his old
colleagues and pupils who had the skill and the tact
necessary for such a delicate case. Ever since that day
Alma, finding no help from the kindly but weak and
vacillating old doctor, and getting nothing but good-
humoured teasing for her fancifulness from Uncle Hugh,
had set her whole soul upon the wish that she might
meet the man from whom she had been told she might
expect the help she craved. As the winter advanced,
and the benumbing influence upon her grew stronger,
this wish had increased until it became a passion, excite-
ing and soothing her at the same time. Then one day
she had suddenly felt conscious of a belief that her wish
was to be fulfilled; and as the day wore on, and the
snow fell thickly, and the heavy clouds brought night
before its time, an impulse, growing stronger as the
hours went by, came upon her to go down to the lake;
and at last, when it had grown quite dark, she had
slipped out of the drawing-room, where she was sitting
with Uncle Hugh, and fastened up the long train of her
dress, and putting on Uncle Hugh's thick military cloak,
had let herself quietly out of the house, and gone down
to the edge of the lake and waited in the falling snow.

"And then, when you came," said Alma dreamily, looking at the golden light on the water as she leaned upon Frank's arm, "I knew at once who you were, though I scarcely remembered your name. And I felt as I looked at you that I had not been mistaken, and that there was help near me. And day by day, as I knew you better, I felt more sure of it, until in all the heaviness and the trouble that I suffered there was always that comfort, and a look in your eyes that gave me patience and strength. But my fancies have gone too, Frank, now, and I can't hear the music as I used to do. Why is that, do you think?"

Frank had rather a fanciful explanation to give. He thought that Alma was only carrying out her destiny, and that, like the heroine of the opera that her father had nursed in his heart of hearts for years before she was born, she had come out victorious from her contest with the beauty of the senses, and that, having found the love she had longed for, her fancy had no need to reach out to shadows for comfort, for her soul had found rest.

THE END.

www.ingramcontent.com/pod-product-compliance
Lightning Source LLC
Chambersburg PA
CBHW031039120726

47905CB00007B/2249